Thirty-One Years
On The Plains And
In The Mountains
Or,
The Last Voice From The Plains

By

William F. Drannan

Double 9
BOOKS

Thirty-One Years On The Plains And In The Mountains

Or,
The Last Voice From The Plains
by William F. Drannan

ISBN: 978-93-59958-93-4

Published by

DOUBLE 9 BOOKS

2/13-B, Ansari Road
Daryaganj, New Delhi – 110002
info@double9books.com
www.double9books.com
Tel. 011-40042856

ABOUT THE AUTHOR

William F. Drannan became a frontiersman and writer recognised for his brilliant reviews within the American West at some point of the nineteenth century. His book, "Thirty-One Years on the Plains and inside the Mountains," offers readers a firsthand account of the adventurous and regularly tough existence on the western frontier. Drannan's book is a captivating memoir that chronicles his widespread travels and exploits inside the untamed American desolate tract. He gives a completely unique angle at the generation of westward growth, recounting his involvement in diverse big historic activities and his interactions with awesome figures of the time. Drannan's adventures encompass serving as a scout and interpreter all through the tumultuous instances of the Indian Wars, prospecting for gold in the Rocky Mountains, and participating within the fur exchange. His narrative is filled with gripping tales of encounters with Native American tribes, outlaws, and the hardships of existence in the barren region. "Thirty-One Years on the Plains and in the Mountains" isn't always best a exciting journey tale but additionally an important historic report. It offers a valuable insight into the challenges and possibilities of existence at the American frontier at some stage in a duration of fast exchange and westward expansion.

CONTENTS

PREFACE

In writing this preface I do so with the full knowledge that the preface of a book is rarely read, comparatively speaking, but I shall write this one just the same.

In writing this work the author has made no attempt at romance, or a great literary production, but has narrated in his own plain, blunt way, the incidents of his life as they actually occurred.

There have been so many books put upon the market, purporting to be the lives of noted frontiersmen which are only fiction, that I am moved to ask the reader to consider well before condemning this book as such.

The author starts out with the most notable events of his boyhood days, among them his troubles with an old negro virago, wherein he gets his revenge by throwing a nest of lively hornets under her feet. Then come his flight and a trip, to St. Louis, hundreds of miles on foot, his accidental meeting with that most eminent man of his class, Kit Carson, who takes the lad into his care and treats him as a kind father would a son. He then proceeds to give a minute description of his first trip on the plains, where he meets and associates with such noted plainsmen as Gen. John Charles Fremont, James Beckwith, Jim Bridger and others, and gives incidents of his association with them in scouting, trapping, hunting big game, Indian fighting, etc.

The author also gives brief sketches of the springing into existence of many of the noted cities of the West, and the incidents connected therewith that have never been written before. There is also a faithful recital of his many years of scouting for such famous Indian fighters as Gen. Crook, Gen. Connor, Col. Elliott, Gen. Wheaton and others, all of which will be of more than passing interest to those who can be entertained by the early history of the western part of our great republic.

This work also gives an insight into the lives of the hardy pioneers of the far West, and the many trials and hardships they had to undergo in blazing the trail and hewing the way to one of the grandest and most healthful regions of the United States. W. F. D.

CHICAGO, August 1st, 1899.

CHAPTER I
A BOY ESCAPES A TYRANT AND PAYS A DEBT WITH A HORNET'S NEST— MEETS KIT CARSON AND BECOMES THE OWNER OF A PONY AND A GUN

The old saying that truth is stranger than fiction is emphasized in the life of every man whose career has been one of adventure and danger in the pursuit of a livelihood. Knowing nothing of the art of fiction and but little of any sort of literature; having been brought up in the severe school of nature, which is all truth, and having had as instructor in my calling a man who was singularly and famously truthful, truth has been my inheritance and in this book I bequeath it to my readers.

My name is William F. Drannan, and I was born on the Atlantic ocean January 30, 1832, while my parents were emigrating from France to the United States.

They settled in Tennessee, near Nashville, and lived upon a farm until I was about four years old. An epidemic of cholera prevailed in that region for some months during that time and my parents died of the dread disease, leaving myself and a little sister, seven months old, orphans.

I have never known what became of my sister, nor do I know how I came to fall into the hands of a man named Drake, having been too young at that time to remember now the causes of happenings then. However, I remained with this man, Drake, on his plantation near The Hermitage, the home of Gen. Andrew Jackson, until I was fifteen.

Drake was a bachelor who owned a large number of negro slaves, and I was brought up to the age mentioned among the negro children of the place, without schooling, but cuffed and knocked about more like a worthless puppy than as if I were a human child. I never saw the inside of a school-house, nor was I taught at home anything of value. Drake never even undertook to teach me the difference between good and evil, and my only associates were the little negro boys that belonged to Drake, or the neighbors. The only person who offered to control or correct me was an old negro woman, who so far from being the revered and beloved "Black Mammy," remembered with deep affection by many southern men and women, was simply a hideous black tyrant. She abused me shamefully, and I was punished by her not only for my own performances that displeased her, but for all the meanness done by the negro boys under her jurisdiction.

Naturally these negro boys quickly learned that they could escape punishment by falsely imputing to me all of their mischief and I was their scape-goat.

Often Drake's negro boys went over to General Jackson's plantation to play with the negro boys over there and I frequently accompanied them. One day the old General asked me why I did not go to school. But I could not tell him. I did not know why. I have known since that I was not told to go and anyone knows that a boy just growing up loose, as I was, is not likely to go to school of his own accord.

I do not propose to convey to the reader the idea that I was naturally better than other boys, on the contrary, I frequently deserved the rod when I did not get it, but more frequently received a cruel drubbing when I did not deserve it, that, too, at the hands of the old negro crone who was exceedingly violent as well as unjust. This, of course, cultivated in me a hatred against the vile creature which was little short of murderous.

However, I stayed on and bore up under my troubles as there was nothing else to do, so far as I knew then, but "grin and bear it." This until I was fifteen years old.

At this time, however ignorant, illiterate, wild as I was, a faint idea of the need of education dawned upon me. I saw other white boys going to school; I saw the difference between them and myself that education was rapidly making and I realized that I was growing up as ignorant and uncultured as the slave boys who were my only attainable companions.

Somehow I had heard of a great city called St. Louis, and little by little the determination grew upon me to reach that wonderful place in some way.

I got a few odd jobs of work, now and then, from the neighbors and in a little while I had accumulated four dollars, which seemed a great deal of money to me, and I thought I would buy about half of St. Louis, if I could only get there. And yet I decided that it would be just as well to have a few more dollars and would not leave my present home, which, bad it was, was the only one I had, until I had acquired a little more money. But coming home from work one evening I found the old negress in an unusually bad humor, even for her. She gave me a cruel thrashing just to give vent to her feelings, and that decided me to leave at once, without waiting to further improve my financial condition. I was getting to be too big a boy to be beaten around by that old wretch, and having no ties of friendship, and no one being at all interested in me, I was determined to get away before my tormentor could get another chance at me.

I would go to St. Louis, but I must get even with the old hag before starting. I did not wish to leave in debt to anyone in the neighborhood and so I cudgeled my brain to devise a means for settling old scores with my self-constituted governess.

Toward evening I wandered into a small pasture, doing my best to think how I could best pay off the black termagant with safety to myself, when with great good luck I suddenly beheld a huge hornet's nest, hanging in a bunch of shrubbery. My plan instantly and fully developed. Quickly I returned to the house and hastily gathered what little clothing I owned into a bundle, done up in my one handkerchief, an imitation of bandanna, of very loud pattern. This bundle I secreted in the barn and then hied me to the hornet's nest. Approaching the swinging home of the hornets very softly, so as not to disturb the inmates, I stuffed the entrance to the hornet castle with sassafras leaves, and taking the great sphere in my arms I bore it to a back window of the kitchen where the black beldame was vigorously at work within and contentedly droning a negro hymn.

Dark was coming on and a drizzly rain was falling. It was the spring of the year, the day had been warm and the kitchen window was open. I stole up to the open window. The woman's back was toward me. I removed the plug of sassafras leaves and hurled the hornet's nest so that it landed under the hag's skirts.

I watched the proceedings for one short moment, and then, as it was getting late, I concluded I had better be off for St. Louis. So I went away from there at the best gait I could command.

I could hear my arch-enemy screaming, and it was music to my ears that even thrills me yet, sometimes. It was a better supper than she would have given me.

I saw the negroes running from the quarters, and elsewhere, toward the kitchen, and I must beg the reader to endeavor to imagine the scene in that culinary department, as I am unable to describe it, not having waited to see it out.

But I slid for the barn, secured my bundle and started for the ancient city far away.

All night, on foot and alone, I trudged the turnpike that ran through Nashville. I arrived in that city about daylight, tired and hungry, but was too timid to stop for something to eat, notwithstanding I had my four dollars safe in my pocket, and had not eaten since noon, the day before.

I plodded along through the town and crossed the Cumberland river on a ferry-boat, and then pulled out in a northerly direction for about an hour, when I came to a farm-house. In the road in front of the house I met the proprietor who was going from his garden, opposite the house, to his breakfast.

He waited until I came up, and as I was about to pass on, he said: "Hello! my boy, where are you going so early this morning?"

I told him I was on my way to St. Louis.

"St. Louis?" he said. "I never heard of that place before. Where is it?"

I told him I thought it was in Missouri, but was not certain.

"Are you going all the way on foot, and alone?"

I answered that I was, and that I had no other way to go. With that I started on.

"Hold on," he said. "If you are going to walk that long way you had better come in and have some breakfast."

You may rest assured that I did not wait for a second invitation, for about that time I was as hungry as I had ever been in my life.

While we were eating breakfast the farmer turned to his oldest daughter and said:

"Martha, where is St. Louis?"

She told him it was in Missouri, and one of the largest towns in the South or West. "Our geography tells lots about it," she said.

I thought this was about the best meal I had ever eaten in my life, and after it was over I offered to pay for it, but the kind- hearted old man refused to take anything, saying: "Keep your money, my boy. You may need it before you get back. And on your return, stop and stay with me all night, and tell us all about St. Louis."

After thanking them, I took my little bundle, bade them good-bye, and was on my journey again. I have always regretted that I did not learn this good man's name, but I was in something of a hurry just then, for I feared that Mr. Drake might get on my trail and follow me and take me back, and I had no pressing inclination to meet old Hulda again.

I plodded along for many days, now and then looking back for Mr. Drake, but not anxious to see him; rather the reverse.

It is not necessary to lumber up this story with my trip to St. Louis. I was about six weeks on the road, the greater part of the time in Kentucky, and I had no use for my money. I could stay at almost any farm-house all night, wherever I stopped, and have a good bed and be well fed, but no one would take pay for these accommodations. When I got to Owensboro, Ky., I became acquainted by accident with the mate of a steamboat that was going to St. Louis and he allowed me to go on the boat and work my way.

The first person that I met in St Louis, that I dared to speak with, was a boy somewhat younger than myself. I asked him his name, and in broken English he replied that his name was Henry Becket.

Seeing that he was French, I began to talk to him in his own language, which was my mother tongue, and so we were quickly friends. I told him that my parents were both dead and that I had no home, and he being of a kind-hearted, sympathetic nature, invited me to go home with him, which invitation I immediately accepted.

Henry Becket's mother was a widow and they were very poor, but they were lovingly kind to me.

I told Mrs. Becket of my troubles with Mr. Drake's old negro woman; how much abuse I had suffered at her hands and the widow sympathized with me deeply. She also told me that I was welcome to stay with them until such time as I was able to get employment. So I remained with the Beckets three days, during all of which time I tried hard to get work, but without success.

On the morning of the fourth day she asked me if I had tried any of the hotels for work. I told her that I had not, so she advised me to go to some of them in my rounds.

It had not occurred to me that a boy could find anything to do about a hotel, but I took Mrs. Becket's advice, and that morning called at the American hotel, which was the first one I came to.

Quite boldly, for a green boy, I approached the person whom I was told was the proprietor and asked him if he had any work for a boy, whereupon he looked at me in what seemed a most scornful way and said very tartly:

"What kind of work do you think you could do?"

I told him I could do most anything in the way of common labor.

He gave me another half-scornful smile and said:

"I think you had better go home to your parents and go to school. That's the best place for you."

This was discouraging, but instead of explaining my position, I turned to go, and in spite of all that I could do the tears came to my eyes. Not that I cared so much for being refused employment, but for the manner in which the hotel man had spoken to me. I did not propose to give up at that, but started away, more than ever determined to find employment. I did not want to impose on the Beckets, notwithstanding that they still assured me of welcome, and moreover I wished to do something to help them, even more than myself.

I had nearly reached the door when a man who had been reading a newspaper, but was now observing me, called out:

"My boy! come here."

I went over to the corner where he was sitting and I was trying at the same time to dry away my tears.

This man asked my name, which I gave him. He then asked where my parents lived, and I told him that they died when I was four years old.

Other questions from him brought out the story of my boy-life; Drake, Gen. Jackson, the negro boys and the brutal negress; then my trip to St. Louis—but I omitted the hornet's-nest incident. I also told this kindly stranger that I had started out to make a living for myself and intended to succeed.

Then he asked me where I was staying, and I told him of the Beckets.

Seeing that this man was taking quite an interest in me, gave me courage to ask his name. He told me that his name was Kit Carson, and that by calling he was a hunter and trapper, and asked me how I would like to learn his trade.

I assured him that I was willing to do anything honorable for a living and that I thought I would very much like to be a hunter and trapper. He said he would take me with him and I was entirely delighted. Often I had wished to own a gun, but had never thought of shooting anything larger than a squirrel or rabbit. I was ready to start at once, and asked him when he would go.

Smilingly he told me not to be in a hurry, and asked me where Mrs. Becket lived. I told him as nearly as I could, and again asked when he thought we would leave St. Louis. I was fearful that he would change his mind about taking me with him. I didn't know him then so well as afterward. I came to learn that his slightest word was his bond.

But visions of Mr. Drake, an old negro woman and a hornet's nest, still haunted me and made me overanxious. I wanted to get as far out of their reach as possible and still remain on the earth.

Mr. Carson laughed in a quiet and yet much amused way and said:

"You must learn to not do anything until you are good and ready, and there are heaps of things to do before we can start out. Now let's go and see Mrs. Becket."

So I piloted him to the widow's home, which, as near as I can remember, was about four blocks from the hotel. Mr. Carson being able to speak French first-rate, had a talk with Mrs. Becket concerning me. The story she told him, corresponding with that which I had told him, he concluded that I had given him nothing but truth, and then he asked Mrs. Becket what my bill was. She replied that she had just taken me in because I was a poor boy, until such time as I could find employment, and that her charges were nothing. He then asked her how long I had been with her, and being told that it was four days, he begged her to take five dollars, which she finally accepted.

I took my little budget of clothes and tearfully bidding Mrs. Becket and Henry good-bye, started back to the hotel with my new guardian, and I was the happiest boy in the world, from that on, so long as I was a boy.

On the way back to the hotel Mr. Carson stopped with me at a store and he bought me a new suit of clothes, a hat and a pair of boots, for I was barefooted and almost bareheaded. Thus dressed I could hardly realize that I was the Will Drannan of a few hours before.

That was the first pair of boots I had ever owned. Perhaps, dear reader, you do not know what that means to a healthy boy of fifteen.

It means more than has ever been written, or ever will be.

I was now very ready to start out hunting, and on our way to the hotel I asked Mr. Carson if he did not think we could get away by morning, but he told me that to hunt I would probably need a gun, and we must wait until he could have one made for me, of proper size for a boy.

The next day we went to a gun factory and Mr. Carson gave orders concerning the weapon, after which we returned to the hotel. We remained in St. Louis about three weeks and every day seemed like an age to me. At our room in the hotel Mr. Carson would tell me stories about hunting and trapping, and notwithstanding the intense interest of the stories the days were longer, because I so much wished to be among the scenes he talked of, and my dreams at night were filled with all sorts of wonderful animals, my fancy's creation from what Mr. Carson talked about. I had never fired a gun in my life and I was unbearably impatient to get my hands on the one that was being made for me.

During the wait at St. Louis, Henry Becket was with me nearly all the time, and when we were not haunting the gun factory, we were, as much as possible, in Mr. Carson's room at the hotel, listening to stories of adventure on the plains and among the mountains.

I became, at once, very much attached to Mr. Carson and I thought there was not another man in the United States equal to him—and there never has been, in his line. Besides, since the death of my mother he was the only one who had taken the slightest interest in me, or treated me like a human being, barring, of course, the Beckets and those persons who had helped me on my long walk from Nashville to St. Louis.

Finally Mr. Carson—whom I had now learned to address as Uncle Kit— said to me, one morning, that as my gun was about completed we would make preparations to start West. So we went out to a farm, about two miles from St. Louis, to get the horses from where Uncle Kit had left them to be cared for during the winter.

We went on foot, taking a rope, or riatta, as it is called by frontiersmen, and on the way to the farm I could think or talk of nothing but my new rifle, and the buffalo, deer, antelope and other game that I would kill when I reached the plains. Uncle Kit remarked that he had forgotten to get me a saddle, but that we would not have to wait to get one made, as there were plenty of saddles that would fit me already made, and that he would buy me one when he got back to town.

When we reached the farm where the horses were, Uncle Kit pointed out a little bay pony that had both his ears cropped off at the tips, and he said:

"Now Willie, there is your pony. Catch him and climb on," at the same time handing me the riatta.

The pony being gentle I caught and mounted him at once, and by the time we had got back to town money could not have bought that little crop-eared horse from me. As will be seen, later on, I kept that pony and he was a faithful friend and servant until his tragic death, years afterward.

In two days we had a pack-train of twenty horses rigged for the trip. The cargo was mostly tobacco, blankets and beads, which Carson was taking out to trade to the Indians for robes and furs. Of course all this was novel to me as I had never seen a pack- saddle or anything associated with one.

A man named Hughes, of whom you will see much in this narrative, accompanied and assisted Uncle Kit on this trip, as he had done the season before, for besides his experience as a packer, he was a good trapper, and Uncle Kit employed him.

CHAPTER II
BEGINNING OF AN ADVENTUROUS LIFE.—FIRST WILD TURKEY.—FIRST BUFFALO.—FIRST FEAST AS AN HONORED GUEST OF INDIANS.—DOG MEAT

It was on the morning of May 3, 1847, that we rounded up the horses and Uncle Kit and Mr. Hughes began packing them.

It being the first trip of the season some of the pack-ponies were a little frisky and would try to lie down when the packs were put on them. So it became my business to look after them and keep them on their feet until all were packed.

Everything being in readiness, I shook hands, good-bye, with my much-esteemed friend, Henry Becket, who had been helping me with the pack-horses, and who also coveted my crop-eared pony, very naturally for a boy. Then we were off for a country unknown to me, except for what Uncle Kit had told me of it.

My happiness seemed to increase, if that were possible. I was unspeakably glad to get away from St. Louis before Mr. Drake had learned of my whereabouts, and up to the time of this writing I have never been back to St. Louis, or Tennessee, nor have I heard anything of Mr. Drake or my ancient enemy, the angel of Erebus.

From St. Louis we struck out westward, heading for Ft. Scott, which place is now a thriving little city in southeastern Kansas, but then the extreme out-edge of settlement.

The first day out we traveled until about 2 o'clock in the afternoon, when we came to a fine camping place with abundance of grass, wood and water.

Uncle Kit, thinking we had traveled far enough for the first day, said:

"I reckon the lad is gittin' tired, Hughes, 's well as the horses, an' I think we'd better pull up for the day."

I was glad to hear this, for I had done more riding that day than in any one day in my life, before.

Uncle Kit told me it would be my job, on the trip as soon as my horse was unsaddled, to gather wood and start a fire, while he and Mr. Hughes unpacked the animals. So I unsaddled my horse, and by the time they had the horses unpacked I had a good fire going and plenty of water at hand for all purposes. Mr. Hughes, meantime, got out the coffee-pot and frying-pan, and soon we had a meal that I greatly enjoyed and which was the first one for me by a camp- fire.

After we had eaten, and smoked and lounged for a while, Uncle Kit asked me if I did not wish to try my rifle.

Of course I did.

So taking a piece of wood and sharpening one end that it might be driven into the ground, he took a piece of charcoal and made on the flat side of the wood a mark for me to shoot at.

"Now Willie," said Uncle Kit, "if you ever expect to be a good hunter you must learn to be a good shot, and you can't begin practicin' too soon."

I had never fired a gun, but I had made up my mind to be a mighty hunter and so started in for shooting practice with much zeal. Uncle Kit gave me few instructions about How to hold the gun, and I raised the rifle to my face and fired the first shot of my life.

I do not know how close my bullet came to that mark, nor how far it missed, for the wood was untouched. But I tried it again and with much better success, for this time I struck the stick about eight inches below the mark. This was great encouragement and from that on I could scarcely take time to eat meals in camp, in my anxiety to practice, and I was further encouraged by Uncle Kit's approval of my desire to practice.

One evening I overheard Uncle Kit say to Mr. Hughes, "That boy is going to make a dead shot afterwhile."

This gave me great faith in my future as a hunter and Uncle Kit and Mr. Hughes seemed to take great delight in teaching me all the tricks of rifle marksmanship.

After we had traveled about two days we came to a belt of country where there were wild turkeys in great numbers, and on the morning of the third day out, Uncle Kit called me early, saying:

"Come Willie, jump up now, an' le's go an' see if we can't git a wild turkey for breakfast." He had heard the turkeys that morning and knew which direction to go to find them.

I rolled out and was quickly dressed and ready.

When near the turkey haunt Uncle Kit took a quill from his pocket and by a peculiar noise on the quill called the turkeys up near to him, then took aim at one, fired and killed it.

"Now Willie," he said, "do you think you can do that to-morrow morning?"

I told him that I thought if I could get close enough, and the turkeys would stand right still, I believed I could fetch one. And I desired to know if it was certain that there would be turkeys where we were to camp that night.

"Oh, yes;" said he, "thar'll be plenty of 'em for some days yit."

Early the next morning Uncle Kit called me as usual, and said, "Git up now, an' see what you can do for a turkey breakfast."

Instantly I was on my feet, Uncle Kit showed me the direction to go, loaned me his turkey-call quill, which, by the way, he had been teaching me how to use as we rode the day before.

I shouldered my rifle and had not gone far when I heard the turkeys, up the river. Then I took the quill and started my turkey tune. Directly a big old gobbler came strutting towards me and I called him up as near to me as he would come, for I wanted to make sure of him.

Uncle Kit had told me about the "buck-ague" and I knew I had it when I tried to draw a bead on that big gobbler. I had never shot at a living thing, and when I leveled my rifle it was impossible to control my nerves.

The turkey seemed to jump up and down, and appeared to me to be as big as a pony, when I looked at him along the rifle. Two or three times I tried to hold the bead on him, but could not. Now I wouldn't have missed killing him for anything, in reason, for I feared that Uncle Kit and Mr. Hughes would laugh at me.

At last, however, the sights of my gun steadied long enough for me to pull the trigger, and to my great delight—and I may as well admit, surprise—Mr. Gobbler tumbled over dead when I fired, and he was so heavy as to be a good load for me to carry to camp.

Now I was filled with confidence in myself, and became eager for a shot at bigger game; antelope, deer or buffalo.

In a few days we passed Ft. Scott and then we were entirely beyond the bounds of civilization.

From that on, until we reached our destination, the only living things we saw were jack-rabbits, prairie-dogs, antelope, deer, buffalo, sage-hens and Indians, barring, of course, insects, reptiles and the like, and the little owls that live with the prairie-dogs and sit upon the mounds of the dog villages, eyeing affairs with seeming dignity and wisdom.

The owls seem to turn their heads while watching you, their bodies remaining stationary, until, it has been said, you may wring their heads off by walking around them a few times. I would not have my young friends believe, however, that this is true. It is only a very old joke of the plains.

The first herd of buffalo we saw was along a stream known as Cow Creek and which is a tributary to the Arkansas river. We could see the herd feeding along the hills in the distance.

Here was good camping ground and it was time to halt for the night. So as soon as we had decided on the spot to pitch camp, Uncle Kit directed me to go and kill a buffalo, so that we might have fresh meat for supper.

That suited me, exactly, for I was eager to get a shot at such big game.

Uncle Kit told me to follow up the ravine until opposite the herd and then climb the hill, but to be careful and not let the buffalo see me.

I followed his instructions to the dot, for I had come to believe that what Kit Carson said was law and gospel, and what he didn't know would not fill a book as large as Ayer's Almanac. I was right, too, so far as plainscraft was concerned.

Uncle Kit had also directed me to select a small buffalo to shoot at, and to surely kill it, for we were out of meat.

It so happened that when I got to the top of the hill and in sight of the herd again the first animal that seemed to present an advantageous shot was a two-year-old heifer.

I dropped flat on the ground and crawled toward her, like a snake. Once she raised her head, but the wind being in my favor, she did not discern me, but put her head down and went on feeding. I succeeded in crawling quite close enough to her, drew a bead on her and fired. At the crack of the rifle she came to the ground, "as dead as a door-nail," much to the surprise of Uncle Kit and Mr. Hughes, who were watching me from a distance.

When the animal fell, I threw my hat in the air and gave a yell that would have done credit to an Apache warrior.

Uncle Kit and I dressed the buffalo and carried the meat into camp while Mr. Hughes gathered wood for the night-fires.

I could scarcely sleep that night for thinking of my buffalo, and could I have seen Henry Becket that night I would almost have stunned him with my stories of frontier life.

The novice is ever enthusiastic.

The following morning we woke up early, and off, still heading up the Arkansas river for Bent's Fort, and from here on the buffalo were numerous, and we had that sort of fresh meat until we got good and tired of it.

The second day out from Cow Creek, in the afternoon, we saw about twenty Indians coming towards us. At the word, "Indians," I could feel my hair raise on end, and many an Indian has tried to raise it since.

This was my first sight of the red man. He looked to me to be more of a black man.

Uncle Kit asked Mr. Hughes what Indians he thought they were. The reply was that he thought them to be Kiowas, and on coming up to them the surmise proved to be correct.

They were Black Buffalo, the chief of the Kiowas, and his daughter, accompanied by twenty warriors.

Black Buffalo, and indeed all the Kiowa tribe, were well acquainted with Uncle Kit and had great respect for him. So a general hand-shaking and pow-wow followed.

Carson spoke their language as well as they could, and consequently had no difficulty conversing with them.

In those days very few Indians knew a word of English, consequently all conversation with them had to be carried on in the several tribal languages or dialects, or in the jargon.

This latter was a short language composed of Indian, French and English words, and was called "Chinook." It originated with the fur traders of Astoria, Ore., and its growth was assisted by missionaries, until it became the means of communication between the whites and the Indians of the coast and interior of the vast Northwest, and even between Indians whose dialects were unknown to each other. In short it was a sort of Indian "Volapuk," and was very easily mastered. There has been a dictionary of it printed, and I have known a bright man to acquire the vocabulary in two or three days.

Black Buffalo and his little band shortly turned about and rode back to their village, which was only two miles away. But they first invited us to visit them, which we did, as not to have done so would have been a violent breach of plains etiquette, that might cause a disruption of friendship.

In the Indian village, after our horses had been unpacked and turned out to graze, Uncle Kit and Black Buffalo strolled about among the lodges or wick-i-ups, of which there were something like fifteen hundred. I followed very closely for I was mortally afraid to get fifteen feet away from Uncle Kit, in that sort of company.

Black Buffalo did us the honor, that evening, to take us to his own private wick-i-up for supper. It was a custom with this, and many other tribes of Indians, that conveyed great distinction to visitors, to kill and cook for them a nice fat dog. However, I was not then aware that I was so distinguished a guest, as indeed neither I nor Mr. Hughes would have been had we not been in the company of Kit Carson. With him we shone by reflected greatness.

While we were out on our walk about the village, Black Buffalo's cook was preparing this distinguishing feast for us.

I had kept unusually quiet all the time we were among the Indians, not even asking one question, which was very remarkable in me. For I presume that on the journey I had asked more questions to the lineal mile than any boy ever had before.

But I ate the dog in silence and liked it. Of course I had no idea what the meat was. So, Uncle Kit observing the gusto with which I was devouring dog, asked me if I knew what the meat was. I told him that I did not, but supposed it to be antelope, or buffalo. He informed me that it was neither, but good, healthy dog.

I thought he was joking, and simply replied that it was mighty good meat, even if it was dog, and gave the matter no further reflection, at the time.

The next day, when Uncle Kit and Mr. Hughes assured me that it was really dog meat, we had eaten the night before, I felt very much like throwing up everything I had eaten at the village, but it was too late then.

After supper, that night in the Indian village, we had what was called a "peace smoke." The Chief selected about a dozen of his braves, and all being seated in a circle, two of our party on one side of the Chief, and Uncle Kit at his right, a pipe was lit and the Chief took one whiff, the smoke of which he blew up into the air. He then took another whiff, and turning to his chief guest, handed him the pipe, who blew a whiff into the air and the second one into the face of the host. This performance having been gone through with for each guest, the Chief then handed the pipe to the first Indian on his right, and thus it went around the circle, each Indian blowing a whiff into the air.

It was considered a great breach of etiquette to speak, or even smile, during this ceremony.

This Indian village was situated at Pawnee Rock, on the Arkansas river, in a beautiful valley, in what is now the southwest corner of Benton Co.,

Kan. The wick-i-ups were made of poles set on ends, gathered together at the top, and covered with buffalo skins from which the hair had been removed.

The Kiowas were, at that time, the most numerous tribe of Indians in the United States.

Early the next morning after our dog-feast and peace-smoke, our party was up and off, and I was particularly glad to get away, feeling that I would rather camp out and feed on buffalo, antelope, jack-rabbits and wild turkey than dwell in the lodges of Kiowas and be "honored" with banquets of the nicest dogs in all that region.

We took the Santa Fe trail and the buffalo were so numerous along the way that we had to take some pains to avoid them, as when they were traveling or on a stampede, nothing could turn or stop them and we would be in danger of being ground to atoms beneath their thousands of hoofs.

In two days more of travel we reached another Indian village, on another beautiful plain, in what is now Pawnee Co., Kan. Here the country was so level that one could see for miles in any direction, and the sun rising or setting, seemed to come up or go down, as a great golden disk, out of or into the earth. We could see many bands of wild horses feeding on the luxuriant grasses, and little did I think, then, that I would live to see the day when that broad and unfenced plain would be converted into homes for hundreds of the pale-faced race.

We were met on the outskirts of the village by White Horse, Chief of the Comanches, who, being an intimate friend of Uncle Kit, shook hands with us and conducted us to his own wick-i-up. There we unpacked the animals and piled up our goods, and White Horse detailed an Indian to guard the packs day and night.

After our horses had been picketed out to grass, the Chief took us into his lodge to dine with him, and here again we had boiled dog and the peace smoke.

White Horse insisted upon our being his guests until morning, it being about noon when we arrived, and as our horses were much jaded we decided to give them the advantage of such a rest.

The Comanche Chief was most exceedingly hospitable, in his way, and would not allow us to eat of our own provisions, but insisted upon our eating with him, and "trotted" out the best "grub" he had.

After breakfast the next morning our horses were brought in by the Indians, who also helped us to pack, and we struck the trail again, accompanied by White Horse and his daughter, who traveled with us all that day and camped with us at night.

That evening Uncle Kit killed a fine buffalo calf, and I thought it the best meat I had ever eaten—even better than dog.

The following morning the Chief and his daughter returned to the village, and we proceeded on our journey.

That day, riding along on my crop-eared pony, about fifty yards behind my companions, I chanced to look behind me and I saw what I thought to be a man, walking on a hill towards us, and he appeared to be at least twenty feet high. As he got further down the hill he appeared to grow shorter, until, I thought, he went down a ravine and out of sight.

I put spurs to Croppy and galloped up to Uncle Kit, and told him I had seen the tallest man on earth, declaring that the man was at least twenty feet high.

"An' you saw a man that high?" said Uncle Kit

"Indeed I did," I replied.

"Sure you saw him?" he asked.

"Yes, sir; and if you will watch you will see him come up out of the ravine, directly."

Uncle Kit, laughing, said: "It was not a man you saw, my boy, but a mirage," and he explained to me the phenomena, which I became familiar with in the years that followed.

Sometimes the mirages present to the vision what appear to be men, at other times bodies of water surrounded by trees, and often houses and whole towns. They appear before you on the dryest plains and then disappear as if the earth opened and swallowed them.

Early in June we reached Bent's Fort and met there Col. Bent and his son, Mr. Roubidoux and his son, and a man named James Bridger, of whom you will see a great deal, later on in this narrative. These men were all traders, buying furs and buffalo robes from Indians, white hunters and trappers.

We remained at Bent's Fort six weeks, and often during that time some one of the many hunters, trappers and traders, that made this place their headquarters, would ask Uncle Kit what he was going to do with that boy—meaning me. To all of which Carson would reply "I'm goin' to make a hunter and trapper of him."

During the six weeks at the fort I was out nearly every day with some of the men, and to me they gave the name of "Young Kit."

By the time we were ready to leave Bent's Fort, Young Kit became quite a rider, and Uncle Kit had been training me in the dexterous use of the rifle, shooting from my knee, lying on my back, resting the gun on my toes, lying flat on my belly, resting the gun on my hat, and in various other positions.

Having disposed of all our blankets, beads and all of the tobacco, except what was reserved for home consumption, we left Bent's Fort, crossed the Arkansas river and followed up Apishapa creek three days, when we came to the Rocky Mountains, among which we were during four days, passing Trinkara Peak then turning south toward a little Mexican village called Taos, where Uncle Kit made his home, he having a house of his own in that village.

On the morning after our arrival at Taos, Uncle Kit said to me at breakfast:

"Willie, there are a lot of Mexican boys here who would like to play with you."

Some of them were standing near in a group, gazing at me in much wonderment.

"But," continued Uncle Kit, "you will have to learn to speak their language in order to have much fun. Go with them if you wish, and tell me to-night how many words you have learned."

Then he spoke to the group of boys in their own tongue and told them I wished to play with them but couldn't speak their language, and wanted to learn.

We had a jolly time that day in many boyish games that I had never seen, and when I came home Uncle Kit asked me how many words I had learned.

"Three," I replied.

"Splendid!" he exclaimed. "'Twont be long fo' you are a fus'-class Mexican."

One evening, after we had been in Taos about two weeks, Uncle Kit told me to put on my best suit and he would take me to a fandango. I was not sure what a fandango was but was willing to experience one, just the same, and, togged out in our best, we went to the fandango, which was simply a Mexican dance. Sort of a public ball.

I looked on that night with much interest, but declined to participate further than that. I learned better in a little while, and the fandango, with the tinkle of guitars and mandolins, the clink of the cavalleros' spurs, and the laugh and beauty of the Mexican senoritas, became a great pleasure to me.

Thus began our life at the little Mexican town of Taos, the home of that great hero of the West, Kit Carson.

CHAPTER III
HUNTING AND TRAPPING IN SOUTH PARK, WHERE A BOY, UNAIDED, KILLS AND SCALPS TWO INDIANS—MEETING WITH FREMONT, THE "PATH-FINDER"

One evening in October as I was getting ready to retire for the night, Uncle Kit said to me:

"Now Willie, to-morrow you must put in the day moulding bullets, for we must begin making preparations to go trapping."

This was pleasant news to me, for I had laid around so long with nothing to do but skylark with those Mexican boys, that life was getting to be monotonous.

The reader will understand that in those early days we had only muzzle-loading guns, and for every one of those we had to have a pair of bullet-moulds the size of the rifle, and before starting out on an expedition it was necessary to mould enough bullets to last several weeks, if not the entire trip, and when you realize that almost any time we were liable to get into a "scrap" with the Indians, you can understand that it required a great number of these little leaden missiles to accommodate the red brethren, as well as to meet other uses.

That evening after I had gone to bed, Mr. Hughes said:

"Kit, what are you going to do with that boy?"

"What boy?" asked Uncle Kit, as if he were astonished.

"Why, Willie. What are you going to do with him while we are away trapping?"

"Why, take him along to help us, of course."

"Thunderation!" exclaimed Hughes; "he will only be a bother to us in the mountains."

I had been with Kit Carson three months, and this was the first time I had seen him, apparently, out of humor. But at Hughes' last remark, he said in a decidedly angry tone:

"Jim Hughes, I want you to understand that wherever I go that boy can go, too, if he likes."

Hughes seeing that Carson did not like what he had said about "that boy," turned the matter off by saying that he had only made the remark to tease the boy.

Next morning Uncle Kit started a Mexican lad out to round up the horses, and the next two days were spent in fixing up our pack- saddles preparatory for the trip.

Our horses were as fat as seals, as there was no end to the range for them in this part of the country.

All being in readiness we pulled out from Taos, four of us, Uncle Kit, Mr. Hughes, myself and a Mexican boy named Juan. The latter went along to bring our horses back home.

We crossed back over that spur of the Rocky Mountains that we had came in through, and struck the Arkansas river near where Pueblo, Colo., now stands, and from here we polled for the headwaters of that river, carefully examining every stream we came to for beaver sign.

We saw abundance of game on the trip, such as antelope, deer and buffalo.

When we had traveled up the river about two days, Uncle Kit thought it was not best to take the horses any further as the country was now too rough for them, so we spent the next two days caching our cargo.

As some may not know what a cache is, I will explain.

Cache is French for "hide." A hole is dug in the ground and the things to be hidden are put in there and covered with brush, then with dirt, then more brush and more dirt, and the whole is covered with turf, to make the surface look as natural as possible, so that it is not likely to be discovered by Indians at a distance.

We having about a thousand pounds of stores to cache, it was no small job.

On the morning of the third day in this camp, we all started out to kill some game for Juan to take back home. Mr. Hughes started out in one direction and Uncle Kit and I in the opposite. We had gone but a short distance, when, looking across a canyon, I saw a herd of some kind of animals and asked Uncle Kit what they were. He told me they were bison, and complimented me on having such good eyes.

Bison, by the way, is the distinctive name in that region for mountain buffalo, all buffalo belonging to the bison family.

We then started on a round-about way to try and get in gunshot of the herd, in which we were successful. When we had got in gunshot of them and he had pointed out the one for me to shoot at, he said:

"Now take a rest on that big rock, and when I count three, pull the trigger, and be sure that you break its neck."

The guns went off so near together that I turned and asked Uncle Kit why he didn't shoot, too, for I did not think that he had fired; but as soon as the smoke from our guns had cleared away, I saw two bison kicking their last.

After dressing the animals we returned to camp and learned that Mr. Hughes had killed two deer, which, with the two bisons, were enough to load the pack-horses.

We were now in the extreme south end of South Park, which was mostly a prairie country, except along the streams, and more or less pine trees were scattered here and there along the hillsides.

Next morning we loaded the pack-horses with the game and Juan started back home, alone, with the horses.

After we had seen him off, we rolled up our blankets and taking enough provisions to last several days, we "packed up our packs" and pulled out up the Arkansas again.

This, to me, was like breaking a colt to the saddle, only I didn't buck.

Notwithstanding I had a light pack, for I was a light subject, it was hard work for me. Mr. Hughes had been out the year before, and being a grown man, it did not worry him as it did me. However, we traveled very slowly, looking well all the time for beaver sign.

In the afternoon of the second day we came to where there was plenty of beaver sign. In fact the trees they had gnawed down were so thick that we could not travel along the river, but had to take to the hillsides.

We camped that night at the mouth of a little stream that empties into the Arkansas, and the following morning, after looking over the trapping ground, the two men selected a place to build our winter quarters, and we went to work. They worked at the cabin while I killed the game for our meat and did the cooking, my outfit being a frying-pan, a coffee-pot and a tin cup for each of us.

They were about two weeks getting our cabin, or dugout, completed. It was made by first digging out a place in the hillside, about twelve feet square, and building up the front with logs, then brush and pine boughs, and then the whole with dirt, the door was made of hewed logs, fastened together with crossed pieces by means of wooden pins, and it was hung on heavy wooden hinges.

Our winter quarters being thus completed, Uncle Kit and Mr. Hughes set out one morning for the cache, intending to return that same evening. Before starting they told me to go out some time during the day and kill a small deer, that I would be able to carry to camp, and have a good lot of it cooked for supper, as they would be very hungry when they returned that night. They started sometime before daylight, and I stayed around the cabin, clearing things up and cutting wood, until about ten o'clock, then cleaned up my rifle and started out to kill the deer. It was an easy matter to find one, for they were as thick in that country as sheep on a mutton farm. But, boy-like, I wandered off up the canyon about two miles before I found a deer that just suited me, and I wanted to see the country, anyway.

At last I found a little deer that I thought about the right thing and I killed and dressed it—or rather undressed it—threw it on my shoulder and pulled for camp.

Instead of going the way I had come, I climbed out on the ridge to avoid the down timber, that was so thick in the creek bottom. When I was near the top of the ridge, I looked off a short distance and saw three Indians, on foot, going down the ridge in the direction of our dug-out.

I had often heard Uncle Kit tell how the Indians robbed the camps of trappers and that they invariably burned the cabins.

As soon as I got sight of the Indians, I dropped back over the ridge, for, luckily, they had not got sight of me. In a few seconds I did some powerful thinking, and I came to the conclusion that it would never do to let them find our dug-out, for while it would hardly burn, they might carry off our bedding, or destroy it. So I crawled up to a log, took good aim at the leader and fired, striking him just under the arm, bringing him down. The other two dropped to their knees, and looked all around, and I suppose the only thing that saved me was the wind was coming from them to me and blew the smoke from my gun down the canyon, so that they did not see where the shot came from.

I heard Uncle Kit tell of lying on his back and loading his rifle, when in a close place, so I did likewise and crawled up to my log again. The remaining two Indians, having looked all around and seeing no one, had got on their feet again, and were standing with bow and arrow in hand, each having a quiver full of arrows on his back, and if they had got sight of me that would have been the last of Young Kit. But I took aim at one of them and fired, with the same result as before. As my second Indian fell, the third one started back up the ridge, in the direction from which they had come, and if I ever saw an Indian do tall sprinting, that one did. I watched him until he was out of sight, and then loaded my gun, shouldered my deer and went to where the two Indians were lying. They were both as dead as dried herring.

I had never seen an Indian scalped, but had often heard how it was done, so I pulled my hunting-knife and took their top-nots, and again started for the dug-out, a great hunter and Indian fighter, in my own estimation.

I hung the scalps up inside the dug-out, directly in front of the door, so that Uncle Kit and Mr. Hughes would see them the first thing on entering the cabin. Then I set about getting supper, all the while thinking what a mighty deed I had done in saving our cabin, which was probably true.

The two men did not return until after dark and they were very tired and hungry, having walked forty miles that day, carrying on the return trip a hundred pounds each. That is a heavy load for a man to carry twenty miles, but they did it, and it was no uncommon thing for the hardy frontiersmen of that day to perform like feats of strength and endurance.

When they pushed open the heavy log door, the scalps were almost in their faces.

"Who did this?" said Uncle Kit, as he threw his heavy pack on the dirt floor.

I told him and he was very much astonished.

"How was it, Willie?" he asked, and I told him the whole story.

While I was telling him the story, as briefly as I could, he showed more agitation than I had ever seen him exhibit.

During all the time I had been with him, he had never spoken a harsh word to me, up to this time. But while we were at supper he said to me:

"My boy, don't let me ever hear of you taking such chances again. Not that I care for you killin' the Injuns, but you took great chances for losing your own hair, for had them redskins got sight of you, by the time they had got through with you, your hide wouldn't have held corn shucks. And it's a mystery to me that they didn't see you."

The following morning after breakfast we all took a trip up the canyon, where I had gone the morning before, and we took with us twelve beaver traps that they had brought up from the cache, and these we set at different places along the stream.

After they were set Uncle Kit asked me if I thought I could find all of them again, and I said I thought I could.

"All right then," he said. "It will be your job to tend these traps, until Jim and me get the balance of the stuff packed up from the cache. Now le's go and see your Injuns."

I took them to where I had shot the two Indians, and Uncle Kit, as soon as he saw them, said:

"They are Utes, and the wust hoss-thieves on the waters of the Colorado. Willie, I'm dog-goned glad you killed 'em. I would a give the best hoss I've got to a been here with you, for I think Old Black Leg would a caught the other feller, afore he got to the top o' the mountain."

"Black Leg" was Uncle Kit's pet name for his rifle.

That night, before going to bed, Uncle Kit said we must be up early next morning, as he and Hughes would have to make another trip to the cache, and that I must tend to the traps and keep a sharp lookout for Indians "But whatever happens," he said, "don't ever be taken prisoner."

They started very early the next morning, and as soon as it was light I struck out to examine the traps. From the twelve I took nine beaver, skinned them, reset the traps, returned to the dug- out and stretched the skins.

The stretching is done by making a bow of a small willow or other pliant wood, for each hide, and then pulling the hide over it. The hides are thus left until they are dry, when the bows are taken out and the hides are packed in a frame made for that purpose, fifty in a bale.

All of this kind of work I had learned at Bent's Fort, while there, from the many trappers there. Besides, Uncle Kit had given me other lessons in the work.

Uncle Kit and Mr. Hughes made a trip to the cache every other day until the stuff was all packed up to our winter quarters.

I had my hands full attending to the traps, as the men brought more of them on the second trip, and they set enough of them to make double work for me. One dozen traps is called a "string," and it is considered one man's work, ordinarily, to "tend a string."

The two men brought all the stuff up from the cache in five trips. On the day the last trip was made, I went out early, as usual, to attend to the traps, of which we had thirty-six. That morning I took twenty-three beaver, and seeing that it would be impossible for me to skin them all, I set about to carry them to the dug-out. If ever a boy worked, I did that day, and had just got through carrying them in when Uncle Kit and Mr. Hughes returned.

After we had got caught up with our work and rested a few days, Uncle Kit said one morning that we must be out early next day and get our work done so that we could go and kill some elk. "For," said he, "we have got to have meat for the winter and we must have some hides for beds."

In those days the trappers made their beds by first constructing a frame or rough bedstand, over which they stretched a green elk hide, securing that by thongs or strings cut from a green deer skin. By lying on these at once, before they are dry, they get shaped to the body and they make a first-class bed for comfort.

We were out early to the traps next morning, and the catch being somewhat smaller than usual, we got through by 11 o'clock, and after eating a "snack"—a lunch—we started on the elk hunt.

After going about four miles we jumped up a band of fifty elk, which was considered a small herd then. But we didn't get close enough to shoot any of them.

"Let 'em go," said Uncle Kit; "no doubt they will go to the quaking-asp grove, and we can git 'em to-morrow." So we returned to camp without any elk. But the next morning we went to the quaking-asp thicket, and there, sure enough, we found the same band of elk, and succeeded in killing five of them. Thus we had enough meat to last a year, if we had wanted that much, and we had skins enough for our beds and moccasins for the winter.

Now we were in no danger of starving, and from now on we could devote our whole attention to the traps.

I had to work very hard that winter, but I was much better contented than when I was with Drake and in the grasp of that old "nigger wench."

Not until now did I tell Uncle Kit of the prank I played on the black tyrant. I also told him why I was so anxious to get away from St. Louis. That it was I feared Drake would discover me and take me back to his farm and the society of his slaves.

Mr. Hughes here interrupted me to say: "Well Willie, you are safe enough from Drake and the wench, but I think by the time you get out o' here in the spring, you would much rather be with them."

I assured him, however, that he was mistaken, and that I was bent on being a hunter and trapper.

"And an Indian fighter?" he added.

"Yes, and an Indian fighter, too, if you like;" I replied.

Well, we remained at this camp all winter, not seeing a person outside of our own crowd, and to take it on the whole, it was one of the most enjoyable winters of my life. It being my first winter in the mountains, I was learning something new every day, and whenever I found the track of any wild animal that I was not acquainted with, I would report to Uncle Kit, and he would go miles with me to see the sign, and would take great pains to tell me what sort of an animal it was and all about its nature and habits.

This was one of the most successful winter's trapping he had ever had, as we were on entirely new ground, where trapping had not been done before, and, moreover, the weather was particularly favorable.

Winter began to break up about a month earlier than usual, it being toward the last days of March when the snow commenced going off. We then took a pair of blankets each, and enough provisions to last us on our trip, and started for Taos, the only kind of provisions we had left being dried elk and venison. It was an easy matter to cure meat in this style in that country, for the air is so light that meat stuck upon the top of a pole eight or ten feet high, will quickly become dried, or "jerked." Trappers seldom take enough flour and coffee to last all winter, as it made too much bulk and weight to pack so far. Sugar was almost unknown in a trapper camp.

The second day after leaving the dug-out we met Juan, the Mexican boy. He was not bringing our horses, but was carrying a letter for Uncle Kit, from Col. John C. Fremont, asking him to come to Taos, as he wished to employ him as guide for his expedition to California.

That evening, after reading the letter, Uncle Kit said: "Willie, I have got to go to California in the summer to pilot Col. Fremont through. Do you want to go along?"

I said I was perfectly willing to go anywhere that he went.

He said: "We will pass through some mighty rough country, and also through the country of the Utes. If you go, you will, no doubt, have plenty of chances to try your hand at shootin' Injuns, for them Utes are tough nuts."

That didn't scare me a bit, for I was now sixteen years' old, had killed and scalped two Indians, and had already begun to consider myself a hunter and Indian fighter from away back. Besides, when the story of my killing the two Indians got out, I came to be generally called "the boy scalper." But Uncle Kit never spoke of me in that way, for he always respected me as a father would his own son.

Now Uncle Kit was anxious to reach Taos and meet Col. Fremont, so we pushed on with all possible speed until the third day from where we met Juan with the letter, we met Col. Fremont at the crossing of the Arkansas river. He had became over-anxious and had started out to meet us.

It was late in the afternoon, so we went into camp and had supper, which consisted of dried venison and water, but for breakfast we had a change of diet, which was dried elk and water.

We learned that Col. Fremont had been detailed the summer before by the government to command an exploring expedition across the continent, and, if possible, find a better route from the "States" to California.

It leaked out that some of the trappers who did not like to have him in the neighborhood of Bent's Fort, for their own selfish motives, had misinformed him that first summer out, as to the lay of the country, hoping thereby to mislead him and his company into the mountains, where they would get snowed in and die of starvation.

Fremont and his party, consisting of twenty-eight men, had started up the Black Canyon, and they did get snowed in and had to stop for the winter.

They ran out of provisions and killed and ate some of their horses, but the other horses died of starvation and six of the men died of scurvy.

It being late when the Fremont party got into the mountains, and the snow-fall being very deep, the game went early to the lowlands and the men were forced to live on salt bacon and horse-flesh. Even that became scarce and the entire company came near perishing before spring.

In the camp with Col. Fremont that evening Uncle Kit and he made their bargain. Carson was to furnish all the horses and was to have the right to take as many extra men and horses as he liked, also the right to trade for furs and send his men and their horses back whenever he desired to do so.

After eating heartily of the dried venison and hearing Col. Fremont's story of the dreadful experiences of his party in the Black Canyon, it was bedtime, and each man rolled himself in his blankets and soon all were sleeping, as tired men can, out on the plains.

We had an early breakfast, each man's hunk of dried meat being handy, so there was really no preparation to be made, except to wash. No compulsion, however, as to that. But having distinguished company, all hands washed this morning before squatting for breakfast.

While we were eating, Fremont asked whose boy I was. Uncle Kit replied that I was his boy, and "a first-class hunter and trapper, and he shoots Injuns purty well, too." He then related the incident of my killing the two Utes.

All arrangements having been made, Uncle Kit agreeing to meet Col. Fremont at Bent's Fort in three weeks, they separated and we pushed on for Taos. On arriving there Uncle Kit hired two Mexicans to go back with

Mr. Hughes to our beaver camp and get the furs, and he gave instructions to take the furs to Santa Fe and dispose of them. Uncle Kit then employed Juan and a Texan boy named John West to assist us in fitting up for our California trip. So at the end of three weeks we met Fremont at Bent's Fort as per agreement.

Fremont's company consisted of twenty-two men, and they were, beyond doubt, the worst looking set of men I ever saw. Many of them were scarcely able to walk from the effects of scurvy and they were generally knocked out.

We had taken with us from Taos a pack-train loaded with vegetables, such as potatoes, onions and the like, and after Freemont's men had associated with those vegetables for a few days, they came out fresh and smiling and were able to travel.

It was about the Middle of May, 1848, that we left Bent's Fort to hunt a new route to the golden shores of California.

The first night out we camped at Fountain Qui Bouille—pronounced Koh-boo-yah—and here a little incident occurred that created much fun for all the party except one—that was me.

As soon as we went into camp, Carson told Johnnie West and me to let Juan take our horses and for us to go out and kill some meat.

We started out in opposite directions, and I had not gone more than a quarter of a mile when I saw a small deer, which I shot, threw on my shoulder and pulled for camp. Only a few rods on the way I came to a little mound of rock about three feet high, and from it flowed a spring of the nicest looking, sparkling water I thought I had ever seen. Being very thirsty, I made a cup of my hat by pinching the rim together, dipped up some of the water and gulped it down, not waiting to see whether it was hot or cold, wet or dry. But a sudden change came over me. I felt a forthwith swelling under the waistband of my buckskin breeches, and I seemed to have an internal and infernal hurricane of gas, which in a second more came rushing through my mouth and nostrils like an eruption from Cotopaxi or Popocatapel. To say that I was frightened would be putting it mild. I rushed down the hill like mad, and fairly flew to camp and up to Uncle Kit, exclaiming as best I could, "I'm poisoned!"

"Pizened?" said Uncle Kit.

"Yes, poisoned;" and just then another rush of gas came through my nostrils.

When the men saw me running so fast they grabbed their guns, thinking the Indians were after me, and quickly surrounded me to hear what was the matter.

Uncle Kit asked me how I got poisoned, and I told him of the spring water I had drank, and asked him if he could do anything to save my life. Then there was another eruption.

Uncle Kit laughed harder than I had ever seen him, but he told me, as fast as he could, that I had drank from a soda spring and that it would not hurt me. Everybody laughed and then all went to the spring to get some of the "poisoned water," which was very good when taken in reasonable quantities and in a reasonable way.

My gun, deer and hat were all lying near the spring, and I secured them, but it was many a day before I heard the last of the "pizen- spring."

Johnnie West came in soon after, having missed all the fun, and Juan and I went with him, taking each a horse, and packed the game into camp.

I was anxious to get away from camp on that little packing trip, hoping the crowd would forget all about the soda-spring before I returned, but I hoped in vain, for when I returned they laughed at and joked me more than ever.

We traveled up the Arkansas river nearly a hundred miles, and as we neared the snow-line the deer and elk were more plentiful and we never went hungry for meat.

At Jimmie's Fork we turned to the left and followed that stream to its head, then crossed over to the Blue river, which is a tributary of the Colorado. Now we were in the Ute country, and had to keep a sharp lookout for Indians. Every evening, after making camp, Uncle Kit would climb to the top of the highest hill near us to look for Indian camps, as it was an easy matter late in the evening to discover their camps by the smoke from their fires. He used to take me along with him, and he would point out different landmarks in the country and would tell me to make close observations, as I would have to return, without him, over the same route and if I were not careful I might lose my way.

On the third day after crossing the divide, we met Tawson, chief of the Apache tribes. Tawson had never met Carson but knew him by reputation; but a number of the warriors were personally acquainted with him.

The Indians all turned about and rode back with us to their village, which was only a short distance away.

Uncle Kit being able to speak Spanish, as were all the Indians in that country, he had quite a talk with the old chief, and in the meantime he had bought all the furs the Indians had to sell.

When we were ready to start from the village, Carson said in Spanish:

"Now, Tawson, I have always been a friend to your tribe and I will tell you what I'm going to do. In about one moon I will start this boy back through your country, with the horses and two other boys- -referring to Juan and West—and if anything happens to them while passing through your country I will hold you personally responsible."

The chief having heard a great deal of Carson, knew he meant just what he said.

The third day after leaving the Apache village we reached the Colorado river, and we had a hard time finding a suitable place to cross. Finally we decided to build a raft of logs and ferry our stuff on that, and swim the horses. This we did successfully, and also cached the furs to keep them safe until my return.

As soon as we crossed the river we began to see signs of the Ute Indians, and Uncle Kit told me to keep my rifle in trim as I might need it soon.

The second day after crossing the river, about 4 o'clock in the afternoon, and just as we had gone into camp, a band of about forty Indians made a dash for our horses. This was the first time I had ever heard the war-whoop, and it fairly made my hair stand on end. Some of our crowd had seen the Indians while yet a distance off, and when the men yelled "Indians! boys, Indians!" I made a bee-line for Croppy, who had by this time fed himself away about fifty yards from camp. When Col. Fremont saw me start on the run, he asked me where I was going. I told him that I was going for my pony as I didn't intend that the Utes should get him.

By the time I got to Croppy I could see the Indians coming, full tilt, and some of the men had already fired upon them. I got back to camp as fast as I could get Croppy to go, and when in a few yards of the camp, I took a rest off of his back and fired, but I missed my Indian. I reloaded as quickly as possible and laid my gun on Croppy's back again, for another shot, and just then it struck me that the reason I missed the first time was because I didn't take good aim.

Uncle Kit had always taught me that it was not the fastest shooting in an Indian fight that did the most execution, and that it was better to fire one shot with good aim than four at random.

When I went to shoot the second time, Uncle Kit was near me, and he said:

"Take good aim, Willie, before you fire."

I did take good aim and had the satisfaction of seeing the Indian tumble to the ground. But whether I killed him or some one else did, I could not say, for an absolute certainty, but I have always thought he belonged to my list.

The Indians were no match for Col. Fremont's men, being only armed with bows and arrows, and they beat a hasty retreat, closely followed for a distance by the soldiers, who, however, did not get any Indians on the run.

When the men returned to camp, and, as usual, after a scrap with Indians, were telling how many red-skins they had killed, Uncle Kit turned to me and asked how many I had got. I said, "one."

"Are you sure?" he asked.

"Well," I said, "I took a rest off of Croppy's back; with a good aim, at the crack of my rifle, the Indian came down."

The crowd went with me to where I had seen the Indian fall, and there he was, as useless for Indian work as Powhattan is.

Col. Fremont then asked the soldiers where were their dead Indians, and Uncle Kit said:

"I reckon Willie is the only one that got his man. Didn't I tell you, Colonel, that he could shoot Injuns?"

However, after looking around awhile, he found five more dead Indians, and, doubtless, more were killed but were carried away by their companions.

The only harm the Indians did our party was to wound two of Fremont's men, slightly.

This was the last trouble we had with the Utes on the trip.

The second day from this little brush we struck a village of Goshoot Indians, and there Uncle Kit bought enough furs to make out his cargo.

We went into camp here for the night, but Uncle Kit and I did not sleep much, as we were up very late as we did not expect to meet again until the next spring, and he had a great deal to tell me before we parted.

The following morning Johnnie West, Juan and I loaded up and started for Santa Fe, and Uncle Kit went on to Los Angeles with Col. Fremont, as guide.

Before I left camp that morning, Col. Fremont, unbeknown to Uncle Kit, came to me and said:

"Willie, in about a year from now I will be on my way back to St. Louis, and I will take you home with me if you would like to go. I will send you to school and make a man of you. You are too good a boy to spend your life here, in this wild country."

But I told him I was perfectly satisfied to remain with Kit Carson.

Had Uncle Kit known of that conversation I think he would have been very much displeased, and it might have caused serious trouble. Therefore I kept my own counsel and did not mention the matter to Carson.

Us boys were four weeks making the return trip to Santa Fe, and we did not see a hostile Indian on the way. I wondered much at that, but a year or two afterward Uncle Kit told me that the Apaches saw us every day and were protecting us, for he had seen Tawson on his return and the chief told him that we had gone through safe.

We arrived at Santa Fe about the first of October, and there I met Jim Hughes, who was waiting our arrival, and I was very glad to see him. I gave him a letter that Uncle Kit had sent him concerning our trapping for the coming winter.

Mr. Hughes said that he was glad that we had got back so early, for it was time we were getting into the mountains for our winter work.

I asked him if we would trap in the same place as the winter before, and he said we would not, as he had brought all the traps out to Taos, and we would go the next winter up to North Park, as he had just returned from there and knew we could put in a good winter's work, as it was new trapping ground that had not been worked, and it was a fine country, too.

Soon as we had got rid of our furs, which Mr. Hughes had sold before our arrival, we pulled out for Taos and begun operations for going to North Park.

All being in readiness in a few days thereafter, Mr. Hughes, Johnnie West and I had started for the new trapping ground, taking Juan along, again, to fetch our horses home. We had to travel over some rough country on the way, but found the North Park a fine region, with scattering pine timber on the hills and quaking-asp and willows along the streams. I have been told that this park is now owned by sheep men, and it is an excellent region for their business.

After looking around over our trapping field Mr. Hughes selected a suitable place for our winter cabin, and we fell to work building it. This time we built entirely above ground with pine logs, an unusual thing for trappers to do.

As soon as our cabin was built, Juan returned to Taos with the horses and we set into our winter's employment.

In those days hunters never wore boots or shoes, but moccasins from the tanned hides of elk. This winter we made enough gloves and moccasins to last us for two years, and each made himself a buckskin suit, out and out.

Game was very plentiful in that country, such as moose, elk and deer, and early in the winter a few mountain buffalo.

We were successful this winter, our beaver catch being nearly eight hundred. The winter was also an unusually long one, lasting until far into April.

After the snow had gone off so that we could travel, Jim Hughes, who had been our foreman, in the absence of Carson, asked me if I thought I could find the way back to Taos, which I said I could. He said that one of us would have to go and get our horses to pack the furs in on.

It was now the spring of 1849 and I was seventeen years old, but it looked to me to be a big undertaking for a boy of my age, a trip of three hundred miles, a foot and alone, with my rifle and blankets; but some one had to go, and I agreed to tackle the trip.

This was on Saturday, and as we never worked on Sundays, except to tend the traps, Mr. Hughes and Johnnie West talked the matter over and decided that before I started away we had better cache the furs and such traps as they would not use in my absence. This was done, so that in the event of their being killed by the Indians, I could find the furs on my return. It was a wise conclusion, as will be seen later on.

It was the custom of the Utes to cross over the mountains in small squads every spring and kill all the trappers they could find and take their traps and furs.

On Monday morning we all set about to cache the furs and traps that would not be used, and it took two days hard work to accomplish the task. Then I made preparations to start on my journey to Taos.

Mr. Hughes thought that as it would be a long and tedious trip, I had better rest up a day or two before starting, but I thought that as I had to make the trip I might as well begin first as last, so Wednesday morning was set as the time for my start.

CHAPTER IV
A WINTER IN NORTH PARK—RUNNING FIGHT WITH A BAND OF UTES FOR MOKE THAN A HUNDRED MILES, ENDING HAND TO HAND—VICTORY

On the day set for my departure, having had our breakfast, Mr. Hughes stepped outside of the cabin, and I was just rolling up try blankets and a piece of dried venison, and Johnnie West was sympathizing with me over the long and lonesome trip that was before me, when all of a sudden Mr. Hughes came bounding into the cabin and exclaimed.

"Get your guns and knives, boys. The Indians are upon us and we must run for our lives."

Each man sprang for his gun, and by this time the Indians were in sight of the cabin and had raised the war-whoop, which, again, raised the hair on the head of your humble servant.

We made for the top of the hill, which was about one hundred and fifty yards from the cabin, and slopped The Indians were by this time at the cabin. Johnnie West counted them and said there were twenty-seven all told.

We each fired a shot among them, but could not tell whether we killed any of them or not. We then started on the run, loading our guns as we ran, the Indians in hot pursuit of us.

After running about two miles, Johnnie West proposed that we make a stand. We stopped on a little ridge, and did not have to wait long until the Indians were in gun-shot of us.

"Now, Willie," said Mr. Hughes, "don't get excited and shoot too quick, but take good aim and be sure that you get your Indian."

As they came up, each of us selected our Indian, fired and each got his man. In a moment the smoke from our guns had cleared away, and the whole band being in sight, Mr. Hughes said:

"Let's run for our lives. There are too many of them for us." And run we did, loading as we flew.

We ran about five miles and made another stand, but not with the same success as before, for we only got one Indian.

We had a running fight all that day and made three or four stands, but could not tell how many Indians we killed, for we would fire at them and then load our guns on the run. They having nothing but loose arrows and tomahawks, we could easily keep out of danger. But they figured on running us down.

That evening near sundown, Mr. Hughes asked me, as I was a little faster on foot than the rest, to drop back far enough to count them, which I did, and found there were eleven of them still in pursuit of us.

When they saw me behind the other two they started the war-whoop and did their best to overtake me, no doubt thinking I was tired out and that the other two had left me. But they were disappointed when I ran on and overtook my friends.

We were now in sight of a large body of timber, and Mr. Hughes thought that if we could reach that by dark we might be able to dodge the Indians and get away from them.

We reached the timber just at dark and tried very hard to dodge our pursuers, but it seemed as though they could scent us like blood-hounds, for we would no more than get stopped and lie down to rest, when they would be upon us.

A number of times during the night we would build up a fire and then go a hundred yards or so from it and lie down to rest, but the redskinned devils kept close to us, and, consequently, we got but little rest during the night.

The following morning we left the timber and took to the prairie. After running some four miles we looked back and saw four Indians very near to us and gaining at every step. Johnnie West proposed that we stop and accommodate them, saying that he felt hungry and tired enough to fight any two Indians in the band. So each man selected his Indian and fired, and we succeeded in killing two of them; the remaining two hid behind some big rocks until the others came up and, again we were compelled to flee.

We ran for about two hours, when we stopped and made another fight and killed two more Indians. This was kept up until late in the afternoon, which made two days and one night that we had been chased by these savages, with not a bite to eat during the whole time, and we were getting so tired that we could scarcely raise the trot.

We were now running down a long slope, when I looked at Mr. Hughes and could see a change in his countenance. There was an expression different from that which I had ever seen on his face before. Just about a half mile ahead of on down a little flat, was a wash-out, and Mr. Hughes said:

"Right down there by that little bunch of willows, at that wash- out, is where I intend to make my last fight. Now you boys can do as you please, but I am exhausted and can go no further."

Before we got to the wash-out, Johnnie West told Mr. Hughes to run straight for the patch of willows, also telling me to turn to the right, while he took to the left, and as soon as we were in the wash-out for me to run to where Mr. Hughes was. This was to be done to cause the Indians to scatter so they would not all be on us at once, there now being seven of them in the gang.

Johnnie West told me to take a bandy-shanked-fellow on the left and he would take one who had two feathers in his hair.

"All right," said Mr. Hughes, "and I'll take the leader."

We all took good aim and each of us brought down his Indian, but we did not have time to load before the others were upon us, and it ended in a hand-to-hand fight, besides it got to where each man had to look out for himself.

One of the Indians came straight for me and dealt me a desperate blow with his tomahawk, but I threw up my left hand and received a severe cut in my wrist—the mark of which I carry to this day—at the same time I struck him with my knife and almost cut him in two As he was falling he threw his tomahawk at me with all the vengeance in him, but missed my head and struck a rock just behind me. I sprang at once and picked it up.

Mr. Hughes was fighting one of the Indians; the other two had attacked Johnnie West, who was on his back with his head against the bank of the wash-out, and they were trying to get a chance to deal him a blow, but he was kicking at them with both feet and was striking so fast with his knife that they had not yet been able to get a lick in on him.

They were so busily engaged with Johnnie that I sprang at once, unseen by them, and buried the tomahawk so deep in the head of one of them that I was unable, for the moment, to recover it. As soon as my Indian was out of the way, Johnnie was on his feet, quick as the twinkling of an eye, and stabbed the remaining one through the heart with his hunting-knife.

In the meantime Mr. Hughes was having a hard fight with his Indian. He succeeded in killing the red fiend but got badly used up. He had a severe wound in the shoulder, also one in the thigh. I received a cut in the wrist, and Johnnie West did not get a severe wound, in fact but little more than a scratch.

The fight and flight being now ended, we went a few rods to a little clump of pine trees, where Mr. Hughes dropped down and said: "Boys, there's no use of talking, I can't go any further; I think I have done my last trappin' and Injun fightin'."

I gathered some limbs and chunks and started a fire, while Johnnie pulled Mr. Hughes' moccasins off and bathed his feet and legs with cold water. They were swollen almost to twice their usual size.

The fire being started, Johnnie proposed that we lie down and take a nap and a rest before starting out to hunt for meat, saying it was impossible for him to stand on his feet any longer. "My legs," said he, "are swollen clear to my body." I was too hungry to sleep, so I proposed that Johnnie stay and care for Mr. Hughes and I would take my gun and go out and kill some game, which was plentiful in this part of the country. I had not gone more than a quarter of a mile when I looked up the ridge and saw a small deer coming down almost in the direction of where I stood, and never before in my life had I cast my eyes on a living animal that pleased me so much as did that one I waited until he was in gunshot and fired. It ran about one hundred yards in the direction of camp and fell dead I dressed it, cut off its head and carried it to camp, and it was all I could do to get along with it in my half-famished condition.

I found Hughes and West both sound asleep by the fire It was not long before I had some of the venison cooked, and I had it fashionably rare, at that. After I had wakened my companions and we had broiled and eaten venison for a time, Johnnie and I rolled some logs together and gathered pine knots and made a good fire. Then we broiled more venison and ate again, until we got sleepy and fell over by the side of the fire, lost to ourselves and Indians. During the night we all woke up again, cooked and ate as long as we could keep our eyes open, and by sun-up next morning there was not enough of that little deer left to feed a cat.

We found ourselves very sore and stiff from the effects of our run, but Mr. Hughes thought we were about one hundred miles nearer Taos than when we started, as we had been running most of the time in that direction, and this was some consolation.

We remained here and rested two days, and as game was plentiful we did not have to go far from the camp to get all the meat we wanted.

On the morning of the third day we started for Taos, which was about two hundred miles away, but all being so badly worn out and Mr. Hughes having such severe wounds, we had to travel slowly, it taking us about two weeks to make the trip. But we had no more trouble with the Indians.

At Taos we met Uncle Kit Carson, who had been waiting our arrival for two weeks. After resting up for a few days, Uncle Kit, Johnnie West and myself started for North Park to pack out the furs. Mr. Hughes stayed at Taos, as he was too badly wounded to accompany us on the trip.

On our arrival at North Park we found everything just as we had left it, except that the traps, which we had not cached with the furs, had been stolen.

On our return trip we camped one evening in a beautiful little valley where the grass was knee high, and along the little stream were green quaking-asp, alder and willows, with scattering pine trees here and there on the hills and in the valley. About sundown that evening the horses commenced to show signs of uneasiness and occasionally they would raise their heads and look in the direction of a little pine grove near by, and snort. Johnnie West, being the first to notice it, said: "Kit, what is the matter with the horses? I believe there are Indians around."

"I don't think so," said Carson, "for I haven't seen any sign of Injuns today."

Shortly after dark that night Uncle Kit went out about fifty yards from camp in the direction of the horses, taking with him neither his gun or his pistol, which was a rare thing for him to do. Just as he was passing around a pine tree a panther sprang at him from the tree. On hearing the rustle in the limbs, Carson jumped back from the tree as far as he could and thus avoided the full force of the blow from the panther. As he jumped back he drew his knife and had a hand-to-hand fight with the huge feline and succeeded in killing it.

Johnnie and I sat at the camp-fire, knowing nothing of the affair until Uncle Kit came in, covered with blood from head to foot, and his heavy buckskin shirt, which had no doubt been the means of saving his life, was torn almost into strings. When he told us he had been engaged in a fight with some kind of a wild animal, Johnnie asked why he did not call for help, and his reply was that he did not have time to call as he had his hands full with the "varmint."

After we had dressed his wounds as best we could, we took a torch and went to the foot of the pine tree, and there lay the panther, dead. He had stabbed it to the heart.

Uncle Kit had a very bad wound in one thigh, also in one arm, so we did not move camp next day, but the day after we proceeded on our journey. We took our furs to Santa Fe, where we disposed of them at a good price, furs being higher that season than usual.

Our furs being disposed of we returned to Taos and rested for about two weeks.

CHAPTER V
ON THE CACHE-LA-POUDRE.—VISIT FROM GRAY EAGLE, CHIEF OF THE ARAPAHOES.—A BEAR-HUNTER IS HUNTED BY THE BEAR.—PHIL, THE CANNIBAL

Uncle Kit, having made quite a sum of money, concluded that he would take a trip over to the headwaters of the Cache-la-Poudre to look for a new field where he could trap the coming winter on a large scale, and wanted Johnnie and I to accompany him, which we did.

Each taking a saddle-horse and one pack animal, we started on the trip, taking a new route to Uncle Kit, as well as to Johnnie and myself.

Carson took the lead, for, like a deer, he could find his way anywhere he wished to go.

We crossed the Arkansas river above Bent's Fort, and from here we traveled along the foothills of the Rocky Mountains, striking the Platte at the mouth of Cherry creek, which is now the center of Denver City, Colo. Here we met Mountain Phil—of whom you will hear more in this narrative. He was living in a wick-i-up and had a squaw for a wife. Uncle Kit and I, being acquainted with him, stopped and had a chat with him while our horses were feeding. Uncle Kit asked him what he intended to do the coming winter, and he replied:

"I will trap for you if you like, but you will have to furnish me with an outfit, for I have none of my own."

"All right, Phil," said Carson, "I will give you a job, but you will have to stop alone, for none of my men will live with you."

"All right," said Phil, "me and Klooch will be enough to stop in one cabin, anyway."

These things being understood we rode off, Mountain Phil agreeing to meet us at Taos about two months from that time.

After we rode away I asked Uncle Kit why no one would live with Mountain Phil. His reply was, "Phil is a very bad man, and I yet have to hear the first man speak a good word for him."

Late that afternoon we saw a little band of Indians—ten in number— coming toward us, and when near them we saw that they were Arapahoes and Gray Eagle, the chief, was with them. Uncle Kit being well acquainted, all shook hands, and the chief insisted on our going to their camp and staying all night with them. Uncle Kit knowing the nature of the Indians, and knowing that Gray Eagle would take it as an insult if we should refuse to visit him, turned about and went home with him. He sent two of his men ahead to the village, and we were met by about five hundred warriors with all the women and children of the village. Just at the outer edge of the village we were honored with what they considered a great reception.

Gray Eagle took us to his own wick-i-up, his men taking charge of our horses and packs. I had learned to speak the Arapahoe language fairly well and could understand anything they said. When supper time came, Gray Eagle came to Uncle Kit and said: "I have a great feast for you; my men have killed a very fat dog; supper is ready, come in and eat."

I remarked to Uncle Kit as we were going to supper, that I was very glad we came home with Gray Eagle, for it had been a long time since I had had a good meal of dog.

Supper being over, the chief got his pipe and selected six men from his tribe and we had a peace-smoke, and he and Uncle Kit smoked and talked nearly all night. During their conversation that night he said that Mountain Phil was a very bad man, and that he would often steal their horses and sell them to the Comanches.

Next morning after breakfast our horses were brought in, saddled up and we were off on our journey again to Cache-la-Poudre.

It might be of interest to our readers to know how this stream acquired its name. There was a Frenchman by the name of Virees Roubidoux camped on the stream spoken of, with a little squad of men; they were attacked by a band of Indians, and the first word uttered by Roubidoux was "Cache-la-poudre," which means in English, "hide the powder," and from that time on the stream has been so called.

We arrived at our proposed trapping field, and after looking over the country we found plenty of beaver sign along the streams and game in abundance, and Uncle Kit decided that there was room enough for four camps.

We returned by the way of Bent's Fort, as Uncle Kit wished to employ the best men he could get to trap for him the coming winter. On our way to the fort, which was four hundred miles from the proposed trapping ground, Uncle Kit told me that he would have to leave me in charge the coming winter, as he was going to the City of Mexico on business, but said that he would come out and get the camps established and return to Taos with the horses before going there.

We found plenty of men at Bent's Fort, and, as usual, they were all broke, having squandered the money earned the winter before for whiskey and card playing. Uncle Kit experienced no trouble in getting all the men he wanted, but had to furnish them with traps and provisions—which took considerable money—he to have half of the furs caught by each of them. Everything being understood we returned to Taos, the men agreeing to meet us there two weeks later. They were all on hand at the appointed time, but there being a large party to outfit it took some weeks to make preparations for the trip, there being eleven in the crowd. It was about the last of October when we arrived at the trapping-ground ready to begin work.

There was a man in the crowd named Charlie Jones, who was an old friend of Johnnie West, and they and I lived in the same cabin that winter. One morning after we had got fixed up comfortably in our winter quarters and Uncle Kit had returned to Taos with the horses, Charlie Jones waked us up very early, saying that there was a light snow and he thought we would be able to get a bear if we got out early. We rolled out, got breakfast and were off as soon as it was light enough to see.

There were three small ridges, all pointing to our cabin; Johnnie West took up the right-hand ridge, Charlie Jones the left and I the middle one. The ridges were open, with scattering pine trees here and there, but along the creek was heavy timber and a dense growth of underbrush. While walking along up the ridge, keeping a sharp lookout for bear, I came in sight of Johnnie West, who beckoned me to cross over to where he was, saying that in the thicket, which covered about an acre of ground, there was a small bear. I proposed calling Charlie Jones over before entering the thicket, but Johnnie said no, as it was such a small bear that Charlie would get mad and would not speak to either of us for a week if we should call him over for such a little bear, "and if we cannot kill that bear," he continued, "we had better quit the mountains."

We both cocked our guns and started into the brush side by side. When near the center of the thicket I saw the bear raise on its haunches. The snow was falling from the bushes so thickly that it was almost impossible to get a bead on him, but I fired, anyway, and hit too low, thus failing to bring him down.

He made a rush for us, but Johnnie had saved his charge in case I failed to kill, but the snow was falling from the bushes so fast and thick that he could not get a shot at the bear as he rushed for us, so we were both compelled to flee for our lives, Johnnie to the hillside, while I took down the canyon, jumping the small logs and falling over the large ones and riding down the brush, while I could almost feel the bear's breath on my posterior at every jump, and had it not been that West had saved his charge, you would now be reading some other book—certainly not this one, as it would never have been written.

Just as we crossed a little opening, Johnnie fired, the ball cutting Bear's jugular vein and also his windpipe, but the bear still seemed to have a "hankering" after me and kept coming for several yards.

After its windpipe was severed, the bear made a louder noise than ever, but not knowing the cause, I thought he was nearer me and I strained every nerve and fibre of my body to widen the distance between us, as I almost imagined his teeth clashing down on me, while Johnnie West was yelling: "Run, Willie; run for your life!"

Well I rather think I was running some about that time, for just then I came to a big log, and I jumped, climbed and fell over it, in fact, I never knew exactly how I did get over it; however, I fell on one side of the log, utterly exhausted, and the bear, not being able to get over, fell on the other side and died.

Of all the hunting and Indian fighting I have ever done, I never had anything to scare me as did that little, insignificant bear.

Charlie Jones, hearing the two shots and Johnnie yelling for me to run, came to the scene and had no little fun with me for running from so small a bear, saying: "If a little bear like that were to come at me, I would take it by the tail and beat its brains out against a tree."

By the time the boys got the bear dressed, I had recovered sufficiently from my run and excitement to help carry the meat to the cabin, which was only a few rods away, as in our foot-race we had been running in direction of the camp. The boys had a great deal of sport at my expense, and many times during the winter I was reminded of the bear hunt, in which the bear hunted me.

After we had got everything nicely fixed up in our new quarters, Johnnie West one evening got down his sachel, took out a book and sat and read till bed time. The following evening when he took the book up again, I asked him what he was reading, and he said, "Robinson Crusoe." I asked him why he did not read aloud so the rest of us could hear, and he did read aloud until bed time. I told him I would give anything if I could read as he did. So he said if I would try to learn, he would teach me to read that winter as good as he could. I assured him there would be nothing lacking on my part, so the next night I took my first lesson. At that time I did not know all the letters, but I was determined to learn to read. In a very short time I had learned all my letters, and being possessed of a great memory, I learned very fast, and Johnnie, seeing I was so determined in the matter, spared no pains in teaching me, and by the next spring I could read Robinson Crusoe myself. Having a start, I could learn of my own accord, and to Johnnie West I am greatly indebted for the limited education I now possess; and were he now living I could not express to him my gratitude for his labors as my tutor in that lonely wilderness, hundreds of miles from any white man's habitation. And, although my education is quite limited, yet what little I do possess has been of great value to me through life.

We had good success trapping this winter, until about the first of January, when we had an unusual heavy fall of snow in the mountains which drove all the game to the lowlands, nothing being left that was fit for meat except a few mountain sheep, and the snow made it very inconvenient getting around to attend to the traps. In the latter part of February I asked Charlie Jones one day to go down to Mountain Phil's camp and see if there was anything that he wanted, as we had kept all the extra supplies at our camp. Mountain Phil and his Klooch—that being the name he called his squaw, which is also the Arapahoe name for wife—were staying alone about ten miles further down the country from where we were located.

On Charlie Jones' return, he said: "It seems that Mountain Phil has been faring better than any of us, for he has been able to kill his meat at camp, thereby saving him the trouble of having to get out and hunt for it."

Johnnie and I did not understand what he meant by this. So, after hesitating a moment, Jones said: "Boys, if I should tell you what I know about Mountain Phil, you would not believe it, but as sure as you live he has killed his squaw and eaten most of her, and he has left his camp."

We insisted that he must be mistaken, but he declared that he was not, saying he had seen the bones in the cabin, and further investigation had developed the fact that he had beyond any doubt killed and eaten his Indian wife.

From that time on, Mountain Phil went by the name of the American Cannibal until his death, which was—if my memory serves me right—in 1863 or '64, at Virginia City, Mont.

After the snow had settled so that a person could travel on top of it, I took my gun and stole out one day to see if I could not kill a mountain sheep. As I clambered up the mountain I looked about one hundred yards or so ahead of me on a cliff of rock, and saw a panther, which I supposed was looking out for the same kind of game that I was. I fired and killed her the first shot and started to skin her, when I heard the kittens, or young panthers, crying up in the rocks near where I had shot the old one. My first thought then was what a nice pet I would have if I could only get hold of those young panthers. I was afraid to crawl into the cave for fear the other old panther might come in on me, so I cut a forked stick and twisted in their fur and in that way managed to pull them out, all the time keeping a sharp lookout for the other old one. I took the two young panthers to the cabin and made pets of them. They grew to be very watchful; nothing could move without their knowing it. The female grew to be very tame, and a more affectionate creature I never saw. But it was different with the male. When he was six months old he got to be very cross, and I had to keep him tied up. One day I went out to feed them and he drew back and slapped me, and I shot him on the spot with my pistol. The female I kept until she was considerably over a year old, when I sold her for one hundred dollars to an Englishman named Mace, and had I only known it, that panther was worth five hundred dollars. I had taught her many tricks.

She could count ten, by putting her paw on the ground ten times, and would do various other tricks, but when asked by any other person than her master to perform, she would shake her head and would not allow any one else to touch her. I always tied her up when going out for a hunt, and when I would return she would cry and scream so shrill that it would almost raise the hat on a man's head until I would untie her. She never was contented until she could get to lick my face, and I never saw a dog more watchful than she.

It was in the month of April that Uncle Kit came in with a pack- train for the furs, the snowfall having been so heavy that he could not get in earlier. Our catch had been light, as we had more snow that winter than has ever been known before or since in the history of that country. Uncle Kit was, however, very well satisfied with our work, with the exception of Mountain Phil, whom he had furnished for the winter, and who had not caught a beaver. We soon had our traps and furs together, loaded up and were on our way to New Mexico.

The third day about noon we reached the Cache-la-Poudre, where we again ran on to the American Cannibal. We stopped here to let our horses feed and to partake of some refreshments ourselves. Uncle Kit, after giving Mountain Phil a lecture for his past conduct, said:

"Phil, if ever you and I are out together in the mountains and run short of provisions, I will shoot you down as I would a wolf, before you get hungry."

Phil asked him why he would do so, and Carson replied: "Because I wouldn't take the chances of being killed and eaten up by a cannibal like you."

It might be well to give a brief description of this cannibal. He was a large, raw-boned man, who would weigh about two hundred and fifty pounds, though he was not very fleshy. He always wore his hair long and never combed it, also wore his beard long and never sheared or combed that. His hair grew down on his forehead almost to his eyes. In fact he looked more like an animal than a human being.

Three days' travel brought us to South Platte, where we crossed the river and made camp on a little stream called Sand Creek. It was our custom to stake our saddle horses out at night as near camp as good grass could be found. The following morning Johnnie West and myself had been out after the pack animals, and on our return when within about a quarter of a mile from camp, we heard a rumbling noise that sounded like a band of buffalo in a stampede. We looked off to our right and saw a large herd of horses, driven by seven Ute Indians, who were pushing them at the greatest possible speed. We urged our horses in the direction of camp as fast as possible. As soon as we were in sight of camp, we gave the alarm and every man sprang to his gun, mounted his horse and was ready to receive them. The Indians did not see us until they had run the herd of horses almost into our camp. Our saddle horses being fresh, we succeeded in killing the seven Indians before they got far away, and captured the herd of horses, which proved to be a herd they had stolen from the Arapahoe Indians the night before, and in less than an hour, Gray Eagle, the Arapahoe chief, came along in pursuit, accompanied by fifty of his select warriors. When Uncle Kit showed him the dead Utes, he walked up to one of them, gave him a kick and said: "Lo-mis-mo-cay-o-te," which means, "All the same as cayote."

Gray Eagle gave us each a horse, thanked us very kindly and returned to his village with his animals.

We proceeded on our journey to Santa Fe, which took us twelve days. Here we met our old friend, Joe Favor, who we had sold our furs to the year before, and who bought them again this season.

Furs being still higher this year, notwithstanding our small catch, Uncle Kit did fairly well out of his winter's trapping.

After settling up with Uncle Kit, Mr. Favor called me into the store and presented me with a single-shot, silver-mounted pistol, also a knife that weighed two and one-fourth pounds, that had been manufactured in St. Louis. We stopped at Santa Fe and rested two days, after which time Uncle Kit, Johnnie West, myself and my pet panther returned home to Taos, which was a distance of ninety miles from Santa Fe.

CHAPTER VI
TWO BOYS RIDE TO THE CITY OF MEXICO. ELEVEN HUNDRED MILES OF TRIAL, DANGER AND DUTY—A GIFT HORSE.— THE WIND RIVER MOUNTAINS

It was now the spring of 1850. I was eighteen years old and beginning to think myself a man. Uncle Kit asked me to go to the City of Mexico, saying that he owed a man there two hundred and fifty dollars, and wished to pay him. He also told me that he would have Juan, the Mexican boy, accompany me on the journey, but cautioned me not to let any one know that I had money. "For," said he, "them Mexican guerrillas would kill you if they knew you had money about you."

The reader can fancy two boys at the age of eighteen, starting out on a trip of eleven hundred miles, over a wild country, with no settlement except hostile Indians and Mexicans, who are worse than Indians if they know a person has money about him. At that time there were no roads across the country in that direction; nothing but a trail—a part of the way not even that—and the whole country full of Mexican guerrillas—or, as we would term them, Mexican robbers—who made it a business to murder people whom they suspected of having money, and who would even massacre whole trains of emigrants, take what money they might have, their provisions and clothing, burn their wagons and drive their stock away. The fact is that many of the depredations committed in those days, for which the Indians were blamed, were done by those fiendish Mexicans.

When the time arrived for starting and we were mounted, Uncle Kit, Johnnie West and Mr. Hughes came out to bid us good-bye.

Johnnie West said: "Well, I am afraid I shall never see you again, for those Mexican guerrillas are worse than Indians, especially when they think a traveler has money about him."

All this helped to put me on my guard, and I didn't even tell Juan that I had money with me.

We started on our journey with two saddled horses and one pack- horse each. We met numerous little bands of Navajoe Indians, but they being on good terms with the whites, gave us no trouble, whatever. We also met numerous little squads of Mexican guerrillas, but they not suspecting two boys as young as we were with having money, did not disturb us. Uncle Kit had sent the shabbiest looking horses along that he had, in order to deceive them. Every band of Mexicans that we met on our trip would ask us where we were from, where we were going and our business. I always told them that I was from Taos, and was going to the City of Mexico to see a friend, and they would pass on.

The first river we came to, Juan asked me if I could swim. I told him that I did not know, as I had never had a trial. We stripped down, tied our clothing about our shoulders and mounted our horses again.

I wanted Juan to take the lead and let me drive the horses after him, but he thought we had best ride side by side and let the pack-animals follow, so in case of accident we could help each other. We made it across safe, and from this time on we never hesitated at a stream.

We were thirty-one days making the trip to the City of Mexico.

I found Mr. Reed at his residence and paid the two hundred and fifty dollars to him. He was much astonished at Uncle Kit sending two boys eleven hundred miles to pay so small a debt, and said that he had not expected to get the money until such time as Carson might be coming that way on other business, for it was so far that he would not have gone after it and taken the chances of crossing the country between the City of Mexico and Taos, as we had done, for the two hundred and fifty dollars.

But Uncle Kit owed this money and had agreed to pay it at a certain time, and he, like many other frontiersman, valued his word more than he did his gold.

We laid over two days at the City of Mexico in order to let our horses rest. The day before we were to start, Mr. Reed, who had invited us to his residence to board while in the City, went out to where our horses were, and seeing that one of the horses had a sore back, told me that he would make me a present of a horse that, if I took good care of, would be able to carry me the entire trip.

I named this horse Mexico, and as will be seen later, he proved to be a noble saddle-horse, which I kept and rode for seven years.

We made the trip home somewhat quicker than we did on our way out, being better acquainted with the country, and so could make better time.

We were just two months making the round trip, arriving at Taos two weeks sooner than Uncle Kit had expected us. Johnnie West and Mr. Hughes were glad to see us return, for it was more than they expected.

By the time my panther had grown to be quite large, and was glad to see me.

On my return to Taos I learned that Uncle Kit and Jim Bridger had formed a co-partnership, for the purpose of trapping the coming winter in the Wind River mountains, which were about seven hundred miles from Taos, and had employed Johnnie West, Charlie Jones and Jake Harrington to trap for them, and in a few days after my return from the City of Mexico we made the start with thirty-two pack-animals, besides our saddle-horses.

Nothing happening worthy of note on our way out, we arrived at our proposed trapping ground, and found plenty of beaver and plenty of fresh Indian sign as well, but the Indians were not apt to give us any trouble at this season of the year, more than to run our horses off, as they would prefer to let trappers alone until spring and then kill them and take their furs.

We established our two camps about four miles apart, and kept our horses in the valley between the two camps; there was an abundance of grass, plenty of game and no end to the beaver. In fact, to take it on the whole, it seemed that this was going to be the loveliest place to spend the winter that we had ever struck, and the boys were all highly elated over their new winter quarters. We had only been in our trapping field about two weeks when Uncle Kit went out one morning to kill a deer and to look after the horses. He had not gone far when he looked across the little valley and saw an Indian driving off our horses. Being in gunshot of the Indian, he fired at him and brought him to the ground. When Uncle Kit returned to camp, he said:

"Boys, I am afraid we have made a mistake in coming here to trap this winter; we must be near the Blackfoot Indians, for I just killed one that was driving our horses off, and I just happened to see him in time to catch him with old Blackleg." At that time the Blackfoot Indians were considered worst tribe in the entire Northwest.

I went at once to the other camp to notify Jim Bridger and his crowd that they might be on their guard. Bridger said he had been expecting it, as he had seen fresh Indian sign out on the ridges some days before, but thought it was getting so late now that they would not give us any more trouble this winter, but that we would have to get out early the next spring.

We stayed here and trapped all winter, with splendid success. Jim Bridger took twelve beaver from his string of traps every twenty- four hours for seven successive days, being the greatest catch I ever knew from one string of traps.

About the last of March we commenced making preparations to leave the mountains, for fear the Indians might come and clean us out.

The day before we were to start there came a heavy fall of snow, and we were not able to move until the first of April, when we made another start for Santa Fe, going via Sweetwater, and we had enough furs to load our entire train.

The second day after leaving camp we were attacked, about noon, by twenty Indians of the Blackfoot tribe, who entertained us for about an hour.

We huddled our horses and used them for breast-works, and killed seven Indians without one of our men being wounded, but we lost two horses.

It might be well to describe the manner in which trappers traveled those days while passing through a country where there were hostile Indians.

Each man would take the number of horses he was to lead and string them out and fasten them together by tying each horse to the tail of the horse ahead of him and the head horse of the string he would tie to the tail of his saddle-horse. This had to be done to prevent a stampede when attacked, and the horses, too, were a great protection to the men, for when they were attacked by Indians the men would ride to the center and use the horses for breastworks in time of battle.

After the fight was over the boys all felt jubilant over their victory. We had no more trouble with Indians for four days, when we reached Rock Creek, a beautiful little mountain stream that pays tribute to the North Platte river. Here was a nice place to camp; plenty of wood and an abundance of grass, and the finest water in the land. Here was a lovely valley, and just off to the northwest was a little hill or ridge, only a short distance from which we made our camp. Some of the men went to getting wood and building a fire, while others were unpacking, not thinking of Indians, and just as the packs were off we were aroused by the war-whoop of a little squad of Indians who were coming over the ridge spoken of. We had a hot little fight, but it only lasted a few minutes, when the Indians withdrew, and Uncle Kit gave orders to follow them, which we did, and had a running fight for about five miles. We captured five horses from the redskins, and in the affair did not lose a man, nor even a horse.

This ended our trouble with the Indians for this trip.

On arriving at Santa Fe, Uncle Kit and Jim Bridger sold their furs to Joe Favor and Mr. Roubidoux for a good price.

Here we met an Englishman, who lived in London, England, and had come that spring from St. Louis, in company with Mr. Roubidoux and Joe Favor.

I had my pet panther with me, and the Englishman took a fancy to her and asked my price for her. I told him that she was not for sale. He offered me a hundred dollars for her. I hated to part with her, but a hundred dollars was more money than I had ever had before at one time, and looked like a big lot to me, so I accepted his offer, and in less than twenty-four hours I was very sorry, for during the time I stayed in Santa Fe, every time that I would pass in sight of her she would cry as pitifully as any child ever heard. Five hundred dollars would not have bought her from Mr. Mace, as he had purchased her with the intention of taking her to England.

Mr. Roubidoux and Joe Favor employed Uncle Kit to go out and trade for buffalo robes with the Comanche and Kiowa Indians. I accompanied him on this trip, and we were out two months, during which time we did not see a white man.

This was the first shipment of buffalo robes that had ever been made from this region, consequently we were able to get them almost at our own price.

As soon as Uncle Kit got out there with his little stock of goods that had been furnished him to trade on, and which consisted of beads and rings and a very few blankets, and the Indians had learned that he would trade for robes, the squaws all fell to dressing them. Among the Indians it was considered disgraceful for men to do such work.

In a very short time there were plenty of dressed buffalo robes, and some very nice ones, and I have seen Uncle Kit trade a string of beads a foot and a half long for a first-class robe, and for a red blanket he could get almost as many robes as he had a mind to ask.

As fast as the robes were bought they were baled, and by the time Uncle Kit pretty well bought up all that were for sale, the wagon- train came and hauled them away.

There were twenty wagon loads of robes and the goods Uncle Kit traded for them would not have cost to exceed seventy-five dollars.

Our work being done, we started for Taos, for it was now almost time to start out for the winter's trapping. On our arrival at Taos we found Johnnie West, who had been loafing around for two months, and who was anxious to get at work again. Uncle Kit hired him to go with us to South Park to trap the coming winter, that being the place he had decided upon for the season's work.

CHAPTER VII
BATTLING THREE DAYS' BATTLE BETWEEN THE COMANCHES AND THE UTES FOR THE POSSESSION OF A "HUNTER'S PARADISE."—AN UNSEASONABLE BATH

All being ready, Uncle Kit, Johnnie West and myself pulled out for South Park. We passed over a high range of mountains, struck the Park on the east side, and a more beautiful sight I never saw than the region was at that time. Coming in from the direction mentioned, one could overlook the entire park, which was almost surrounded by snow-capped mountains, and the valley, several miles below, which was about eighty miles long and from ten to twenty miles wide, was as green as a wheatfield in June. When we were near the valley we could see elk in bands of a hundred or more, with small herds of bison scattered here and there in the valley, and antelope by the hundred.

I had often heard of a hunter's paradise, and when I got sight of this lovely valley, with its thousands of wild animals of almost every description known to the continent, I made up my mind that if there ever was such a place as a hunter's paradise, I had surely found it. The high mountains with scattering pine trees on the sides; the snowy white peaks above the timber line, and the many little mountain streams and rills that paid tribute to the main stream that coursed this beautiful valley, all combined to form a scene of magnificent grandeur. The quaking-asp, balm and various other kinds of small timber that grew along the streams all helped to add to the beauty of the scene.

We crossed over to the west side to a cove that ran back some twelve miles from the main valley; here, we decided, was the best place to establish our winter quarters. Every little mountain stream in the valley was alive with beaver, and Uncle Kit thought it so late that we would not be bothered by the Indians that fall, but, that we would have to get out early the following spring. Feeling perfectly safe, we built our cabin this winter entirely on top of the ground, consequently we were not long in getting our winter quarters completed and were soon ready to start in trapping. We had excellent success this winter; very little snow to contend with, making it much better getting around than usual and an easier task to look after strings of traps.

In those cases each man had his string of traps, and it was his business to go to each trap every day, take the beaver out, skin them, set the traps, carry the skins home and stretch them. Sometimes we would trap as far as seven miles from camp, that being the outside limit. After we had trapped here about three weeks there came a light fall of snow which drove most of the game to the valley, and we experienced no trouble in getting all the meat we wanted close to camp, in fact we could often kill deer and antelope from our cabin door.

The second morning after the snowfall, Uncle Kit, Johnnie West and myself all started down the valley to took after our traps. We went about a mile together, I left the other two, my traps being the farthest away, some three miles down the valley. After leaving the other two I struck out down the valley on a turkey trot, that being my usual gait when alone. I had not gone far when I heard two gun shots. Thinking that Uncle Kit and Johnnie had been attacked by the Indians, I turned in the direction that I heard the shooting, and ran back much faster than I had come, but had not gone far when I saw ahead of me, up the narrow valley, a band of about twenty bison coming direct for me. I thought by shooting the leader it might check their speed and perhaps cause them to change their course. So I brought my gun to my face and dropped the leader, but it neither caused the others to halt or change their course, and they were making a bee line for me, and there was not a tree in reach large enough for me to climb nor a place of any kind that I could hide.

Now I was not long in making up my mind that I had a first-class foot-race on my hands—as an Irishman might say—and after running some distance I looked back and saw the bison were on me at every jump. Had I only known the nature of bison, which I learned afterward were not so vicious as buffalo, I could have turned to the right or left and they would have passed on; but thinking that they were after me, I got out like a quarter-horse, putting in my best licks to try to reach a wash-out that I knew of ahead of me. Thinking that if I only could reach that ditch I might have some possible show for my life, I lost no time in getting there, but got right down to business and did the prettiest running I have ever done in my life. Every time I looked back I saw that the rushing herd was closer upon me, until they were within a few feet, and by the time I reached the ditch I fancied that I could feel the breath from the nostrils of a half dozen bison on the rear base of my buckskin trousers. Then into the ditch I went, head-long and into about four feet of water. It seemed to me that those buffalo were half an hour crossing that ditch, but I stood perfectly quiet in the water up to my waist until they had all passed over.

The ditch being deep and the banks perpendicular, I had to wade the water for some distance up the ditch before I could find a place where I could climb out. I had just scrambled up the bank and shaken myself, when up came Uncle Kit and Johnnie, who had heard the report of my gun and had come to see whether or not I had killed anything.

"Rather cold to go bathing," said Uncle Kit. "When I go bathin' I allus pull off my buckskin suit."

But I told them I considered myself lucky to be able to find a suitable place to go swimming just at that time, and congratulated myself on being all there.

Aside from my race with the bison, I put in a very pleasant winter, and Uncle Kit said he had never spent as pleasant a time in the mountains as he did that winter in South Park. "In fact," said he, "it was more like a pleasure trip than anything else."

Our camp at this time was near where the town of Tarryall has since been built, and we ranged our horses in the extreme south end of the park, where they had the best kind of grazing the entire winter.

It was in the latter part of March—this now being the spring of 1852— when Uncle Kit made a trip to the south end of the park to get our horses, thinking we had stayed there about as long as it was safe.

During his absence Johnnie West and I were busily engaged in making preparations to start for Bent's Fort, as soon as Carson should get back with the horses. On his return he informed us that he would not leave the park until about the first of May, which was a surprise and disappointment to us both, as we had made all calculations on getting started the following day. We asked what was up that we were to be detained so long.

"On my trip for the horses," said Carson, "I saw some Injuns of the Comanche tribe, and they told me that them and the Utes war goin' to have a battle as soon as the Utes can cross the mountains, and the place for the battle decided on is in the south end of the park." He also said that with all the Indian fighting he had been mixed up in he had never before had an opportunity to see two tribes come together, and that he would not miss seeing it for any consideration.

In those days each tribe of Indians had their own scope of hunting and trapping ground, and if one tribe was caught intruding upon the rights of another tribe it was apt to cause trouble.

As I have said before, South Park was a hunter's paradise in the winter, and added to this, in the summer almost the entire valley was covered with wild strawberries. Along the many little mountain streams were abundance of wild gooseberries, blackberries and wild currants, while on the hillsides were acres of wild raspberries. In fact almost every variety of berries that there grew west of the Missouri river could be found in South Park; while the streams were full of the finest quality of mountain trout as well as many other kinds of fish.

The two tribes of Indians mentioned had been in dispute for a number of years as to their boundary line, each claiming South Park, and this battle had been arranged the fall before by the chiefs, also the place decided upon for the battle, which was to be on a little stream in the extreme south end of the park, that has since gone by the name of Battle Creek.

Battle Creek heads in the Pike's Peak range of mountains, and runs almost due west. The particular spot selected for this battle was on this creek, about two miles from where it empties into the stream that runs through the park.

No better place could have been selected for the fight. There were scattering pines here and there, with not a bush of any kind to interfere with their wild charges, and a gentle slope from each side to the stream which we might call the dead line.

The Comanches were to occupy the south side, while the Utes were on the north.

As this battle was to settle for all time the long-disputed right of these two powerful tribes, it was likely to be no tame affair.

This was what might be called a civil war between two tribes of Indians. They had quarreled so long over this portion of the country that the two chiefs had met and decided to have it settled for, and the conditions of the battle were as follows: In the event of the Comanches being victorious they were to have South Park; the summit of the Rocky Mountains to be the boundary line. And in the event of the Utes being victorious, the boundary line was to be at the foot of the Rocky Mountains on the eastern slope, the country in dispute comprising all of the territory between the Arkansas river and South Platte, including South Park.

About two weeks before the time set for the battle, the Comanche warriors began to arrive. Some brought their families while others did not.

Uncle Kit, being well acquainted with the Comanche chief, as well as the most of his warriors, loaded up all his furs and we moved over near the Comanches' quarters a few days before the battle was to take place.

As the Comanches came in they would pitch their wick-i-ups back on the hill about a quarter of a mile south of the little stream, which was to be their line of battle. They were all on hand before any of the Utes came across the mountains.

About two days from the time the last of the Comanches came to the ground, there was a little squad of Utes came in and pitched their camp about the same distance from the little stream as the Comanches, only on the opposite side.

This little squad of Indians came on ahead to ascertain whether they would be able to cross the mountains, and if they did not return in so many days the others would take it for granted that all was clear and would follow, which they did, and a few days later the entire Ute nation was there.

The battle did not begin for two or three days after all the Utes were on the ground, thereby giving both sides ample time to kill plenty of game to last them through the war.

During the time they were preparing for battle, neither tribe seemed to make any attempt to molest their enemy in any way whatever, but apparently looked upon it as a matter of business and proposed to fight it out on the square.

During the time we were awaiting the battle, Kiwatchee, chief of the Comanches, who was a very intelligent Indian in his way, and could speak French fairly well, and who was also an intimate friend of Kit Carson, came to Uncle Kit and said:

"I know you are a great chief and I want to hire you and your men to help me whip the Utes.

"If you help me fight the Utes I will give you five ponies each."

Kit Carson declined by telling Kiwatchee that he did not come to fight, but as he had never witnessed a war between two tribes of Indians, he had come merely to look on, and as the war was for the purpose of settling a dispute between the two tribes, he did not think it would be right for him to interfere. Kiwatchee insisted on our entering into the battle and asked how many horses we would take to help him fight the Utes. But Uncle Kit told him he would take no hand in the affair.

We were camped on the hill near the Comanches, where we could overlook the entire battle-ground, as well as the Ute camp. We dared not go near the Utes, for they were not at all friendly toward the pale-faces, and in case the Utes were victorious we would have to flee with the Comanches.

The day before the battle was to take place, Kiwatchee came and said to us:

"To-morrow we will fight."

We asked him how long he thought the battle would last. Kiwatchee said he thought he could whip the Utes in one day.

The following morning about sunrise, just as we were eating breakfast, the two chiefs commenced beating their war-drums, which was a signal to call their men together. The war-drum, or what the Comanches call a "tum-tum," was made of a piece of hollow log about eight inches long, with a piece of untanned deerskin stretched over one end. This the war chief would take under one arm and beat on it with a stick. When the tum-tums sounded the first morning there was great commotion among the Indians. At the first tap the war-whoop could be heard, and in a few moments both tribes of Indians were down at the little stream, each formed in line on his own side.

On arriving at the stream the tum-tums ceased and were not heard again till the Indians were formed in line of battle and each war- chief passed down in front of his men, after which they again commenced beating on the tum-tums, and at that the arrows began flying.

Now the fun had commenced in earnest, and of all the war-whoops I ever heard they were there, and the more noise the Indians made the harder they would fight.

After they had fought for about two hours they seemed to get more cautious than at the start, and would look for some advantage to take of the enemy.

They fought hard all day; sometimes the Comanches would cross over to the same side with the Utes, and I saw many hand-to-hand fights with tomahawks and knives. At other times the Utes would cross over on the Comanche side of the stream, but would soon retreat again, and each side would resume their old position for a time. About sunset both tribes withdrew, apparently by mutual agreement, each side returning to camp for supper.

I did not learn how many Comanches were killed that day, but there were some twenty odd wounded, and some of them fatally. The night was made hideous by the shrieks and cries of the squaws and children of the warriors who had been killed or wounded during the day.

Neither tribe put out picket guards during the night.

The next morning about sunrise the war-chiefs were out beating on the tum-tums. The warriors did not hasten around so briskly as the morning before, however, they were soon at the spot and ready for battle.

After going through the same manoeuvres as the morning before, the war-woops rang out loud and shrill, and again the arrows began to fly. The contestants fought hard all day again, without ceasing. About the middle of the afternoon the Comanches made a desperate charge on the Utes, crossing the creek and fighting them at close quarters. Among the Comanches was one Indian in particular that I was acquainted with, that I saw engaged in a number of hand-to- hand fights, and always came out victorious, but he got badly used up during the day. This Indian went by the name of White Bird, and he was beyond doubt the worst disfigured piece of humanity I ever saw, but he fought on, and he seemed to say by his actions:

"I am slightly disfigured, but still in the ring."

About sundown the two armies again withdrew for refreshments and repairs.

That evening after eating my supper! went over to White Bird's wick-i-up and found him sitting there, bloody from head to foot, with a huge cut on one cheek, another on one side of the head, and numerous other wounds, making him the most horrible specimen of humanity that I had ever seen living. He had not even washed the blood from his face or hands, but was sitting there telling his squaw and children how many Utes he had killed during the day, apparently as cool and unconcerned as though nothing had happened him. But he was not able for duty the next day, and died about ten o'clock.

We never learned where the Indians buried their dead, for they took them away during the night and disposed of them in some manner.

There were more Indians killed and wounded the second day than the first, and that night the Comanches had a big war-dance over the scalps they had taken.

The morning of the third day each tribe marched down at about the usual hour and resumed their positions in the line of battle, and that morning they fought more cautiously than before, until about ten o'clock, when the Utes made their first big charge on the Comanches, and they had a hard fight, which resulted in the death of many Indians, and the Utes retreated with considerably the worst of it.

In this charge we counted over forty Utes that were killed and scalped.

After the Comanches had driven the Utes back, Johnnie West and I went down within about fifty yards and sat there until the war was ended. About the middle of the afternoon of the third day, the old war-chief of the Comanches rushed up and commenced to shout, "Co- chah! Co-chah!"

which meant to go ahead, or, in other words, to charge. Johnnie West, who understood the language, turned to me and said:

"The Comanches are going to make another charge."

Sure enough, they did; crossing the creek and made a desperate rush for the Utes, but the Utes could not stand the pressure and retreated, the Comanches following them to the top of the hill where the Utes were camped, it being understood between the two chiefs that, when either army or tribe was driven back to the top of the hill, they had lost the battle.

The Comanches now returned, singing and shouting at the top of their voices, and in a short time a little squad of Comanches came in with about one hundred head of Ute horses. We never learned whether they had captured the horses or whether they had won them in the battle.

That night the Comanches had another big war-dance, and while the unfortunate squaws and children were weeping over the loss of their fathers and husbands, the victorious warriors were dancing, singing and shouting, and while dancing, each warrior would try to show as near as he could the manner in which he killed and scalped his enemy, and of all the silly maneuvers a white man ever witnessed, it was there at that war-dance.

The next morning there was not a Ute to be seen, all having left during the night.

The day following, the Comanches broke camp and started back for their main village on the Arkansas river. We broke camp and started out ahead of them, and in four days reached Bent's Fort, where Uncle Kit sold his furs to Colonel Bent and Mr. Roubidoux.

These two kept a boarding-house at the Fort, and this being the general loafing place during the summer season for most of the trappers in this part of the country, they also kept whiskey, and after the trappers had sold their furs, many of them would stop around the Fort and pay board for about three or four months during each summer, and by the time they were ready to start trapping again, Col. Bent and Mr. Roubidoux would have all of their money back for grub and whiskey, and, in fact, many of them would be in debt to them.

There being so much stock around the Fort the game was driven back so far that it became necessary to go considerable distance to get any. Col. Bent and Mr. Roubidoux proposed to hire Johnnie West and I to hunt for them for two months, saying that they had not had fresh meat half of the time the past spring. We agreed to work for them for two months, they being willing to pay us fifty dollars each per month, with the understanding that in case we kept them in meat all summer they would pay us extra wages. They now having some thirty odd boarders, it took a great deal of meat, and having to go some distance for game we had to pack it on pack-horses. We hunted for them two months, and at the end of that time we had kept them in meat and had enough ahead to last them one month longer.

It now being time to start out to look for trapping ground for the coming winter, we went to Col. Bent for a settlement, and after he had counted out our hundred dollars each he asked us how much extra wages we thought we should have. I told him I was perfectly willing to leave it to Mr. Roubidoux, and Johnnie being willing to do that also, Mr. Roubidoux told the Colonel to pay us twenty dollars each, extra, all of which was agreeable to us, and they engaged us to hunt for them the next summer at seventy-five dollars per month.

We returned now to Taos to prepare for the winter's trapping.

CHAPTER VIII
KIT CARSON KILLS A HUDSON BAY COMPANY'S TRAPPER, WHO WAS SPOILING FOR A FIGHT.—SOCIAL GOOD TIME WITH A TRAIN OF EMIGRANTS

Arriving at Taos I learned that Uncle Kit had his trapping company already organized for the coming winter, consisting of himself, Jim Bridger, Jim Beckwith, Jake Harrington, Johnnie West and myself, six in all.

Early in the fall of 1852 we pulled out for the head of Green river, which was a long and tedious journey, being more than eight hundred miles from Taos and over a rough country. We took the trail along the foot of the Rocky Mountains, running north until after crossing North Platte. Here we struck across the Bad Lands, and I thought that if there ever was a place rightly named, it surely was this section of country. We were three days crossing this God-forsaken country; and we would often travel a half day without seeing a living thing of any description. From there we struck across the main divide of the Rocky Mountains, and were three days crossing over to the headwaters of Green river, and were somewhat disappointed when we learned that Green river had been trapped over by the Hudson Bay Company the year before. However, we were there, and it was too late to look up another trapping-ground, so we occupied some of the old cabins that had been erected by the Hudson Bay Company and went to trapping.

Notwithstanding the country had all been trapped over, we had fair success, or, at least, much better than we expected. We stayed there and trapped until some time in February, when we pulled up and moved down Green river nearly twenty miles and there we trapped for two weeks, but not with as good success as we had had at the old camp.

We again moved camp down to what was known as Hell's Hole. There we found about forty French Canadians trapping for the Hudson Bay Company, who, by the way, had plenty of bad whiskey. They were not very friendly toward the new arrivals.

Among the party was a big fellow by the name of Shewman, that seemed to think himself a very bad man; he did not appear to have any love or respect for any American trapper, which was the case with the general run of those French Canadians who were in the employ of the Hudson Bay Company.

This man Shewman seemed to have a great antipathy toward Kit Carson.

If the reader will pardon me, I would like to say just here, that while Kit Carson was the last man to offer an insult, yet, at the same time, if challenged, he would fight any man living rather than be called a coward, and in those days the character of men concerning whom this work is written quarreled but very little. If a man insulted another, ten chances to one he would be challenged to fight a duel; and in such a case he would either have to fight or be branded as a coward, and the sooner he left the crowd the better it would be for him, for he could see no peace while remaining with them.

The third day we arrived at the place spoken of, this man Shewman got pretty well ginned up and started out to look for Uncle Kit, saying that he had heard a great deal of Kit Carson and of his fighting proclivities, and that he would lick him on sight. One of Shewman's friends, knowing Kit Carson by reputation, tried to induce him to let Kit alone and have nothing to do with him, but the more they said to him the madder he got, until finally he was raging with anger.

It happened that while he was in his rage, Uncle Kit, Jake Harrington and I, knowing nothing of Shewman's mad fit, started out to look after our horses and had to pass near their camp. Just as we were passing by their cabin, Shewman said:

"There goes the d—d white-faced American now. Look at him, he looks just like a coward, and he is a d—d cowardly cur, just like all the rest of the Americans."

Uncle Kit stopped and addressed him in the following manner:

"I am an American and I feel proud of the name, but I would have you understand that I am no coward. I will fight you any way that you wish."

Shewman said: "If you want me to kill you, get your horse and I will get mine, and we will get one hundred yards apart and start at the word. After we start, each fire when we please."

This Uncle Kit agreed to, saying: "There is my horse, I will be ready in three minutes. Get ready as soon as you please; as you seem to want to fight, I will accommodate you."

I had been with Uncle Kit now since 1847, and this was the first time I had ever seen him in any serious trouble, and I was surprised at the cool and unexcited manner in which he talked to Shewman. He was apparently as cool as though he was just in the act of starting out buffalo hunting. There was a smile on his countenance when he was talking to Shewman about the fight that was to take place, in which one of them was to lose his life.

I had been with Kit Carson long enough to know better than to say anything to him, but Jake Harrington followed him out to where his horse was, and started in to try to talk him out of the notion by telling him that Shewman was drinking. He turned to Harrington and said: "Jake, I thought you were an American, and would fight for the name." Harrington, seeing that Uncle Kit was determined in the matter, said no more.

Carson went out to where his saddle-horse was feeding, caught him and took a half-hitch around his nose with the riatta, jumped on him without any saddle, and by this time Shewman was on his horse also, with his rifle in hand.

Up to this time I had not said a word to Uncle Kit, but as I came up I asked him if he was not going to get his gun.

"No," said he, "this is all the gun I want;" and he took out his pistol and rode away a few rods, so that Jake Harrington and I would not be in range of the bullets from Shewman's gun, and stopped to wait for Shewman to give the word. A number of Shewman's friends tried to persuade him not to start, but their talk only seemed to add to his rage. After they had exhausted all their persuasive powers, and seeing that he was so determined in the matter, they let him go.

He cried out in French that he was ready, and at that moment they both started their horses at full speed toward each other. When within thirty yards, Shewman fired, and at the crack of his gun, Jake Harrington clapped his hands and shouted: "Good! good! Uncle Kit is safe."

We could not see any sign of his being hit, and when a few yards nearer each other, Uncle Kit fired, and Shewman fell to the ground mortally wounded, the bullet passing through his body just above the heart.

Shewman lived until Uncle Kit got to him, then he acknowledged that it was all his own fault, and that it was good enough for him.

As soon as the fight was ended, Jake Harrington and I ran into camp to notify the rest of our crowd, thinking that we would have to fight the entire Canadian outfit of trappers, but we found it quite different, for after the fight they were more friendly toward us than before. We stayed two days and helped to bury Shewman.

This was the first white man that I had ever seen buried in the Rocky Mountains.

We rolled him up in a blanket, laid him in the grave and covered him with dirt. The funeral being over, our party started for Bent's Fort.

The third day's travel brought us to Sweetwater, where we came to the top of a hill, from which we could overlook the entire valley, which was covered with wagons and tents. This was a large train of emigrants from various portions of the East who had started the year before and had wintered on Platte river, the edge of settlement, and when spring opened they had resumed their journey.

After supper that evening, Uncle Kit suggested that we visit the emigrant camp and see the ladies, which did not altogether meet with my approval, but rather than be called bashful, I went along with the crowd. I was now twenty-one years of age, and this was the first time I had got sight of a white woman since I was fifteen, this now being the year of 1853.

I had been out in the mountains a long time, and had not had my hair cut during that time, but took excellent care of it. I always kept it rolled up in a piece of buckskin, and when unrolled it would hang down to my waist.

There was a number of young ladies in the train, and they were not long in learning that I was the most bashful person in the crowd, and they commenced trying to interest me in conversation. At that time I only owned two horses, and would have given them both, as free as the water that runs in the brook, if I could only have been away from there at that moment. Seeing that I had long hair, each of them wanted a lock. By this time I had managed to muster courage enough to begin to talk to them.

I told them that if they would sing a song, they might have a lock of my hair.

A little, fat Missouri girl, spoke up and said: "Will you let any one that sings have a lock of your hair?"

I assured her that I would.

"And each of us that sing?" interrupted another young lady.

I said each one that would sing could have a lock, provided there was enough to go around.

I now had the ice broken, and could begin to talk to the ladies and crack a few jokes with them.

The little, fat, chubby young lady, that first started the conversation, sang a song entitled "The Californian's Lament," which was as follows:

Now pay attention unto me,
All you that remain at home,
And think upon your friends
Who have to California gone;
And while in meditation
It fills our hearts with pain,
That many so near and dear to us
We ne'er shall see again.

While in this bad condition,
With sore and troubled minds,
Thinking of our many friends
And those we left behind,
With our hearts sunk low in trouble
Our feelings we cannot tell,
Although so far away from you,
Again we say, farewell.

With patience we submitted
Our trials to endure,
And on our weary journey
The mountains to explore.
But the fame of California
Has begun to lose its hue—
When the soul and body is parting
What good can money do?

The fame of California
Has passed away and gone;
And many a poor miner
Will never see his home.
They are falling in the mountains high,
And in the valleys, too;
They are sinking in the briny deep,
No more to rise to view.

This I thought the prettiest song I had ever heard in my life. Environment so colors things. In other words, "circumstances alter cases."

The lady at once demanded a lock of my hair as compensation for services rendered, and I removed the buckskin wrap and told her to take a lock, but cautioned her not to take too large a bunch, for fear there might not be enough to go around. The young lady, seeing that I was very bashful, had considerable trouble in finding a lock that suited her. A number of the young ladies sang together, after which several of them took the scissors and cut a lock of hair from the head of the young trapper.

I wondered at the time why it was that all the young ladies had a pick at me, for there was Johnnie West, a fine looking young man, who was continually trying to engage some of them in conversation, but they did not want to talk to any one but me, and it amused Uncle Kit not a little to see the sport the young ladies were having at my expense.

Before leaving, I told the young lady who sang the first song that I thought it was the prettiest song I had ever heard, and requested her to sing it again. She replied that she would if I wished, and she did.

The next day about ten o'clock as we rode along, feeling drowsy from the warm sun, Jake Harrington turned around in his saddle, yawned and said: "Well, Will, can't you sing the song for us that you learned from those little Missouri gals last night?"

I told him I thought I could, and commenced clearing up my throat, at which the entire crowd smiled above a whisper; but I surprised the crowd by starting in and singing the song just as I heard the young lady sing it the evening before. Every man in the crowd took off his hat, and they gave me three cheers.

On arriving at Bent's Fort we learned that furs were high, and notwithstanding our catch was light, Uncle Kit did fairly well.

He sold his furs again to Col. Bent and Mr. Roubidoux.

After Uncle Kit had settled up with all the other boys, he called me into the tent and said:

"Willie, I have settled with all the men now but you; how much am I owing you?"

Up to this time I had never received any wages from Uncle Kit, nor had I expected any, for I did not think that I had done enough for him to pay for my raising. I had always felt under obligations to him for picking me up when I was without a home and almost penniless, and had, as I considered made a man of me.

Uncle Kit told me that I was old enough now to do a man's work, and that I was able to fill a man's place in every respect. He took his purse from his pocket, counted me out one hundred and fifty dollars in gold; and not until then had I known that he had ordered me a fifty dollar suit of buckskin made at Taos, the fall before; and not until then had he told me that he was to be married on the tenth of July, and wanted Johnnie West and I to be there without fail. I asked him who he was going to be married to. He said her name was Rosita Cavirovious. She was a Mexican girl who lived in Taos. I did not know the lady but was acquainted with some of her brothers. I told Uncle Kit that I would surely be there.

Uncle Kit and Jim Beckwith now started for Taos, and Johnnie West and I began making preparations to start in hunting for Col. Bent and Mr. Roubidoux, as per contract nearly one year before.

Col. Bent said that he was very glad that we were ready to start in hunting, as they had been out of fresh meat at least half of the time that spring.

In that country bacon was high, being worth from twenty-five to thirty cents per pound, and early in the spring higher even than that.

This spring, as usual, there were some thirty trappers congregated at Bent's Fort, apparently to eat and drink up what money they had earned during the winter.

CHAPTER IX
MARRIAGE OF KIT CARSON.—THE WEDDING FEAST.—PROVIDING BUFFALO MEAT, IN THE ORIGINAL PACKAGE, FOR THE BOARDING-HOUSE AT BENT'S FORT

Johnnie West and I started with a saddle-horse each and four pack-mules for a buffalo hunt; I still riding Croppy, the pony Uncle Kit had given me at St. Louis, but he was getting old and somewhat stiffened up in his shoulders.

We traveled up the Arkansas river to the mouth of the Purgatoire—pronounced in that country Picket Wire—which was about thirty miles from Bent's Fort. Seeing a small band of buffalo some distance away, we took the pack-saddles off of the mules and turned them out to graze, mounted our saddle-horses and were off for the herd; but the wily beasts got wind of us and started off before we got within gunshot of them. After running them about a mile we overhauled them, both fired and each killed a yearling calf while on the run. I fastened my rifle to the pommel of the saddle, drew my pistol, and there being a very fine heifer that had dropped back to the rear, I spurred up by the side of her and was just in the act of firing, when old Croppy stepped into a prairie-dog hole and fell with me.

Johnnie West had just fired his second shot and killed a fine three-year-old heifer, when he looked and saw old Croppy lying there, and I stretched out beside him, apparently dead. The first thing I knew after the fall, Johnnie West was sitting by my side slapping me in the face with his hand.

I was badly bruised but no bones were broken, and as soon as I recovered sufficiently to know for a certainty that I was not dead, an examination of old Croppy developed the fact that his left shoulder was badly broken. I being too chicken-hearted to shoot him, got Johnnie West to put him out of his misery, and now I was left afoot and thirty miles from home. Johnnie West went back and got our pack-mules. We dressed our buffalo and had plenty of meat to load all of our mules, and some to leave there for the hungry cayotes. That night while we were cooking some of the meat for supper, the cayotes raised a howl and it seemed as though they would take possession of our camp in spite of us; but by firing a shot among them once in a while, we were able to keep them at bay.

In those days hunters never took along anything to eat, for a man that could not kill what he could eat was considered worthless.

The following morning we loaded our meat on the mules, lashed my saddle on top of one of the packs and started for Bent's Fort. I being bruised and crippled up from the effects of my fall, Johnnie let me ride his horse and he walked almost the entire way home.

Mr. Roubidoux on learning that I had left old Croppy dead on the prairie, said: "I have got the best buffalo horse on the plains, and I will make you a present of him;" and turning to his herder, he said, "go and bring Pinto in."

When the spotted horse was brought in, Mr. Roubidoux said: "Now, Will, I am going to make you a present of this horse, and I want you to keep him to remember me by."

I thought this the prettiest horse I had ever laid eyes on, and he proved to be as good a buffalo horse as Mr. Roubidoux had represented him to be.

On the third day of July, Johnnie West and I having enough meat ahead to last several days, we pulled out for Taos to attend the wedding of Kit Carson. Arriving there, Uncle Kit took us to his house.

He brought my new buckskin suit, and I know it was the handsomest of the kind I had ever seen. On the front of the trousers was the finest of bead work, representing horses, Indians, buffalo, deer and various other animals; and on the coat the same, except they were worked with beads and porcupine quills.

I was now twenty-one years old, and had never attended a wedding. The ladies present all being of Catholic faith, Uncle Kit and his bride were married in the Catholic church by the priest.

There were at that time about five hundred inhabitants in Taos, and every man, woman and child attended the wedding of Kit Carson.

After the ceremony was over all marched down about three blocks to where there had been a whole bullock roasted, also three sheep. The tables used were made of rude boards split out with a froe. There were no table-cloths, no tea or coffee, but plenty of wine and an abundance of meat, that all might "eat, drink and be merry."

While we were at the supper table Uncle Kit happened to get sight of Johnnie West and I, and, taking each of us by the hand, he led us over and gave us an introduction to his wife, and this was the first time I had ever been introduced to a lady. Uncle Kit introduced me as his Willie. Mrs. Carson turned to me and said:

"Ge-lem-a mo cass-a la-mis-mo ta-casso tades vases; meaning, Willie, my house shall be your home at any and all times."

As I do not write Spanish, I simply give the sound of her words as she spoke them-or as I would.

I was highly pleased with the manner in which Mrs. Carson addressed me, for no lady had ever spoken so kindly to me before, and I had supposed that after Uncle Kit was married I would have to hunt another home.

Supper being over, all repaired to the dance hall and enjoyed themselves dancing until sunrise the next morning, when they returned to the tables for breakfast. This time they had coffee and tea, but during the entire feast they did not have a bite of bread on the table.

Here I met Jim Beckwith, of whom there will be much more said at intervals later on.

Jim wanted me to accompany him to California the following spring, saying that he knew of a pass through the Sierra Nevada Mountains, which, if we could manage to get the tide of emigration turned that way, we could establish a toll road and make a fortune out of it. I said I would not promise him now, but would give him an answer later on.

The wedding being over, Johnnie West and I, after bidding Uncle Kit and his wife good-bye, started for Bent's Fort. Col. Bent and Mr. Roubidoux wanted to employ us to hunt for them the coming winter. Johnnie thought he could do better trapping, but I hired to them to hunt until the following spring.

Col. Bent always had from six to twenty boarders, having six men of his own, and I kept them in meat all winter, alone.

About the first of April—this being in 1854—I settled up with the Colonel, and having written Jim Beckwith the fall before that I would be on hand to go with him to California, I now pulled out for Taos.

I visited with Uncle Kit and his wife while at Taos, and found that what Mrs. Carson had said at the feast was true, for I was as welcome at their home as though I was one of the family.

Jim Beckwith had everything in readiness for our trip across the Sierra Nevada Mountains.

The day before starting, Uncle Kit asked us what route we would take. Jim said that we would go around by the headwaters of the Gila river, this being a tributary to the Colorado. On this trip we would cross that part of the country which is now Arizona. Uncle Kit said this was a good route, and that he had gone over it twice in company with Col. Fremont. He drew a diagram of the country, showing the route by streams, mountains and valleys; telling us also what tribes of Indians inhabited each section of the country that we would pass through. Among the different tribes spoken of was the Pimas, whom he said were friendly toward the whites, and insisted on our calling on that tribe, provided we went that way.

He had been at their village in 1845, and at that time they had told him he was the third white man they had ever seen.

The reader will understand that all the Indians in that section of the country at that time could speak Spanish, having learned it from the Aztecs, a tribe that lived in Old Mexico and were of Montezuma's race. They often came out into that country to trade with the other Indians.

All being ready we bade Uncle Kit and his wife good-bye, and were off for California. We crossed the Rocky Mountains up the Arkansas river and took the trail made by Col. Fremont in 1848 to the summit of the Rocky Mountains. We then crossed over the mountains onto the headwaters of the south fork of Grand river, and from here we headed almost south, passing through a country that had all been burned over. We could look ahead for miles and see nothing but burnt hills. Game was so scarce that we could barely kill enough to supply us with food, until we struck the north fork of Gila river. Here we found plenty of game. We traveled down the Gila three days, which brought us to the Pima—or as was sometimes then called Peone—village. This village was situated in a lovely valley about twenty miles long and ten wide. The soil was very fertile. The surrounding mountains were very high and covered with fine timber, while the foothills were luxuriant in the finest quality of bunchgrass, and along the little mountain streams were cottonwood and willows.

The Indians here were fairly well civilized, a fact worthy of note, as they had never had a missionary or priest among them. They also had a different mode of worship from the tribes of the Northwest. Their place of worship was what might be called a large shed constructed by setting posts in the ground and covered with poles, brush and the leaves of the century plant, these leaves being from three to five feet long and from six to ten inches wide. Their houses were also covered with these leaves.

I never saw but two of these plants in bloom. One was about fifty miles north of Sacramento and the other in Golden Gate Park, near San Francisco. It was said they held their flowers four months. These flowers are very eing four inches across and look as though they were made of

a

_.. to return to my story. These Indians had three days of worship, also three days of feasting. On assembling at their place of worship, the chief chose four men from the audience, whom we would term preachers, but which they called abblers. They never pray, but the abblers stand up and talk to the audience, during which time the Indians preserve the very best order. The abblers tell them what they must do and what they must not do. When ready to break up, all join in singing, but never sing before preaching. Just how they learned this mode of worship was a mystery to me, and is yet, for that matter. We attended service while in the village and after preaching was over many of them invited us home with them.

There were about five hundred men in this tribe, all of whom were apparently very industrious, raising corn, melons, red pepper and other vegetables in abundance. They raised some very large melons, which were not excellent in flavor, however.

The Pimas were very kind to us while we were with them, often taking us out to their truck patches and pulling nice, large melons for us. I asked a very aged Indian where they got their seed corn, but he did not know, saying they had raised it ever since he could remember. They did their plowing with wooden plows, which they made themselves, being pulled by oxen that were hitched to the plows by a strong stick in front of their horns. For harrows they used brush, and they had shovels made of wood to dig with.

Notwithstanding they were in one sense uncivilized, they showed us more hospitality during the time we were with them than most white people would have shown to strangers.

These Indians keep their age by taking a piece of horn, pressing it out flat and punching a hole in the center. When a child is a certain age he has one of these tied about his neck, and every year the child is supposed to cut a notch in the piece of horn. I did not learn how old they had to be before they were supposed to keep their own age.

We found the chief of the tribe to be very obliging. He told us the Apaches were bad Indians, and that they had killed many white people— men, women and children.

When we were ready to leave the village, the chief came out and bade us good-bye, and gave us a cordial invitation to call on him when passing through the country.

We crossed the Gila river near where Colville now stands. Here wa. tribe of very indolent Indians, that during this season of the year did no. wear a stitch of clothing of any kind whatever. They were known as the Yumas.

We both emptied our rifles before crossing the river, knowing that they would get wet in crossing. I fired at a bird across the river and it fell to the ground.

At the crack of my rifle the Indians ran a few paces from me, dropped down and stuck their fingers in their ears. They told us in Spanish that they had never seen a wah-hootus before, meaning a gun with a loud report.

When Jim Beckwith went to fire his gun off, the squaws all ran away, but the bucks, being more brave, stayed, but held their hands over their ears. This tribe lived principally on fish.

The reader will remember that I had traveled over this same country in the year 1849 in company with Kit Carson and Col. Fremont, when on our trip to California.

After traveling about five miles we crossed a little sage-brush valley that was almost covered with jack-rabbits, and they were dying by the thousand. We could see twenty at one time lying dead in the sage-brush.

That night we camped on what has since been known as Beaver creek, and here we had to strike across the San Antonio desert, and having been across the desert I knew it would be eighty miles to water. Having two parafleshes with us for such emergencies, we filled them with water to use in crossing this desert.

A paraflesh is made of rawhide expressly to carry water in, and are frequently used to peddle milk by the Mexicans.

The second day from Beaver creek we reached a little stream near the Goshoot village, this being the place where Uncle Kit finished buying furs to load his pack-train in 1848.

The next morning we reached the village. I had not seen any of these Indians for five years. Then I was a mere boy and now a grown man, but every one of the Goshoots knew me and were glad to meet me. We stopped that day and visited with them, and bought some venison and frigoles, or beans.

The next morning we resumed our journey to Los Angeles, crossing the extreme northeast part of Death Valley. From here on the country was all new to me, and had it not been for the kindness of the Goshoot Indians, we would have perished for the want of water.

When I told a good Indian in that village where we were going, he sat down and with his finger marked a diagram in the dust, showing the lay of the country that we must pass ever, every little blind spring near the trail, the different mountains and valleys, and made it so plain that we could scarcely have made a mistake on the trip.

On arriving at Los Angeles we found only one white man in the place, and he was the only person in the whole town that could speak the English language. He had arrived there some years before, married a Mexican woman and had got to be very wealthy. He tried to induce us to go farther up the coast, telling us if we started for San Francisco the country was full of Mexicans, and that they despised all Americans and would be sure to murder us on our way; but as we had started for San Francisco, we were determined to see that city if possible. After laying over one day with the old American we resumed our journey.

The next place we struck was Monterey, where is now the famous Hotel del Monte, about two hundred miles from Los Angeles. Here we did not find a man who could speak a word of English, and we found the Mexicans still more selfish than in Los Angeles.

We began to think that the old white man had told the truth, for we would not have been surprised at any time to have been attacked by a band of Mexicans.

While here I saw two persons that I thought to be curiosities. They were of Indian parentage, light complexion and had eyes of a pink color. One was a boy about twenty years old and the other a girl of sixteen, and were brother and sister. It was claimed that they could see well after night, but could not see their way on a bright, sunny day.

These Indians were said to be of the Mojave tribe, that inhabited a portion of the country some six hundred miles east of Monterey, near the Mojave desert. I have since learned that such freaks are called albinos.

The reader will no doubt wonder why we came this round-about away to get to San Francisco. The reason is that in coming a more direct course we would have passed through a country that was infested with wild tribes of Indians; that is, tribes hostile to the whites. There being only two of us the chances were it would have proved a very unhealthy trip for us at that time.

CHAPTER X
ROBBER GAMBLERS OF SAN FRANCISCO.— ENGAGED BY COL. ELLIOTT AS INDIAN SCOUT.—KILLS AND SCALPS FIVE INDIANS.—PROMOTED TO CHIEF SCOUT

Arriving at San Francisco we found things very lively, this being about the time of the greatest gold excitement in California. Here was the first city of note that I had been in since leaving St. Louis; here also was the first time I had seen gambling going on on a large scale. There were all kinds of games and all kinds of traps to catch the honest miner and rob him of his money that he had labored hard to dig out of the ground.

That night Jim Beckwith and I took in the sights of the city. We went to the different gambling houses and had just finished our tour and were on our way back to the What Cheer house—that being the hotel at which we put up—the leading hotel in the city then. We were just passing one of the gambling dens, when we saw two men coming out of the door leading a man between them who was crying like a child, and exclaiming: "I am ruined! I am ruined!"

We learned from the two men that he had come to the city that day with eight hundred dollars in gold, had bought a ticket for New York, and it was his intention to sail for that city the following morning. But he had gone out that night to have a farewell spree with his friends, got too much booze, started in gambling, thinking he might double his money by morning; but like thousands of other miners in those days, he "played out of luck," as they termed it, and had lost every cent he had. We walked on down to the hotel, and in a few minutes the three came into the hotel also, the one still crying like a baby. The proprietor only laughed and said it was a common occurrence for men to come to the city with even twenty thousand dollars, gamble it off in less than a week and then return to the mines to make another stake. But he said he had never seen a man before that took it as hard as this one did.

It was all new to me, and a little of it went a long ways.

That night after Jim Beckwith and I had retired, I told him that I had seen all of San Francisco that I cared to, and was ready to leave. However, we stayed two days longer, after which we pulled out for the Sierra Nevadas, by the way of Hangtown, a little mining camp situated at the American Fork. Here we crossed over a pass that Jim had told me of more than a year previous, which led us to the headwaters of the Carson river.

I proposed we give it the name of Beckwith Pass; and from that day to this it has been known by that name, and since has been made a splendid stage road.

After traveling down the Carson river some distance, we met a party of miners who informed us that a few days previous a band of Indians down on the Humboldt had made an attack on an emigrant train, cut off a portion of the train, stampeded the teams, killed all the people of that part of the train and burned the wagons.

They also informed us that Col. Elliott was down on what was known as Truckee Meadows with a company of soldiers, but, so far, was having very poor success killing Indians.

Col. Elliott had been sent out there with four companies of cavalry to protect the emigrants against the Pah-Ute or Piute Indians, which were very numerous down on the Humboldt, and around the sink of the Carson and as far up the mountains as Lake Tahoe.

Jim being very well acquainted with Col. Elliott, proposed we go around that way, thinking that the Colonel might be able to assist materially in turning the tide of emigration through his pass, his object being to get as much travel that way this fall as possible, and the following spring he would establish a toll road through that pass.

Col. Elliott was pleased at meeting Jim, and in the conversation said: "Beckwith, I am very glad, indeed, to see you. You are just the man I have been wanting this long time, for I haven't a scout in my entire command that is worth a cent to scout for Indians. I don't believe there is one of them that would dare to leave headquarters fifteen miles alone, and I want to employ you as chief of scouts."

Jim thanked the Colonel kindly for the honor, but told him he could not accept the offer as he had another matter he wished to attend to, and told him of the scheme he had on hand. But, he said, he had a young man with him that he could recommend highly for that position, and he gave me a great send off as a scout.

The Colonel insisted on our going with him to his private quarters for supper, which we did, and after having a pleasant visit with him, we returned to our own camp for the night.

When we were ready to take our departure for the evening, Col. Elliott said: "Mr. Drannan, can I see you privately to-morrow morning at nine o'clock?"

I told him that I would call at his quarters at that hour.

After Jim and I had reached our camp I asked him why he had misrepresented me to Col. Elliott in the way he had, when he knew I had never scouted a day in my life, knew nothing of scouting and had done very little Indian fighting.

Jim said: "You are a young man and have been among the Indians long enough to be pretty well acquainted with their habits. There is not a single fellow in Elliott's outfit knows as much about scouting as my black horse, and if you ever intend starting in, now is your chance. That is the reason I gave you such a send off to the Colonel."

After thinking the matter over, I concluded that Jim was right in regard to it, and now was a good time to make a start.

After breakfast the next morning I met Col. Elliott at his quarters at the time appointed. He invited me in and set out a bottle of whiskey and a glass. I thanked him, but declined to drink.

"Where were you raised," said the Colonel, "that you do not drink whiskey? I thought you grew up in the Rocky Mountains."

I told him that I did, but was not raised to drink whiskey. I also told him that I had been brought up, since a boy fifteen years old, by Kit Carson.

The Colonel asked me many questions about Indians, their habits, my idea of fighting them and so on, after which he asked me if I would like a position as scout. I told him I would, provided there was enough in it to justify me.

The Colonel made me a proposition of one hundred dollars a month and rations, I to furnish my own horses. I could also turn my extra horses in with the Government horses and it would cost me nothing to have them herded. I accepted his proposition, agreeing to start in on the following morning. I also had an agreement with him that when I did not suit him, he was to pay me off and I would quit. Also, when he did not suit me, I was to have the privilege of quitting at any time, all of which was satisfactory to him, and I started in on the following morning as per agreement.

That evening about sunset three of Col. Elliott's scouts came in, and he gave me an introduction to them, telling them that I was going to be a brother scout. After supper I had a long talk with one of them, in which he posted me somewhat as to the different watering places, grass, etc.

From him I learned that they had not seen an Indian for three days, but had seen any amount of sign, every day, which was evidence that there were plenty of Indians in the country.

The following morning when I went for my orders I was much surprised at the Colonel saying: "Oh, damn it! I don't care. Go any way you please and as far as you please. The other boys say there is not an Indian in fifty miles of here, and if you find any you will do better than any man I have sent out, so far."

When I went to order my lunch, and told the negro cook to put up enough to last me until the next night, he looked at me and said: "Whar you going, boss?" Jim told him I was going out to get some cayote scalps. I now mounted Mexico—the horse that Mr. Reed had given me at the City of Mexico—and started off on my first scouting trip, taking an easterly direction until I had struck the old emigrant road.

After I had left camp the other scouts were talking among themselves, and none of them thought I would ever return. One of the scouts told Jim that I was the biggest fool that he had ever seen, to start out scouting in a strange region and not ask anything about the country, grass, water, Indians, or anything else.

"Don't be alarmed about that boy," said Jim, "he'll take care of himself in any man's country."

I had been taught by Uncle Kit that when I attempted to do a thing to carry it out at all hazards, if it was in my power to do so.

After I had ridden about twelve miles or so, and was just entering the mouth of a little ravine, on looking up the same ravine I saw three Indians who had just hove in sight over the hill. I dropped back from their view as quick as I could, which only took about two or three jumps of my horse.

The Indians having their backs toward me, I was confident they had not seen me. They were heading for the emigrant trail, that being what we called the wagon road across the plains in those days.

I rode around the point of a hill and tied my horse in a washout where he would be hid from view, climbed up the top of the hill and saw five warriors, riding direct for the trail. After watching them for a short time I hurried back to my horse, mounted him and rode as fast as Mexico could conveniently carry me over this sagebrush country—about a quarter of a mile in an opposite direction to which the Indians were traveling. Riding up to the head of a little ravine, where I could tie my horse in a place where he would not be discovered by the redskins, I dismounted, tied my horse and crawled up through the sagebrush to the top of the hill, where I could watch the movements of the Indians.

This was a rolling country, low hills covered with a heavy growth of sagebrush, and not a tree of any description to be seen anywhere.

I had discovered my game, but how to capture it was what puzzled me.

The reader can have a faint idea of the situation of a young man in a strange country and a sandy, sagebrush plain, who did not know where to find either water or grass. If I returned to headquarters they would escape me, and this being my first time out in the scouting business, I could not afford to let them get away. So, after holding a private council with myself, I decided these Indians were spies, who were scouting for a large party of Indians that were somewhere in this part of the country, and that they were looking for emigrants, and in case they did not see any such that day, they would no doubt go to water that night.

I laid there on the hill watching their movements and trying to devise some plan by which I could capture them then.

Could I only have had Jim with me, how easy it would have been to follow them to their camp that night, kill and scalp them and capture their horses.

In those days an independent scout was entitled to all the stock captured of the enemy by him.

I watched the Indians until they got to the emigrant trail, where they stopped and held a council, apparently in doubt as to which way they should go. After parleying for some five minutes they struck out on the trail. I watched them for about two miles, then they passed over a low range of hills and were out of sight.

I now mounted Mexico and rode as fast as I could, not directly after them, but as near as I could to keep out of their sight; and at the same time I felt confident that should they discover me, that there was not an Indian pony in that whole country that could catch Mexico, either in a short or long distance.

After riding some five miles or so, I dismounted and tied my horse to a sagebrush, and climbed to the top of the highest hill between me and where I supposed them to be. I discovered them about a mile away, and they were just leaving the trail, riding up a ravine that led to the north. They dismounted and put their ponies out to grass. There also appeared to be a little meadow where they stopped, and I concluded there must be water there, too. I took in the situation at a glance and could see that I would have to ride a long distance to get near them. Just immediately beyond them was a little hill that sloped off down to the meadow on which they were camped, but in any other direction a person could not ride without being discovered.

I went back to my horse, mounted and took a circuit of about ten miles, having to travel that distance in order to keep out of their sight. Coming in from the north, I rode almost to the top of the hill; here I dismounted, tied my horse, crawled to the top of the hill, and on looking down could see them almost under me, the hill was so small and steep. They were busily engaged in skinning a jack-rabbit, and about that time I felt as though I could eat a hind quarter of it myself if it had been cooked; for I had been too busily engaged that day to stop and eat a lunch.

Here I lay in the sagebrush trying to devise some plan by which I could do away with them and capture their horses.

It was now about four o'clock in the afternoon, and this being about twenty miles from headquarters, I would not have time to ride there and return with soldiers before they wold break camp in the morning.

For me to attack them alone looked like a big undertaking.

There being a little grass for their horses, I now concluded they would remain until morning. So I crept back to where my horse was tied, took out my lunch and sat down and ate it, at the same time debating in my mind the best course to pursue.

I remembered what Col. Elliott had told Jim, that he did not have a scout that dared go fifteen miles from camp and now if I should return to camp and report what I had seen, he would start soldiers out, and by the time they could reach the ground the Indians would be gone, and there would be nothing accomplished, consequently I would, no doubt, be classed with the balance of the scouts in the opinion of the Colonel. While on the other hand, should I be successful in laying a plan by which I could do away with the Indians and take their scalps to headquarters as evidence of my work, it would give me a reputation as a scout.

I was confident they had not seen me that day, and knowing, too, the Pah-Utes had not been disturbed by Col. Elliott's scouts, they would no doubt lie down when night came, and I might steal a march on them and amid their slumbers accomplish the desired deed.

Having been brought up by one of the bravest frontiersmen that traversed the plains at that time, and who always taught me to respect a brave man and hate a coward, I made up my mind to make the attack alone, provided the Indians did not put out guards that night.

After I had finished my lunch I examined both my single-shot pistols—I still having the one presented to me by my old friend Joe Favor, three years before at Bent's Fort, also the knife, which the reader will remember weighed two and one-fourth pounds— and creeping back to the top of the hill I watched them cook and eat the jack-rabbit. As it grew dark I drew nearer, and when it was about as dark as it was likely to be that night, I crept up to within a few yards of them. They had a little fire made of sagebrush and did not lie down until very late.

I was so near that I could hear them talking, but I could not understand their language, as I had never been among them, but I was confident they were Pah-Utes, because I was in their country.

After they had smoked and talked matters over, which I supposed was in regard to the next day's scouting, they commenced to make preparations to sleep. In the crowd, apparently, were three middle-aged warriors and two young ones, not yet grown. The three older ones laid down together, while the two young ones made their beds about fifteen feet away from the other three.

After they had become quiet I commenced crawling closer, as there was some fire yet and I wanted to get their exact location before I made the attack.

I felt confident that I could kill one of them the first blow with my knife, and then I could kill the other two with my pistols. But this would still leave two to one and I with nothing but a knife; however, after going this far I was determined to make the attack at all hazards.

When I had crawled up within a few feet of their bed, one turned over and muttered something in his own tongue, which I could not understand. I made sure I was not detected, and after lying still for some time I concluded they were all asleep, and I soon made up my mind that I had better make the attack at once and have the matter settled one way or the other. After taking in the entire situation I decided to make the attack with my knife. I took the pistol from my right holster in my left hand, thereby giving me a better chance after emptying the one pistol to easily grasp the other one with my left hand.

I knew that if I could get a fair lick at one of them with my big knife, which I always kept as sharp as a razor, that he would make little, if any, noise. My plan of attack being completed, I crawled up near their heads, and all appeared to be sound asleep.

I decided to take the one on my right first, so that in case the other two should attempt to arise I would be in a position to shoot the one on my left and at the same time cut the other one down with my heavy knife. But it was my intention to kill all three of them with my knife, if possible, in order to save both pistols for the two young ones, as I expected a hard fight with them, for I felt sure they would be on to me by the time I got through with the other three, at the very best I could do.

I now raised up on to my feet and aimed to strike the one on my right about the middle of the neck. I came down with all my might and killed him almost instantly. I served the second one the same way, but by this time the third one had raised to a sitting position, and I struck him in the shoulder and had to make a second lick to kill him. By this time the other two had been aroused, and, as near as I could tell in the darkness, one of them was crawling in the opposite direction on his hands and knees, while the other one was coming at me on all fours. I shot him with the pistol that I held in my left hand, and I then thought I was almost safe. Just at that moment the other young buck was on his feet, with bow in hand but no arrows. He dealt me a blow on the side of the head, which staggered me but did not knock me down, and before I had time to recover, he dealt me a second blow, but it did not stagger me so much as the first, but it brought the blood quite freely from my nose, at the same time I made a side stroke at him, but struck too low. I then drew my other pistol from the holster and fired, shooting him through the chest, and though he fell mortally wounded, he again raised to his feet and dealt me another blow, which was a great surprise to me, but just one stroke of my big knife severed his jugular and he yielded up the ghost.

Now my task was done. At the risk of my life I had accomplished the desired end, and my reputation as a scout would be established.

I knew the other scouts were having some sport at my expense while I was away, for I had overheard two of them in a conversation that morning make some remarks about Col. Elliott's tenderfoot scout.

I had said nothing to them, but this made me all the more determined in the undertaking, and now I had turned the joke on them, and, as the old saying goes, "he who laughs last laughs best."

I could see by the light in the east that the moon would be up in a short time, so I went and got my saddle-horse from where I had tied him, and who, by this time was very thirsty and hungry, as he had had nothing to eat and no water since morning. I watered him, then picketed him out for about two hours on the little meadow, by which time the moon had risen.

I then scalped the five Indians and tied their scalps to my belt. They would be good evidence of my day's work when I should meet the Colonel at his quarters. This being done, I tied the five Indian horses together and started for headquarters, arriving there about noon the next day.

Just as I had put the horses in the corral and before I had time to dismount, Col. Elliott's orderly came on the dead run, saying: "Col. Elliott wishes to see you at his quarters at once."

I turned about and rode over to the Colonel's tent, and when I had saluted him, he said: "Sir, whose horses are those you just turned into that corral?"

I said: "Sir, those are my horses, as I understand that any stock captured from the Indians by an independent scout, he is entitled to."

"Mr. Drannan, do you tell me that you captured those horses from an Indian?"

I said: "Col. Elliott, yes, sir; and here is something more I captured with them." At that I threw down the five scalps at his feet.

He looked amazed as he gazed at the scalps, but said nothing for a few moments.

About this time the orderly announced Jim Beckwith at the door. The Colonel said let him come in, and just as he entered the door, Col. Elliott said:

"Beckwith, where do you suppose this scout got those scalps?"

Jim picked up the scalps, examined them thoroughly, and said: "I'll bet my black horse that he took them from the heads of five Pah-Ute Indians."

The Colonel smiled and said: "Drannan, if you will tell us all about the whole affair, I will treat."

I related the adventure in brief. Dinner being ready, the Colonel set out the whiskey and cigars and told me to call on him that afternoon, as he wished to have a private conversation with me.

I picked up the five scalps and started to dinner, and as I passed by the kitchen I threw them under the negro cook's feet and told him to cook them for dinner for my friend and me—referring to Jim Beckwith. When he saw the scalps he exclaimed: "Laws a massa, boss! whar you git dem skelps? Marse Meyers said dey wasn't an Injun in fifty miles o' hyar."

While we were eating dinner, Jim said to me: "Don't you know them fellers didn't think you'd ever come back?"

I asked him what fellows, and he said: "Why, those scouts. One of them told me you was the d—est fool he ever saw in his life, to go out scouting alone in a strange country, and that the Pah-Utes would get you, sure."

I said I did not think it worth while to ask those scouts anything about Indians or anything else, for I didn't think they had been far enough from camp to learn anything themselves.

That afternoon when I was announced at the Colonel's tent, I was met in a somewhat different manner by him to what I had been that noon, for he raised the front of the tent and said: "Come right in Drannan, why do you hesitate?"

After having a social chat with him and rehearsing to some extent the fight which took place the night before between myself and the five Pah-Utes, he proposed to make me chief of his scouts. He said: "Now, Drannan, I will tell you what I wished to see you about. I have five scouts besides you, and I am going to make you chief of all my scouts, and you can handle them to suit yourself."

I told the Colonel that I did not desire any promotion whatever, for in the first place I would not be doing my self justice, and that it would not be doing justice to the other scouts, and I thought it would be of more benefit to both him and his other scouts, to go alone, as I had started out.

He asked me why I would prefer going alone. My reply was that a person in that business could not be too cautious, and I did not know what kind of men he had, and just one careless move would spoil the plans of the best scout in the world.

The Colonel admitted that I was right, but insisted on selecting one man from his five scouts to assist me, saying: "If he don't suit you, after trying him two or three days, report to me, and you may select any one from my scouts that you like." And to this I consented. I told him that I would be ready to start out the following morning, and if he had any orders to give me to give them now, as I would start very early. He said that he had no orders to give, but that he had selected Charlie Meyers to accompany me; and he proved to be a good man and a good scout.

CHAPTER XI
A LIVELY BATTLE WITH PAH-UTES.—PINNED TO SADDLE WITH AN ARROW.— SOME VERY GOOD INDIANS.—A STUTTERING CAPTAIN.—BECKWITH OPENS HIS PASS

The next morning I ordered three days' rations for two men, and Charlie Meyers desired to know if I was going to Salt Lake City or New York. I told him I was going out hunting, and if I struck fresh signs of game I proposed tracking it to wherever it went.

That day we took the divide between Carson and Humboldt, south of the emigrant trail, making a ride of forty miles that day, and then a dry camp—a camp without water. The following morning we rode about five miles, and came on to a big Indian trail that had been made the evening before. We pushed on as fast as we could, all the time keeping a sharp lookout, for we were now in the heart of the Pah-Ute country, and could not be too careful. About half past three o'clock we came to where the Indians had camped the night before, on a tributary of the Humboldt. At this camp three antelope had been devoured, so we knew that there had been a large band of the redskins at that feast. It was also evident that they were not very far ahead of us, as their fires had not entirely died out.

Continuing the pursuit we were now getting close to the emigrant trail, and it was plain that the Indians had headed west, which convinced me that they were looking for emigrants, and if so they would not go far before they would either go into camp or leave the trail. It proved that after following the emigrant train a short distance they had taken to the hills. The country was a sea of sagebrush, and frequently we would start a jack-rabbit or antelope that we would have been pleased to roast for supper, but dared not shoot.

When near the top of a hill I would dismount, and leaving my horse with Meyers, would crawl to the summit of the hill and peep over in order to discover whether or not the Indians were in sight, and then return, mount my horse and ride at a rapid gait until near the top of another hill, when the same maneuver would be repeated.

At last we came to a sharp ridge and I dismounted. I remarked that if we did not find those Indians soon we would have to make another dry camp that night. It was now nearly sunset, and on crawling to the top of the ridge and looking down on a nice little valley not more than a half-mile distant, I saw that they had just gone into camp and had not yet got all their ponies unpacked.

I had a good chance to make a rough estimate of their number, which I thought to be about two hundred warriors.

I rushed back to Meyers and told him that I had located them, and that one of us would have to ride back to headquarters that night and report, and asked him whether he would rather go or stay and watch the Indians.

"Why not both go," he asked.

I told him that by the time the cavalry could get there the Indians might be gone, and one of us must stay and see where they went to.

We were now, as near as we could tell, about thirty-five miles from camp, as that afternoon we had been traveling west, in the direction of headquarters.

After thinking the matter over, Meyers concluded that he would rather make the ride than stay. I told him to be off at once, but before starting, he said to me: "Suppose the Indians should discover you while I am away?"

I replied that I would like very much to have them discover me, when I knew the soldiers were in sight or within ten miles, for I would like to run them into such a trap, and that I was not afraid of any horse in their band catching Mexico in any distance.

I instructed Meyers not to spare horseflesh on the way, and to tell Col. Elliott to start two companies of cavalry as soon as possible.

We shook hands and he started, and that was once that he made good time. It being after seven o'clock when he started, he reached camp at fifteen minutes after eleven that night.

When he had gone I started in to lay my plans for the night.

It was yet so light that I could get a good view of the surrounding country, and about three miles from the Indians' camp I could see the highest hill anywhere around. I decided at once that if I were on that high hill I could see every move of the Indians, besides I could look up the Humboldt and see the soldiers, or at least the dust raised by them, while they were yet a long way off.

This peak lay north of the trail, and the trail ran east and west.

As soon as it was dark I mounted my horse and rode to the peak and tied him to a sagebrush in a sinkhole, that looked as though it might have been put there on purpose, for my horse was hidden from every direction.

I now went to the top of the hill, and there being a dense growth of sagebrush, I was perfectly safe from discovery when daylight should come.

I did not have to wait long after daylight, for just as the sun was creeping up over the hill and shedding its rays on the little valley where the two hundred braves had had such a pleasant night's rest, dreaming, perhaps, of emigrants, horses, provisions and other stuff that they would probably capture the following day, I looked up the Humboldt and saw the two companies of cavalry coming.

The Indians seemed in no hurry to leave, and were perhaps waiting for the five scouts to return and report, never thinking that they had been killed and scalped, and that the same paleface who did the deed was then watching their every movement and laying plans for their destruction.

I got my horse in about a minute, mounted and rode across the country to meet the cavalry, taking a route so that I would not be seen by the Indians.

I met the soldiers—who were commanded by Capt. Mills and Lieut. Harding—about four miles from the Indian camp, and they came to a halt.

I told them about the number I thought there were in the Indian band and the lay of the country, as nearly as I could. The Captain and Lieutenant stepped to one side and held a council, and after talking the matter over they called me and said they had about decided to attack the enemy from both above and below at the same time, and, as I had seen the ground, they asked my opinion in the matter. I told them I thought it an excellent plan, and then Capt. Mills turned to Lieut. Harding and said: "Which do you prefer, to make the upper or lower attack? Take your choice."

He then asked me if they could get to the head of the ravine that the Indians were camped on and not be seen by them. I told him that I could show them a ravine that led from the emigrant trail to the head of the valley on which they were camped, and marked out a plat of the country in the dust, showing the course each company would have to take, telling them that the company making the upper attack would have to travel about a mile farther than the one making the attack from below. He then asked me if the companies could see each other before the Indians could see them. I informed him that they could not, but that I could show him a hill where he could station a man and he would be able to see both companies, but the Indians could not see him, and when the company from above should reach the top of the hill that man could signal to the other company to charge.

At that time Lieut. Harding turned to Capt. Mills and said: "If the boy scout will go with me I will make the upper attack, as he has been over the country and knows the lay of the ground."

Of course I consented, and we marched to the mouth of the ravine just mentioned.

I pointed out the hill referred to, and the Lieutenant placed a man on top of it, and we proceeded.

Just before we reached the top of the other hill, Lieut. Harding halted and formed his men in line, placing them about ten feet apart, saying: "I have only a hundred soldiers, but I want it to appear that I have a thousand."

When we first came in sight of the Indians, some were lying stretched out in the sun, some were sitting down, while a few were out looking after their horses, everything indicating that they had just had their breakfast and were lounging around, not having the slightest idea of an enemy in twenty miles of them, and we took them wholly unawares.

When the Lieutenant formed his men in line before raising the top of the hill, he asked me to take charge of his left wing and he would take charge of his right. As soon as we came in sight of the Indians, he gave the order to charge.

This was the first thing of the kind I had ever witnessed, and when I cast my eyes down the line of soldiers I thought it the grandest sight I had ever seen. This was also the first engagement for either of the companies.

In all the scrimmages I had been in with the redskins, the one that made the most noise was the best Indian fighter; so when the Lieutenant gave the order to charge, I raised a yell, as I thought this to be one of the essential points of a charge, and wondered why the rest of the boys did not do the same. However, after hearing a few of my whoops they picked it up, and each began yelling at the top of his voice, and by this time we were among the Indians.

The two companies had about the same distance to run after sounding the charge, but Lieut. Harding was at the scene of conflict a few moments ahead of Capt. Mills, thereby giving the Indians time to scatter. This was attributed to the fact that Capt. Mills had to charge up grade while Lieut. Harding had down grade, which they had not thought of before making the arrangement, and the ground being mostly sand made a great difference in the speed of the horses.

Meyers and I made a rush for the Indians' horses, but the soldiers all stuck together, and seeing that a number of Indians were at their horses already and mounted, we abandoned the idea at once. Had one platoon made a dash for the horses and stampeded them, we would no doubt have got more Indians.

After emptying both of my single-shot pistols I drew my knife, and just at that moment an Indian shot Meyers through the arm with an arrow and he sang out to me that he was wounded. Another Indian then made a dash at Meyers with his bow and arrow in hand, so I charged after him and made a slash at him with my knife, but he saw me in time to slide off on the opposite side of his horse. I could not stop the blow so I struck his horse in the back and brought him to the ground, and the Indian ran for dear life.

About this time a soldier came riding along, and I knew from his actions that his pistol was empty (the soldiers had no firearms in this engagement except pistols), and I asked him why he did not draw his sabre and cut them down. He said he had no orders to do so.

To that I did not reply, but I thought this a queer way of fighting Indians, when a soldier had to stop in the midst of a battle, fold his arms and stand there to be shot down while waiting orders to draw his sabre. A moment later they received orders to use their sabres, and they went to hewing the Indians down.

I saw an Indian with two or three feathers in his hair, and I took him to be the war chief. He was coming direct for me with bow and arrow in hand, and I made a desperate rush for him and made a strike at him with my knife, but he threw up his arm and knocked off my lick, at the same time a measly redskin shot me through the calf of my leg, pinning me to the mochila of my saddle.

The mochila is a large covering for a saddle made of very heavy leather and comes low on the horse's side, thereby affording great protection to horses in cases like this. This shield is of Spanish origin, but they were used by all mountaineers as well as Mexicans.

I was leaning over when the arrow struck me and pinned me to the saddle, so that I could not straighten up, for I was almost on the side of the horse when I received the arrow.

Capt. Mills, seeing the predicament I was in, came to my rescue and cut the war chief down with his sabre, just in time to save me from getting another arrow.

The Captain pulled the arrow out of my leg, which had a very large spear made of hoop iron, and it tore a bad hole in my leg when he pulled it out. By this time the redskins were scattering in all directions, some on foot and some on horseback.

As soon as I was free I saw a band of about fifty horses not far away, and asked the Captain to detail some of his men to assist me in running them off. The Captain dashed off to his orderly who he told to take a platoon of men and go with the boy scout to take charge of those horses.

In this charge we got fifty-two horses and killed four Indians. We drove the horses out on the hill where they would be out of the way and where the Indians would not get them, and the Sergeant left his men to guard them until further orders.

As I rode back to the scene of battle I looked up the road and saw four wagons coming. I asked the Sergeant where those wagons were going, and he said they were ambulances, coming to haul the wounded to headquarters, saying they had started at the same time the cavalry did but could not keep up, consequently they did not arrive until after the battle was over.

About the time I returned to the battlefield the bugle sounded calling the soldiers in from the chase, and on looking over the ground, four dead soldiers and twenty-seven wounded were discovered. There were sixty-three dead Indians in sight, and more, no doubt, were scattered around in the sagebrush.

The battle being over we had our breakfast. I also had my horse put out to grass, as he was very hungry, not having had anything to eat since noon the day before, and not much then.

After breakfast was over the soldiers buried their four dead comrades and loaded the wounded into the ambulances and started for headquarters, arriving there about nine o'clock that night. Charlie Meyers had a wound in his arm that laid him up all summer, and I was not able to ride for two weeks; although I had the best of care.

From that time on I was known as the boy scout, and the next day after our return, Col. Elliott appointed me chief of scouts with rank and pay of captain, which was one hundred and twenty-five dollars per month. He also provided me with private quarters, my tent being pitched near his own, and notwithstanding that I was only a mere boy the other scouts all came to me for orders and counsel, and I often wondered why men who knew nothing of scouting nor the nature of Indians would stick themselves up as scouts.

Two weeks from the time I got wounded the Colonel asked me if I thought I was able to ride, saying that the news had just come to him that the Indians had attacked a train of emigrants, killed some of them and driven off their stock. This depredation he said had been committed in the Goose Creek mountain country about one hundred and twenty miles east of us. Col. Elliott said that he was going to send out a company of soldiers there, and if I felt able I might accompany them, which I did.

All being in readiness, I selected two scouts to assist me, and we pulled out, taking with us a pack-train with one month's provisions.

We had a rough and tedious trip, as not one of the entire crowd had been over the country and did not know a single watering place, so we had to go it blind, hit or miss. I had not gone far when I found that I had made a sad mistake, as notwithstanding my leg appeared quite well when I started out, yet, after one or two days' riding, it got quite sore and pained me severely, and the longer I rode the worse it got.

Five days' ride and we were at the place where the emigrants were camped. Another small train had pulled in with them as they were afraid to cross the desert alone.

That night Capt. Mills called the men of the train together to ascertain whether or not they wished to look after their stock, but they did not seem to know themselves what to do. They were quite sure that the Indians had driven the stock south, as they had tracked them some distance in that direction. Capt. Mills asked me what I thought of finding the stock, and I told him that if it was driven south, of which the emigrants seemed quite sure, it was more than likely that the Indians and stock were several hundred miles away, and that it would be next to impossible to get any trace of them, and in my opinion it would be like trying to find a needle in a haystack.

After considering the matter the emigrants concluded that I was right.

Those of them who had lost all their stock were a pitiful sight indeed, women and children were weeping, and particularly those who had lost their husbands and fathers in the fight with the Indians.

There were no women and children killed, as the Indians did not attack the train, being apparently only bent on capturing the horses and cattle. They had killed the guards and also the men that ran out to protect the stock.

One who has never witnessed a like affair can scarcely comprehend the situation of a widow left out there with three or four children in this desolate region, utterly destitute. It was a gloomy situation, indeed, and a sight that would cause the hardest-hearted man to shed tears.

Those who had lost their stock made some kind of arrangements to ride with those that had come later.

The day before starting the emigrants rolled all their wagons together that they did not have teams to haul, also the harness, and in fact everything they could not haul, and burned them, so that the Indians would not derive any benefit from them.

I merely note a few of these facts to give the reader a faint idea of the trials, troubles and hardships that the early settlers of the "wild West" had to pass through, not only in crossing the plains, but, as will be shown later in this book, in many instances after settling in different parts of this western country.

The day before starting, Capt. Mills suggested that as my wound was giving me so much trouble, I should return to headquarters in company with the train of emigrants, and asked how many men I wanted to guard them through. I told him that I would not feel safe with less than twenty men. The Captain thought that twenty would not be sufficient, so he made a detail of twenty-five men and issued rations to last us eight days.

Capt. Mills and the men he had reserved remained in this section of country to guard emigrants that might be traveling westward, as the Indians were now working in this part of the country since our battle with them on the Humboldt.

Having completed all arrangements we pulled out with one hundred and twenty-five wagons, all told, in the train, but as some of the oxen were very tender footed we had to travel very slowly. I divided my men into squads of twelve each, and changed guards at morning, noon, evening and midnight.

I also started six guards ahead every morning, with instructions to keep from one to three miles from the train on either side, according to the lay of the country. The second day one of the scouts returned from the south and reported having seen six Indians southwest of the train; this was about ten o'clock in the forenoon. I turned and rode off with the scout, saying nothing to anyone in the train. He piloted me to where he had seen the Indians, and sure enough there were the tracks of their ponies in the sand. The scout returned to the train and I followed the trail of the Indian all day, but never got sight of an Indian. When dark came I turned about and rode to camp, arriving there at twelve o'clock that night.

The people in the train were very much pleased to see me return, for they had felt much uneasiness as to my safety, fearing that I might have fallen into the hands of the Pah-Utes. This ride, however, laid me up for two weeks, and I had to go the balance of the way in an emigrant wagon.

The captain of this train had a jaw breaking name that I never heard before or since. It was Sam Molujean, and I know he was the most excitable man that I ever saw. When Capt. Molujean got excited he could not talk at all for stuttering, so one day the guards concluded to have a little sport at the expense of the Captain. We were now nearly opposite where about a month previous a battle with the Pah-Utes had been fought, and the advance guards were riding back to the train—it now being time to corrall for dinner. They met Capt. Molujean, who asked if they had seen any Indians.

One of the guards informed him that there were sixty-odd up the ravine. This set the Captain wild. He wheeled around and rode back to where I was in the wagon and started in to tell me what the guard had said, but he could not utter a word.

After listening to him a minute or so I told him if he would get some one to tell what he wanted I would answer his question. I suppose I was somewhat impatient, as I was suffering from my wound. At this one of the guards rode up with a smile on his face, and I asked him if he could tell me what Capt. Molujean was trying to say to me. He related to me what they had told him in regard to the sixty-odd Indians up the ravine, referring to the Indians that had been killed in battle between the soldiers and Pah-Utes.

We had a good laugh at the Captain's expense, after which I told him the Indians the guard had reference to were all good Indians.

"Oh! is that so?" he exclaimed, and these were the first words he had been able to utter. "But," he continued, "I did not know there were any good Indians in this country; I thought all of them were savage." I told the Captain that those Indians were dead, and that all dead Indians were good ones. This was a stunner for the Captain, and I do not think that the joke has ever penetrated his massive skull.

We did not see any more Indians or any sign of them on the trip.

On reaching headquarters we found Jim Beckwith awaiting our arrival. He had been out with three other men whom he had hired to help him blaze a road across the mountains through his new pass. He had finished his work on the road and returned to Col. Elliott's camp, knowing that if he could get one train to go his way it would be a great help toward getting the tide of immigration turned in that direction the following season.

Here Beckwith took charge of the train, Col. Elliott recommending him very highly, and telling the emigrants that if they would only obey his orders he would pilot them through in safety.

Before starting, Jim asked me to come over and spend the winter with him, saying that he was going to build a cabin on the other side of the mountains, lay in a big supply of provisions, and as after that he was going to do nothing, he wanted me to help him.

I promised to go and winter with him if it was possible for me to do so, as at this time I did not know but what I might have to go to San Francisco to have my leg treated the coming winter.

From here the emigrants were to pay Jim to pilot them across the mountains to a little mining camp called Hangtown, which was about one hundred and twenty miles east of Sacramento. They made the trip without any trouble. I saw one of the emigrants the next spring and they spoke in very high terms of Jim Beckwith.

CHAPTER XII
COL. ELLIOTT KILLS HIS FIRST DEER, AND SECURES A FINE PAIR OF HORNS AS A PRESENT FOR HIS FATHER.— BECKWITH'S TAVERN.—SOCIETY

Two weeks after the incidents related in the previous chapter, Capt. Mills came in with another train of emigrants, not having seen an Indian on the trip, and from this time on there was no danger of such trains going from that region through Beckwith Pass, and as the road was now broken by the other train, these emigrants could cross the Sierra Nevadas without a guide.

About this time four men with pack animals came along who claimed to be from Salt Lake. They reported that they had seen Indians one day traveling east of headquarters. I took two men and started out and was gone about a week, but did not see an Indian, or a track or sign of one, and when we returned the Colonel concluded that he had been misled by the packers.

Col. Elliott now ordered me to take fifty men, with two weeks' provisions, and go as far as we could with that amount of rations, or until we should meet some emigrants. We were gone about three weeks, but did not see either Indians or emigrants. The fact is, that it was getting so late in the fall that the Indians had all gone south, and the emigrants were not moving on the desert at that season.

On our return the Colonel had everything ready and we pulled out for San Francisco. We camped the first night at Steamboat Springs, a place that has since grown to be a famous health resort. On the second day we passed over the country where now stands Carson City, the capital of Nevada. At that time, this region, like all of that country then, was a wild, unsettled, sagebrush desert, or mountain wilderness.

The morning we left Eagle Valley the Colonel rode in advance of the column with me, and I saw there was something on his mind. In a little while he said he would like to kill a deer with big horns, so that he could send it—the horns—to his father in New York, who had never seen a deer, and he added that notwithstanding he—the Colonel—had been on the Pacific coast two years, he had never killed a deer in his life. I told him that I would fix it for him to get one the very next day, and he was as pleased as a child.

That night we camped by a big spring at the mouth of a great canyon, and about the spring stood a number of large pine trees. Many persons who had passed that way had carved their names in the bark of the trees, and among the names were two that were quite familiar to me. One of these was the name of Capt. Molujean—I wondered how he had done it without stuttering—and the other was the name of James Beckwith. On the same tree was written with lead pencil: "Sixty miles to Beckwith's Hotel."

On my favorite horse, Pinto, I rode out with the Colonel for a deer hunt. While riding along the canyon about two miles from where the command had camped, I saw a large doe crossing the canyon and coming down the hill toward us. I signaled the Colonel to halt and I shot the doe, breaking her neck, while sitting on my horse. I then told the Colonel to secrete himself behind a tree and he would soon see the male deer, and he would stand a good show to get a fine pair of horns. In a few moments two deer came tracking the one I had shot.

"Be ready, now," said I, "and when he stops let him have it." So when the deer were within about fifty yards I gave a keen whistle and they stopped, stock still. The Colonel fired and brought the big buck to the ground. The other, which was a small one, started to run, but I sent a bullet after it that made more venison.

We now had plenty of meat, and the Colonel was as proud over killing that deer as I was over my first pair of boots.

We stopped here until the command came up, dressed the venison and went on our way rejoicing.

Soon we were ascending the Sierra Nevada Mountains, and about three o'clock we struck the snow-line.

To one who has never gone from comparative summer in a few hours' ride, to the depths of winter and a considerable depth of snow, the sensation is a strange one. Of course, I had often done that before. But having more leisure to think of it now, and having more to do with the snow, I thought of its strangeness, and I am reminded of a little girl whom I have become acquainted with long since those days, and the effect that the first sight of snow had upon her. She was born in San Francisco, and had not seen any snow up to the time when she was three years old. Her parents were coming east with her on a railroad train, which runs over about the same ground that we were on at the time I was there with Col. Elliott. Awakening in the morning in a sleeping-car on top of the Sierras, the little one looked out, and seeing the vast fields of whiteness, she exclaimed: "Do look, mamma; the world is covered with sugar."

As we ascended the mountains the snow became so deep in a little while that we were forced to camp. The next morning the herders were directed to take the stock ahead in order to tramp down the snow to make a trail, but in four miles it became so deep that it was impossible to proceed further in that manner, and then the Colonel detailed fifty men to shovel snow, but having only a few shovels, wooden ones were made that answered the purpose, and while we were shoveling, the horses were also frequently driven back and forth over the trail, and in three days we had a passable road for the wagons.

At the end of the three days we reached the edge of the snow on the opposite side of the mountains, and there being a beautiful camping ground and the first night out of the snow for some time, the luxury of it was fully appreciated by all hands.

On a pine tree here I again saw signs of my old friend, Jim Beckwith, for there was written: "Twenty miles to Beckwith's Hotel." So you see that even in that faraway country, and at that early day, even the pioneer had learned the uses of out-door advertising.

The next morning we took an early start and traveled hard all day, anticipating with much pleasure that at night we should enjoy all the luxuries of the season at Beckwith's Hotel. And we did, to the extent that this region and the markets of San Francisco could afford.

We reached [Transcriber's note: unreadable text] about sunset that evening, and the command went into camp and I went to Jim's new log house. He had built one and had started in to build the second, having two carpenters at work finishing them up.

After supper Col. Elliott and all his officers, both commissioned and non-commissioned, came to Jim's house, where, after a social chat and having cracked a few jokes, which latter was really a part of the business connected with this life, Col. Elliott pulled off his overcoat, laid it and his hat on a bed, stepped up near the table and said:

"Mr. Beckwith, I wish to say a few words to your friend, Mr. Drannan, in behalf of myself and the other officers present." Jim told him to go ahead, which he did, telling how faithful I had been and what valuable services I had rendered both to him and the emigrants. He went on and made quite a lengthy speech, in conclusion of which he said: "Mr. Drannan, as a slight token of our appreciation of your services while with us, I now present to you this pair of glasses," whereupon he handed me a fine pair of field glasses which he took from his overcoat pocket, "and here are two navy revolvers that Capt. Mills and Lieut. Harding wish to present to you as a token of their friendship."

This took me wholly by surprise, as I had not expected anything of the kind, and I was so dumbfounded that all I could say was to thank them for the presents, the thought never having entered my head that my services had been so highly appreciated by the officers of those four companies.

Col. Elliott said that in case he should go out on the plains the following summer, which in all probability he would, he wanted me to go with him without fail. I promised him that I would, provided I was in the country when he started out.

After Col. Elliott had closed his remarks and taken his seat, Jim Beckwith arose and made quite a speech in his plain, rude language, addressing his remarks principally to Col. Elliott, in which he said: "Colonel, I would not have recommended this boy to you so highly if I had not been with him long enough to know that when he starts in to do a thing he goes at it for all there is in him, and, as I told you, he has been with Kit Carson ever since he was a boy, and I knowed that if he didn't have the everlasting grit in him, Kit Carson wouldn't have kept him around so long. I am very glad indeed, Colonel, that he has filled the bill, and now the Injun fightin' is all over for this season and 'twill be some time before we all meet again, if we ever do. I have nothing of value to present to you, but such as I have is as free as the water in the brook."

At this he produced a gallon jug of whiskey, set it on the table, gave us some glasses and told us all to help ourselves. This wound up the evening's exercises, and after each had tipped the glass about three times we broke up the lodge and each went on his way rejoicing.

Before the Colonel left that night he told me that we would divide the captured horses the next morning. I told him that all I wanted was the five horses that I had captured from the five Indian scouts when I first started in to scout for him, but the next morning [Transcriber's note: unreadable text] out when the horses were brought in and made the division. There were sixty-three of them, and he left fifteen to my share.

I stayed at Jim Beckwith's for about two weeks, and his carpenters having the houses completed, we saddled up four horses and took them to Hangtown. It was a distance of twenty miles to Hangtown, which at that time was one of the loveliest mining towns in California. There were between four and five thousand inhabitants in and around the place. During the day it appeared dead, as there was scarcely a person to be seen on the streets; but at night it would be full of miners, who, it seemed, came to town for no other purpose than to spend the money they had earned during the day.

This winter passed off, apparently, very slowly, being the most lonesome winter I had put in since I struck the mountains.

Along about the middle of February our groceries were running short and Jim went to Hangtown for supplies. On his return he brought me a letter from Col. Elliott, asking me to come to San Francisco at once.

I asked him what he thought of it, and he told me by all means to go.

I told him I would have to stop in San Francisco and buy me a suit of clothes before going out to the fort to see Col. Elliott. He thought this was useless, saying: "Your buckskin suit that Kit Carson gave you is just what you want for a trip like that."

I thought that if I wore such a suit in civilization the people would make light of me, and I hated the idea of being the laughing stock for other people.

Jim said: "It is Col. Elliott you are going to see, and he would rather have you come that way than any other."

I took my suit down and looked at it, and it was a fine one of the kind. I had never worn it since Uncle Kit's wedding, so it was practically new. I decided to wear it, and the next morning I started for San Francisco, Jim accompanying me to Hangtown to take the horses back to his ranche.

At Hangtown I took the stage for Sacramento, which, by the way, was the first time I had ever ridden in a stage-coach.

We started from Hangtown at five o'clock in the morning and at twelve o'clock that night the driver drew rein at the American Exchange Hotel in Sacramento. The coach was loaded down to its utmost capacity, there being nine passengers aboard. The roads were very rough at this season of the year—being the latter part of February—and I would rather have ridden on the hurricane deck of the worst bucking mustang in California than in that coach.

This hotel was kept at that time by a man named Lamb.

That night when the proprietor assigned the passengers to their respective rooms he asked us if we wished to take the boat for San Francisco the next morning. I told him that I did, whereupon he asked me if I wanted my breakfast. I told him that I did, saying that I didn't want to go from there to San Francisco without anything to eat. This caused quite a laugh among the bystanders; but I did not see the point, for at that time I did not know that one could get a meal on a steamboat, for I had never been near one.

Just as I stepped on the boat next morning, a man rushed up to me with a "Hello there! how are you?" as he grasped me by the hand. Seeing that I did not recognize him, he said: "I don't believe you know me." I told him that he had one the best of me. He said: "You are the boy scout that was with Capt. Mill last summer, and you rode in my wagon." Then I recognized him. His name was Healey, and at the time was running a restaurant in San Francisco, and he insisted on my going to his place when I got to the city, which invitation I accepted. His establishment was known as the Miners' Restaurant.

Mrs. Healey and her little daughter, eleven years old, knew me as soon as I entered the door, and were apparently as glad to see me as though I had been a relative of the family.

The next morning when I offered to settle my bill they would not take a cent, but requested me while in the city to make my home with them.

That day I went out to the Fort, which was three miles from the city, and on arriving there the first man I met was Lieut. Harding, who at once conducted me to Col. Elliott's quarters.

That afternoon we made the rounds of the Fort, and Col. Elliott, when introducing me, would say: "This is the 'boy scout,' who was out with us last summer, and whom you have heard me speak of so often."

I made my home with Col. Elliott and his wife during my stay at the Fort, which was two weeks.

CHAPTER XIII
SOMETHING WORSE THAN FIGHTING INDIANS.—DANCE AT COL. ELLIOTT'S.— CONSPICUOUS SUIT OF BUCKSKIN.—I MANAGE TO GET BACK TO BECKWITH'S

That night Mrs. Elliott had every lady that belonged around the Fort at her house, and she took the "boy scout" along the line and introduced him to every one of the ladies. This was something new to me, for it was the first time in my life that I had struck society, and I would have given all of my previous summer's wages to have been away from there. I did not know how to conduct myself, and every time I made a blunder—which seemed to me every time I made a move—I would attempt to smooth it over, and always made a bad matter worse.

Next morning at the breakfast table I told the Colonel and his wife that I was going back into the mountains as fast as I could get there. I knew I could track Indians, and fight them if necessary, but I did not know how to entertain ladies, especially when my best clothes were only Indian-tailored buckskin.

Mrs. Elliott assured me that she would not have had me come there dressed differently, had it been in her power to prevent it. "Dressed otherwise than you are," she said, "you would not be the same 'boy scout' that my husband has told us so much concerning."

Of course this was encouraging, and I concluded that I might not have been so painfully ridiculous as I had supposed. For, be it known, I had been scarcely able to sleep the night before for thinking of what an outlandish figure I had cut that night before all those high-toned ladies, and of the sport my presence among them must have created.

However, I felt much better after the pleasant way in which Mrs. Elliott declared she looked at it, and with renewed self-complacence proceeded to discuss with the Colonel his plans for the next summer's campaign.

He informed me that he intended to go out with four companies of soldiers, and would locate a short distance east of last year's quarters, at a place where the town of Wadsworth has since been built. Plenty of good water and an abundance of grass were there, and with two companies he would make his headquarters there. The other two companies he would send about one hundred miles further east, to the vicinity of Steen's Mountain, and it was his wish that I should take charge of the scouts and operate between the two camps.

Notwithstanding I had a good home with Col. Elliott and his wife as long as I wished to remain, it seemed to me that this was the longest and lonesomest week I had ever experienced. Everything being so different from my customary way of living, I could not content myself.

The day before I was to start back home it was arranged that I should return to Jim Beckwith's ranche and keep the Colonel posted by letter in regard to the snow in the mountains, and when he would be able to cross. Then I was to join him at Beckwith's.

The following evening Mrs. Elliott gave a party, which was attended by all the ladies and gentlemen of the garrison. There was to be a general good time, perhaps the last party of the season, as it was approaching the time for preparations for the next campaign against the Indians.

When all the guests had arrived and the spacious house was a blaze of light and happiness—fair women smiling and their musical voices fairly making a delightful hub-bub of light conversation, and the gentlemen, superb in their gold-trimmed uniforms, or impressive in full evening dress—the manager of the dance sang out for all to take partners for some sort of a bowing and scraping drill that is a mystery to me to this day. I had seen the fandango in Taos, and elsewhere in the Mexican parts of the southwest, but this was the first time I had seen Americans dance, and it was all appallingly new to me.

I sat in a corner like a homely girl at a kissing-bee, and had nothing to say.

After the crowd had danced about two hours, the floor-manager sang out, "Ladies' choice!" or something that meant the same thing, and to my surprise and terror, Mrs. Elliott made a bee-line for me and asked me to assist her in dancing a quadrille. I had no more idea of a quadrille than I had of something that was invented yesterday, and I begged her to excuse me, telling her that I knew nothing whatever of dancing. She declared, however, that I had looked on long enough to learn and that I would go through all right. I hung back like a balky horse at the foot of a slippery hill, but between Mrs. Elliott and the prompter I was almost dragged out on the floor.

The reader may be able to conceive a faint idea of my situation. I was now twenty-three years old, and this was the first time I had been in civilization since I had left St. Louis, a boy of fifteen. Here I was, among those swell people, gorgeous in "purple and fine linen," so to speak; ladies in silks, ruffles and quirlymacues, gentlemen in broadcloth, gold lace and importance, and I in only buckskin from head to foot. I would have freely given everything I possessed to have been out of that, but my excuses failed utterly, and finally I went into it as I would an Indian fight, put on a bold front and worked for dear life.

I found it quite different to what I had expected Instead of making light of me, as I feared they would, each lady in the set tried to assist me all she could.

When on the floor it seemed to me that every man, woman and child were looking at me, as indeed they were, or rather at my suit of buckskin, that, worked full of beads and porcupine quills, was the most beautiful suit of its kind I have ever seen. But it was so different from the dress of the others that it made me decidedly conspicuous. When on the floor and straightened up I felt as if I were about nine feet high, and that my feet were about twenty inches long and weighed near fifty pounds each.

The prompter called out, "Balance all!" and I forgot to dance until all the others were most through balancing, then I turned loose on the double-shuffle, this being, the only step I knew, and I hadn't practiced that very much. About the time I would get started in on this step the prompter would call something else, and thus being caught between two hurries I would have to run to catch up with the other dancers. However, with the assistance of Mrs. Elliott, the other good ladies, the prompter, and anybody else in reach, I managed to get through, but I had never gone into an Indian fight with half the dread that I went into that dance, and never escaped from one with more thankfulness.

The following morning, after bidding Col. Elliott, his wife and all the other of my new-found friends good-bye, I started on my return to Beckwith's ranche, perfectly willing to resign my high- life surroundings to go back to the open and congenial fields of nature and an indescribable freedom.

I found Beckwith suffering severely from an old arrow wound that he had received in a fight with the Utes near Fort Hall in 1848.

CHAPTER XIV
DRILLING THE DETAILED SCOUTS.—WE GET AMONG THE UTES.—FOUR SCOUTS HAVE NOT REPORTED YET.—ANOTHER LIVELY FIGHT.—BECKWITH MAKES A RAISE

It was late spring when the snow began to melt, but it went away very fast when it once started. About the first of June I wrote to Col. Elliott that by the tenth of the month he could cross the mountains. He did not arrive until the 20th of June, then I joined him and we started across the mountains.

By direction of the Colonel each of the captains detailed four men from their respective companies to be my assistants, and at my suggestion young men were chosen, such as myself, who could ride forty-eight hours, if necessary, without stopping, and I asked for men who were not afraid to go alone, not afraid to fight, and, above all, men that would never allow themselves to be taken prisoner.

The command having been drawn up for dress parade, the orderly sergeants called their rolls, and whenever a man's name was called whom the captains wished to de-tail, he was directed to stand aside. Up to this time the men did not know and were wondering what was up. Col. Elliott informed them after the drill was over, and said to them:

"Soldiers, this man, Capt. Drannan, is now your chief, and you will act according to his orders at any and all times. He will instruct you when to meet him at his private quarters."

The next three days were spent in drilling the scouts to mount and dismount quickly, to shoot at some object when on the dead run, to lie on the side of the horse and shoot at an object on the opposite side while running at full speed, and a great deal of other work of that kind.

Three days later we started east, Capt. Mills and Lieut. Harding with their companies, expecting to go about one hundred miles before locating permanently for the summer. I started out in advance of the command with my entire force of scouts. We traveled about fifteen miles together, when we separated, four taking the north side of the emigrant trail, with instructions to keep from four to five miles from it; four keeping the trail and four, with myself, south of the trail. I gave the men north instructions in case they should find an Indian trail to follow it until they were sure the Indians were making for the emigrant trail, and then dispatch one man to notify the men on the trail, the other three follow the Indians, and at the end of three days all were to meet at a certain point on the trail where, we expected to meet the soldiers.

The second day out we struck an Indian trail south of the road, but it being an old one we did not follow it but made a note of the number we thought there were in the band, an that night we pulled for the emigrant trail, expecting to meet the soldiers there.

We did not meet the soldiers, but met the four scouts who had traveled on the emigrant trail.

We got no word that night from the men north, but according to agreement we went to a hill near by and built two fires of sagebrush, that they might know where we were, and if in need of assistance they could dispatch, but did not see nor hear anything of them.

The next morning I kept the emigrant trail myself, sending the other squad of men south, with instructions to meet me at Humboldt Wells, telling them about the distance it was from where we were then camped, and describing the place to them. There we would wait until the command came up, as we were now running short of rations. That day the party south struck the same trail that we had seen the day before; two of them followed it and the other two came to camp to report. The party that had started out north of the trail got into camp just at dusk, tired and hungry, and the following morning at daylight the other two from the south came into camp. From what I could learn from them the band of Indians they had been following were traveling along almost parallel with the emigrant trail, looking for emigrants, as it was now getting time that the emigrants were beginning to string along across the plains en-route for the gold fields of California.

Our provisions had run out, so we sat up late that night awaiting the arrival of the command, but we looked in vain.

The following morning, just as I could begin to see that it was getting a little light in the east, myself and one assistant scout crawled out quietly, without disturbing the other boys, to kill some game. We had not gone far from camp when we saw nine antelope; we both fired and both shot the same antelope. We dressed the game and took it to camp, arriving there just as the other two scouts came in from the south. The boys were all up in camp, and considerable excitement prevailed among them, they having heard two shots, and thought the Indians had attacked us. They were all hungry as wolves, so we broiled and ate antelope almost as long as there was any to eat.

Almost the entire scout force were from New York, and were new recruits who had never known what it was to rough it, and they said this was the first meal they had ever made on meat alone. After breakfast was over, it now being understood that we would lie over until the supply train should come up, my first assistant scout and two others took a trip to a mountain some two miles from camp, which was the highest mountain near us, taking my glasses along to look for the supply train. In about two hours one of the scouts returned to camp in great haste and somewhat excited, saying that about fifteen or twenty miles distant they had seen a band of Indians who were traveling in the direction of camp. We all saddled our horses, left a note at camp informing Capt. Mills where we had gone and for what purpose. We started for what has ever since been known as Look-out Mountain—of course not the famous Lookout Mountain of Tennessee—and there joined the other three scouts. From the top of this mountain we could get a good view of the Indians through the field glasses. We watched them until about one o'clock, when they went into camp in the head of a little ravine some five miles distant—This convinced us that there was water and that they had stopped for the night. We located them as well as we could, and the entire scout force, being thirteen all told, started across the country for their camp.

Seven of this number of scouts had never seen a wild Indian and were over anxious to have a little sport with the redskins. The Indians, being in a little ravine, we were able to get within a half a mile of them before they could see us. After advancing as far as we thought prudent, one of the scouts and myself dismounted and crept through the sagebrush within three hundred yards of them. Their fire was yet burning and the Indians were lounging around, everything indicating that they had just cooked and eaten their dinner. I counted them and made out twenty-one, my assistant scout made twenty-three, and instead of being Pah-Utes, as we expected, they were Utes. The boys all being anxious to try their hand, I decided to make the attack at once. Returning to where I had left the other scouts, I told them my plan of attack, telling them to bear in mind that one shot well calculated was worth three or four at random. I also told them as soon as I gave the war- whoop for each of them to make all the noise he could.

Now we all mounted, and by riding up a little ravine we were able to get within fifty rods of them before they could see us.

Before making the charge I told the boys to draw their pistols, and when the pistols were emptied to draw sabres and cut the savages down before they could get to their horses. We rode slowly and cautiously until almost in sight of the Indians, when I gave the word "Charge!" and all put spurs to their horses, raised the yell, and one minute later we were in their midst, arrows and bullets flying in all directions. I received an arrow wound in the calf of my right leg, the man immediately on my right got shot through the left or bridle arm, and one of the raw recruits got his horse shot from under him.

He did not wait for orders, but drew his sabre and went to work cutting them down as he came to them. When we first made the charge some of the Indians made a desperate attempt to get their horses, but the scouts shot and cut them down, not allowing one of them to mount. The Indians, much to my surprise, fought as long as there was one of them left standing. The battle lasted about fifteen minutes, and when it was over we counted the dead Indians and found the number to be nineteen, but there were twenty-one horses, so we were confident that two Indians either escaped or fell in the sagebrush where we could not find them.

We gathered up the horses and ropes that belonged to the Indians. The man that had his horse killed in the battle, caught the best horse in the band, threw the saddle on him and started for camp, considering we had done a good day's work. As we rode down the ravine in the direction of the emigrant trail some of the boys looked in that direction and saw the smoke curling up from a camp- fire.

"The command has arrived!" shouted one of the boys.

I proposed that we give the Captain a surprise. We all dismounted, and each fastened a scalp to the browband of his bridle, and when the Captain saw us coming and saw that each had a scalp, he said: "Boys, let's give them three cheers." At that the valley rang out with the yells.

This pleased the new recruits that had been engaged in the battle, and I can truthfully say that I never saw the same number of green men equal them in the first engagement, for every one of them fought like heroes.

We dismounted, turned our horses over to the herder and called for supper. This was the first square meal that it had been our pleasure to sit down to for four days, and this was where none of us shrunk from duty, in the least.

By this time the wound in my leg was beginning to pain me, and gave me more trouble than I anticipated. The next morning it was badly swollen, and I was not able to ride horseback for several days.

That morning we pulled for Steen's Mountain, which we supposed to be about forty miles from where we were camped.

Not being able to ride horseback, I rode in one of the ambulances.

From here we kept guards out on each side of the trail, with orders to keep from five to six miles from the train, and if any Indians were seen to report at once.

The second day in the afternoon Capt. Mills established his headquarters about one mile from the trail, in a beautiful spot; plenty of water, an abundance of good grass, and a few pine trees scattered here and there, making it an unusually pleasant place for quarters that summer.

Not being able to ride, I stayed in camp, but sent all the other scouts out. The second day my first assistant returned and reported having found the trail, as he thought, of about fifty Indians, traveling west, and about parallel with the emigrant trail.

The next morning I started my assistant and three scouts after the Indians, with orders to report as soon as they had the redskins located.

They were gone four days and no word came from them. I began to be very uneasy, as well as Capt. Mills, thinking something must have happened them or they would have returned, as they only took three days' rations with them. I took four other scouts and went on their trail.

The reader will understand that in this country the soil is somewhat sandy, and a horse is easily tracked. Our horses being shod, it was easy to distinguish their tracks from that of the Indians' horses. My wound gave me much trouble, but we followed the trail of the other scouts for some distance after striking the trail of the Indians, and their horses being shod, we could easily track them, but finally they became so obliterated that we could see no more trace of the shod horses. We sought in vain to get some sign of them, and came to the conclusion that while the scouts were trailing the Indians another band had stolen up behind them and either killed or taken them all prisoners, for we could get no trace of them, nor have they ever been heard of since. As soon as I returned to quarters, by the consent of Capt. Mills, I detailed two men of my scout force to carry a dispatch to Col. Elliott. As the Indians were now too far west for Capt. Mills to attempt to follow them, I sent the two best men I had to bear the message to the Colonel. They made the trip in two nights, riding at night and lying over in the daytime. The next day after the Colonel received the dispatch his scouts discovered the same band of Indians, and Col. Elliott sent one company of soldiers out at once after them. The soldiers overhauled them at Clover Valley, which was about forty miles south of the emigrant trail, and attacked the redskins, but they were too much for the soldiers. In the engagement the loss to the command was sixteen men killed, and I never knew just how many were wounded or how many Indians were killed. The soldiers had to retreat. All I ever learned from this battle I learned from the dispatch bearers, as they stayed at Col. Elliott's quarters until after the soldiers had returned from the engagement.

From this on I kept scouts out south of the trail continually.

One evening one of the scouts came in and reported having seen a little band of Indians some twelve or fifteen miles south of the trail. The other three scouts that were out with him remained to watch the Indians while he came to report. The scout was not able to tell just the number, as they were some distance away. The other three scouts secreted their horses, crawled to the top of the highest hill near by and lay there in the sagebrush and with glasses watched the Indians, who were traveling almost in the direction where the scouts lay, bearing a little south, so that the scouts did not have to change their hiding place. I mounted my horse for the first time since I had been laid up, and in company with five other scouts, including the one who had brought the message to me, started to investigate the matter.

We rode to where the other three scouts had been left, and they were awaiting our arrival. They had lain on the hill and watched the Indians go into camp and then returned to where the dispatch bearer had left them.

After holding a council for about five minutes we all mounted and rode as near the Indians as we considered safe, and dismounted. Taking another scout who had been watching them, I crawled as near as we dared to their camp to try to ascertain their number. We decided that there were about fifty. It was perilous to get very close for the reason that the Indians had a number of dogs, and when we would get too near the dogs would begin to bark, and three or four Indians would raise up and look about and every Indian in the band would listen. When we returned to where we had left the other scouts they were all prepared for an attack, but I told them there were too many for us to tackle alone. Besides, they were Utes, the worst Indians in the whole country to fight.

We were now about fifteen miles from headquarters, so I dispatched two men at once to Capt. Mills in all haste, requesting him to be there by daybreak, if it were within the bounds of possibility. This being a sandy, sagebrush country, one could not ride at full speed, but the scouts made good time, nevertheless, and Capt. Mills and his command were with us before daylight. We met him about a mile from where the Indians were camped, and I told him how the ground lay and the general surroundings as best I could, and I suggested that as on account of the dogs I had not been able to locate the horses of the Indians, it would be advisable to wait until daylight to make the attack.

We waited about an hour, when the Captain said he thought it was light enough to kill Indians. He gave orders to mount, drew his men up in line and rode back and forth, up and down the line, instructing them how to proceed, saying:

"When I give the word, 'charge!' every man draw his pistol, and when within fifty yards, begin to fire. Don't fire at random, but take good aim, and when your pistols are empty draw your sabres and cut them down. Don't let one escape. Don't wait for further orders; you have them, now carry them out."

Capt. Mills rode to the left wing and asked me to take the right. I told him I thought it best that myself and the scout force should make a dash for the Indian horses as soon as he made the charge, for if we could succeed in getting the horses we need not let one Indian escape.

It was now so light that we could see their ponies on the hill just beyond their camp. All being ready, and I having instructed my assistants, the Captain ordered them to charge. I made a dash to the right with my entire scout force. This was a great surprise to the redskins. They were nearly all abed yet, except a few of the earliest risers. Those who were up made a desperate rush for their horses, but unavailingly. We got there first and stampeded the herd. Some of the horses were picketed, but we cut the ropes as fast as we came to them, and before any of the Indians could get to their horses we had them on the dead run.

Taking a circuitous route we drove the horses around between the scene of battle and head-quarters. When about a mile distant my first assistant and myself returned to the battle ground leaving the other scouts to guard the horses. We arrived at the scene just in time to see the last Indian fall. When it was good light the Indians could be seen lying around in every direction. The orderly sergeant and two privates were looking around in the sagebrush, thinking there might be some of them hiding there, and all of a sudden two young bucks started up and began to run, and for about three hundred yards they had what I thought to be the prettiest race I had ever witnessed. The two Indians on foot and the soldiers on horseback, running through the sagebrush and every man in the crowd, from the Captain down, yelling at the top of his voice. Here I did the poorest shooting that I had ever done in my life, emptying one of my revolvers and not touching an Indian. But the soldiers finally got them.

We counted the dead braves and found them to be forty-eight in number.

In this engagement Capt. Mills did not lose a man, and only one was wounded. This was the result of making the attack so early in the morning. Had it been later, after the Indians were all up, they would have made a harder fight.

The battle being over we all started for headquarters, feeling jubilant over the victory.

We reached headquarters at ten o'clock in the morning, after which Capt. Mills told us we had done enough for one day, and that all could take it easy for the rest of the day. The next morning I struck out east on the emigrant trail, sending one man north and one south of the trail, each taking three days' rations, our object being to meet emigrants, if there were any, and guard them through to Capt. Mills' quarters, as it was now time for the emigrants to come stringing along; a time that heretofore among the Indians had been considered a harvest in this section of the country.

The first day in the afternoon I rode to a high hill, took my glasses, and looking east I saw a train of emigrants stringing along. This was the first train of the season. The scout from the north and also the one from the south had got sight of them, and were pulling for the trail. We pushed on and met the train just as it was pulling into camp. I called for the captain and he came forth. I told him we were scouts for Capt. Mills, and were out for the purpose of protecting emigrants. The captain, as well as the people in the train, were very much pleased to know that they were going to have protection after that through the hostile country. They had been troubled more or less by Indians all the way through Utah, having a great deal of stock, both horses and cattle, stolen by the Indians, as they supposed, but among men who were better informed it was the supposition that they were stolen by white men, for in those days there was a set of white men in Utah much worse than Indians.

On learning that I had been in California they had many questions to ask about the gold fields of that noted country. They were expecting to find gold by the bushel when once there.

This was a large train, there being one hundred and twenty wagons all told. The next morning I sent out one of my scouts north of the train, the other one ahead, with instructions to keep from one to two miles in front, and I went south of the trail that day. This was done so that if the scouts should see a large band of Indians they could notify the emigrants and give them a chance to prepare for the battle, but we experienced no trouble on this trip.

We were two days traveling from where we met the train to Capt. Mills' quarters, and from here the Captain sent a sergeant and twenty men to guide the emigrants through to Col. Elliott's headquarters.

This kind of work was kept up for about a month, every week, and sometimes two or three trains of emigrants would pass by, but we experienced no serious trouble the remainder of the season with Indians.

During this summer the officers in looking through their glasses from different high points around, discovered a beautiful valley, which we afterwards learned was named Thousand Springs Valley. Capt. Mills came to the conclusion that this valley at this time of the year was headquarters for the Utes, and not thinking the distance was so great sent another scout and myself to investigate.

It may be well to mention the fact here, that in these regions the air is so rarified and clear that distances are very deceptive, objects appearing to be much closer than they really are.

We started with three days' rations, and on the third day in the afternoon we struck the valley, just at its mouth on the desert, but the water was warm, and we traveled some distance up the valley, finding the springs numerous, but all warm. We also found an abundance of grass and plenty of Indian sign, but not fresh. It appeared that a large number of Indians had wintered there. After looking the valley over we returned to camp, but by a different route from the one we came. We saw no Indians or fresh sign of them until the second day of the return trip, but about two o'clock we came in sight of four Indians traveling eastward. We tried to attack them, but our horses being much jaded, the Indians outrode us, so we had to give up the chase. We were of the opinion that the four Indians were scouts for a big band making its way to winter quarters.

A short distance north we secreted our horses in a ravine, and watched for the Indians from the top of a high hill until noon the next day, but all in vain, for we did not see an Indian. We returned to camp, our horses worn out and half starved. The part of country we passed over on this trip is now the most northeastern portion of Nevada, and just what it is good for I have never been able to learn.

After lying around here watching for emigrants about two weeks longer, and making two different trips east on the emigrant trail, Capt. Mills now concluded that there would be no more emigrants that fall, so we pulled up and moved to Col. Elliott's quarters. We kept scouts out on the trip, but did not see an Indian or even a fresh trail on the trip. On arriving at Col. Elliott's quarters I could see that he was not pleased with the way things had gone with his command during the summer. His men had had two engagements during the season, and had got the worst of it both times.

He had lost twenty-six men, and not a scalp to show for them.

Capt. Mills felt quite jubilant. He had over sixty Indian horses that he had captured, over sixty scalps, and had not lost a man, with the exception of the four scouts. Col. Elliott did not have much to say, but the Lieutenant declared that the Colonel was very jealous of Capt. Mills over the past summer's work.

After remaining at headquarters about a week we pulled out across the Sierra Nevada Mountains, along the same route that we had taken the fall before, somewhat earlier, and winter not having yet set in, we experienced no trouble in crossing. The first night we camped at the head of Eagle Valley, and from there to Jim Beckwith's ranche it was sixty miles.

I being over-anxious to see Jim, saddled up my Pinto horse the next morning and started for his place, making the ride in one day. On my arrival I found Jim doing a rushing business in the hotel line, but was just in the act of selling out his hotel to a man from Sacramento. Beckwith had sold all my horses during the summer at what I thought a good figure, having got fifty dollars per head all around.

The command came on two days later, pitched their tents and stayed two days, having a red hot time. The men had plenty of money, and Jim Beckwith, who was now running a saloon in connection with his hotel, had plenty of bad whiskey. The Colonel put very little restriction on his men while they remained there, allowing them to have a general spree, for they had been where there was no chance to spend their money, and the little they had was burning their pockets.

Jim Beckwith made a handsome little clean-up during the two days they were camped there.

When the Colonel was ready to pull out for San Francisco he came to me and invited me to come to the Fort and spend a few months during the winter. I told him I did not know where I would winter, but preferred to seek quarters where I could hunt for a livelihood. I told him I did not wish to put in another winter lounging around as I did the last one. The Colonel made me a proposition to come to the Fort after I had visited my friend, Jim Beckwith, saying that he would organize a hunting party among the officers and take a trip north of San Francisco on the Russian river.

The country to which we wished to go is now Sonoma County, Cal., of which Santa Rosa is the county seat. In fact the region is now called Santa Rosa Valley, and it is well named, for it is a great garden of roses and other beautiful flowers that grow indigenously and in luxurious profusion. At the head of the valley are the famous geysers of California.

The Colonel, after dividing the horses with me, started for the Fort, I agreeing to join him there in a few weeks for the hunt.

After remaining at Jim Beckwith's for a few days, he and a gentleman from Sacramento came to a trade, Jim selling out "slick and clean."

Jim had too much money to stay in the mountains. I saw $12,000 weighed out to him in gold-dust, and I don't know how much coin he had, but there were several thousand dollars of it.

"Now we will go to San Francisco for the winter," said he, "and will have a good time. You stay with me this winter, and it shan't cost you a cent."

We took our horses and started for Sacramento, making the trip in four days Here we boarded a boat for the bay.

In those days persons speaking of going to San Francisco, always spoke of it as "going to the bay."

The second morning after our arrival, I found at the feed-yard, where my horses were, a gentleman awaiting my arrival, who wanted to buy my stock.

I sold all of the horses to him except Mexico and Pinto—they were not for sale at any figure.

I stayed around the city for two weeks, until it became monotonous. Jim Beckwith had lots of money, and it looked to me as though he wanted to get rid of it—as soon as possible. He would get just so full every day, and when he was full of whiskey his tongue appeared to be loose at both ends. It now being the first of December, I saddled my horse and rode out to the Fort, and on arriving there I found all anxious for the hunt. Col. Elliott had been talking the matter up among them. It took about three days to prepare for the trip, and I kept hurrying them up, all that was in my power, for I did not want to fool around there until the good ladies took it in their heads to have another dance, as it was not a dance that I was hunting. I had had enough of that on my other visit to satisfy me for some time to come.

CHAPTER XV
A HUNT ON PETALUMA CREEK.—ELK FEVER BREAKS OUT.—THE EXPEDITION TO KLAMATH LAKE.—A LIVELY BRUSH WITH MODOC INDIANS

The hunting party made up at the Fort was ready early in December, and we pulled out, promising to be home by New Year's day, at the latest.

At this time there were no steamers running across the bay in the direction we wished to go, so we hired a tug to take us over to the mouth of Petaluma creek, near which we proposed to pitch our hunting camp. Here was live-oak timber, with now and then a redwood, and in places the chapparal was thick, and there was no end to deer sign.

We had plenty of shelter in case of storm, having two good-sized tents in the outfit and only six men, not counting the darkey cook, who, however, always does count in an expedition like that. In the party I was the only one who had ever hunted any. Three of the others had never fired a shot at larger game than a jack- rabbit. Col. Elliott had once killed a deer, of which I made mention in a preceding chapter.

The following morning after breakfast I told them to select their course for the day's hunting, and I would go in an opposite direction.

"Why do you wish to go in an opposite direction?" Lieut. Harding asked; "Why not all go together?" I replied that after we got out in the woods I did not think they could tell a man from a deer, and I did not want to be shot by a white man out here in this country.

Capt. Mills proposed that three go at a time, two officers and myself, by so doing there would be no danger.

This being satisfactory, Lieut. Harding, Capt. Mills and myself took the first turn. Neither of them had ever hunted any, and both were as ignorant in that line as I was when I started out from St Louis in company with Uncle Kit Carson, which, by the way, I had told them something about the night before, while sitting around the campfire.

When we were all ready for the hunt and had started to walk away from the tent, Capt. Mills requested the Colonel to have the horses in readiness to pack the deer in. We had not gone far until I asked them if they could not walk without making so much noise. Lieut. Harding said he did not see what difference it made how a person walked, and I had to stop and explain matters by telling them that a deer depended as much on his ears as he did on his eyes, and if we did not walk easier the deer would hear us before we could get sight of them, and it seemed to me that they had stepped on every stick along our way and had rubbed against every brush that we passed near. Having been trained to hunt since a boy of fifteen years old, it became second nature for me to slide along without making a particle of noise.

After traveling a short distance we saw four deer coming toward us, and I pointed out an opening and said: "When they get to that place I will stop them; be ready, and when I count three, fire." When the deer were all on the selected spot I gave a keen whistle, which caused them to stop and throw up their heads. I counted three and fired, but did not hear the report of the other guns. Just as I turned to see what was the trouble, Capt. Mills fired, but Lieut. Harding stood and held his gun at a "ready" and did not fire at all. He said the sight was so pretty that he did not think of his gun. I killed my deer, and the Captain wounded his by breaking one fore leg. The other deer gave a few jumps and stopped, and I took the Lieutenant's gun and shot it dead. We now had two deer and were only about a mile from camp. I left the two officers to dress the venison and I went back to camp after a horse to pack it in. While I was away, and before they had got the fallen game dressed, two other deer came along within gunshot of them. The two officers fired at them and killed one deer, both claiming the honor of the fatal shot. Now we had plenty of meat for a start, and would, no doubt, get more before we consumed that.

After arriving at camp with the deer I directed Jake, the negro cook, to get an early dinner, as I wanted to take a big hunt that afternoon.

While at the dinner table I suggested that as they could find deer anywhere around there, for they were as thick as sheep and not very wild, that they might kill that kind of game, while I would mount Pinto and prospect for larger, for I thought there were elk in that country, and if that was true we wanted some of them.

After dinner I mounted my horse and was off for an elk hunt. After riding up the river about three miles I could see any amount of sign. Dismounting and tying my horse, I took an elk trail where a band had just crossed the trail on which I was riding, and I did not follow it very far until I came in sight of the elk. There were eight in this band, and I had to take a roundabout course to get in gunshot of them, but when I finally did get a shot at them I killed an elk that carried the largest pair of horns I have ever seen, with one exception. I unjointed his neck about a foot from his head and dressed him, but left his hide on. The head and horns were all I could lift as high as the horse's back.

When I rode up to camp and the negro cook saw that head of horns he exclaimed: "Hello, Marstah; what you got dar? You must hab killed de debbil dis time, suah."

From the negro I learned that the officers had all been out, and had seen more or less deer and had done more or less shooting, but had only killed one small doe.

That night the elk fever raged high in camp, as that pair of horns had set them all wild to go elk hunting the next day. That night we ordered an early breakfast, so as to get an early start to our hunting ground.

After riding up the river the next morning, to where I had killed the elk the day before, we all dismounted and tied our horses. I asked them which they preferred, to go single or two together, and they thought it the best plan to go in couples.

Being somewhat acquainted with this kind of game, and knowing where to find them at this time of day, I told them what ridges to take to lead them to the main divide, also what our signals would be to come together.

Capt. Mills and I took up the center ridge, the two other couples going on ridges each side of us, but not in sight. After going about a mile or so we heard two gunshots to our left, and in a few moments we could hear elk running. The underbrush was so thick that it was difficult to get a shot at them on the run, so, seeing an opening that they were sure to cross, provided that they did not change their course, I had the Captain to stand by the side of a big tree and level his gun at the opening, and when an elk darkened the sight to fire, which he did, and got a fine elk. I fired also, but did not get my elk. He was as proud over killing that elk as I was over killing my first buffalo.

We hunted until about four o'clock that afternoon, and several shots were fired, but the Captain was the only one who got an elk that day. So we loaded that one, and the one I had killed the day previous, on to our horses and returned to camp with about all the meat the horses were able to carry.

The next morning I told the other men that as they now knew the elk range and how to hunt them, and could get along without me as well as not, that I would hunt for a grizzly bear, and if I could only kill a grizzly I would be ready to go home. I spent the next three days bear hunting, and saw any amount of sign, but only saw one bear and did not get a shot at it.

After being out about two weeks, and all having enough of hunting, they thought, to last them a year—as they had killed more or less deer, and one of them had killed an elk—and time being about up for the tug to come after us, we pulled up camp and started for the bay, arriving there on the 19th. The tug arrived on the 20th, about noon.

We reached San Francisco that evening, about dark, unloaded our baggage and meat, hired a man to watch it that night and we saddled up and rode out to the Fort.

The following morning I returned to the city, hired a team and took our baggage, as well as the meat we had killed, back to the Fort.

I was hailed several times while passing through the city by parties who wished to buy my mammoth elk horns, but I would not sell them, having already given them to Col. Elliott.

I stayed around the city until the middle of February, not knowing what to do to kill time, and loafing is the hardest work I ever did.

About this time Col. Elliott received orders to go out into southeastern Oregon, as soon as the weather would permit, and establish a fort at Klamath Lake. As soon as he received these orders he came to the city and hunted me up, and wanted me to go with him, at the same time insisting strongly on my joining his command; saying: "If you will enlist I am sure I can bring enough influence to bear to procure a Lieutenant's commission for you."

I told him emphatically that I would not enlist, as I intended to be a free man all the days of my life, "And when I scout for you," I said, "if I fail to do my duty, or shirk in the least, all you have to do is to say so, and I will quit then and there, and at the same time if you ask anything that I consider unreasonable, I will quit you cold."

The Colonel, however, accepted me as an independent scout.

I requested him to procure some one that was familiar with that country to go along as guide, but he told me that I would be around the city, and would have a better chance to find a suitable person than he would, and requested me to find a man and he would be satisfied with the selection.

During my stay in the city I saw a great many men who claimed to know all about that country, and who were anxious for the trip, but when I would question them they did not know any more about the country than I did, and I had never been in that region.

Finally the time was set to start, which was the first of June.

Before starting this time I had an understanding with Col. Elliott regarding the stock that might be captured by the scouts; he agreeing to let the scouts take the stock captured by them and divide it equally among themselves.

After having started, the Colonel was undecided as to where he would cross the Sierra Nevada Mountains. At that time there was no map of the country between California, Oregon and Nevada, but finally he decided to cross over the Beckwith Pass. After we had crossed the mountains we turned north, crossing the Truckee river where Reno now stands. From here we traveled across the sagebrush plain to Honey Lake.

So far we had no trouble with Indians, and the command stopped to let the horses rest a few days.

While lying there Col. Elliott requested me to take four other scouts and go north four days to prospect for water and grass, for this was now a strange country to all of us.

My companions were John Reilly, Fred Miller, John Boyd and George Jones, of whom there will be more said later on, and who were my companions the rest of the summer, or, as long as I was able to scout. Altogether there were twelve scouts in my company.

In the evening of the second day of our trip we camped at a nice little spring. We got into camp just at sundown, and having seen considerable Indian sign during the day, I had the boys stake their horses near the camp, and I took a look around on the ridges to see if there were any camp-fires in that part of the country. I was gone for about three hours, and the boys got quite uneasy while I was away. I only saw one Indian camp, which was northeast of our camp, and not having discovered it until after dark I was unable to tell just how far it was away. On my return I told the boys that we would have to stand guard that night, each one taking a turn of two hours, and as soon as supper was over we put the fire out so as not to give the redskins any advantage in that way. The next morning we got breakfast, and as soon as it was light George Jones and I went to the nearest ridge to look for Indians. I saw them just breaking camp, and they were about two miles away. That day we had to travel very cautiously, being in an entirely new country and knowing it to be full of hostile Indians.

That night we camped on a small stream which afterwards we found to be a tributary of McCloud's river. From what we had seen, there appeared to be plenty of water and grass, and from the Indian sign we had seen, they appeared to be in large bands, so we concluded to return to the command. The first day on our return trip, just about noon, as we were looking for a place to stop for lunch, we were discovered by about twenty Indians. The red devils made for us, and their war-whoops sounded as though they were bloodthirsty. They came pell-mell over the hills and hollows in hot pursuit of us, and I tell you things looked a little blue; only five of us and at least twenty Indians, and no telling how many there would be in a short time.

I told the boys that we would give them a round, anyway; and I had four men that were not afraid to face an Indian even in a hand-to- hand fight, if necessary; and then one feels more brave when he knows that he has got companions who will stay with him till the last dog is hung.

We rode to the top of the ridge, stopped and drew our revolvers, and when they were close enough we fired two shots apiece in succession and then put spurs to our horses and ran nearly a mile, when, on looking back, we saw that we were outriding them. We rode a mile further to the next ridge, just dropped over out of sight, and stopped and reloaded the empty chambers of our revolvers.

We knew now that we had the best horses, and the boys were all anxious to give them another round; so we waited until they were in pistol shot—as we felt more bold, knowing that if we could not whip them we could outrun them—and taking good aim this time we fired three shots each, making fifteen shots in all.

We saw a number of Indians fall to the ground, but did not stay to count them as we were just then in somewhat of a hurry.

We rode on again, they continuing to follow us. When we were far enough ahead again and in a suitable place, we stopped, reloaded and waited for them to come up, but they seemed to have changed their minds and didn't appear as anxious to ride in our company as they had on the start, for now they kept out of pistol shot. One of the boys dismounted and said: "I believe I can reach them from here," and taking a rest over his horse's back, fired and killed a horse. This caused a scattering among them, and if our horses had been fresh we would have tried to kill the whole outfit.

George Jones remarked that he guessed the red devils had enough of it already, and we rode on. They made two circles around us, keeping out of gunshot, and then rode away.

We pushed on with all haste possible, expecting that they had gone away to get reinforcements and follow us up, but that was the last we saw of them.

That night we made a dry camp, and did not build any fire for fear that they might be on our trail, and the next morning we were off very early. We rode until about ten o'clock, when we struck plenty of grass and water. Here we stopped, and one man stood guard on the hill while the others ate breakfast, and we were agreeably surprised at not seeing any more Indians on the trip.

We got back to the command the evening of the sixth day, and informed Col. Elliott that there was plenty of water as far as we went, and abundance of grass, also no end of Indian sign.

The command made preparations to move on again, and two days after our return we started, but moved slowly and cautiously, making only from ten to fifteen miles a day. Now we had twelve scouts in all, and it was our business to guard the command while traveling, and, in fact, at all times when there was a possibility of an attack, and we had to watch out north, south, east and west, lest a large band of Indians should make an attack unawares and get the better of the expedition.

We traveled in this manner until reaching the little stream spoken of, where the scouting party had turned back, not having met any trouble.

The Colonel thought it best for me to take a part of my scouts and go ahead again and prospect the country for water and grass.

After giving my other scouts particular orders to keep A sharp lookout for Indians, and to scout the country thoroughly for eight or ten miles in every direction daily, I took my same four men that were out the trip previous, four days' rations, and started out again.

All my talking did not prevent a surprise, for the second day after our departure the Indians made an attack on the herders, captured twenty-two horses in broad daylight and killed one of the herders. The same evening about sundown they made an attack on the command, and after a hard fight for an hour or more, the Indians retreated, leaving sixty dead Indians on the battlefield, there being eleven soldiers killed and twenty wounded.

On my return Col. Elliott told me not to leave the camp so far any more, for, said he, "I am satisfied if you had been here we would not have had the surprise."

I told the Colonel what kind of country we would have for the next seventy-five miles; plenty of water and grass, abundance of game and the country full of hostile Indians.

The reader will understand that this was the year 1856. The Klamath Indians and the tribe afterwards known as the Modocs, of whom mention will be made later on in this work, were one and the same tribe; and up to this time they did not know what it was to be whipped. Besides there had been but little travel through this part of the country without experiencing a great deal of trouble with those Indians.

CHAPTER XVI
MORE FISH THAN I HAD EVER SEEN AT ONE TIME.—WE SURPRISE SOME INDIANS, WHO ALSO SURPRISE US.—THE CAMP AT KLAMATH LAKE.—I GET ANOTHER WOUND AND A LOT OF HORSES

When we pulled out for Klamath Lake we traveled from five to ten miles a day and kept scouts out in all directions. While riding along one day with my four assistants, a few miles in advance of the command, we came to a beautiful body of water which is now known as Clear Lake, which is the head of Lost river. Here we dismounted, and on looking into a brush shanty that stood on the lake shore, I saw more fish than I had ever seen before at one time. The little shanty was filled to its utmost capacity with fish, hanging there to dry for winter use. Further on we found numerous other similar shanties, all containing like quantities of drying fish. These were the Indians' dry-houses. They had caught the fish and hung them there to dry in the hot summer's sun. Such was their food in winter when the land game was scarce.

After our fill of admiring the beautiful lake and resting our horses, we mounted and started back to the command. We had gone only a short distance, when, all of a sudden, on reaching the top of a little hill, we were met by twelve Indians, who had not seen us, nor us them, until within a hundred yards of each other.

There was only one thing to do and that was to fight, for they were directly between us and the command, and the braver we were I thought the better; so I gave orders to charge, but the Indians did not stand fire. We got three of them that first round and in another hundred yards we got three more, but their horses being fresh and ours somewhat jaded, they outran us and got away.

These were the first Klamath Indians I had got close enough to, to see how their moccasins were made, and for a person engaged in the business that I was then in, it was quite essential to be able to tell the tribe an Indian belonged to by his track. And here I will state that not any two tribes cut and make their moccasins alike and at that time I could tell an Indian by his track, if he belonged to any tribe that I was familiar with.

Here we laid over three days to let our horses rest up a little. While here we had all the fish that we wanted to eat, for the lake was literally full of the finest in the land.

In a southwesterly direction we could see, by looking through our field glasses, a large valley, which Col. Elliott thought to be the country which he was ordered to go to.

The second day after leaving Clear Lake we struck another lake. We did not name it, but it has since been known as Tule Lake, and is the outlet of Lost river, but has no visible outlet itself. Here we laid over two days, after which we pulled out up the valley. Two days more and we were at Klamath Lake, and here Col. Elliott established his headquarters and started in to fortify himself against the Indians, which were very numerous in this country at that time.

John Riley, Fred Miller, John Boyd, George Jones and myself took four days' rations and started out to investigate the surrounding country north of headquarters.

The next afternoon about three o'clock we saw a band of Indians some distance away as they were passing over a somewhat uneven country. We were not just able to tell the number in the band, but thought there must be about twenty, and they were driving some loose horses.

We stopped to consider the matter as to what was best to be done. George Jones said: "Boys, we have been out all summer and have not got a single horse to pay for our trouble, and I think I could fight like the devil if there was a good band of horses at stake." The balance of the crowd seemed to think likewise, so we concluded to follow up the Indians and give them a round. We started at once, but before overtaking them they had pitched camp on the shore of Lake Klamath.

After it was quite dark, George Jones and I crawled around near the camp and counted twenty Indians.

Our intention had been to stampede the horses in stead of making an attack on the Indians, as we thought the number too great to tackle, but an investigation developed the fact that they had turned their horses into a little peninsula that ran out into the lake, and had pitched their tents so as to hold their horses in there. Riley said there was only one of two things to do, and that was to make the attack or crawfish. We were all well armed, the other four having each a six-shooter and a sabre, and I had my big knife, which was almost as good as a sabre, and two six-shooters.

We laid and watched their movements until all turned in for the night.

They were badly scattered, making it worse for us than if they had been in a bunch. We waited until about eleven o'clock, when we thought they were all asleep, and having laid our plans of attack, we all crawled up abreast to within a rod or so of where some of them were lying, and each drew his pistol and sabre.

Taking our pistols in our left hands and sabres in the right, we made a rush for them, intending to cut the first ones down with our sabres, and if we got into close quarters we could use both at the same time.

In such cases it is quite essential that a scout should be able to use his pistol in his left hand, which had been part of their drill duties before starting out scouting.

As soon as the attack was made some of the Indians arose on their feet, and we tried to cut them down as fast as they arose, but it was so dark that it was difficult to distinguish our own men from the Indians.

The Indians fought us with their tomahawks, and it was not long until we were all mixed up together, and a person had to look close before striking, for fear of making a mistake. After fighting some time I had two hand-to-hand encounters, but was victorious in both of them. Just as I had finished the second one I got a tremendous blow from behind that caught me on the shoulder, and it knocked me as blind as a bat. When I tried to rise I would stagger and fall like a drunken man. After making the third attempt to get on my feet, and seeing it was no use and being afraid my own men might mistake me for an Indian, I laid down as still as I could until the fight was ended.

About this time my shoulder commenced to pain me fearfully, and it was a hard matter for me to lie still. I could then see a very little, but to me everything was still. Just then I heard George Jones' voice. He was asking where Will was. I did not hear any reply, and a moment later he hallooed at the top of his voice. It sounded to me as though he was a long ways off, but at the same time he was within four rods of me. I made out that time to answer so he could hear me, and in a moment they were all by my side. Some one raised me up, while another ran to the lake and got his hat full of water. They removed my clothing sufficiently to exam me my wound, and found that my shoulder blade was broken in two places. When I was able to talk, the boys asked what they had better do, saying they had the last Indian killed. I said if you are sure you have them all killed, build a fire and put out guards until morning, and we will return to headquarters with the stock.

George Jones, feeling much concerned about me on account of my wound, proposed to ride to headquarters that night for the surgeon, but I told him it was not necessary, that I would be able to ride to headquarters the next day.

I took a sup of brandy, which we were never without on a trip like this, and drank a cup of coffee, after which I felt much better, but could not move my left hand or shoulder without much pain.

The next morning as soon as it was light enough to see to scalp an Indian, the boys took twenty-one scalps, and we had fifty-two horses, some of which were extraordinary good ones of that class. That was ten horses each and two over. After having counted them, George Jones said: "I think Will ought to have the two extra horses, for he is the only one that got wounded in the fight."

The boys were jubilant over their victory and the band of horses, but were very sorry to have one of their comrades so badly used up. After they had breakfast over, the saddle horses were brought in, my horse was saddled for me and they assisted me in getting on him, or rather put me on, for I was almost as helpless as a child.

My shoulder they had tied up as best they could with two handkerchiefs, and one of the boys leading my horse, we started for headquarters. We were about twenty miles from the command, but I never rode fifty miles that seemed as far as that twenty miles did. When we arrived at camp my shoulder was badly swollen, and it took the surgeon a long time to get it set just to his notion, or, at least it seemed so to me, and when he did finally get it set he gave me something to put me to sleep.

However, I was not able to ride any more that summer. All that I was able to do was to sit in camp, hear the reports of scouts as they came in and give orders.

It had been six weeks since I was hurt, and it was getting late in the fall and the weather looking somewhat blustery, I told the Colonel I thought I would go back to San Francisco and winter there.

Up to this time the surgeon had not allowed me to ride on horseback, but I had come to the conclusion that I could now stand it to ride without any serious difficulty, and I was anxious to get back before winter set in.

When I told the Colonel my intentions, he said: "How in the name of God will you get to San Francisco? If you were well and able to ride I could not spare an escort sufficient to guard you through."

"It don't matter about the escort," I said, "when I get ready I will go if I have to go alone."

"Young man," said he, "you must be insane to even think of such a thing."

"Colonel," I said, "you may call it what you please, but I mean just what I say; and I suppose that as you have been out all summer, having no chance to either send or receive any mail, that you would like to send out after that."

Said he, "I have no one to send, that could make the trip without asking a larger escort than I could spare."

I told the Colonel that I could select two men from his command, either of whom I could take and make the trip safely, or the two would make it alone with perfect safety.

The Colonel replied, "If I could only think so I certainly would ask them to go;" and he asked who the parties were to whom I had reference. I told him they were Messrs. Jones and Riley, who had been my assistant scouts the past summer.

The Colonel asked when they would be in camp. I told him they had just returned a few minutes previous. He said: "Tell them I will see them at your quarters at seven o'clock this evening." I assured him that they would be there, but up to this time I had not mentioned or even hinted at such a thing to them, but being desirous of seeing them before the Colonel had a talk with them, I set about to find them. I found them in their quarters and told them of the proposed meeting and the object, and asked them what they thought of it.

George Jones said: "As far as I am concerned, I think I can make the trip alone, for I can see an Indian just as far as he can see me, and just as quick, and I am perfectly willing to take the chances."

"And how with you, Riley?" I asked. He replied: "I will go if I can get permission."

At seven o'clock, sharp, all hands met at my tent. The Colonel opened the conversation by saying: "Gentlemen, our chief scout, Mr. Drannan, has concluded to leave us and go to San Francisco to spend the winter, and under the circumstances I don't want to see him go alone. Do you men feel like accompanying him and bringing our mail back on your return?"

George Jones said: "I can only speak for myself. I will accompany him alone and bring the mail back if no one else feels like going." At this Riley said he was willing to accompany George on the trip if necessary.

Col. Elliott straightened up and said: "Boys, I don't believe you realize the danger you will necessarily have to encounter in making this trip. Think the matter over thoroughly until to-morrow evening, by which time you will be able to give me a decided answer;" and then the Colonel departed, requesting us all to meet him in his quarters the following evening at seven o'clock, sharp. After he had gone George Jones asked me how long I thought it would take us to go to Sacramento. About fifteen days was my estimate, and I was of the opinion that we would best go an entirely different route to what we came. Before leaving my tent they had made up their minds to tackle the trip anyway, let it go as it might, and the time set to start was ten days from that.

The following evening we all went to the Colonel's tent at the hour agreed upon. He asked the boys as soon as they entered if they had made up their minds to tackle the trip, and they both told him they had. He then asked me when I would be ready to start, and I told him in ten days.

George Jones then asked the Colonel what length of time he would give him and Riley to make the trip in. "I will give you a month and a half," was the reply.

Five of us had fifty-two horses that we had captured from the Indians. I called the other four together and told them if they would let me pick six horses from the band they might have the remainder. This being agreeable, the day following the horses were driven into the corral and I selected my six. Jones and Riley put in a good portion of the day in saddling and riding them to see whether they were broke or not, and we found them all to be fairly well broken to ride.

The next day I told the Colonel that I was ready to resign my position as chief of scouts, for you will have to appoint another man, and you had just as well do it first as last.

"No," said the Colonel, "when you are ready to start, I will give you a voucher for your pay up to that time, and when you get to San Francisco you can get your money."

We commenced making preparations to start, but did not let it be generally known until the day before starting, and then everybody wanted to write a letter to send out, and by the time we were ready to start we had a pack-horse loaded with mail.

The Colonel sent a long letter to his wife, and told me a lot of stuff to tell the other officers, of which I did not remember one- fourth.

Finally we were rigged up and ready to start, but we had a hard time to get away, for Dick Jones wanted me to tell Jim Johnson so and so. Another had some word to send to a friend, whose name I had never heard before, and never thought of after I was out of sight.

After shaking hands all around, and Col. Elliott telling me a lot of stuff to tell his wife and numerous other ladies which he knew I would not repeat the half of, for he knew that there was not another man in San Francisco that hated to try to talk to ladies as much as I did. If we had not jarred loose and rode off I suppose we would have been there all day, and we would have had enough word to carry in our heads, that had it been written, would have made a book that Webster's Unabridged Dictionary would be small compared with it, and again shaking hands we waved our hats at the many soldiers standing around and rode away.

CHAPTER XVII
DISCOVERY OF INDIANS WITH STOLEN HORSES.—WE KILL THE INDIANS AND RETURN THE PROPERTY TO ITS OWNERS.—MEETING OF MINERS.—IN SOCIETY AGAIN

On our return trip we took the divide between the Klamath River and Tule Lake. I had told Col. Elliott before starting that I intended to pass west of the snowy butte instead of east of it, as we did coming in.

This butte has since been called Shasta Mountain, and it is one of the grandest sights that ever the eye of man beheld. It flouts the skies with its peaks of everlasting snow, gleaming like a vast opal under the sunshine, or peeping out in rainbow-tinted glints, from among the rifts of the clouds that rake along its sides. Often long streams of glittering white stretch from its peaks, far out into space, and these are called "snow-banners."

My object in passing west of Shasta was to strike the headwaters of the Sacramento and follow that river to the city of Sacramento. Late in the evening of the fifth day we struck a beautiful region, since known as the Shasta Valley.

While we were looking ahead through our field glasses and laying out our route for the next day, we discovered a great cloud of dust, which seemed to be not more than five or six miles away, and just beyond a low range of hills that we could overlook. We secreted our horses and watched the dust, but we had not watched long before about sixty horses came in sight, driven by five Indians. We could note that there were a number of mules in the band, and that two of the redskins carried rifles.

We were not long in making up our minds that this was stolen property, and that they had done murder and had taken the stock and were getting away as fast as they could. Otherwise they would not have those rifles.

In those days Indians knew very little about using guns, and the mules we knew did not belong to them, for they did not have any mules, only as they could steal them from the emigrants.

We watched them until they came to a nice little stream, where they stopped, staked their saddle-horses out, and as it was almost night, we were confident from their movements that they were going into camp. Being not more than three miles from where we were, we staked out horses on the grass, ate a cold lunch, and it now being dark we started afoot for the Indian camp.

We did not get in sight of the Indians any more until within a quarter of a mile of their camp.

They had a little fire of sagebrush and had not lain down yet, but were watching the horses very closely. They stayed up until about eleven o'clock, and every few minutes some of them would go out to where the horses were feeding and look all around.

The moon being full, it was a very bright night, and we could see well.

Finally the horses all got quiet, and the Indians, after building up a little more fire, all laid down by it for a nap.

After they had lain there some little time, I told the boys now was our time, for as soon as one of them woke up he would go out to the horses again.

George Jones requested me not to take any hand in the fight for fear I might get my shoulder hurt over again, as it was not well by any means. I told him I would not unless I thought it really necessary; but if it was I would give them a shot anyway, just for luck. I gave George Jones one of my revolvers, so he took a revolver in each hand, and Riley had a revolver in his left and his sabre in his right hand. We now started to crawl up to where the Indians were no doubt fast asleep.

I crawled up with the balance, in case the boys got in close quarters, thinking that a shot might help them, but George Jones assured me that by taking one of my revolvers they would get three the first shot and then they would have three more shots for the other two, so that before any of them got to their feet we would have them all.

It being an unusually bright, moonlight night, we were able when near them, by the aid also of the little fire which was yet burning, to get their exact position, which was a great help in making an attack.

When within ten feet of the Indians, Jones and Riley both rose to their feet and fired three shots, Jones firing both pistols at once, and they killed two Indians as they lay and killed the third one as he raised to his feet.

The other two ran, not offering to fight at all, but Jones and Riley got them before they had gone further than a few steps.

This fight occurred about sixteen miles east of Yreka, near Little Shasta. We rebuilt the fire by throwing some sagebrush on, and in their outfit we found two scalps taken from white men, and which looked to have been taken in the last twenty-four hours; two rifles, but no ammunition, and I don't think they would have known how to use them if they had had ammunition. They were armed with bows and arrows, and some had knives.

I stayed and looked after the captured horses while the other boys went back after our own horses. On their return I laid down and slept awhile, but the other boys did not lie down at all that night, for there was not much night left by the time they got in with our horses.

The following morning, as soon as it was light enough to see, we counted the horses and found there were fifty-five of them.

After getting our breakfast we started back on the trail the Indians had come, that being the course we wished to go. We traveled hard all day, and just at night we came to a little stream running across the valley, that we had looked at through the glasses the evening before. Here we went into camp for the night, and on looking across the valley on the opposite side of the river we could see through the field glasses a number of little wreaths of smoke curling up into the air, and they were scattered along the foothills here and there for several miles.

I knew at once they were not from Indian fires, for I could not see a lodge, and they were too badly scattered to be an Indian village.

Just what it was we could not make out, but we stopped on the little stream that night, which is now called Shasta river. I slept but very little, as my broken shoulder was commencing to bother me again from riding. I was up and down all night long, and was around among the horses many times.

The next morning we were up and had our breakfast and started very early. We had not gone more than two miles, when, on looking ahead, we saw twelve men coming on horseback. Through my glasses I saw they were white men, and told the boys so. George Jones could not believe they were white men until he looked through the glass, when he said: "Well, I'll be d—d if they ain't white men."

We altered our course so as to meet them, and less than a half hour's ride brought us face to face.

There was a man by the name of Wm. McConnell riding in the lead, and on meeting us the first word uttered by any of the party was by McConnell. He said: "Where in the name of God did you get those horses?" While I was telling him where and how we came in possession of them, George Jones took the five Indian scalps from the pack and said:

"And there is something else we got at the same time we got the horses."

Then he took the two white men's scalps from the pack, also the two rifles, and they were also satisfied that the scalps were the scalps of the two white men who had been herding this same band of horses and mules, for the hair was similar in color to that of the two herders. One of them had dark brown hair and the other one had rather light hair.

From this company of men we learned that near us there was a mining camp, the stock belonged to the miners, and that the two men killed had been herding the horses and mules about three miles away from camp. This was a new camp called Greenhorn Gulch.

The herders always brought the horses to camp every night, but the last two nights they had failed to bring the stock in, and this man McConnell had raised the crowd to hunt the stock, being satisfied that the two herders were killed and the stock driven away by the Indians.

After giving them a brief outline of our little fight with the Indians, our business there, etc., McConnell asked us how much the miners would have to pay us for our trouble. I told him that we did not make any charge, but that if the miners felt that it was worth anything to them to have their horses brought back, they could pay us just what they felt like giving. McConnell said for us to ride back to camp with them and he would call a miners' meeting that afternoon and state the case to the miners, and he was satisfied they would do what was right.

We drove the stock to where they were accustomed to being corralled at night and corralled them, and made camp for the night, for I was needing rest, very much, on account of my shoulder.

This man McConnell was erecting a store building about half way between Greenhorn Gulch and a new discovery that had recently been made, some two or three miles off.

About two o'clock Mr. McConnell came to our camp and told us to come along with him to a certain miner's cabin, and that the miners would all be there and we would see what could be done. When we got to the cabin, sure enough every miner was there.

Mr. McConnell called the house to order, stated the object of the meeting and made quite a little speech. He told the miners that we had brought the stock home, told where and how we came in possession of it, and that he, as well as eleven other men that were present, had seen the five Indian scalps, also two scalps of white men that he was confident were the scalps of the two herders, and had also seen their two rifles.

After Mr. McConnell had addressed the crowd in a very genteel manner he set a hat on the newly constructed miners' table and said: "Now, gentlemen, how much will each of you give? I will give twenty dollars." At the same time he threw twenty dollars in for a starter. The other miners followed suit, all contributing liberally, and the amount raised reached three hundred and fifty dollars.

After the money was counted they asked us if we were satisfied with that amount.

We told them that we were, and that if they had not given us anything it would have been all right, for we only considered that we had done our duty, which we would expect any man to do for us under like circumstances.

The morning following, before starting out again, we obtained information from Mr. McConnell concerning our trip down to Sacramento that was of great value to us. He directed us by way of Scott's Valley, and told us we need not have any fear of trouble with the Indians, which was a great relief to us at that time.

We found it a splendid trail, and made the trip from the mining camp to Sacramento in nine days. Mr. McConnell thought it would take us twelve days, but having plenty of horses along we could change when we liked, and by doing so could make good time.

The next day after arriving at Sacramento we got our horses on pasture, and the following morning took the boat for San Francisco.

The next morning after arriving at San Francisco we went to the Miners' Restaurant to see my old friend, Healey, and they were all very glad to see us.

After breakfast we hired a team and started to the Fort with our baggage.

They were all greatly astonished when we told them that we had made the trip alone.

As soon as I arrived at the Fort I went to see the surgeon, and he told me that my shoulder was in a dangerous condition, and that I would have to stay around the Fort so that he could see me at least every other day for several weeks.

There was a great commotion at the Fort when the news spread abroad that we had arrived from Fort Klamath, for every one that had a friend away with Col. Elliott's command expected a letter, and we had to have a postmaster appointed to distribute the mail.

During my stay at the Fort I made my home at Mrs. Elliott's.

While I was away with Col. Elliott, Jim Beckwith had been at the Fort a number of times, and each time had left a letter for me requesting me to come to see him as soon as I got back.

After resting a few days I started to the city to look Jim up, and found him without any trouble. His money was about all gone, and he was anxious for me to go to the mountains with him on a trapping expedition the coming winter, saying he was tired of laying around doing nothing but drink whiskey.

We made arrangements to start in two or three weeks from that time, provided my shoulder would permit. Jim agreed to go to Sacramento when we were ready to start and get my horses, and I returned to the Fort to have my broken shoulder taken care of.

Now, as I have said before, I don't think there was ever a young man that suffered from bashfulness as I did during what time I was in the company of ladies.

At that time I thought Mrs. Elliott was doing all she could to tease me, but since I have grown older and learned a little more about civilization, I am convinced that it was for my own good, thinking that I might overcome my timidity to a certain extent by having me go in society. Nearly every day while at the Fort she would either ask me in the afternoon to go in company with her to visit some lady friend, or would want me to stay at her house to receive some lady company, and frequently I have accompanied her to a neighbor's house where there were young ladies, and I would have given every horse that I owned to have been away. But Mrs. Elliott had been almost like a mother to me, and I could not refuse to go with her when she requested me to do so. After I had been at the Fort about two weeks Mrs. Elliott said she was going to give another party, but I told her I had a lawful excuse this time for not dancing, as the surgeon would not allow me to dance on account of my shoulder. Among the balance of Mrs. Elliott's lady friends was Lieut. Jackson's wife, who, by the way, was one of the loveliest and best women I have ever met. Her husband had been ordered the past summer out to Arizona, and was at that time establishing a new fort, which was known afterwards as Fort Yuma.

Mrs. Jackson was expecting to go soon to join her husband at Fort Yuma, and as I was going on to the waters of the Gila, trapping, she insisted on my waiting and going in company with them. Finally, after stopping around the Fort three weeks, the surgeon told me by a certain time, which was nearly a week, I might start out, and if I was careful I would be perfectly safe.

I went down to the city, and Jim Beckwith and I agreed on the time to start, after which I returned to the Fort.

The evening before I was to start, every army officer at the Fort, there being twenty-eight in number, and every lady, married and single, came to Mrs. Elliott's house. When I asked her what all this meant, she said: "I suppose they have come to bid you good- bye." But it was not long until I knew the object of the meeting, for some one in the crowd sang out: "Choose partners for a quadrille!" and in a jiffy there was a double set on the floor, and the floor manager said: "All ready."

The musicians took their seats, and the same prompter stood there that prompted for them the time I attended that other party of Mrs. Elliott's.

The music started up, and I commenced to realize that I was attending a party, or the party was attending me, one of the two. They danced nearly all night, and had what they called a nice time, while I sat back in one corner scared half to death for fear they would call "ladies' choice;" and I knew Mrs. Elliott or some other lady was sure to come for me, and as my shoulder was getting most well, I was afraid that I could not get clear on the plea of being a cripple.

When the party broke up, Mrs. Jackson insisted on my paying them a visit at Fort Yuma, as it would not be a great ways from where I was going to trap the coming winter.

The next morning when I rode off, and different ones were waving me adieu, Mrs. Elliott told me to be sure and pay them a visit when I came to the city.

CHAPTER XVIII
TRAPPING ON THE GILA.—THE PIMAS IMPART A SECRET.—RESCUE OF A WHITE GIRL.—A YOUNG INDIAN AGENT.—VISIT TO TAOS.— UNCLE KIT FAILS TO RECOGNIZE ME

The same day that I left the Fort, Jim Beckwith came down to the boat bringing my horses, twelve in number, and after buying our outfit for camping, provisions, and so on, we bought quite a lot of beads, blankets, cheap rings and such goods as we could trade to the Indians for furs.

The following day we pulled for the trapping region, by way of the old San Jose mission, and from there to the old mission of San Gabriel, thence across the Mojave desert. From there we struck out for the mouth of the Gila river, and crossed just where it empties into the Colorado. We then traveled up what is known as Salt river, some distance from where we crossed the Gila. This was early in January, and we found plenty of beaver that were easy to catch.

No trapping had been done in that region for several years. Besides, we thought at the time, and it so proved, that we were entirely out of the way of hostile Indians.

Here we put in two months trapping, with splendid success. Then, as it was getting too late in the season to trap, Jim proposed that we take our little stock of goods, or a portion of it, and visit the Pima tribe of Indians, which we found to be not as great a distance away as we had supposed, it being only about forty miles to their village.

They all knew us and were glad to see us. The chief and some other of the head men were out on their annual hunt, and we did not get to see them, as we only stayed two days, during which time they treated us the very best they knew how. They had plenty of vegetables such as turnips, onions, potatoes, sweet potatoes, etc.

While on this visit a certain young Indian got to be a great friend to me, but I am sorry to say that I have forgotten his name. He had a sister whose name was Nawasa, who also got to be a warm friend of mine, and I must say, that, although an Indian, she was a lady in her way, and I thought, really, that she was the best looking Indian I had ever seen.

The evening that we were to start back to our camp, Nawasa came to me and told me in Spanish that her brother wanted to see me, and that he had something to tell me. I started off with her, and after we had gone a short distance I asked her where her brother was, and she pointed to a bunch of bushes, saying he was there.

On my arrival at the spot I asked him what he wished to say to me. I knew he had something private and important to say, otherwise he would not have called me to an out-of-the-way place like that.

He raised to his feet and looked around to see if there was any one in sight, and said in Spanish:, "Sit down here, me and my sister have something to tell you."

He started in by saying that the Apaches were very bad Indians, and that they had killed many of my friends; which showed that he considered all white people my friends.

"Six or seven years ago," he continued, "they killed a man, his wife, and two boys, and took two girls prisoners. A long time ago the smallest girl died and the big girl buried her."

At this, Nawasa spoke and said: "Many times I have gone with her to the village and heard her sing a pretty song, but I could not understand a word of it."

I asked if this girl was living yet.

Nawasa said: "Yes, I see her every few days."

I asked her what size the girl was, and from what I could learn she was almost grown.

I asked her if the girl was satisfied, and she thought she was not, saying she was held a prisoner and had to do the work for the Indian families, or lodges, as she termed them. She said the work consisted of getting the wood and water, and whatever little cooking was to be done.

The reader will understand that while the Apaches were hostile toward the whites, and the Pimas were not, yet the two tribes were always on peaceable terms. But I could see at a glance that those two Indians felt a deep interest in that white girl. I asked Nawasa how far it was to where the white girl was. After studying awhile, she said it was about six hours, meaning six hours' ride.

I asked her when she would see the girl again, and she made me understand that if it would please me, or be of any benefit to the girl, she could see her most any day, saying that she went near the village to gather huckleberries, this being the time of year the red huckleberries are ripe in this country.

I told them that I would come back in four days, and then I would go with them to that place to gather huckleberries.

I wanted to look over the ground before laying my plans for taking the girl, provided she wished to leave the Indians.

This ended the conversation, so we went back to camp, where I found Jim Beckwith and a crowd of Indians joking, smoking and having a good time generally, for, as I have said before, this was the most sociable tribe of Indians that I ever saw.

On our arrival at camp, Jim asked me in Spanish where I had been, and when he saw the Indian girl, said: "Oh, I see; you have been off courting;" and then he and the Indians had a laugh at my expense.

I did not say anything to Jim about what I had heard until the next day.

We started early in order to make the trip in one day. I told him the story just as I had it from the two Indians, and told him that I was going to try to get the girl away from the Apaches if she wanted to leave them.

I rode along some distance, apparently in a deep study, and he finally turned to me and said:

"I think you had better let that gal alone, for then. Apaches is the wust Injuns in the hull country. If you make the attempt and they ever git on your track, they'll run you down in spite o' you."

To the readers of this book I will say I never was more astonished in my life, than I was to hear Jim Beckwith talk as he did. In all the time that I had been with him, this was the first time I had ever seen the slightest indication of his showing the white feather, as we termed it. It seemed to me he had lost all his nerve.

I said: "Jim, my mind is made up; if that white girl is dissatisfied and wants to leave the Indians, I am going to make the attempt, and trust to luck for the balance."

From that time until the day I was to go back to the village, he tried in every way he could think of to persuade me not to make the attempt, but I told him there was no use talking, that I looked upon it as being my duty, knowing that the girl was a slave to those Indians.

On the day appointed I saddled Mexico and started for the Pima village. I met the two young Indians about two miles from the village, where they had come to meet me, and they were both riding one horse, Nawasa riding behind her brother. When I met them she jumped off from behind her brother and said she wanted to try my horse to see how he rode, and she got on Mexico behind me and rode to camp.

I stayed at the village that night, and the next morning the three of us started out to gather huckleberries.

After we were on the ground and were busying ourselves gathering berries, Nawasa said:

"If you will go on that little hill"—pointing to a hill near by— "at noon to-morrow, I will bring the white girl here to this tree, and you can see her for yourself."

She made me promise her not to go any nearer the Apache camp at this time, for, said she, "If they suspect anything wrong, the white girl will be traded off to the Indians in Mexico for a slave."

After making arrangements to meet the next day, Nawasa rode off toward the Apache town, and her brother and I rode back to the Pima village. The following day I rode back in company with my young Indian friend to within two or three miles of the berry-patch, where we separated, and I rode out to the ridge that Nawasa had pointed out to me the day previous.

I saw them standing by the tree, as she had said. I put my glass to my eyes and saw sure enough that it was a white girl with Nawasa, and that she looked very sad.

I then rode back to the Pima village. That same night the two young Indians both came home, but they would not say a word while at camp. It seemed that they would not under any consideration have let any of the other Indians know what they were up to, so the next morning when I started home they took their horses and rode with me about two miles.

After we had got away from the village some distance, I asked Nawasa if the white girl still wanted to leave the Apaches, and she said, "Yes, she would like very much to leave them, but was afraid; as the Apaches had told her that if she ever tried to get away and was caught, she would be sold to the Mexican Indians as a slave, and there she would have to work in the fields, which would be much harder work than she has to do where she is."

I told Nawasa that if she would bring the white girl out on the same ridge that I had rode on, I would give her five strings of beads, and I would give her one string to give to the white girl. She promised that she would try, and that she would do her best.

I agreed to be back in eight days and see what arrangements had been made, and to let her know when I would be ready to take the girl.

When I got back, Jim asked me what I would do with the girl if I was successful in getting her away from the Indians. I told him I would take her to Fort Yuma.

"And what in the name of God will you do with her when you get to Fort Yuma?" said Jim.

I told him that if Mrs. Jackson was there, which I was confident she was, that I would leave the girl with her, and that I had no fears but that the girl would be taken care of in the very best manner that Mrs. Jackson could provide for her.

Jim said: "If the girl is satisfied with the Injuns, why don't you let her alone? She don't know anything but Injun ways, and she never will."

I told him that my mind was thoroughly made up, and I would rescue that girl from the Indians or lose my scalp in the attempt. And now don't say any more about it, for it will do no good.

He said: "Go ahead and do as you please, as you have always got to have your own way about things, anyhow."

I said: "Yes, Jim; when I know I am right, I propose to have my own way."

This ended the conversation, for the time being, at least, for Jim saw that I was determined in the matter, and he said no more about it.

On the day appointed I took my two favorite saddle-horses and rode over to the Pima village. I started very early and arrived at the village about four o'clock in the afternoon.

After knocking about the village for a little while, my two Indian friends proposed that we take a ride.

Of course I knew the horseback ride was only a ruse to get a chance to tell me the plans laid by herself and the white girl for her escape, although she said that she just wanted to try my Pinto horse to see how he would ride.

And here I will say that I don't believe there was another Indian in that village who had any idea of the scheme that was being worked up between myself and those two Indians, for they would never say a word to me while within earshot of any of the tribe.

The other Indians thought I was courting Nawasa, and it was always the custom among those Indians for a young couple never to ride out alone.

It has always been a mystery to me why those young Pimas took such a deep interest in the white girl, for they were merely untutored Indians, having only a few years since seen the first white man, and had not seen many since then.

But those two young Indians seemed to be as kind-hearted persons as I ever met, and were the most intelligent Indians I ever saw, who were not educated, and I often regretted that I did not take them to some school and have them educated, for it would have been a great benefit to the people on the plains at that time.

But to go on with my story. We took our ride, and as soon as we were well away from the village Nawasa told me that she had seen the white girl and completed plans for her escape. She said that after making arrangements with the girl, she—Nawasa—had not gone to the Apache village, but had met the girl at the huckleberry patch most every day.

She said: "The girl will come to the berry-patch every day until we go there for her, provided the Indians with whom she lived would let her go, that she might be there to-morrow, and she might not come till the next day. The girl is willing to go with you, and we will go to the berry-patch to-morrow and wait till she comes."

The next morning the three of us started out ostensibly to pick berries.

After we were out of sight of the village the young Indian man took my Pinto horse and started in the direction of Fort Yuma, it being understood that he was to stop about half way between Fort Yuma and the place where we would meet the girl. He was to wait there until the middle of the afternoon, and if we were not there by that time he was to return to camp.

Nawasa and I went on to the berry-patch, but the white girl was not there. We had not waited long, however, until Nawasa looked up and said in Spanish, "There she comes now."

I looked and saw the girl running. She did not discover us until she was within about fifty yards of us, and when she saw us she stopped very suddenly and hung her head.

I did not know at the time whether she was ashamed or whether she had been with the Indians so long that she was really afraid of a white person; but Nawasa was not long in getting to her, and the girl would look at me and then look back, as though she had a notion to go back to the Apache village.

When I rode up to where she was, she dropped her head and would not look up for some little time.

I saw that her face was badly tattooed, but her body was not, and as she stood there, apparently undecided what to do, she was to me an object of pity, and her dejected countenance would, I think, have appealed strongly to even Jim Bridger's heart.

I told Nawasa to help her on behind me, for we must be off quick. Nawasa said: "She don't want to go." I then spoke to the white girl in Spanish, and said: "My dear girl, why do you hesitate? Get up behind me and I will take you to your own people. Why do you want to stay here and be a slave for those Indians?"

I wish I could give in detail the persuasive language used by that untutored but kind-hearted Indian girl, to get her to leave the Apaches. She would tell her that if she would only go with me that I would take her to her own people, and would tell her how happy she would be with them.

After a great deal of persuasion, as I sat on my horse I reached down and took her by one arm and told the Indian girl to help her up behind me. She took her by the foot and helped her on my horse, and mounting her own horse we flew out of that section about as fast as our horses were able to carry us.

I was riding Mexico, and he was one of the swiftest horses in that country, and he had great endurance, also.

We rode some distance before I said anything to the girl, though Nawasa had kept along at our side, talking to her all the time to keep her spirits up. Finally I spoke to her in the English language, but it was some time before I could get her to utter a word; I don't know whether it was through fear or bashfulness.

Four miles' ride brought us out of the timber into an open prairie, with low hills covered with bunch-grass, and here and there a bunch of prickly pears, so rank that one dared not attempt to ride through them. There were little mountain streams running through the country, with no kind of timber but willows, strewn here and there along the banks.

On we went, over the hills and across the valleys, putting our horses down to what they could stand and at the same time keeping a sharp lookout behind to see if the Indians were trailing us.

Our course for the first twenty miles, to where we met the young Indian, was a little north of west, and from there almost due west.

About two o'clock we arrived at the point where we were to meet the young Indian, and found him there, waiting.

We dismounted, and I was not long in changing my saddle from Mexico to my Pinto horse. This horse would weigh nearly eleven hundred pounds, and had good life and splendid bottom.

By this time the white girl was beginning to talk some.

After having my saddle changed and on my horse, the Indian girl told her she would go no farther with us. She told Nawasa that she was afraid to go with me, as she was afraid that I would take her to Mexico and sell her for a slave, where she would have to work in the fields. But Nawasa assured her there was no danger, saying: "Esta umbra mooly ah-me-go," meaning, "This man is a great friend of mine;" and she again told her not to be afraid, for I would take her to her own people.

This seemed to give her some encouragement.

After the young Indian had shown me the direction to Fort Yuma, by landmarks, etc., I asked him how far it was.

He stepped out by the side of my horse, and after taking a good look at him, said in Spanish: "About three hours, or perhaps three and a half." I then told Nawasa to help the girl up again, and she did so.

When we were about to start, the two Indians came up to us and said: "Adios anlyose," which means, "Good-bye, my friend;" at the same time shaking hands with us both.

After riding a short distance I commenced talking to her in our own language.

It seemed that she had almost forgotten English, and when she would try to talk it she could not join the words together so as to make much sense of it. It was hard to understand her, but between English and Spanish together she could manage to talk so that I was able to understand her. However, her English seemed to improve by degrees, and I asked her if she would not be glad to get back to her own people, so they could dress her up and make a lady of her.

I do not believe that the poor girl had really thought of or realized her rude condition.

She said: "No, I can never be a white girl," and at the same time commenced crying, and said in broken English, "Now I remember seeing my mother dressed all nice, and plenty more women all dressed nice." It seemed after talking to her in her own language a short time she could call back to memory things that she had forgotten altogether.

I asked her how long since she was taken by the Indians. She had to study some time before she could answer, but finally in broken English, intermingled with Spanish, she said she thought seven years.

I asked if she was taken alone. She said, no, she had a little sister taken at the same time she was. I asked her where the little sister was, and she replied that she had died, and she thought she had been dead about three years.

I asked her if the Indians had killed her father and mother. She said: "Yes, and my little brother, too; and burned our wagon and all that was in it."

Then I said to her: "I don't see how you can love those Indians who had killed your father, mother and brother." She replied that she had no one else to love.

I then said to her, "You will soon be among friends, for I am taking you to a woman that will be as good to you as your own mother was," and at that moment we hove in sight of the Fort. I pointed to the Fort, and told her there was where the woman lived that I was taking her to.

We were now safe from an attack from the Apaches, and only a few minutes later I drew rein at Fort Yuma.

I first rode up to the guard, whose beat was in front of the Commander's tent, and asked where Lieut. Jackson's quarters were. He pointed to a tent not far from where we then were, saying: "That is his tent, and his wife is there, too."

As I rode to the Lieutenant's quarters, all eyes were turned in our direction. Mrs. Jackson came to the door of the tent and recognized me at once, and her first words were: "Chief, in the name of common sense, where are you from, and who is this you have with you?"

I said: "Mrs. Jackson, this is a girl I rescued from the Indians. She has no parents and no relatives, that she knows of, and I have brought her to you, thinking you would be a friend to her."

The reply of that noble woman was, "I will, with all my heart," and at that she assisted the girl in getting off the horse and led her into her own tent.

By this time Lieut. Jackson and all the officers of the Fort were there, and it seemed to me that the Lieutenant would never quit shaking my hand, and when he went to introduce me to the other officers who were present, laughingly said.

"What shall I call you? I have known you as the 'Boy Scout,' also as the 'Chief of Scouts.' I have known you when you were giving lessons in hunting, and now you have come in from a hostile Indian country with a white girl riding behind you. What shall I call you?"

I said: "Lieutenant, call me Will Drannan, the trapper, for I am now engaged in that business."

"Yes, I see you are," responded the Lieutenant with a hearty laugh, "and I see you have had splendid success in your new enterprise." He then asked me if I had trapped the girl.

I told him that I did not trap her, but that I got her away just the same.

The Lieutenant then introduced me to the officers, and had the orderly take charge of my horses. I was never kept more busy in my life answering questions than I was for the next two hours, relative to the girl and my plan of rescuing her.

Among the officers was a captain by the name of Asa Moore, who had heard all about this massacre only a short time after it occurred, and he said he thought there were some of the relatives living somewhere in California, but he did not know just what part of the state.

I had forgotten to say that on our way to the Fort I asked her name. It seemed at first that she had forgotten it, but after studying some little time she tried to speak the name, which at that time I understood to be Otus, but I have learned since that her name was Olive Oatman. She did not seem to remember her given name. The Indians had a name for her, but I have forgotten what it was.

Lieut. Jackson invited us into his tent, but when we got to the door it was barred.

Mrs. Jackson asked us to wait a few minutes until she got some clothes on Will's girl.

A few minutes later, when we were called into supper, Mrs. Jackson had washed the girl and had her dressed in calico.

Mrs. Jackson told us that after she got her dressed, the girl sat down and wept bitterly and said she did not know how to wear such clothing.

I remained at the Fort two days, and I must say that this girl improved both in talking and in manners during the time I was there far beyond our expectations.

When she would appear down-hearted or discouraged Mrs. Jackson would talk to her in such a kind and motherly manner that the girl would cheer up at once and would be anxious to try to make something of herself.

After spending two days at the Fort, and knowing that Jim Beckwith would be uneasy about me, I commenced making preparations to return.

Mrs. Jackson promised me that she would give the girl the very best care possible while she remained with her, and if she could hear of any of her relatives she would see that she got to them safely.

With this understanding I left the girl with Mrs. Jackson, but before I was ready to start the Lieutenant came to me and asked if I did not want a job of scouting. I told him that I did not at present, that I was going to Santa Fe and did not know when I would return again.

He then handed me a letter of recommendation, saying, "If you ever happen to want a position scouting, just show this letter and it will be of some benefit to you," and he assured me that if at any time he could assist me in any manner he would cheerfully do so.

When I was ready to start, Miss Oatman asked Mrs. Jackson what she should say to me. Mrs. Jackson told her to tell me good-bye, and tell me that she was very thankful to me for all I had done for her. But the poor girl could not remember it all. She could only remember the words "Good-bye, I thank you," at the same time shaking hands with me.

This was the last I ever saw of the girl, but have heard various reports concerning her since. I have been told that Mrs. Jackson raised money at the Fort to send her to San Francisco to have the tattoo marks removed from her face by the celebrated Dr. Fuller of that city, but they having been formed with vegetable matter, he was unable to remove them. I was also informed that she was afterwards sent to New York for the same purpose, but with no better success.

Only a short time ago, since coming to Idaho, I heard that she had really found some of her relatives somewhere in the state of Oregon, where she remained and raised a family; while a still later report is that she is married to a rich merchant and is living somewhere in the state of New York.

I have often thought of this poor girl since, and it has always been a question in my mind whether I did right in taking her away from the Indians after she had been with them so long; but if I did do right, and she or any of her relatives should by chance see this work and glance over its pages, I wish to say that to that kind-hearted Indian girl of the Pima tribe, Nawasa by name, and her brother belong the praise of rescuing Olive Oatman from the Apache Indians.

In the first place, had it not been for her and her brother, I would never have known of the girl, and even after I knew she was there, I could not have done anything without Nawasa's assistance, for she could not have worked more faithfully and earnestly if there had been a thousand dollars in the operation for her.

On my return trip I rode the first day to the Pima village and remained there that night.

I hired my young Indian friend to go among the Apaches and trade beads for furs, and he went home with me.

Nawasa was very anxious to know how I got through with the girl, but did not dare say anything while in camp; so the next morning when her brother and I were leaving she caught a horse and rode with us some distance. As soon as we were out of hearing of the other Indians, she and her brother commenced asking all sorts of questions concerning the girl; whether I thought she would be happy with her own people or not.

Those Indians had learned in some way that somewhere, a long distance away, the white people had great villages, and Nawasa asked if I thought the white girl would be taken to the large cities.

The young Indian and I arrived at our camp about four o'clock that afternoon and found Jim Beckwith in a splendid humor, for he was glad to see me. He had given up all hope of ever seeing me again, for he thought the Apaches had followed me up and killed me. I told him what I had brought the young Indian for, and he was well pleased with the arrangement.

We fitted him out with beads that cost us twenty dollars, and tin pans and blankets, agreeing to come to his village in two weeks for our furs.

When the two weeks were up we took our pack-horses and went to the village, and to our surprise he had traded off the beads and blankets to much better advantage than we could have done ourselves.

For this favor we gave him in compensation two pairs of blankets, four brass finger rings and four strings of beads; and the young fellow thought he had been well treated for his trouble.

It was now getting late in the season, and after buying all the furs the Pima tribe had we commenced making preparations to pull out for Taos, as we had about all the furs we could pack on our horses to advantage, having fourteen pack-horses in all.

We packed up and started, and made the trip without anything of consequence happening on the way. We did not see any hostile Indians and had very good success, only losing one pack and horse while crossing a little stream, the name of which I have forgotten; and arrived at Taos in the latter part of June.

It was late in the afternoon when we rode up to Uncle Kit Carson's home. He and his wife and little child were out on the porch, and as soon as we rode up, both recognized Jim Beckwith, but neither of them knew me, for when they had seen me last I was almost a beardless boy, and now I had quite a crop of beard and was a man of twenty-five years of age.

"Hello, Jim!" were Uncle Kit's first words, and he and his wife came out to the gate to shake hands with him.

"Well, how are you, anyhow; and how have you been since you left, and who is this you have with you?" said Uncle Kit, the last in a low tone of voice.

I had dismounted some yards distant, and on the opposite side of the pack-horse from them. Jim told Uncle Kit that I was a discouraged miner that he had picked up in California, saying: "He don't amount to very much, but I needed some one for company and to help me through with the pack-train, so I brought him along."

By this time I had made my way through the bunch of pack-horses and walked up to Uncle Kit and spoke to him, and I think I got the worst shaking up that I had had for a long time, and I don't think there ever was a father more pleased to see his son return than Uncle Kit was to see me.

Our horses were turned over to the hired man, who took care of them, and the next two days were spent in visiting Uncle Kit and his wife. Of course I had to tell them of the hardships I had undergone during my absence from home; my adventures, narrow escapes, etc.

I learned that Mr. Hughes had died during my absence; I also learned that Johnnie West was at Bent's Fort.

After resting two days we packed up again and started for Bent's Fort. Uncle Kit went along with us to assist in making a good sale of our furs, and we arrived there just in time, as the last train was going out for the season, and we sold them for a good price.

Here I met Jim Bridger, Johnnie West and a number of other acquaintances and friends who supposed I had been killed and scalped by the Indians. I was sorry to learn that Johnnie West, like the majority of the old frontiersmen, had fallen into the habit of drinking up every dollar that he earned.

While we were here, Uncle Kit made a proposition that himself, Jim Beckwith, Jim Bridger and myself take a trip to the head of the Missouri river and put in the winter trapping.

He said he wanted to make this trip and then quit the business, saying: "I have business enough at home to attend to, but I have always had an anxiety to take a trip to the headwaters of the Missouri river."

The four of us returned to Taos, arriving there just in time to celebrate the Fourth of July, arriving on the second, and now I was home again in my fine buckskin suit. The night of the fourth we all attended a big fandango, and had a huge time. I was somewhat over my bashfulness by this time, and by the assistance of Mrs. Carson and two or three other ladies present, I was enabled to get through in pretty good shape. After that night's dancing, I felt that if I were back at the Fort, where I tried to dance my first set, I would show them how dancing first began.

CHAPTER XIX
A WARM TIME IN A COLD COUNTRY.—A BAND OF BANNOCKS CHASE US INTO A STORM THAT SAVES US.— KIT CARSON SLIGHTLY WOUNDED.— BECKWITH MAKES A CENTURY RUN

We remained at Taos until August first, then, all being ready for our northern trip, each man taking his own saddle-horse and five pack horses, we made the start for the headwaters of the Missouri river. We crossed the Platte where it leaves the mountains, and the next day we met a band of Arapahoes, who informed us that the Sioux were on the war-path, and that Gen. Harney was stationed on North Platte with a considerable body of soldiers. The day following, after having crossed the Cache-la-Poudre, we reached Gen. Harney's camp. The General, being a good friend of Uncle Kit and Jim Bridger, insisted on our being his guests, so we took supper with him and camped there for the night.

While at the supper table, Jim Beckwith told the General who I was and what I had been doing the last three years, following which I took Lieut. Jackson's letter from my pocket and handed it to the General. I had never seen the inside of the letter myself. The General read the letter the second time, and looking up at me, he said:

"Yes, I'll give you a job; you can start in to-morrow if you like."

Before I had time to answer him, Uncle Kit spoke up, saying: "General, I have employed him for the next six months and I cannot get along without him."

At this the General said: "Mr. Carson, your business is not urgent and mine is, and I insist on the young man taking a position with me for the remainder of the summer."

I said: "General, I did not show you that letter with the intention of asking you for employment, but simply to show you the standing I have with the people where I have been."

"Young man," he replied, "I don't wish to flatter you, but there is not a man in my service that I could conscientiously give such a letter."

When he saw that we were determined to proceed, he tried to persuade us that we could not make it through, "For," said he, "the whole country is full of hostile Indians between here and there, and they are killing emigrants every day." Which was true.

The following morning we pulled out again, aiming to push through and get into the bad lands as quickly as possible, knowing that when once in there we would not be attacked by a large band of Indians, there being no game in that region for them to live on.

The second day out from Gen. Kearney's quarters, about the middle of the afternoon, we were looking for a place to camp for the night, when we saw eleven Indians coming for us full tilt. Jim Bridger was riding in the lead, I being the hindmost one. Jim being the first to see them, he turned as quick as a wink and we all rode to the center. Each man having a saddle-horse and five pack-horses, they made good breastworks for us, so we all dismounted and awaited the impolite arrival. I drew my rifle down across the back of one of the horses when the Indians were two hundred yards away, and Uncle Kit said: "Don't fire yet. All wait until they get near us, and I will give the word for all to fire at once. Each man take good aim, and make sure of his Indian; use your rifles first and then draw your pistols."

He did not give the word until they were within about one hundred yards of us, and when he did, we all fired. I saw my Indian fall to the ground. We then drew our revolvers, and I got in two more shots before the Indians could turn their ponies so as to get away.

At the first shot with my revolver I did not see the Indian fall, but at the second shot I got my man.

We killed seven from the little band, only leaving four. They seemed to realize at once that they had bit off more than they could chew, and in about three minutes they were out of sight, and that was the last we saw of them.

We did not get a man wounded, and only one horse hurt, and that very slightly.

This was our last trouble with Indians until we were across the Yellowstone.

The next day after crossing that river we saw on our right, about a quarter of a mile away, twenty Crow Indians coming for us. They gave us chase for five or six miles, until we struck suitable ground. As soon as that was obtained we stopped to make a stand, and as soon as they were in sight around the hill they were within gunshot, and we all fired. I think I wounded my Indian in the leg, and killed his horse. Jim Beckwith said he saw three Indians fall to the ground. This, however, was the last trouble we had with the Crow Indians on that trip.

The next day we arrived at Fort Benton, on the Missouri river. There we met a number of trappers in the employ of the Hudson Bay Company, and not an independent trapper in the outfit. Strange, but true, the trappers in the employ of that Company always hated the sight of an independent trapper.

Here we stayed over two days, trying to gather some information as to our route, and, strange as it may seem, we could not find a man who would give us any information as to the route we wished to go, which was only about two hundred miles from there.

Trapping had never been done in that region, and these men knew that this was because of hostile Indians there. They were not men of sufficient principle to even intimate to us that the Indians were dangerous in that section, but let us go on to find it out for ourselves, hoping, no doubt, that the Indians would kill us and that there would be so many independent trappers out of the way. From here we took the divide between the Missouri river and the Yellowstone, aiming to keep on high land in order to steer clear, as much as possible, of hostile Indians.

Uncle Kit said he was satisfied that there was a large basin somewhere in that country, but did not know just where or how to find it.

It was in the evening of the fifth day when we came upon a high ridge, and almost due west of us and far below we could see a great valley, since known as Gallatin Valley, where Bozeman, Mont., now stands.

When we came in sight of this beautiful region, Uncle Kit said: "Boys, this is the country I have been looking for, and I'll assure you if we can get in there and are not molested, we can catch beaver by the hundred."

We had not been bothered by Indians, nor had we seen any sign of them since we left Fort Benton.

We had been on high ground all of the way, and we thought now when once in this valley we would be entirely out of the way of the Crows, and the Bannocks and Blackfoot Indians would be the only tribes to contend with.

From where we first saw the valley, we started to go down the mountain. The next day, as we got lower, we could see plenty of Indian sign. Striking a canyon, that we thought would lead us down to the valley, we gave it the name of Bridger's Pass, which name it has to-day. As we neared the valley we saw more Indian sign, and from the amount of it, it seemed that the country must be alive with them. When within about five or six miles of the valley, we saw a band of Indians to our right, on the ridge.

Jim Bridger said: "Boys, they are Crows, and we are in for it."

They did not come in reach of us, but kept along the ridge above us. We could see by looking ahead that near the mouth of this canyon there was a high cliff of rocks.

We expected to be attacked from those rocks, and we had to be very cautious in passing this point. But to our surprise they did not make the attack. Here we began to see beaver sign in abundance. I don't think that I ever in my life saw as much of it on the same space of ground as I saw there, for every little stream that emptied into that valley was full of beaver dams.

The Indians kept in sight of us until we struck the valley, which was just at sunset. We traveled until dark, when we stopped and built up a big fire. As soon as our fire was burning good we mounted our horses and rode about one mile on to open ground. Dismounting, we loosened all our saddles, both pack and riding- saddles, and picketed all our horses as close together as we could.

We made our bed in the center, keeping a guard out all night. Jim Beckwith was the first man on duty, and my turn came second. By the time I went to relieve Jim the moon was up, and he told me to keep a keen lookout in the direction of the creek, "For," said he, "I am almost sure I saw an Indian in that direction about half an hour ago."

Of course this put me on my guard, and I kept my eye peeled in great shape. About my second trip around the horses I looked in the direction of the creek and thought I saw an Indian coming on all fours.

He would only come a few steps and then stop. Being below me, I could not get him between me and the moon, so I concluded I would meet him half way. I got down on all fours and watched him, and when he would start I would move ahead, keeping my eye on him, and when he would stop I would stop also.

This I did so that to move at the same time he did, he could not hear the noise made by me. When I was close enough I laid flat on the ground, shut my left hand, and placing it on the ground, resting my gun on my fist, took good aim and I got him.

At the crack of my gun the whole crowd were on their feet, and a moment later were at the scene of war. We went to the place where it lay, and beheld a very large white wolf lying there, "dead as a door nail."

This was the first time I had ever made such a mistake, and it was some time before I heard the last of it.

The next morning when we got up, instead of being one band of Indians in sight, there were two. We made up our minds that we had discovered the finest trapping ground in America, and had a poor show to get away from it, but we went ahead and got our breakfast, just as though there were no Indians in sight of us, but we concluded we had better leave this part of the country, so we pulled out southwest across the valley, having no trouble until we struck the West Gallatin river.

Here the beaver dams were so thick that it was difficult to find a place to cross. After prospecting some little time, we struck on a buffalo trail crossing the river, and we concluded to cross on that trail. I was in the lead, but did not proceed far until we saw the mud was so deep that we had to retrace our steps. When we faced about to come back, of course I was thrown into the rear, and just as we had turned the Indians made an attack on us from the brush. I fired four shots at them at short range with my revolver, the others firing at the same time. Just as we were out of the brush, my favorite horse, Mexico, which was the hindmost horse in my string, was shot down, having five or six arrows in his body. I sprang from my saddle and the other boys halted until I cut my dying horse loose from the others, which was only a second's work, and we made a rush for the open ground, which was reached in a few jumps. The Indians did not show themselves on the open ground, but kept hid in the brush. We rode up and down the stream for an hour and a half, but could not find a place that we could cross for Indians and mud. Every place we would attempt to cross, the Indians would attack us from the brush.

This, however, was all an open country, excepting immediately along the stream, where was an immense growth of underbrush. After making several attempts to cross and being driven back, Jim Beckwith proposed that we put spurs to our horses and ride as fast as they could carry us for three or four miles up the river, that we might be able to cross before the Indians would be able to get there, "For," said he, "this brush seems to be full of redskins."

This being agreed to, we all started at full speed up the river, and after running some distance we saw a large buffalo trail leading across the river. Jim Bridger being in the lead, said: "Here is a big buffalo trail, let's try crossing on it." We were about one-fourth of a mile from the river, and Uncle Kit, who from some cause had dropped behind, sang out: "All right, let's hurry and get across and out of the brush on the other side before them redskins get here."

At this we all made a rush for the river, and just as we were going out on the other side the Indians attacked us from the brush. They shot Uncle Kit's hindmost horse down before he was out of the mud and water, and he had to get off in two feet of mud and water to cut his dying horse loose from the string of horses. We killed two Indians here. Uncle Kit, while he was down cutting his horse loose, shot one who was just in the act of striking him with a tomahawk. We made our way to open ground as quick as possible, rode about a half a mile and then stopped and loaded our pistols.

Uncle Kit said: "Boys, how in the world are we to get out of this? The whole country is alive with Indians."

Jim Bridger said: "Kit, you are the man that got us in here, and we will look for you to get us out."

"All right," said Kit, "mount your horses and let's be off." And he gave orders to ride abreast when the ground would permit.

By riding in this manner we could corral quicker. What is meant by corralling is that each man has his string of horses as we have before stated, and when attacked each man rides to the center, and the horses are a great protection to the men in time of battle. We traveled some four or five miles without seeing an Indian, but all this time we were on open ground.

Finally we came to a little stream, a tributary to the Madison river, and when crossing this we were again attacked by the Indians, who were secreted in the brush.

This was a surprise, for we had not seen an Indian since we left the West Gallatin. Here we had a fight that lasted full twenty minutes. We were about the middle of the stream when they opened fire on us.

Uncle Kit said: "Come ahead, boys;" at the same we commenced firing at the Indians, and every foot of that stream had to be contested, from the middle, where they first opened fire on us, to the shore. I saw two dead Indians in the water, and there might have been more, but I did not have time to stop and look for Indians, either dead or alive. I had seen the time that I was hunting for Indians, but at this particular time I didn't feel as though I had lost any.

Uncle Kit was now in the lead and I was bringing up the rear. Just as we were out of the water and he was removing the saddle from his horse, he got two arrows through his buckskin hunting shirt, and was very slightly hurt.

We managed to stand them off until he removed the saddle from the dying horse to another, after which we pulled for open ground, all escaping unhurt, excepting the slight scratch Uncle Kit received from the arrow.

The redskins did not follow us away from the creek.

As soon as we were on open ground we stopped and built a fire and dried our clothing, for we were as wet as drowned rats. To build a fire we had to pull small sagebrush that grew here and there in the open prairie in that country. While we were drying our clothing and eating a lunch, we had our horses feeding near us, but did not dare let them scatter for fear of an attack, which we were liable to experience at any moment. After we had our clothing pretty well dried out and having had a little something in the way of refreshments, on looking off to the northeast about two miles distant, we saw a big band of buffalo and a lot of Indians after them.

We concluded that we had remained here long enough, so we mounted and pulled out again.

The balance of the day we kept on open ground, and saw numerous little bands of Indians, but were not molested by them until late in the afternoon.

About sundown, while traveling down a little narrow valley, all of a sudden about fifteen Indians, all well mounted, made a charge on us. We corralled at once. By this time our horses had learned to corral pretty quick, and when they were in gunshot we opened fire on them. I fired at one with my rifle and got him, for I saw him fall to the ground, and I got another with my pistol. I do not know how many were killed, but they went away a much less number than they came. We all escaped unhurt, but Uncle Kit lost another horse, making in all four horses that day.

We moved on again and traveled about five miles and made another camp, but did not build a fire. Our horses were picketed near camp, and that night we stood guard the same as the night before, but I did not see any Indians crawling up on all fours. The morning following we were off very early, and traveled some four miles before we came to water. Coming to a nice little brook, we stopped and took our breakfast. Here we had a chance to have killed an antelope, but did not dare shoot.

After taking something for the inner man, we proceeded on our way. We did not have any more trouble with Indians, not even seeing any until we got to what is known as Stinking Water or Alder creek, near where Virginia City, Mont., now stands. In traveling down this stream, which is quite crooked, and just as we were rounding one of those points of the hill running down to the creek, riding in the lead I saw two Indian wick-i-ups about half a mile ahead, just in the edge of the brush. I at once gave the signal to turn back, and we got out of sight without being discovered by the Indians.

We turned our course, somewhat, making a circuitous route, and when we were just opposite the wick-i-ups, Jim Bridger and Uncle Kit climbed to the top of the hill, taking my glasses with them, and took in the situation. When they returned to where we were they were feeling much more encouraged, saying: "Thank God we are rid of the Blackfoots and Crows; those are the Bannocks. We are now in their country, and they are not so numerous nor so hostile as the Crows and Blackfoots." That night we camped on Stinking Water, near Lone Butte, picketed our horses close around camp and stood guard the same as the two nights previous.

The next morning we were up early and off again, aiming to cross the main divide and go over to Fort Hall, expecting to find there a great many trappers and raise a crowd sufficient to come back and trap on the Gallatin river this winter.

At that time Fort Hall was a great rendezvous for trappers.

Now we were beginning to feel more encouraged and to think our chances were pretty good, but that evening, while traveling up Beaver Canyon, which, I think the railroad runs up now, from Pocatello, Idaho, to Butte City, Mont., the Bannocks attacked us about fifty strong.

They held us there for about an hour, and had it not been for a thunder storm that came up, I don't think one of us would have got out of that canyon, for they had us completely surrounded. They killed two horses from Jim Bridger's string and wounded Uncle Kit in one shoulder severely.

When the thunder storm came up the Indians were gradually closing in on us, and it commenced to thunder and lightning, and it actually rained so hard that one person could not see another two rods before him.

While it was raining so hard, we mounted and rode out of the canyon.

I never saw it rain harder in my life than it did for a half hour. When we were on open ground and it had quit raining, we stopped, and Uncle Kit said: "Now who says the Almighty didn't save us this time by sending that shower of rain just at the right time?"

That night we camped near the summit of the Rocky Mountains, dividing the waters that run into the Pacific and Atlantic oceans. Uncle Kit suffered all that night from his arrow wound, the arrow going under his shoulder blade, and when we examined the wound we found it much deeper than we had any idea of. This was the last trouble with Indians on that trip.

The next morning we started very early, and were three days making Fort Hall, having no trouble whatever on the way. On arriving at the Fort we were very much disappointed in regard to raising our crowd to go to the head of the Missouri river to trap the coming winter. There were only about twenty trappers at Fort Hall at that time, and they appeared to have no particular objections to living a little while longer. Those of them who had never interviewed the Blackfoot and Crow Indians personally were pretty well acquainted with them by reputation, and they said they did not care to risk their lives in that country. We remained here two weeks, after which time—Uncle Kit's wound getting considerable better—Jim Bridger, Uncle Kit and myself concluded to go on to the waters of Green river and trap the coming winter.

While here, Jim Beckwith fell in with a man by the name of Reese, who said he had trapped on the headwaters of Snake river the winter previous, and that trapping was good there. He induced Beckwith to go to that section of the country, saying it was only one hundred miles from Fort Hall. This trapping ground was immediately across the divide of the Rockies and south of the Gallatin, where the Blackfoot and Crow Indians were so bad, but Reese thought they could get out the next spring before the Indians could get across the mountains.

So he and Beckwith started, and at the same time we pulled out for the head of Green river. They went to the head of Snake river, and I afterwards learned that they trapped there all winter with splendid success, but trapping being so good they stayed too late in the spring. One morning about the last days of April, after they had just eaten their breakfast and were making preparations to go to look after their traps, they were attacked by about one hundred Blackfoot Indians. Reese was killed the first shot, and Jim then saw that his only show was to run, which he did. It was about sunrise when they made the attack. Jim Beckwith fled, with the Indians in hot pursuit. It was claimed to be one hundred miles from there to Fort Hall, and that same evening, before dark, he was in Fort Hall, and he went all the way on foot.

In this run Beckwith burst the veins in his legs in numerous places, making him a cripple for life. The last time I saw him was at his own home, near Denver, Colo., in 1863. At that time he was so badly crippled that he had to walk with two canes, and after telling me the condition he was in, he showed me a number of running sores that were caused by the bursted veins. For Jim Beckwith, now dead and gone, I will say, he was a hero in his day. For bravery he was far above the average, and at the same time he was honorable and upright. He was a man whose word was as good as gold, and one who was possessed of great strength and had a constitution equal to that of a mustang. The worst thing that could be said of Jim Beckwith was that he was his own worst enemy, for he would spend his money for whiskey as fast as he earned it.

Uncle Kit, Jim Bridger and myself wintered on the waters of the Green river and trapped, but had very poor success, this country having been trapped over so much that the beaver were scarce and hard to catch, and Uncle Kit's wound bothered him all winter, and in fact as long as he lived.

After winter had broken up we started for New Mexico, via North Park. Our idea in taking that route was to avoid the hostile Sioux.

We were successful in getting through without having any trouble with Indians, whatever, arriving at Bent's Fort about the first of June. We sold our furs again to Col. Bent and Mr. Roubidoux. Joe Favor having gone out of business, I engaged with Col. Bent and Mr. Roubidoux to go among the Arapahoe Indians to trade for furs and buffalo robes.

CHAPTER XX
CARSON QUITS THE TRAIL.—BUFFALO ROBES FOR TEN CENTS.—"PIKE'S PEAK OR BUST."—THE NEW CITY OF DENVER.— "BUSTED."—HOW THE NEWS GOT STARTED

Uncle Kit Carson pulled out for home and when he was starting he said he had done his last trapping and he was going home to his sheep ranch and take things easy. "For," said he, "I had the wust luck last winter that I ever had in my life, when I had 'lowed to have the best. I'm gittin old enough to quit."

Before he left he told me that whenever I felt like it he wanted me to come to his place and make my home as long as I pleased.

Col. Bent fitted me out with twenty-five pack animals and two Mexican boys to assist me, and I started for the Arrapahoe country, one hundred and twenty-five miles distant. I was supplied with beads, blankets and rings to trade to the Indians for furs and buffalo robes.

On my arrival at the Arrapahoe village I learned that there were not many furs on hand, as the Sioux had been so hostile the past fall and winter that the Arrapahoes had not been able to trap or hunt much, consequently we had to visit all the little hunting parties belonging to that tribe, in order to get furs and robes enough to load our pack train.

After remaining about two weeks I got a fair load and started on my return, making the round trip in little over one month, having had no trouble whatever with Indians or otherwise. On my return to Bent's Fort I found John West, who had been trapping in the Windriver mountains in company with two other men I did not know. They had been successful the past winter and had sold their furs for a good price, and now Johnnie had plenty of money and was having what he termed a glorious good time, spending from ten to forty dollars a day.

After I had settled up with Col. Bent and Mr. Roubidoux I went to Taos with the determination that I would take it easy the balance of this season.

Col. Bent offered to bet me a horse that I would not stay in Taos one month. He told me that if I would go to Taos and rest up a month and return to the fort and hunt for them the balance of the season he would make me a present of a better horse than the other one he gave me, but I told him that he was mistaken, and that he never owned a better horse than Pinto. I knew that Pinto was getting old and had had many a hard day's ride, but I could get on him to-morrow morning after breakfast, and be in Taos before sundown, which was a distance of eighty miles. I made a bargain with them to return to the fort in a month from that time and hunt for them until something else turned up.

On my arrival at Taos I found Jim Bridger stopping with Uncle Kit, and he made me a proposition that we go and stop with the Kiowa tribe that winter and buy furs and buffalo robes. I agreed to that provided that Col. Bent and Mr. Roubidoux would agree to buy the furs and robes of us. They were the only traders in that country since Joe Favor had retired from business.

In one month I returned to the fort as per contract and started in hunting.

There was so much stock around the fort that I had to go from ten to twenty miles to find deer, and sometimes further to find buffalo.

After I had hunted about three weeks Jim Bridger came over to try to make a bargain with the company in regard to buying furs and buffalo robes.

Up to this time the Kiowa had not traded any at this fort. In fact, there had been but little trading done among them, yet they were in the heart of the buffalo country in the fall of the year, being located on the Arkansas river, one hundred miles west from the Big Bend. We made a bargain to work for Bent and Roubidoux by the month, they to furnish us.

They thought the best plan would be to buy a load of robes and return with it, and then go back again, for by so doing we would not have to run chances of being robbed by other tribes as we would by waiting until spring to pack over to the fort.

We started about the first of November for the Kiowa village, with thirty-two pack-horses and a Mexican boy to help us. This was just the time of year that the buffalo were moving south for the winter, and they travel much slower and are much harder to frighten than in the spring when they are traveling the other way. I attributed this to their being so much fatter in the fall of the year, for in the fall one would never see a poor buffalo except it was either an old male or one that had been crippled; and their hides are much more valuable than those taken off in the spring.

On arriving at the village we found that the Indians had a new chief, whom neither of us were acquainted with. His name was Blackbird. The old chief, Black Buffalo, who fed us on dog meat when we were on our way from St. Louis to Taos, ten years before, having died, Blackbird was appointed in his place, and we found him to be a very intelligent Indian. He said his people were glad to have us come among them and that they would be pleased to trade with us.

We stayed there about two weeks before offering to buy a hide or fur of them, but would show our goods quite frequently in order to make them anxious, and by doing so we would be able to make a better bargain with them.

After staying there about two weeks we told the chief that on a certain day we would be ready to trade with his people, putting the date off about one week.

When the day arrived the Indians came in from all quarters to trade furs and robes, bringing from one to one dozen robes to the family. The squaws brought the robes, and the bucks came along to do the trading, and we got many a first-class robe for one string of beads, which in St. Louis would cost about ten cents. We traded for enough furs in one day to load our entire pack-train of thirty-two horses.

The next morning we loaded up our furs and pulled out, telling the chief that we would be back in one moon—meaning in their language, one month—which would keep us busy, it being about four hundred miles to Bent's Fort, and as we were heavily loaded we would have to travel slow. The Mexican boy would ride ahead and the pack horses would follow him, while Jim and I brought up the rear. We experienced no trouble in getting all the buffalo meat we wanted, for those beasts were quite tame at this season of the year, and they would often come near our camp. So near, in fact, that we could sit in camp and kill our meat.

Upon our arrival at the fort Col. Bent and Mr. Roubidoux were well pleased with the success of the trip, and we at once started back after the second load. We found more furs and robes there awaiting our arrival than we could load on our horses. In all we made four trips that winter, and Col. Bent told me some time afterward that they cleared a thousand dollars on each cargo.

When spring came Jim Bridger and I went to Taos and visited Uncle Kit for about a month.

This was now the spring of 1859 and the excitement over the gold mines around Pike's Peak was running high. We all knew where Pike's Peak was, for any day when it was clear we could see it very plainly from Bent's Fort or Taos, but we did not know just where the mines were. Jim proposed that we take a trip out there and see about the mines. So we talked the matter over until I was finally attacked with that disease which was then known as "the gold fever."

About the first of June we made a break for the gold fields. We crossed the Arkansas river near Fountain ca-booyah (or something like that)—(Fountain qui Bouille, Boiling Fountain)—and did not go far from there until we struck a wagon road, which showed there had been much travel, and we could see that it had not been long since a wagon passed.

We were very much surprised at a wagon road in this portion of country, but there it was just the same. We did not travel on this road very far until we overtook a large train of emigrants, and on making inquiry we learned that they were on their way to Pike's Peak.

Jim Bridger laughingly remarked: "If you are not careful you will pass Pike's Peak before you go there, for there is the mountain," pointing to the Peak, the foot of which we were just then passing. At this another man said: "We are going to Cherry creek to the mines. Do you know how far it is?"

I told him it was twenty miles to the head of Cherry creek. He then asked me how far it was to Denver. I told him I had never heard of any creek or river by that name in this country. "But," he said, "I mean Denver City." But Jim and I had never heard of the place. He said Denver City was on Cherry creek in the gold mines.

We passed on, crossing the main divide between the Arkansas and the Platte rivers, striking the head of Cherry creek, then traveled down Cherry creek to the mouth, on a now well-beaten wagon road, the dust in places being six inches deep or more.

When we were within a mile of the mouth of Cherry creek I looked ahead, and for the first time I saw Denver, there being then as I supposed about fifty tents and campers' houses in the place. We stopped to take a look around and saw people coming in, every hour of the day, over the Platte and Arkansas river routes, and could see all kind of conveyances from a hand cart to a six-horse team. While there I saw a number of carts come in drawn by men alone, all the way from two to eight men to the cart.

After stopping around Denver two days and taking in the sights, we pulled out for the mountains to a place called Gregory, about forty miles from Denver, where it was reported they were mining.

The mines were located on North Clear creek and there were only two claims being worked.

Gregory, the man that this little camp was named for, was working a claim and said he was taking out some gold, and a man by the name of Greene Russell was working another claim.

They were both old Georgia miners.

This man Russell told me how the excitement got started. He said that himself, Gregory and Dr. Russell, a brother of his, and three other men had come out there the fall before, and early that season had discovered gold on Cherry creek, and also a little on the mountain stream where they were then at work. Dr. Russell being a man of family, concluded to return to his home that fall. He and the rest of the crowd cautioned him to say nothing about what they had struck, for they did not consider they had found anything to warrant an excitement and a stampede, as it was termed in mining parlance. The Doctor promised he would not mention it even to his most intimate friends. But it seems he did not keep his word, but commenced to spread the news as soon as he struck the settlements, telling wonderful stories of the gold around Pike's Peak, which set the people wild. They seemed to think there had been another California struck which caused a repetition of the stampede ten years before. During the winter the news spread all over the State and they came from every quarter.

Russell continued: "Now you can see the effect of it. If I had known my brother would have told such outrageous stories I would not have allowed him to go home." He said he thought there were a few claims outside of the ones they were working that would pay, but beyond that he did not think it would amount to anything.

After remaining here one week we concluded we had gold mining enough to last us some time, so we started back for the foot of the mountains, and the first night we camped at the place where Golden now stands, the place where South Clear creek flows from the mountains.

At this time there were at least five hundred wagons to be seen at one sight, camped on this creek. We camped near the crossing of Clear creek, and there was almost a constant stream of people coming in.

Late that evening four men came into camp with four yoke of oxen, a wagon, and an outfit for mining and with a good suppy of grub— enough to last them a whole season. They camped that night a few yards from us. On finding that we had just returned from the mines they came over to learn what news we had. We told them what we had seen and what Mr. Russell told us.

After they had heard our story, one of them said. "Well, boys, I'm a goin' back to Missouri. What are the balance of you goin' to do?"

They talked the matter over for some time and finally all concluded that old Missouri was a pretty good country and they would all start back in the morning.

One of the crowd said: "What will we do with our provisions? We can't haul it back for our cattle are so tender footed now that they can hardly travel." Another said: "What we do not want ourselves we will give to those hand-cart men over there." But another one in the crowd who perhaps was more like the dog in the manger that could not eat the hay himself nor would not let the cows eat it, spoke up and said: "No, we will not do any such thing! What we do not want to take along to eat on our way back we will throw in the creek."

The next morning after they had eaten breakfast two of them got up into the wagon and selected what provisions they wanted to take along with them, after which they threw the remainder out on the ground and the other two carried it and threw it into the creek. It consisted of flour, dried fruit, bacon, sugar, and I noticed one ten gallon keg of molasses.

I was told that this was an everyday occurrence. As we had seen the elephant and had about all the mining we wanted, for awhile, at least, we saddled up our horses and started for Taos, by the way of Bent's Fort.

Three days' ride took us to Bent's Fort, and we had a thousand and one questions to answer, for this was the first news they had got from the mines around Pike's Peak.

CHAPTER XXI
A FIGHT WITH THE SIOUX.—HASA, THE MEXICAN BOY, KILLED.—MIXED UP WITH EMIGRANTS SOME MORE.— FOUR NEW GRAVES.—SUCCESSFUL TRADING WITH THE KIOWAS

While at Fort Bent we bargained again to go and trade with the Kiowas, on the same terms that we were employed upon the preceding winter, and we could commence at any time we pleased.

We then started for Taos, and when we got there found Uncle Kit suffering very much with his last arrow wound. The doctor had told him that it had never healed inside and that it might be the death of him.

We remained at Taos until time to go to the fort, doing nothing in particular, but hunting a little and occasionally attending a fandango. During this time, however, unbeknown to us and the people at the fort, the Comanches and Sioux had been fighting among themselves, having been so bold as to come on to the Arkansas river and murder a number of white people. Had we known this we should not have made the attempt to go over that country. Or had Bent and Roubidoux known it they would not have asked us to go. But, somehow, it seemed always my luck not to see trouble until I was right in it.

On our arrival at the fort they were anxious to get us fitted out and started as soon as possible. Mr. Roubidoux said: "Last winter you made four trips for us; now every extra trip you make this winter we will give you fifty dollars extra, apiece," which we thought a great layout.

We started out with thirty-two pack animals and the same Mexican boy as assistant that we had the previous winter.

While passing through the Comanche country we met a young man of that tribe with whom I was on good terms, having done him a favor during the war between his tribe and the Utes, for which he felt very grateful to me. After learning where we were going, he said: "Look out for the Sioux, for they have killed lots of white people this fall near Pawnee Rock." But he did not tell us that his tribe and the Sioux were at war.

When we had passed nearly through the Comanche country we thought they were all west of us, for we saw where a large band of Indians had crossed the road going South. This we did not exactly understand, for we well knew that neither the Comanches nor Kiowas had hunt-parties out this time of year, as the buffalo were moving South, and the Indians could kill all they wanted near the villages.

It was about noon when we crossed the Indian trail and that was the general topic of conversation the balance of the day. If they had been on foot we could easily have told what tribe they belonged to by their moccasin tracks, but they all being on horseback left us to guess.

We made an early camp so that if it became necessary we could move that evening, but we built no fire.

As soon as we had decided on our camping place and while Jim and Hasa, the Mexican boy, were unpacking and arranging the camp, I rode about two miles from camp to high ground to look for Indians. When I was on the highest point I could find, I saw a little band of Indians coming from the South, and making their way for the river below us. They were about ten miles away and I could not tell by looking through my glasses just the exact number, but I could see them plain enough to tell they were not Comanches.

On my return to camp I told Jim Bridger what I had seen and he at once declared that they were Sioux, and said we were sure to have trouble with them before long.

We decided to remain there that night, and I agreed that I would stand guard while Jim and Hasa slept. I stood guard until the morning star rose, and I turned in, telling Jim to get an early breakfast and call me, which he did. The boy brought in our horses, saddled them and tied them near camp. The pack animals were also feeding near camp.

Just as we had finished our breakfast and it was getting good daylight, I cast my eyes in the direction of our horses and saw that a number of them had raised their heads and were looking off down the river as though they had seen something. I sprang to my feet and saw nine Indians coming up the river in the direction of our camp, but they were apparently sneaking along slowly. I could see at once by their movements that they did not think they were discovered yet. I said to Jim: "The Sioux are on us," and he sprang to his feet, saying, "Let us mount our horses and meet them before they get among our pack horses," which we did, at the same time telling Hasa to keep the horses together.

We started to meet them on the dead run, and I wish to say here now, that Jim Bridger, though a very brave man, was very exciteable when in an Indian fight, and as we started I said to him: "Now Jim, for God's sake keep cool this time and make every shot count."

When within about a hundred yards of the Indians, and our horses doing their best, I raised my rifle and fired, killing the leader dead. I then drew my pistol and raised the yell. About that time, from some cause, Jim's horse shied off to the right, so when we met the Indians he and I were about thirty or forty yards apart. Jim claimed that his horse scared at something in the sage brush.

Two of the Indians that seemed to be the best mounted made a break for our horses, which I discovered after I had fired two shots from my pistol. I wheeled my horse and made a rush for them, leaving Jim to take care of the other three that we had not yet killed. But the redskins had got too far the start of me, and being on good animals they beat to the pack horses, and before I got in gunshot of them they had killed both the boy and his horse. Had the poor boy kept his presence of mind he might have saved himself, but I think he got excited and did not try to get away.

I got one of them, but the other having the fastest horse, outran me and made his escape. I think he had the fastest horse I ever saw under an Indian in my life. Jim Bridger killed one of the remaining three, and the others got away. Three out of nine escaped, and had it not been for Jim's horse getting scared I don't think they would have killed our Mexican boy.

We dug a grave and buried the poor fellow as best we could under the circumstances, scalped the Indians, packed up and pulled out, leaving the poor unfortunate lad to rest on the lonely banks of the Arkansas river. The Indians we left a prey to the many wild animals that roamed the hills and valleys.

We traveled on with heavy hearts, expecting at any time to be attacked again by another band of these "noble red men," fearing that we might not be so successful the next time.

In the afternoon we came to where the Indians had had another fight with what we supposed, and which afterwards proved to have been emigrants, returning from Pike's Peak. Here we saw four fresh graves, and from the general appearance of things we concluded that the fight had been in the morning, which also proved to be the case.

We were now satisfied that the big trail we had seen the day before was made by Sioux, and that they had split up into small bands to catch small trains of emigrants.

Being satisfied that these emigrants were not far ahead of us, we made up our minds to push on and try to overhaul them, as much for our own protection as anything else.

Jim Bridger told me to take the lead and ride as fast as I wished, and he would make the pack animals keep up; also telling me when on high ground to take my glasses and look for Indians.

After traveling about two hours, putting in our best licks, we came in sight of the train. We then pushed on with new courage and overtook the emigrants just as they were going into camp for the night. I rode up and asked if they had any objections to our camping with them. "Certainly not," replied one of their crowd, "and if you can fight Indians we will be pleased to have you camp and travel with us also."

We dismounted, unpacked and turned our pack animals loose with the emigrants' stock, but picketed our saddle animals near camp. Those people told us of their fight that morning with the Indians. Just as they were hitched up and were in the act of pulling out, the Indians attacked them, about forty strong. They only had twenty- four men and the Indians killed four of their number, and theirs were the graves we had seen that morning.

They didn't have an Indian scalp, nor did they know whether or not they had killed an Indian.

Jim then told them about our fight with the nine Sioux and of losing our Mexican boy. "But," said he, "to show that we got revenge look as this collection of hair," and he produced the six Indian scalps we had taken.

Jim added that if his horse had not got scared upon making the charge, we would have got them all before they could have reached the boy.

They offered to furnish two men to look after our pack-train if we would scout for their train and travel with them as far as we were to go their route, which was about one hundred and fifty miles.

There were eight wagons in the train, composed of two and four horse teams.

When we were ready to start Jim told me to go ahead, saying: "You have a pair of glasses and your eyes are better than mine, and I will bring up the rear, so there will be no danger of a surprise party."

This being agreed to, I started ahead of the train and rode about five miles in advance all the time, keeping my eyes peeled for Indians. In the forenoon I saw a small band of the savages, but they were a long way off and were traveling in the same direction we were. I was sure they could not see us, for I could only see them faintly through my glasses.

That evening we made an early camp at a place we named Horse-shoe Bend, and I am told that the place is mentioned yet by that name. It is a big bend in the Arkansas river almost encircling two or three hundred acres, and where we camped it was not more than a hundred yards across from one turn of the river to the other.

That night we drove all our horses into the bend and did not have to guard them or keep out a camp guard. I remained out in the hills, about three miles from camp, until dark, selecting a high point and with my glasses watching all over the country for Indians. The boys were all well pleased when I returned and told them there were no red-skins anywhere near, and that they all could lie down and sleep that night. They turned in early.

The next morning we broke camp early, and about eleven o'clock came on to four emigrant wagons returning from Pike's Peak. The Indians had stolen the horses.

There were sixteen men in the party and they had been there three days and had not been two miles away from camp. They made some kind of arrangement with the train we were with to haul their things to St. Joe, Missouri, and left their four wagons standing by the roadside.

We had no more trouble while with this train, and everything moved along nicely.

When we were near Pawnee Rock, where we were to leave the train, and some twenty miles from the Kiowa village, I met about thirty Kiowa Indians going out to run the buffalo near there. Of course they all knew me, and after shaking hands we stopped to await the arrival of the train. When it came in sight and the men saw the Indians all around me they thought I had been taken prisoner. They at once corralled their wagons for a fight, and all the talking Jim Bridger could do would not make them believe otherwise, until he rode out to where we were. When he told me this I thought to have a little sport with the boys before leaving the train, and I proposed to Jim that we start to the wagons with the Indians riding on either side of us, so as to make it appear they had taken both of us prisoner. But Jim thought it would not do, as they were so excited they would shoot at our Indians before we were near the wagons. So we rode to the train and told the emigrants that these Indians would not molest them, and that they were my friends.

When I told the Indians the cause of their corralling their wagons, they all had a hearty laugh and called the men squaws. The Kiowas said that their people would be glad to see us at their village, and that they had plenty of robes to trade for beads, rings and blankets. So here we bade the emigrants good-bye, they keeping the Sante Fe trail east, while we turned due south, and in company with the thirty Kiowas, rode that evening to their own village. Chief Blackbird met us at the outer edge of the village and invited us to his wick-i-up. We told him that we had come to trade with his people, and that in four days we would be ready for business.

Jim Bridger and I had talked the matter over concerning this tribe and the Sioux, for we well knew that if they and the Sioux were on friendly terms we would get home safe, if not, we would have a hard time of it.

I proposed to Jim that we make Blackbird a present of something, and while he was in the best of humor I would ask him the question. Jim thought it a capital idea, and before supper I went to our cargo and got three rings and three strings of beads. After supper I gave one string of beads and one ring to Blackbird, one to his wife and one to his eldest daughter, who was about grown. We then sat down and had a social smoke and a friendly chat. By this time Blackbird was beginning to think I was a pretty good fellow, so I asked him if the Sioux were good Indians. He said: "Yes, the Sioux are my friends."

That was all I wanted to know, and I did not ask him any more questions, nor did I tell him of our trouble with the nine Sioux. I told him we wanted to hire four young men from his tribe to go to the fort with us. He said: "All right, I'll see tomorrow."

Our idea in wanting the young Kiowas along, after finding they were on good terms with the Sioux, was that we knew when we were in company with the Kiowas the Sioux would not give us any trouble.

The day following, in the afternoon, Blackbird came to us and told us that there were four young men who wanted to go with us and asked how long we would be gone. We told him we might be gone one moon, perhaps not so long. He wanted to know what Indian country we would pass through. I told him none but the Comanches, for they were terribly afraid of Navajoes. We assured him that we would not pass through their country.

On the day appointed for the sale of our goods, the robes came in by the hundreds. I never saw anything equal it.

We conducted our sale something like an auction. I would hold up a string of beads and show them to the crowd; an Indian would step forward and offer a robe for two strings of beads. Another would offer a robe for one string. This was our idea for appointing a certain day for trading with them, for the more Indians present the better prices we were able to get for our goods.

We went there this time with about the amount of goods we had always taken before to trade for a train load of robes, and we sold our entire stock the first day. We could have traded ten times that amount. Moreover, we got about one-half more than we could pack at one trip.

We knew before we started in to sell that there was a greater number of robes in the village than at any time we had visited it before, as we had been pretty well over the village, and I had never seen the like of robes and dry buffalo meat before, nor have I since. Every wick-i-up was hanging full. The Indians said it had been the best season for buffalo they had seen for years.

I never saw people more busy than the squaws were. All were dressing buffalo hides, and every family had from three to one dozen robes, and this was the best day's sale we ever had, as it seemed that the Indians were crazy for the rings and beads.

I just mention these facts to show the reader how the people took advantage of those Indians, for at that time they did not know the value of money and had no use for it except as ornaments. They would pay a big price for a half dollar, but every one they got hold of they would hammer out flat, punch two holes through it and put it on a string; then the chief or some of his family would wear them on their backs or fasten them to their hair and let them hang down their backs. I have seen strings of flattened out half dollars two feet long worn by the chief or some member of his family.

When we went to pack up we could only get two-thirds of our robes on the animals so we left the remainder in charge of Blackbird, and he agreed to look after them until we returned. I told him if he would take good care of them I would bring him a big butcher knife when I came back.

So we started for Bent's Fort accompanied by four young Kiowas. We had loaded our horses unusually heavy this trip, each animal packing thirty robes.

Two of the Indians rode in front of the pack-train with me and the other two behind with Jim. Our idea in traveling that way was that in case we should meet a band of Sioux, these young Indians would tell them we were their friends, and no matter how bitter they felt toward us they would pass on.

We traveled three days before we saw any Sioux. It was our custom to always stop and unpack and let our horses rest and feed about an hour.

That day we had just unpacked and turned our horses loose to feed and were ready to eat a cold lunch, when we looked up the ridge and saw twenty Sioux Indians coming down the ridge in the direction of our camp. I told one of the Indians that we had better go and meet them. He said he would go and for me to stay in camp. I told him to tell them to come down to camp and get something to eat. So he started off in a trot to meet them, and when he came up to them he stood and talked with them for some time, after which they turned and rode off in another direction. When the Indian boy returned I asked him why they did not come down to camp and have some dinner. He said they had plenty to eat and were in a hurry.

Jim Bridger said to me in our own language: "If we had not had those young Kiowas with us by this time we would have been in a hurry, too." These were the last Sioux we saw on the whole trip.

When we returned to the fort and reported our troubles to Col. Bent and Mr. Roubidoux, they felt very bad over the loss of the Mexican boy, Hasa, but they complimented us on the way we had managed. They asked me what I had agreed to pay the Indians. I told them I had not made any bargain whatever, and that we had not agreed to pay them anything, nor had they asked it. But we thought that under the circumstances we did not consider it safe to attempt to make another trip that fall or winter without an escort of that kind, and we couldn't expect those Indians to make the trips free of charge. Col. Bent told me to make my own bargain with them, and he would pay the bill whatever it might be.

This was the first time these young Indians had ever been in civilization, so I took them around the place and took particular pains to show them everything. When we had been all around and I had showed them everything out doors, I took them into the kitchen of the hotel. When they saw the cook getting supper on the stove they said it was no good, for they could not see the fire and they did not understand how cooking could be done without it.

After they had seen all there was to be seen I took them in where the two proprietors were, and after telling them that they would hire them all winter, providing they did not ask too much, I asked them what they were going to charge us for the trip they had already made.

The most intelligent one spoke up and said: "Give me one string of beads and one butcher knife for the trip already made, and give me one butcher knife for the next trip." I then asked the others if they were satisfied with that, and they said they were; so I paid them off by giving them a butcher knife that cost about fifty cents in St. Louis and one string of beads that would perhaps cost ten cents. They thought they had been well paid for their trouble, and I could see that they had not expected so much. This was no doubt their first experience in hiring out.

The next morning Col. Bent and Mr. Roubidoux said to Jim and I: "Now boys, we will make you a present," telling us that their horses were in the corrall, and for us to go and pick out a saddle horse apiece. They told us that all the horses in the corrall were theirs, and we might take our choice, and that we could turn our other horses into the herd for as long as we liked.

I selected a black horse and saddled him, and he seemed to be quiet and gentle.

There were some trappers at the fort who were going to South Park to trap the following winter. When I led the horse out to get on him they asked if it was mine. "Yes," I said. They asked what price I had set on him, and I said one hundred dollars. They said they would give me that for him if I would wait for my money until spring when they returned from South Park. I asked them if they were going to trap for Col. Bent and Mr. Roubidoux, and they said they were. We then walked into the store and I asked Col. Bent and Mr. Roubidoux if they would go these men's security for one hundred dollars. They said they would, and I told the trappers the horse was theirs. Mr. Roubidoux asked me if it was the horse he had given me. I told him it was and he said: "You did well, for I bought that horse of an emigrant last summer and have never been able to get any money out of him. I think you will have to take a lot of my horses to sell on commission, for I see right now you can beat me selling horses all hollow."

We remained at the Fort three days this time, after which we rigged up and started for the Kiowa nation again with more goods to trade for buffalo robes. We made the trip in eleven days, being the quickest we had yet made over the road.

We found the chief in an excellent humor, and he was as well pleased over his new butcher knife as a boy would be over his first pair of red topped boots.

We found the Indians anxious to trade robes for our trinkets and we had no trouble in getting a load and more than we could pack again. We made five trips that fall and winter with the very best success, keeping those same four Indians with us all winter.

CHAPTER XXII
A TRIP TO FORT KEARNEY—THE GENERAL ENDORSES US AND WE PILOT AN EMIGRANT TRAIN TO CALIFORNIA.— WOMAN WHO THOUGHT I WAS "NO GENTLEMAN."—A CAMP DANCE

Jim Bridger proposed that he and I make a trip to Fort Kearney together, and remain there until the emigrants began to come along, thinking that perhaps the Sioux would be so bad on the plains again that summer that we might get a layout scouting for trains going to California. Both of us were well acquainted with a greater part of the country to be traveled over, and there were few other men as well posted as to where the Indians were likely to make attacks, which was one of the most essential requirements in scouting with a train.

About the first of April we started, by the way of Denver City, for Fort Kearney, and as it had been nearly a year since we had seen the first named place we found quite a change there. Instead of a tented town, of shreds and patches, we saw a thriving village that had some quite comfortable wooden houses and an air of distinct civilization. To-day Denver is probably the best built city of its size in the world, but there was a time after this present visit of mine and Bridger's when the place became almost deserted. That was when the Union Pacific railroad was being constructed to Cheyenne, leaving Denver one hundred and eight miles due south. Then, all the people in Denver who could raise any sort of a team, took their household goods and gods, and in some cases the houses, and struck out for Cheyenne. Many who were too poor to get away became enormously rich, afterward, from that very fact, for they became possessed of the ground, and when the Kansas Pacific railroad was projected, and afterward constructed, Denver took on such a boom that real estate nearly went out of sight in value. The poor ones became wealthy, and nearly all of the Cheyenne stampeders returned. Following this, some years afterward, the discovery of silver carbonates in California Gulch, where Leadville now stands, gave Denver another boom that made the place the Queen city of the Plains, for good and all.

We reached Fort Kearney before the emigrants had got that far out, and found Gen. Kearney in command. He was glad to see us, and told us that if we needed any references to send the parties to him and he would give us a send-off that would be likely to fix us all right, and we knew that it would.

"I predict more trouble," said he, "on the plains this summer than there ever has been in any season previous to this, from the fact that the northern Sioux are, even at this early date, breaking up into little bands, and no doubt for the express purpose of capturing small bands of emigrants crossing the plains the coming summer."

The first train that came along was from Illinois and Missouri. It was on the way to California and was composed of sixty-four wagons. The company was made up of men, women and children, nearly all of the men having families. They camped about a mile from the fort, and at near sundown Gen. Kearney proposed that we go over and see the ladies. So we rode over—the General, Jim Bridger and I.

Arriving at the camp we were astonished at seeing that the emigrants had no system whatever in forming their camp or corralling their wagons and stock, all being scattered here and there, hodge-podge.

I remarked to Gen. Kearney that they had certainly not met with any trouble from Indians so far, else they would have been more careful. The General replied that they would learn before they got much further.

When we arrived at their camp quite a crowd gathered around us, and among the balance was one man apparently forty years old, who walked up to Gen. Kearney and said: "How are you, John?" that being the General's first name.

Gen. Kearney looked at him for a moment, then shook hands with him and said: "You seem to know me, but you have the best of me. If I ever saw you before I don't remember when or where."

The gentleman then said: "When we used to go to school together you were the only boy in my class that I could not throw down, but I believe that I could to-day."

They had been schoolmates in Ohio and this was the first time they had met since they quit school. "Of course," said Gen. Kearney, "you had the advantage of me, for you knew I was out here, while I never dreamed of you being in this country."

We soon learned that the emigrants had heard about the hostility of the Sioux Indians, and were dreading them very much.

After the General and his old schoolmate talked over by-gone days for awhile they commenced asking him all sorts of questions relative to the Indians on ahead.

The General gave his views regarding the outlook for the coming summer, and after having "said his say" about the noble red men, a number of the emigrants thought they would turn back the next morning.

Gen. Kearney said to them: "Here are two as good mountaineers as may be found west of the Missouri river and I believe that you could hire them to go the entire trip with you at a reasonable figure, and I feel sure they will be able to render you valuable service, while passing through the Indian country, they being well posted as to where the Indians would be most likely to make an attack. They are also well informed as to water, wood and grass, and the different drives to be made between camping places, &c."

When we were just ready to mount our horses to return to the Fort for supper, a number of the men came to Jim and me and asked how much per month or per day we would take to go with them as scouts through the Indian country. We told them to get their supper over and call their men together, and we would go back to the Fort and get our supper, after which we would come down to their camp again and talk matters over and see if we could make a bargain. By this time a number of ladies had gathered around, and among them was an old lady who said: "You two gentlemen with buckskin coats on can come and take supper with us in our tent."

Gen. Kearney said: "You had better accept the lady's hospitality, for you have a great deal to talk about."

We thought this a capital idea and took supper with the emigrants, and the General returned to his quarters But before going he gave all, both ladies and gentlemen, a cordial invitation to come to the Fort the next day and pay him a friendly visit.

After all were through eating supper, Jim Bridger asked how many men they had in their train, but no one was able to tell. When he asked who their captain was a man replied that they did not know they had to have a captain. Jim with an oath said: "What in the name of God do you think those soldiers over there would do without a captain, or at least an officer of some kind?"

Then he told them they had better form in line and see how many men they had, and elect five men to transact business with us. They formed in line and counted and there were one hundred and forty men in the train, and not one of them had ever been on the plains before, and, of course, not one of them had ever seen a hostile Indian.

They then proceeded to elect the five men to transact the business with us, after which Jim turned to me and said: "Now make your proposition." I suggested that as he was the oldest, he should go ahead and make the bargain, whereupon he said: "All right. Gentlemen, I will make you an offer; if you see fit to accept it all right, and if not there is no harm done. We will scout for you for six dollars per day from here to the foot of the Sierra Nevada Mountains, and you board us and herd our horses with yours. We must have charge of the entire train, and we want at least two or three days in which to organize and drill before leaving this camp, and after the lapse of five days if this community is not satisfied with our work, we will quit, and not charge you a cent for what we shall have done at that time, and if our work is satisfactory we will expect our money every Saturday night, for it is the money we are after and not the glory. Now, gentlemen, take the matter under consideration and give us an answer to-morrow morning after breakfast."

On the following morning one of the men from the train came to the Fort very early to inform us that they had decided to accept our proposition.

We told him to go back to camp and have all the teams hitched up and we would be down after breakfast and put in a few hours drilling the teamsters.

We numbered the wagons by putting the figures on the end-gates of the wagons, telling each teamster to remember his number, and when forming a corrall, no matter what the occasion might be, for the even numbers to turn to the right and the odd numbers to the left, forming a circle with the teams inside of the corrall or circle of wagons.

For the benefit of the reader who has not had the fortune—or misfortune, whichever he deems it—to have traveled in an Indian country where the corrals are necessary in order to protect the traveler from the Indians, I will give a more detailed description of how they are formed:

By having each wagon numbered every man knew his place in the train, and when it was necessary to corral, one-half of the teams would turn to the right and the other half to the left. Each would swing out a little distance from the road and the two front teams- -numbers one and two— would drive up facing each other. All the rest of the wagons would drive up forming a circle, with the teams on the inside of the corrall, and the back or hind ends of the wagons pointing outwards. The two hindmost teams would now swing together as in the front, closing the rear gap in the circle. This also served the purpose of a pen in which to run the stock in the event of an attack, thus preventing the possibility of a stampede.

Our object in drilling the teamsters was to teach them how to form a corrall quickly in case of an attack while under way.

After drilling a while we told the committee to select eight men from their train to assist in scouting, we preferring young men with horses of their own or such as could get horses, and those men to be exempt from guard duty except in cases of emergency. They proceeded at once to select the eight men for assistant scouts, after which we told them to appoint a sergeant, or whatever they chose to call him, to command, respectively, every platoon of twenty men, the hundred and forty being organized in such squads.

This was the hardest task, apparently, for the committee, as no one wanted to serve in that capacity, each one having some excuse or other, but they finally completed the appointments and then Jim said to me:

"Now, Will, you take entire charge of the scouts, and I will take charge of the balance of the men," telling me that in the day time on the move he would assist me in scouting all he could, but after the train was corralled to handle the scouts to suit myself.

I told the newly appointed scouts to saddle their horses and we would have a little exercise. I took a piece of pine board box cover, sharpened it and stuck it into a prairie dog hole. This board was about twelve inches wide and two or two and a half feet long. I drew a mark about thirty feet from the board, telling them to fire when they reached this mark. I had them all mount and start about a hundred yards from the board, and when at this mark to fire at the board while at full speed, each taking his turn.

Out of eight shots only one hit the board, and that was made by the last one that fired.

I told them that such shooting would never do at all if they expected to fight Indians, so I mounted my horse and asked them which hand I should use my pistol in. All cried out: "Use your left hand!" I said: "All right, I will shoot across my bridle reins." I had one of the boys get on his horse and whip mine down to a dead run, and with my pistol in my left hand I put two bullet holes through the board while passing it.

This was a surprise to all of them, as they had never seen shooting done that way before, but they were all eager to learn.

After practicing this feat awhile I started in to teach them to mount quick. This was the hardest thing for them to learn, and all of their horses were trained to stand perfectly still until they straightened up in the saddle.

And here I will say that in scouting it is very essential to have a horse that is quick to start.

The way we used to train our horses to start was by having some one stand behind them with a whip and strike them just as we jumped into the saddle. This taught both horse and rider to be very agile, as we would have to get on our horses almost on the dead run when in close quarters with the Indians.

That evening near sunset another train drove up from Missouri. There were twenty wagons and they were desirous of joining our train. The committee came to us to see what they thought of letting them in. We told the committee that we were willing to take them in by their paying one dollar a day. This being agreeable to the committee and newcomers agreeing to pay the per diem we took them in.

The morning of the third day, after organizing we pulled out, Jim Bridger staying with the train all day. I dropped four of my men behind the train, telling them to keep about half a mile from it and at the first sight of Indians to get to the train as quick as possible and report to Jim Bridger, who would signal me at once by firing two shots in quick succession, otherwise there was to be no shooting in the train during the time we were in a hostile country.

All went smoothly until the fifth day. We were then on the north side of the South Platte and my new assistant scouts were beginning by this time—or at least some of them were—to be anxious for a little sport with the Indians.

I had told them the day before that they might expect to see Indians at any time now, as we were then in the Sioux country.

The morning of the fifth day I started two scouts ahead of the train, telling them to keep about two miles ahead of the wagons, two to drop behind the train and two south, and to keep on the highest ground they could find. Taking the other two with me I struck out north of the road, this being where I most expected to find Indians. After riding five or six miles we came up on to a high point where I took out my glasses and made a survey of the surrounding country. I saw a large band of Indians traveling almost parallel with the wagon road and moving in the same direction the train was going. I should judge them to have been about ten miles away. Anyway, they were so far that I could not tell their number, but I thought there were in the neighborhood of one hundred and fifty in the band.

I showed them to my associates by allowing them to look through my glasses. I then showed them a route to take and designated a certain point for them to go to and remain, until I should come to them, and I started alone after the Indians to try to get closer to them and also get their general course of travel so as to come to some conclusion as to what their intentions were. I succeeded in getting within about four miles of them and at getting a good view of them as they were passing over a little ridge. I saw that they had no squaws with them, and I knew then they were on the war-path.

After taking a good look at the redskins I got back to my two scouts as quickly as possible. Shortly after joining them I saw nine Indians coming toward the road, about three or four miles away from us, we being between them and the road, making them about eight miles from the road.

I started one of my men to the train on a double quick to inform Jim Bridger of what we had seen and also to bring at least four or five good men and horses back with him, telling him where to meet us on his return.

I was thoroughly convinced that these nine Indians we had seen were scouts for the large band ahead of us, and my object was to capture them and not let one of them get back to the big band of warriors that we had seen.

The other scout and I secreted our horses and watched the nine Indians on the sly, until the other man returned bringing three men with him from the train. By this time the Indians were within two miles of the train, and we had swung around so as to come in behind them and were only about a half mile from them. We followed them leisurely until they were passing over a little ridge near the train, when we put spurs to our horses and rode at a lively gait. I told my men to save their ammunition until they were near them and take good aim so that every man would get his Indian the first shot, and to not get excited or scared, for if all would keep cool we would be able to get all of them without much trouble.

It so happened that just as we came on to the ridge that the Indians had passed over a few minutes before, they came in sight of the train, which was then not more than half a mile away. They stopped and were looking at the train.

Jim Bridger's quick eye had caught sight of them, and not knowing but it was the big band coming, he had the wagons corralled to prepare for an attack.

When we came to the top of the ridge mentioned we were not more than three hundred yards away from them and I immediately ordered a charge.

I was on Pinto, and he knowing what was up, was ready for a chase. In fact, I could not have held him had I been so disposed.

The warriors were so engrossed looking at the train, no doubt thinking what a picnic they would have with them, that they did not see us until I was almost ready to fire. I was somewhat in advance of the rest, my horse being the fleeter, and when within about a hundred yards I raised in my stirrups, brought my rifle to my shoulder and fired, killing one Indian, and the boys claimed that I killed a horse from under another one at the same time. They were sure the same bullet killed both, for both fell at the crack of my rifle.

As soon as I had fired I drew my pistol and told them to do likewise, also telling them to be sure and make every shot count.

If ever I saw a horse that enjoyed that kind of sport—if I might call it such—it was old Pinto.

The Indians made an effort to turn to the north, but I was on the left of my men and my horse was fleet enough to head them off. I crowded them so close that they headed straight for the train; in fact, I think they were so scared that they did not know where they were going.

At the first fire with our pistols three of the Indians fell, leaving four yet mounted and one on foot—the one whose horse I had shot at the first fire. I saw the Indian on foot making for some sage brush near by and sang out to a man named Saunders, who was on a fine grey horse, to run that Indian down, which he did, killing him the second shot, so he said afterwards.

About this time I saw Jim coming, with six or eight men following him closely. Then we all commenced yelling at the top of our voices, which excited the Indians still more. Whether they saw our men coming or not I do not know, but two of them ran almost right up to them and were shot down at a distance of thirty or forty yards.

We succeeded in getting the other two, not letting one escape to tell the tale; thereby accomplishing just what I started to do when I first got sight of them.

After the last Indian had fallen, I rode to where Jim was and told him of the big band of Indians I had seen that day, and suggested that we had better go to Barrel Springs that night, which was about four miles further on, as I thought that the best place to be in camp in case we were attacked by the Indians. In this he agreed with me.

By this time my men were all on the battle-field, and most of the men from the train, also a number of the women who had come out to see the dead Indians. I asked one of the boys to go with me to scalp the Indians, after which I would go to the train as I wanted to change horses, but none of them knew how to scalp an Indian, so Jim and I had to teach them how.

One old man, who was looking on, said: "I would not mind shooting an Indian, but I would not like to scalp one of them."

After scalping the nine Indians we rode to the train and showed the scalps to the women. One young lady said to me:

"I always took you to be a gentleman until now."

I said: "Miss, I claim to be only a plain plains gentleman, but that at any and all times."

She said: "I don't think a gentleman could be so barbarous as you are."

"My dear lady," I replied, "the taking of these scalps may be the means of saving the train," and then I explained why we always scalped the Indians when we killed them. I told her that the Indians did not fear death, but hated the idea of being scalped.

About this time Jim Bridger came up and gave a more through explanation of the scalping business, and I did not hear anything more of it at that time. But Jim often teased the young lady spoken of, who had a lovely head of hair, by remarking what a fine scalp it would make for the Indians.

I changed saddle horses and then myself and two assistants rode out north to watch the movements of the main band of Indians.

Before starting out Jim gave us the password of the pickets, which was "Buffalo."

We rode until near sunset before we got sight of the big band of Indians again, they having gone into camp about four miles west of Barrel Springs, where our train was camped, and only about a half mile from the trail or wagon road.

I crawled up as near their camp as I dared to go, and watched them until about nine o'clock that night, at which time a number of them had turned in, apparently for the night, and a number were around their horses all the time, giving us no opportunity whatever, to stampede them, which was my intention, provided they gave us the least show. I told my assistants there would be no danger whatever, until daybreak the next morning, and we would return to camp and sleep until near daylight.

When we got to the train Jim had not gone to bed yet. I told him where we had located the main band, and as near as I could the number of the Indians—about one hundred and fifty—but that I did not anticipate any trouble during the night.

Jim said he would sit up until four o'clock the next morning. "At which time," said he, "I will call you and you can take as many scouts with you as you like and watch every move made by the Indians, and if they start this way telegraph me at once and I will have everything in readiness to receive them, and I think we will be able to give them quite an interesting entertainment."

What we meant by the term telegraphing was sending a messenger as fast as he could ride, as there were no other means of transmitting messages quickly.

The next morning at four, sharp, Jim woke us up. He had our horses there, ready to saddle.

I sent three scouts north of the trail, three south and took the other two with me to look after the Indians.

We arrived at the place where we had been secreted the evening before, just as the Indians were breaking camp. They started toward the road, and I watched them till they struck the road and headed toward the train.

I then dispatched one of my assistants to the train, which was nearly four miles distant, telling him to spare no horseflesh, but make the trip as quick as his horse was able to carry him and notify Jim of the Indians' movements. The other scout and I stayed to watch the Indians. They traveled along the road at their leisure until they got in sight of the train, but Jim had all in readiness for them. He had raised the tongues of the two lead wagons— which in forming a corrall always stood face to face— about six feet high and had the nine scalps we had taken the day before, strung on a line and swung under the wagon tongues so as to be readily seen by the Indians. As soon as the Indians came in sight of the train he had all the men form in single line on the outside of the corrall, while all the women and children and all the stock were on the inside.

They circled around the entire train, taking in the situation but keeping out of gunshot. Seeing that the emigrants, much to their surprise, were ready to receive them, and seeing no chance to stampede their stock, they rode off on the hillside about half a mile away and held a council for about half an hour, after which they all mounted and rode away. They were not disposed to tackle a greater number than they had, especially when their antagonists were armed with guns, while they had only bows, and arrows, and tomahawks.

Our men were well armed with such hand-guns as were then in existence. Some had squirrel rifles, others yager's, shotguns and pistols. In fact, about all makes of firearms were represented in that emigrant train.

This was the first big band of hostile Indians that any of the people had ever seen, and Jim said there was the "wust" hubbub inside that corrall he had ever heard, notwithstanding he had cautioned them to be quiet.

The most nervous of the women, at sight of the Indians, commenced crying and screaming, while those more brave tried to reconcile those that were half frenzied from fright, and keep them quiet. Some were afraid to have their husbands stand outside the corrall for fear they would be killed by the redskins; but had it not been for that line of men standing on the ouside of the wagons, and those scalps dangling from the wagon tongues all of which led the Indians to believe that the pale-faces were anxious to entertain them for awhile at least, they undoubtedly would have attacked that train that morning.

My assistants and I watched them all that day, and the train, after the Indians had gone, moved on. The Indians went back and took the trail of the nine scouts that they had sent out the morning before, tracked them to where their dead bodies lay, and taking four of the bodies with them, moved on eastward. We selected a high point and watched them until they had gone about ten miles, and then we turned and followed up the train, which camped that night at the head of Rock Creek. When we arrived and reported that the Indians had left the county they were the happiest lot of people I ever saw. It seemed that they thought this was the only band of Indians in the country.

The next day being Sunday Jim proposed that we lay over and rest, saying that he was about worn out himself and that he was satisfied that the scouts were in the same condition. This was satisfactory to all, so we did not move camp that day.

Up to this time we had not killed any game, although we had seen plenty, there being considerable buffalo in this part of the country yet, but it had been contrary to orders to shoot while traveling, and I want to say right here that the people of this train were always obedient to our orders during our travels with them.

I told them I would go out and kill a buffalo that day provided I could find one not too far from camp. A number of men in the train wanted to go with me for a buffalo hunt. "The more the merrier," I said, so we and started, six of us together.

About two miles from camp we saw a band of fifteen that had not yet seen us. We at once dropped back over the hill and taking a circuitous route, we rode on the opposite side of them from camp, and cautiously to within about a hundred and fifty yards, when they raised their heads, took a good look at us and started off toward the train. I told Saunders as he was on a fast horse to take one side and I would take the other and let the other boys bring up the rear, as by so doing we could drive them near camp and save packing the meat so far. When we were in the valley just below camp

I told each man to select his buffalo and fire, which they did, when within a quarter of a mile from camp. We then all commenced yelling like Indians, and Jim Bridger said that he never saw a crowd of men get to their guns as quick as the men in the train did, for they actually thought we were Indians.

We succeeded in killing four buffalo out of the band, the last one being within a hundred yards of camp. We dressed them and all hands volunteered to carry the meat to camp where it was turned over to the committee to be distributed among the people of the entire train.

This was a great treat to them, for they had been living on bacon for a long time, having no fresh meat whatever.

It was twenty-five miles from here to the next place where we could find water and a suitable camping place where we would also have a good chance to protect ourselves from Indians. So we pulled out early, I distributing my scouts as usual, only that I went alone and had a hard ride for nothing.

After I had gone quite a distance I saw what I supposed to be Indians; but they were a long way off. The thought struck me that it was the was the same band we had seen before and that they were sneaking around intending to steal a march on us and attack the train while traveling and stampede the stock, which was often done when no scouts were kept out for their protection. I started to follow them up and did not find out my mistake until I struck the trail of my supposed band of Indians which to my surprise proved to be a buffalo trail and instead of Indians I had been following a band of buffalo all day.

That night I laid out and the people in camp were very uneasy about me, thinking I never would return, as they thought I must have been killed by Indians. Jim told them not to be alarmed as I would turn up all right the next day.

On a trip of this kind I usually took a lunch along with me; but not expecting to be out long this time I did not take anything to eat, so I had to starve it out until I got back to the train, which was the next day at noon.

I did not see any fresh Indian sign on the entire trip; neither did the other scouts see any sign of them, and we concluded that if we did not have any trouble for three days, we would be out of danger of the Sioux, for by that time we would be out in the Bitter Creek country and there was no fear of Indians there.

All went along smoothly and we did not see or hear of any more Indians until we got to Fort Bridger. Here I met one of Gen. Connor's men who told me that the Utes were very bad in the vicinity of Fort Douglas near Salt

Lake, that being the place where Gen. Connor was stationed at that time. He said that they had not been able to get a fight out of the Indians yet, although they had followed them around a great deal.

We decided to take Sublet's Cutoff, leaving Salt Lake City about one hundred miles south, as Jim said he would rather fight Indians than Mormons.

Six days after leaving Fort Bridger I met two of Gen. Connor's scouts in Cash valley, and they told us the Utes were very bad farther West, and advised us to take the Goose Creek route to avoid the Indians. We took their advice.

Here was a scope of country that neither Jim nor I had ever been over, it being a new road just made the year previous.

After traveling four days on this road, late in the evening of the fourth, I discovered a little band of Indians about six or eight miles from the road on a stream that I have since heard called Raft river, which is a tributary of the Snake.

We watched the band until dark and then rode as near as we thought safe. I then left my horse with my two assistants and crawled up near the Indian camp and tried to get a count on them. When I got near them I found that they were Bannocks and were not warriors, but apparently a hunting and fishing party, and were an old men and women. I went away without molesting or even allowing them to know that I had been there.

Four days' travel from here brought us into a section of country where I had done my first scouting, on the waters of the Humboldt. The first day after striking the Humboldt, three of my men and I late in the afternoon, ran on to a small band of Utes, eleven in number. I thought we had discovered them and got away without being noticed, so I told the boys that by making a circuit of about one and a half miles we would have the advantage of the ground and would be on to them before they knew it.

On arriving at the place where I expected to make the charge I was disappointed to find that they were mounted and on the move, they having no doubt gotten sight of us when we first saw them. We gave chase but they had too far the start of us, and after running about two miles we ended the pursuit.

There was no more trouble until we got to where Wadsworth now stands. Here, one morning about sunrise, as the herders were bringing in the stock, five Indians rushed in and tried to stampede the animals, but the herders happened to see them in time to give the alarm. Jim and I having our horses tied near the camp, were out after them quicker than I can tell it. We got two of them, and I think the other three must have thought themselves extremely lucky that they got away with their scalps.

The only damage done by them was that they scared the herders out of a year's growth, and just where those Indians came from I never have been able to tell, for I made it a rule to circle the camp every evening and look for Indians and Indian signs.

This was the only time on the trip that I had an Indian steal a march on me, and this was the last trouble we had with Indians on this trip. Ten days travel brought us to the foot of the Sierra Nevada Mountains at the head of Eagle Valley.

Jim knowing that they wanted to lay over the next day, it being Sunday, he selected a lovely camping ground in a pleasant pine grove and went into camp about the middle of the afternoon.

As soon as we had got into camp, Jim and I went to the committee and told them they did not need our services any longer as there would be no danger whatever from here on of Indians, they being now out of the hostile country entirely.

When the women folks learned that we were going to leave they proposed giving a farewell party that night. Having musicians in the train, they selected a nice level spot, and all who desired to participate congregated there and had an enjoyable time. I think they enjoyed that dance out in that lovely forest as much as though they had been dancing in the finest hall in San Francisco; and I think even the old people who were religious were so overjoyed to know that they were once more safe from the much dreaded and barbarous red men of the plains, that they almost felt like dancing themselves.

Although I had been with this train just two and one half months I had been in company with the ladies but very little, for I had never been in in daylight only just long enough to eat my meals and change horses, consequently I was but slightly acquainted with any of them. This was the first dance on the trip, and it was surprising to me to see how sociable the ladies were with me, and had it not been that I was so bashful, I might have had a pleasant time.

When the dance was over, about ten o'clock that night, one of the committee got up and made us quite a speech in behalf of the people in the train, telling us how much they appreciated the interest we had taken in guarding their train through safely, and after he was through talking he gave each of us a letter of recommendation, which had been drawn up that evening while the dance was going on. I think those letters were signed by every man in the train, and a great many of the ladies had signed them too. The speaker concluded his remarks by asking us to remain with the train as long as we desired, and our provisions should not cost us a cent, nor for having our horses herded with theirs. It being too late in the fall to return to Fort Kearney, we accepted their kind and liberal offer and concluded to travel with them a few days.

We remained with them until near Sacramento, and here I met my old friend Johnnie West. He was beginning to look very old, considering his age. He told me he had quit drinking and was going to lead a different life from this on; that he had taken up a ranch five miles from Sacramento on the river and invited us home with him.

We accepted the invitation, and bidding the people that we had been traveling with nearly three months, good-bye, we left them and went with Johnnie to his ranch.

When we were ready to leave, I think every person in the train shook hands with us.

CHAPTER XXIII
BRIDGER AND WEST GIVE CHRISTMAS A HIGH OLD WELCOME IN SACRAMENTO. —CALIFORNIA GULCH.—MEETING WITH BUFFALO BILL.—THIRTY-THREE SCALPS WITH ONE KNIFE

On our arrival at Johnnie West's ranch we found that he had quite a comfortable house, considering that it had been built by an old trapper. He had five acres under cultivation, and had raised a promiscuous lot of very desirable produce, especially in the way of vegetable truck.

We remained with West two months, putting in our time hunting, fishing and loafing. It being near Christmas now, the question arose as to what we would do to celebrate that festive season. Jim was for going to San Francisco and Johnnie wanted to go to Sacramento. I told them it was immaterial to me where I went. But all this time I was afraid that if John West got to town in company with Jim Bridger that West would break his oft-repeated resolutions and there would be a big run on the reddest kind of paint. I told Jim my fears and proposed that we remain at home and take our Christmas there. But Jim couldn't see it in that light, and said one little spree wouldn't hurt Johnnie, so the day before Christmas we pulled out for Sacramento. That same evening Jim and Johnnie both got loads that they ought to have gone after about nine times, if they just had to pack them, and the result was that it was my busy day keeping them out of the calaboose. I promised the police I would put them to bed and make them stay there until morning.

Next morning, the first thing after we had dressed, Jim said: "Well boys, let's go and have a Christmas drink." I said: "Boys, I will take one drink with you and then quit. Now if you fellows want to make brutes of yourselves and get into the lock-up, just go ahead, but I am going to go home as soon as I get my breakfast." So we went down the street and into the first saloon we came to and called for egg-nogg. I remained with them until they were drinking their fifth drink. I could not do anything with them, so I told them I was going to breakfast, and they could do as they pleased. This was the first time in my life that I had ever been placed in a position where I was actually ashamed of my associates. I was so disgusted when I left them that morning to go to my breakfast that I thought I would go home and leave them. But after eating my breakfast, being, perhaps, in a better humor, I started out to hunt for them. I do not wish to try for a moment to lead the reader to believe that I do not like the taste of liquor, for I am confident at that time I really liked it better than either of my associates, but I always despise the effect, and that seemed to be what they, like thousands of other, drink it for. It always seemed to me that when a man is drunk he is more disposed to show the brute that is in him than to act a gentleman.

After looking around some little time I found Jim Bridger in a saloon so drunk that he could scarcely walk. I asked him where Johnny West was, and the bar-keeper told me that the police had taken him to the station-house. I asked what for, and he said for trying to shoot some one.

I watched for an opportunity and took both of Jim's pistols and knife away from him and gave them to the clerk at the hotel. Afterwards I walked to the station-house to see what the charge was against Johnny West. The man told me the charge was drunk and disorderly and shooting a pistol inside of a house. I asked him if he would let Johnny out if I would pay the fine. He said: "Yes. As soon as he is sober to-morrow morning, you can come around. The charges will be twenty dollars."

If the reader ever had any experience with a drunken man, which to me is the most disgusting thing on earth, he can realize something of the time I had with those two men, for it took me all the next day to get Johnny West home and get him reconciled.

He was determined to return to Sacramento, and it took me two more days hard work and coaxing to get Jim Bridger home. I have it by good authority that this was the last drunken spree that Johnnie West ever took. He remained on his ranch some six years longer and having accumulated considerable wealth, sold out for a good price and returned home to his relations in Texas, and there died a short time afterwards;

Jim Bridger and myself stayed at Johnny's until about the middle of January. This now being 1861, we started for New Mexico, via Los Angeles, with the intention of laying over in Los Angeles until we could cross the Rocky Mountains. There was a good wagon road from Sacramento to San Jose, and from San Jose to Los Angeles.

At this time the Indians were all peaceable through California, the only trouble with them was their begging. At that I think, beyond any doubt, that they could beat any class of people it has ever been my misfortune to meet.

We arrived at Los Angeles on the fifth of February. It being one of the Spanish feast days, they were having a great time. The Spanish population of this place having now become reconciled, we were treated with due respect while we remained here, being about one week, during which time we lived on fruit. For here were fruits and flowers, world without end. Beyond any doubt, this is the greatest place for flowers that I have ever seen.

Soon we pulled out for New Mexico, keeping on the north side of the Colorado river until above the head of the Grand Canyon, this being pretty well up in the Rocky Mountains, and here near the head of the Grand Canyon we began to see more or less Indian sign, but we were undecided as to what tribe of Indians they belonged.

The second day after crossing the Colorado river we ran on to a band of Indians, but to our satisfaction they were of the Pima tribe, and the same young Indian whose sister had assisted me in rescuing the white girl Olive Oatman, was with them.

As soon as he saw me, he ran to meet me and shouted "Kain, igo,"—meaning "Hello, friend,"—and shook hands with me.

The Pimas were out on their annual hunt for that season, and we had to remain with them two days. Being acquainted with them all, and as I have said before, when one is out in a hostile Indian country, sometimes the company of friendly Indians is quite acceptable.

After leaving here we would be compelled to pass over a small portion of the Ute country, and game being plentiful at this time, we feared they might be out on a hunt, and just at present we were not hankering after sport of the Indian fighting kind. So I proposed to Jim Bridger that we hire four of these young Pimas to accompany us through the Ute country, knowing that the Pimas were on good terms with all their neighboring tribes. Jim said that we had nothing to give them, having neither jewelry or beads with us.

I told him that I would spare them a horse if we could get them to go, I had four horses with me, while Jim only had three. He told me to go ahead and make any kind of a bargain with them I liked and he would stand his portion.

That night after supper while we were sitting around the camp fire, smoking and cracking jokes—for an Indian enjoys a joke as well as any one—I got up and told them that we would, after leaving their country, have to travel over a small portion of the Ute country, and they being hostile towards the white people, we did not feel safe to try to cross their country alone, I told them we were very poor, having no beads nor blankets to spare, but if four of their men would accompany us for three days, I would give them a good horse.

The young Indian said: "You have been a good friend to me, and me and my friend will go with you across the Ute country. We don't want your horse, but when you come back you can bring us some beads."

This we agreed to do, and the next morning we started early, accompanied by four young Pima Indians.

During the first two days' travel from the Pima camp we saw not less than two hundred Indians of the Ute tribe, camping the second night within a quarter of a mile of a large village of them, but having those Pimas with us they did not offer to molest us.

When we were approaching a village two of the Pimas would ride ahead and tell the Utes that we were their friends. They traveled with us four days, when we concluded we were safe and they returned to their crowd of hunters, and we proceeded on our journey, crossing the main divide of the Rocky Mountains at the head of the Blue river, striking the head of the Arkansas river as soon as we were across the main divide.

The day we crossed the divide we went into camp as soon as we were out of the snow on the east side. That night when it was dark we could see down the Arkansas river a great number of camp fires, and what this all meant was a mystery to us. We knew that we were then in the Comanche country, but we could not think that they were up in that region so early in the season. We were both somewhat restless that night, sleeping but very little, fearing that these were camp-fires of the Utes, and if so we were sure to have trouble with them before we could get out of this part of the country.

We were not in much of a hurry to start next morning, but I took my glasses and selecting a high point for a general look, was agreeably surprised to see that the camp was one of wagons and tents. That made us feel considerably better. We packed up at once and went down to see what it all meant.

On arriving we found a company of miners. The gold in California Gulch had just recently been discovered, and that was attracting them. As soon as we learned the cause of the excitement, we struck camp and walked up the canyon to where they were at work. They were taking out gold in great quantities, but we only remained until next morning, when we packed up and started for Taos, going via the place where Colorado City now stands—a deserted village near the present city of Colorado Springs. We were now in a country where we were perfectly safe, so far as Indians were concerned, and we could travel at our ease.

On our first day's travel, after leaving the mining we passed through the country where I did my first trapping in company with Uncle Kit Carson and Mr. Hughes, and as we were riding along I pointed out to Jim the place where I took my first Indian scalp. This was the first time I had ever mentioned it to him and he said that Uncle Kit had told him all about it a long time ago.

On our arrival at Taos we found Uncle Kit suffering severely from the effects of the arrow wound that has twice before been mentioned in this history. He and his wife were glad to see us, and Uncle Kit insisted on my remaining with him and taking charge of his stock. He now had several bands of sheep and some four hundred head of cattle, and not being able to ride and look after the camps, he wanted me to ride from one camp to the other and look after the business in general, for which he offered to pay me well. I agreed to work for him at least two or three months and perhaps longer, provided I liked the business.

After I had been one month at work a wholesale butcher came over from Denver to buy cattle and sheep. I went out and showed him Uncle Kit's, after which we returned to Taos and he closed a trade with Uncle Kit, agreeing to take one hundred head of cattle and one thousand head of sheep. The price to be paid for them I never knew, but he paid a certain portion down and the balance was to be paid the coming October, in Denver City.

I remained with Uncle Kit until the first of October, looking after things in general, when he asked me to accompany him to Denver City, which was one hundred and eighty miles from Taos.

About the middle of the afternoon of the sixth day we rode into Denver, from the southwest. When near where Cherry creek runs through the city we saw an immense crowd of people in the streets, so we pushed on to see what the excitement was.

When near the crowd we met three or four men on horseback riding up the street. We asked what was causing the excitement. One of them replied: "Oh, nothing, only they are going to hang a man down there in a few minutes."

This being the first opportunity I had ever had to see a man hung, we stayed and saw it through. We rode up to the edge of the crowd, which was about forty yards from the scaffold where the hanging was to take place, and had been there but a few moments when we saw the sheriff coming with the prisoner, having a very strong guard of some two hundred men all well armed. As soon as the prisoner stepped on to the platform some one handed him a chair to sit down in.

The sheriff turned to the prisoner and said: "Mr. Gordon if you have anything to say, now you have the opportunity. I will give you all the time necessary to say what you wish."

The prisoner rose to his feet and brushed his hair back, apparently cool, but the moment he commenced to talk I could see the tears begin to trickle down his cheeks.

I thought it a most pitiful sight. He did not talk long, but briefly thanked his friends for their kindness towards him during his confinement, and said: "Gentlemen, I think you did very wrong in holding out the idea to me that I would come clear, when you knew very well that there was no show whatever for me," and took his seat.

A gospel minister then stepped upon the platform and engaged in prayer. When he rose from praying the prisoner was weeping bitterly. The sheriff then stepped up to him and said: "Come, Mr. Gordon, your time is up," and he took him by one arm and another man by the other, and when he raised to his feet they tied his hands behind him, tied a cloth over his face, led him on to the trap and the sheriff placed the rope around his neck and started down the steps to spring the trap, when the prisoner sang out: "Come back, Meadows, come back!"

The sheriff turned and walked up to where the prisoner was, and he said:

"Meadows, fix the rope good so it will break my neck, for I want to die quick."

After the sheriff had fixed the rope he stepped down and sprung the trap, and from where I was I could not see that Gordon made the least struggle after he dropped.

Just as we were ready to leave here who should step up but our old friend Mr. Joe Favor, whom we had not seen for a long time. He insisted on us going to his store, telling us where to put our horses. So, after putting our horses up, we went around with him.

On arriving at Favor's place we found that he had a number of his St. Louis friends with him, who had only arrived a few days previous to this. After introducing us all around, he said: "I want you two men to come over and take supper with me. I have just ordered supper at the Jefferson House."

Uncle Kit tried to excuse himself on the grounds that we were not dressed well enough to go into company, we having on our buckskin suits. But his answer was:

"I would not have you dressed otherwise if I could, so be sure and come with your side arms on" having reference to our revolvers and knives. He then addressed his conversation to me for a few moments by asking what I would take to tell him the honest truth as to how many Indians I had scalped with the knife that he gave me, seeing that I still carried it.

I said: "Mr. Favor, I could tell you just the number, but it would be out of place for me to do so." He asked why, and I said: "Mr. Favor, up to this time I don't think I have ever given you any reason to doubt my word, but if I should tell you the honest truth as to the number of Indians I have scalped with that knife I fear you would doubt me."

By this time a number of his St. Louis friends had flocked around me, and it seemed as if they would look through me. Mr. Favor assured me that he would not doubt my word for a moment, but I told him his friends would. They assured me that they would not, saying from what they had heard of me from Mr. Favor before seeing me, they felt satisfied that I would tell them the truth.

I said: "Gentlemen, if I had gotten one more scalp I would just have even thirty-four, but as it is I have just taken thirty-three scalps with this knife. I mean from Indians that I killed myself. I have taken a number that were killed by others, but I did not count them."

The crowd then turned their attention to Uncle Kit Carson, and while at the supper table those St. Louis parties asked him what he would take to sit down and give them a true history of his life and let them write it up and have it published. To this he would not hear. They then came at him in a different manner by asking what per cent, of the net proceeds he would take. To this he said: "Gentlemen, if there is anything on earth that I do dislike it surely is this thing called notoriety," and he continued by saying, "There is a part of my life that I hate to think of myself, and a book written without the whole of my life would not amount to anything."

After supper we returned to the store and those men talked with Uncle Kit until near midnight about this matter. By this time he had become impatient and said: "Gentlemen, there is no use talking, for I will not submit to a thing of this kind, and you will oblige me very much by not mentioning it any more." So that ended the conversation concerning the matter, for the time being, and Uncle Kit and I retired for the night.

The morning following I walked down to the store and Mr. Favor told me there had been some parties looking for me, and left word for me to meet them at the store at ten o'clock.

I sat down and waited until they came at the hour appointed. A gentleman in the crowd named Green Campbell seemed to be their spokesman. And, by the way, this same Mr. Campbell has since grown to be very wealthy and now resides in Salt Lake City, and a few years ago was nominated on the Gentile ticket for Governor, but was defeated.

Mr. Campbell said to me: "There are five of us that have been mining here this summer and have done very well, but we are not satisfied. We want to go on to the waters of the Gila river and prospect this winter, and have been trying for several days to find some one that could guide us to that country, and Mr. Favor having recommended you to us very highly, we wish to make some kind of a bargain with you if we can, to guide us to that part of the country. Is it safe for a small party to go in there?"

I said: "Mr. Campbell, it depends altogether in what part of the country you want to go. I could take you on the waters of the Gila river where you would be perfectly safe, but whether it would be where you want to go or not is the question." I drew a diagram of that part of the country as best I could, showing the different tributaries to the river, pointing out the region where they would be safe and also that which they would not dare enter on account of the hostile Apache Indians.

Mr. Campbell asked me if I would remain with them until spring. I told him I would, and they made me a proposition, which I accepted. They were to furnish all the pack animals necessary for the outfit and to board me, I to furnish my own saddle-horses. I advised them to go to Taos with a wagon and team, and buy their pack animals there as they would be able to get them much cheaper than in Denver. They proposed that I go to Taos and buy the pack animals and have everything ready by the time they would arrive, as they had business which would necessarily detain them for at least two weeks. This I agreed to do.

That afternoon I was walking down the street near the Planters House when I met a policeman in great haste, making his way for the hotel mentioned. As he approached me he said: "I deputize you to assist me in making the arrest of those stage drivers in the Planters' House." This was a crowd of men who were driving stage at that time for the notorious Slade, of whom more will be said later on.

I had left my side arms at Mr. Favor's store, not thinking I would have any occasion to use them, but at the request of the policeman, I entered the hotel and found a general row proceeding. As soon as we entered the door two or three of the crowd made for me, I backed off and defended myself the best that I could, until I had backed to the end of the hall. The door at the end of the hall being shut, I could back no farther. Here I sparred with them for some time, when one of them struck at me with all vengeance and just grazed the side of my face. As I threw my head and shoulders back to dodge the blow I knocked the whole upper portion of the glass door out. Just at that instant Wm. F. Cody, better known as Buffalo Bill, seeing the predicament I was in, and seeing that I was unarmed, caught me by the shoulders and jerked me through that window much quicker than I could tell it. He handed me one of his pistols and said: "Come on pard, and we will take them fellows or know the reason why."

When we entered the door they had the policeman and bar-keeper both cornered behind the bar, but seeing that we were prepared for them, strange to say, not one of them drew his pistol, but all surrendered at once, and the entire crowd, six in number, were escorted to the cooler.

The name of this policeman was William Deecy, and he is now living in Boulder, Montana. I saw him less than one year ago, and we enjoyed a good laugh as we rehearsed the affair of the Planters' House.

That afternoon after having his business attended to, Uncle Kit went to Mr. Favor and said: "Joe, I want you and your friends from St. Louis to come and take supper with me this evening at the same hotel where we had supper last evening."

When Uncle Kit spoke in this manner Mr. Favor felt sure that he had changed his mind in regard to having his life written up, and before going to supper, in the absence of Uncle Kit, Mr. Favor asked me about it. I told him he had not. Whereupon he proposed betting me a new hat that those parties would write up his, Kit Carson's, life. I said; "Not by his consent." "Yes," said he, "by his own consent."

This bet I accepted, and that night Mr. Favor and all of his St. Louis friends accompanied us from the store down to the hotel for supper. There was one gentleman in the crowd who was a splendid talker, and apparently an intelligent man, and when at the supper table that night, he mentioned the matter to Uncle Kit again of having his life published. On turning his eyes to the refined gentleman, he said: "I would have you understand that when I say anything I mean it. I told you in plain English last evening that I would not submit to anything of that kind, and now don't compel me to talk too harsh, but please drop the subject at once."

Mr. Favor, who had been watching very close all this time, could see at once there was no use in talking any more about the subject and turned the conversation as quickly as possible and there was no more said about it.

That night while in a conversation with Buffalo Bill he told Uncle Kit and I that he would be going out to Bent's Fort in a few days and proposed that we join him there and have a buffalo hunt before I went away. We promised that we would meet him.

The next morning Uncle Kit and I mounted our horses to start on our return trip to Taos, and when we rode up in front of the store, Mr. Favor told me to come in and get my hat. I told him no, that I would not take it now, but let it go until next spring when I returned. He said to call and get it any time, saying: "You won it fair."

After we had ridden but a short distance I told Uncle Kit how I came to win the hat, and he said: "I think them St. Louis men are gentlemen, but I don't propose to have any one write up my life. I have got plenty to keep me as long as I live and I do not like notoriety." And just here I would say, that to a man that roughed it out on the plains in those days as we old frontiersmen had to do, they did not feel that a history of their lives would be fit to go before the public, for as Uncle Kit said: "A man on the frontier had to undergo many hardships, that if written up true, just as they occurred, people in the civilized countries would not believe them when they read it."

On my arrival at Taos I bought ten Mexican jacks or burros to use for pack animals on the trip that we were about to start upon. After that we started for Bent's Fort where we joined Buffalo Bill and Col. Bent and struck out for the "Picket Wire" — Purgatoire — on a buffalo hunt.

Here we found buffalo plenty and enjoyed two days successful hunting, and I must say that a more jolly crowd I was never out with than those three men were on a trip of this kind. Buffalo Bill, who was as good-natured a man as a person would wish to meet, was able to furnish amusement for the entire crowd. Col. Bent himself was no mean Nimrod, and Uncle Kit did not take a back seat on such occasions.

This was the last hunting expedition that it was ever my pleasure to go upon in company with Mr. Cody, and it was not my pleasure to meet him again for a number of years afterwards.

From here Uncle Kit and I returned to Taos, and I commenced making preparations for the trip to the waters of the Gila.

CHAPTER XXIV
FACE TO FACE WITH A BAND OF APACHES.—THE DEATH OF PINTO.—THE CLOSEST CALL I EVER HAD.—A NIGHT ESCAPE.—BACK AT FORT DOUGLAS

On the arrival of Mr. Campbell and party we packed up and were off to the waters of the Gila. Our crowd consisted of Green Campbell, of Missouri; Thomas Freeman and David Roberts, of Illinois, and Marlow Pease, of Massachusetts.

I took three saddle horses with me and they each took a saddle horse and three extra horses belonging to the company. We did not lose any time getting across the main divide. Being late in the fall we had great fear of becoming snow-bound on the trip. We left the head of the Arkansas river some fifty miles to the north so as to be able to cross the river without having the snow to encounter. After we were across the main divide I told them there would be no danger of being snowed in now. So they would stop occasionally from half a day to three days in a place to prospect what they called the most favorable looking places for the yellow metal and most generally finding a little gold, but not as they considered in paying quantities, and while they were prospecting it was my business to scout all around the camp to prevent a surprise party by the reds and to kill game to live on.

We arrived at the Gila, striking the middle fork a little more southwest than I had ever been before. I told them we were now in the Apache country and that those were the worst Indians we had to contend with. We found a nice place for a camp and Mr. Campbell proposed to build a log cabin in order to protect ourselves against the Indians, but I told them I thought they had better prospect a week or ten days first, and if they found it to pay them we could build a cabin, and in the mean time I would try and locate the Indians and watch their movements.

The first four or five days I didn't go very far away, but made an entire circuit of the camp every day. After being here five or six days, I struck out in a southwesterly direction, intending to go about ten or fifteen miles from camp.

Up to this time I had not seen any fresh Indian sign whatever, and had about concluded that we would not have any trouble this winter with them. After riding about ten miles or so I came to a nice little brook, and there being fine grass, I stopped and let my horse feed for an hour or more. I was riding my old Pinto that day and he was also feeling fine.

About one o'clock I mounted Pinto and started south, striking for a high mountain, from which if I could once reach the top, I could, with the aid of my glasses, see all over the entire country. While climbing this mountain I ran on to a bear cub. Seeing that he was very fat, I shot him and lashed him behind my saddle, and was soon climbing the mountain again, which was, in places, steep and very rocky, with scattering pine trees here and there. After going about a half a mile and just as I came to the top of a steep little pitch, I came face to face with a band of Apache Indians. I did not take time to count them, but thought there were about eighteen or twenty of them, I fired four shots in quick succession. The first two shots I killed two Indians, but the other two I could not tell whether I got my men or not, as I was just in the act of turning my horse when I fired. They fired a perfect shower of arrows at me. To run back down the mountain the way I came was a matter of impossibility, as it was both steep and rocky, so I took around the side of the mountain, thinking that I would be able in a few moments' run to reach the top of the mountain, where I could have a better show to defend myself.

I had to ride all over my horse to avoid the arrows, first on one side, hanging by one foot and one hand, then on the other side.

I had not run more than one hundred yards until I knew there was something wrong with my horse, for he had always before seemed to know when I was in a tight place and seemed eager to carry me out of danger. I gave him the spurs three or four times but he did not increase his speed in the least, and then I knew well that he had been shot, and it always seemed a miracle to me that I went through all that and did not get shot also.

It is quite useless for me to say I thought my time had come. On looking ahead some fifty yards I saw a pile of rocks about four or five feet high, which I made a bee line for. Getting to the rock pile I dismounted and ran between two large rocks where poor old Pinto tried to follow me, but he received two more arrows in his hip and one in his flank. He fell to the ground, and after falling raised his head, and looking toward me, whinnied.

The poor faithful old fellow lay there and would whinny for me at intervals as long as he lived, which was perhaps half an hour. The reader can fancy my condition just at this time. Here I was almost surrounded by hostile Indians and the only friend that I had with me dead. I did not expect to ever get away from there, for I expected that while a part of the Indians guarded me the balance would go off and rally reinforcements.

I had made up my mind to fight them to the last and kill as many as I could before they got me. They made three desperate charges for me before dark, but as luck would have it I was always loaded for them. I piled up rocks as I could get them loose in a manner to give me protection from every quarter, but expected they would reinforce and attempt to starve me out.

Just as it was getting dark, two of the Indians crawled up to within thirty feet of my rock pen. I was watching them, and just as they rose up to fire I fired and brought one of them to the ground, thereby making another good Apache. The other one ran away, and it being somewhat dark, I did not get him.

This made the fifth Indian I had killed since I had been in my little rock pen and I had fired eleven shots. After it was good and dark I made up my mind that I would get out of there sometime during the night, for to remain there till the morrow only meant death, and I might as well lose my life in trying to get away that night as to remain there and be killed the next day. I felt sure they had a guard around me, but I made up my mind to make a desperate effort to get away. I crawled to where my dead horse was laying, which was only a few feet from my rock house, cut the latigo, removed my saddle from the dead horse, lashed it to my back, taking the mochilar or covering for a saddle, which I have described heretofore, I took my knife and cut a hole in the front portion of the mochila where the pommel of the saddle protrudes, so that I was able to stick my head through. The mochila was good as a shield, for an arrow would not go through it except at very short range. I cut the reins off of the bridle, and as the bit was a very heavy one, I thought it would answer pretty well as a sling shot in close quarters.

I had no idea of getting out without a desperate fight with ninety-nine chances against me to one in my favor. After I had my rig complete I started to crawl away flat on the ground like a snake, I would crawl for a short distance, then stop and listen. It was very dark, there being no moon in the fore part of the night. I was expecting every minute to feel an arrow or a tomahawk in my head. After working my way down the hill some hundred yards or so, I came to a tree and raised up by the side of it. I stood and listened for some time, but could not hear anything of the Indians, so I struck out in the direction of camp, walking very cautiously for some little distance.

After traveling about six miles I felt comparatively safe, knowing they could not do anything toward tracking me until morning and did not think they would even be able to track me then.

I passed over a great deal of rocky country where there was but little vegetation. Finally I laid down to wait until morning, and I must say that I never had been out in all my life when I actually longed for daylight to come as I did that long and lonely night, and I believe that I would freely have given five hundred dollars to have had a man there with me that night; not that I was afraid of Indians, for I considered that I had given them the slip, and did not believe they would be able to overtake me before I would reach camp even though they should be able to track me the next morning.

I thought of my dying horse who had been such a faithful servant and carried me out of so many tight places, and when I would think of him I could fancy that I could see him raise his head and whinny at me as he had done that evening in his dying moments, seemingly asking me for help, and I could not keep the tears from my eyes. As soon as it was light I started for camp, arriving there about ten o'clock that morning. The men in camp had given me up and did not expect to ever see me any more, thinking that the Apaches had got me. I told the men that we would have to leave this part of the country now, and that too, just as soon as I could get a bite to eat and get my saddle repaired. While the boys pulled up and started to move camp I saddled up another horse and took my back track, traveling very cautiously, thinking they would try to follow me out, and I wanted to watch their movements and see whether they had reinforced or not. I told the boys to move northeast and where to camp, the place being ten miles from where we were then, and not to build any fire that night, also that I would be in camp some time before morning this time, I was very cautious not to be surprised the second time. I rode back within a mile of where my dead horse lay, but could not see any Indians, so I finally concluded that it had been a small hunting party, and seeing that they could not scare me out of my rock pen by their ferocious charges, accompanied by a war-whoop that would make the hair stand on the bravest mountaineer's head, they had abandoned the idea altogether and had no doubt left the ground before I started to crawl away from my rock pen, which had been the means of saving me from falling their victim.

I returned to camp, arriving shortly after dark. We moved north, the men prospecting the country as we went and I scouting, keeping a sharp lookout to prevent a surprise party, but we did not see any more Indians during the entire winter. We struck the Colorado river at the mouth of the Green river.

Mr. Campbell concluded that he would go to southern Nevada; taking a southwesterly course from Green river, I piloted them about one hundred miles and they now being in a country where they were perfectly safe as far as hostile Indians were concerned, I left the party, and the most of them it has never been my pleasure to meet since. I met one of the party by the name of Freeman in Seattle in the year of 1889. At that time he was settled down in his old neighborhood in Illinois and had a wife and five children. I can truthfully say that I never met five better and more agreeable men to travel with in all my career than those men were. While with them I never saw one of them apparently out of humor with his companions or heard one use any kind of language than that of a gentleman. Leaving the party I struck for Salt Lake City. I had no trouble in finding the way, or otherwise, and arrived at Fort Douglas about the first of March.

On arriving here I found General Connor just making preparations to move with almost his entire force against the Ute Indians, who at this time were concentrating their forces in Cash Valley, and committing a great many depredations in that part of the country.

CHAPTER XXV
THREE THOUSAND DEAD INDIANS.—A DETECTIVE FROM CHICAGO.—HE GOES HOME WITH AN OLD MORMON'S YOUNGEST WIFE AND GETS INTO TROUBLE.— THE FLIGHT

Gen. Connor offered me a position as scout, which I accepted, and on the sixth day after my arrival at Fort Douglas, in company with two other scouts, I struck out in advance of the command. In the forenoon of the eighth day from the fort we found the Indians on a tributary of Cash Valley in a deep canyon and fortified. They had cut logs and rolled them down the hill, piling them on each side of the canyon, several feet high and had intermingled them with brush. This was the first fortification I had ever seen built by Indians.

We returned and met the command that night, and when we were making our report to the General he asked me what the fortifications looked like. I told him that I could not think of anything to compare them to, but that I thought they could be swept very easily by a Howitzer from above and below. He asked me if I would accompany one of his commissioned officers that night to see the fortifications, and I told him I would. After supper that evening a Captain came to me, whose name I am sorry to say I have forgotten, and asked me if I was the man that was to accompany him to the Indian fortifications. I told him that I was, and he asked what time we had better start. I told him we had better start at once as there would be a moon in the fore part of the night, but that the after part would be very dark. So we mounted our horses and were off.

We rode to within about three-quarters of a mile of the fortifications and there we remained until it was light enough to see, and then the Captain took out his glasses and scanned the whole country as well as the fortifications. After looking about half an hour the Captain asked me what I thought of it, and what would be my plan of attack. I told him that I had no idea, as I had never seen Indians fortified before. He said it would be a bloody fight, I said yes, but I thought the blood would all be on one side. "Yes," replied the Captain, "we ought to clean them out without losing ten men."

We went to our horses, mounted, and rode back to the command as quick as we could, meeting it about four miles from the fortifications, piloted by the two scouts that had been out with me the day before.

The Captain and Gen. Connor had a long conversation as we moved along. When within a mile of the mouth of this canyon Gen. Connor formed his men in line, one half to go on each side of the canyon in which the Indians were fortified, and the cannon were placed at the mouth of the canyon.

I did not see any Indians of any account until the command to fire was given. When the soldiers commenced to fire—there being about twelve hundred—it frightened the Indians so that they came running out from under those logs and brush like jack rabbits and were shot down like sheep. In all my experience in the Western wilds I never saw such a slaughtering as there.

The Indians had been taught by the Mormons that if they would fortify themselves in that way the whites could not harm them, teaching them also, that the Lord would protect them, which was a great thing for the white people, for it came so near cleaning the Utes up that there was only a little remnant left, and they never gave the white people any more trouble. Thus white people were enabled to pass through that country unmolested. Heretofore it had been one of the most dangerous parts of the country. For all this I have ever since believed that the Mormons, unintentionally, did the Gentiles a great favor.

After the battle was over, and as scouts are at liberty to go where they please, I rode over the battle-field in company with the other scouts and I never in all my life saw such a mangled up mass as was there. Men, women and children were actually lying in heaps, and I think all that got away were a few that hid among the logs and brush.

In this battle the Captain told me they did not lose a man, and had only four wounded, while he counted over three thousand dead Indians.

When I returned to Salt Lake City I was astonished to see the manner in which the Salt Lake papers abused Gen. Connor for slaughtering the Indians in the manner he had, when they (the Mormons) had planned the slaughter, although not meaning for it to be a slaughter of Indians.

Gen. Connor said that the Mormons had thought that the Indians would fortify themselves, and when attacked by the soldiers, they would wipe them (the soldiers) off the face of the earth. The idea had been so thoroughly instilled into the minds of the Indians by the Mormons that the Lord would protect them if only fortified in this manner that they depended most altogether on the Lord to protect them.

The third day on our return trip we came to a little place called Ogden. Here the General made preparations to leave the command and go ahead, accompanied by one company, of cavalry. When they were ready I was directed to accompany him, which I did. He and I rode in the rear of the company. After riding some little distance Gen. Connor said: "Drannan, I think I can put you on the track of a good thing if it would suit you." I asked him in what way. He asked me if I had not heard of the Mountain Meadow massacre in Utah. I said: "Certainly, many times." He said: "Now be honest with me and tell me who you think did that horrible work." I told him the Mormons, and the Mormons alone.

He then told me there was a man at the fort from Chicago trying to work up the case and if possible to find out just by whose authority the Mormons had massacred those emigrants, and he said: "From what I have seen of you, I think you would be just the man to help him work up the case."

I said: "General, I think you are mistaken. I never did any detective work among the white people, and I fear I am not good enough a talker to obtain the desired information." The General said: "All right, we'll see."

We reached the Fort that night at dark, having ridden forty miles that day. That evening the General told me to come to his quarters the following day at ten o'clock and he would introduce me to the gentleman referred to.

I went to the General's quarters and the gentleman was present. His name was Howard. By whose authority he was working up this case I never learned, but, however, after questioning me for some time as to what I knew of the Mormons, he asked me what I would charge him per month to go along with him, play the hypocrite, and try to help work up the case. I told him it was all new work to me; that I knew nothing of detective work whatever. I said that if it were a case of Indians it would be quite different, but I did not think I would be of much service to him working among the Mormons.

He proposed that he would furnish me a suit of clothes suitable for the part I was to play, furnish money to pay my expenses, such as hotel bills, whiskey bills, ball-room bills, and pay me fifty dollars per month, I to do as he told me, or as near as I could. "And, at the end of one month," said he, "if your work does not suit me, or if I don't suit you, I can pay you off and you can go your way; or if you stay and we work up this case as I anticipate, as soon as the work is completed I will pay you one hundred dollars per month instead of fifty."

Under these conditions I went to work for him, and the next two days were spent in drilling me on Mormon phrases, their customs And so on, he having been there some three months, had got pretty well posted on the Mormon doctrine.

When I got my new suit of clothes on and he got my hair fixed up just to suit him I looked in the mirror, and I could hardly believe that it was Will Drannan.

The third day we mounted our horses and started across the country to a little town called Provo, which is about forty miles from Salt Lake, if I have not forgotten. Here, we are both Mormons, are brothers, and our business buying cattle; looking around to see who has cattle to sell. We arrived at Provo on Sunday evening and made the acquaintance of two young men who were Mormons. They asked us to go to church with them. "All right," said Mr. Howard, "but where will my brother and I stay to-night?" The eldest of the two young men said: "One of you can stay with me and the other can stay with Jim," referring to his chum. So it fell to my lot to go with Jim after church.

On our way to church, naturally enough the boys asked our names, and Howard spoke up and said: "My name is George Howard, and this is my brother Frank." And I will tell you now with all candor I did not feel right over this, for it was the first time in my life that I had ever lived under an assumed name, but I had agreed to do what I could, and although I would have given the best horse I had to have been out of the scrape, yet I was into it and I was determined to go through with it if possible. That evening when we came out of church Jim gave me an introduction to his two sisters and they asked me to walk home with them from church, and I did so.

After conversing with them for some time and getting a little acquainted with them, I asked the girl on my left how old she was, and she said she was seventeen. I asked her how long she had lived in this country. She said: "My father was one of the first settlers in this country. He came here among the first emigrants and I was raised here in this country."

"Is that so?" I asked. "Then you were here in this part of the country at the time of the Mountain Meadow massacre?" "Yes," said she, "but you know we must not talk about that." "Well," said I, "you know they were all Gentiles that were killed and what's the difference?" "Well," she said, "I think it was all wrong any way."

I asked her if her father was in that fight and she said: "Let's don't talk about that, please don't ask me any more questions about it."

By this time we had reached the gate, and the conversation stopped for that time. The next day I tried to get a chance to talk to her, but my efforts were all in vain. That afternoon I met Howard and told him of the conversation I had with the young lady, and he insisted on my working on her father if I could get a chance to have a private conversation with her.

On Wednesday night there was to be a big dance at the church, and it being free to all, we attended it. In the mean time I had engaged the company of those two young ladies for the dance. I paid all due respect to the young lady, but did not mention the affair of which I was desirous of obtaining information until we were returning from supper to the church, when I again made mention of the affair in such a manner that I did not think she would suspect anything wrong. But she gave me to understand in plain language that she would not converse on that subject under any circumstances.

I saw there was no use to waste any more time with her and did not mention the subject again.

We remained in this place ten days, during which time I formed the acquaintance of an old man by the name of Snyder, who had five wives, three of them living at his residence in the town and the other two on his farm in the country. Being a brother Mormon, Mr. Snyder one day during my stay there invited me home with him for dinner, and on entering the dining room he introduced me to his three wives, the youngest of the three being about twenty years old, while Snyder was sixty-one years old.

That afternoon Howard and myself were taking a walk, and by chance met this young Mrs. Snyder, whom I introduced to my brother. He asked to accompany her on her walk, to which proposition she unhesitatingly assented, and he walked on home with him.

Her husband was not at home, but before Howard left the gate he heard one of Snyder's other wives say to her: "I'll tell on you, and you will not get to go out again."

This convinced him that there was a great deal of jealousy existing between Mr. Snyder's wives. He said she was well posted in everything pertaining to the Mormon doctrine, and at the same time bitterly opposed to their proceedings.

The afternoon following George Howard and I took a stroll down to Salt Lake City, which was a distance of three miles.

We had been in the city but a short time and were walking up Main street, when on casting my eyes across the street I saw old man Snyder standing talking to Porter Rockwell and Bill Hickman. They were just across Main street immediately opposite us, and George had not yet got sight of them. Those two men were supposed to be Brigham Young's "destroying angels," and their business was to put any one out of the way who had fallen under the ban of the Mormon Church.

These two men had been pointed out to me before, and as soon as I got sight of them I said in a low tone: "There are the leaders of the Danites."

When he looked across at them old man Snyder was pointing his finger direct at us, and Rockwell and Hickman seemed to be very eager to get a good look at us.

George said: "This is no place for us. Let's get back to the Fort." And all the talking I could do I could not make him believe that we were perfectly safe there in the city in broad daylight. His very countenance showed uneasiness to extremity. He had been there long enough to be thoroughly posted in all their laws, customs, etc., and didn't seem to think it would be healthy for us there from that time on. However, I can truthfully say that we made the trip to the Fort in much less time than we did from the Fort to town, notwithstanding it was all up grade.

On our arrival at the Fort we went to Gen. Connor's quarters and told him the whole story just as it occurred. The General said: "The thing is up with you now Howard, you might as well quit and go home. You can do no more good here now. You are perfectly safe here in the Fort, but the moment you are out of sight of it you are in danger of your life. But you will have one company of cavalry to protect you when you go to leave the Fort."

It was really laughable to see the way Howard would tremble and shake while Gen. Connor was talking to him, and he was anxious to get out of the country and wanted me to go with him, it being the wrong time of year to catch a train going East. He thought if he could get to Fort Bridger, which was one hundred miles east of Fort Douglas, he would be safe from the Mormons, and would stand equally as good a show to strike a train going eastward as he would at Salt Lake.

Before we were ready to start for Fort Bridger there came a man to Fort Douglas who had been wagon boss for Maj. Russell the year before. He had just received a letter from his former employer requesting him to come at once to Fort Kearney. He was anxious to find some one to travel with, as it was not safe for one to travel alone in that country, and it was a long and tedious trip this time of year.

The Pony Express was then running, but outside of that we were not likely to see any one on the trip.

They insisted on me accompanying them, and being anxious to cross over on the other side of the mountains, I agreed to join them. Having two saddle horses myself I told them three horses between them would be enough, for in case of emergency I would use one of my horses for a pack animal. The next two days were spent in getting ready for the trip, Mr. Damson, the wagon boss, having procured three horses for himself and Howard, Mr. Howard thinking it might not be conducive to his health to leave the Fort to look for horses.

Getting everything in readiness, we made the start just at dark, going the Emigrant canyon route, striking Echo canyon fifty miles from Salt Lake City, making the trip that far without stopping to let our horses feed or even to eat anything ourselves. We did this because we wished to get beyond the Mormon settlements without being discovered by them. We reached Fort Bridget the third day and there took in two more companions, John Scudder and John Korigo, who had been at work at the Fort all winter hauling wood for the Government. They had earned a little money and were returning to their respective homes, one living in Missouri and the other in Pennsylvania. We were now five in number and calculated to make Fort Kearney in fifteen days, which, if I remember rightly, is called six hundred miles from Fort Bridger.

We crossed Green river and took the Bitter creek route, thinking that would be the safest from hostile Indians; but when we got to the head of Bitter creek the Pony Express rider informed us that the Indians were very bad on the North Platte river, having killed two express riders the week before.

This frightened the boys badly, for not one of them had ever been engaged in an Indian fight, and all were free to admit that they were not hankering after experience of that kind.

After we struck North Platte we saw considerable Indian sign every day, but it was evident that the reds were in little bands.

From now on we made a dry camp every night, always stopping in the middle of the afternoon to let our horses graze while we did our cooking to avoid building our fire after dark. Then we would mount and ride until after dark and make a dry camp. This was done in order to avoid an attack while in camp, but we made the entire trip without seeing an Indian.

On my arrival at Fort Kearney I met my old friend Jim Bridger, who was waiting there for a man by the name of Jim Boseman, who was on his way with a large train of emigrants to the eastern part of Montana, the same country that Bridger, Kit Carson, Beckwith and I passed through in 1856 when the Indians were so bad.

Jim Bridger had met Boseman the fall before and had promised to pilot him through to that part of Montana, for which he was to receive five hundred dollars, it also being understood that, there would be at least fifty men in the train and all well armed.

Bridger was just in receipt of a letter from Boseman stating that he would be there on or about a certain date with two hundred men, most all of whom had families.

Jim was very anxious to have me join him, offering to divide the spoils.

I told him it would be folly for me to accompany him, as he would be able to handle the train alone and would then have the five hundred dollars himself, and furthermore, I did not care for work of that kind that summer, as I would rather return to Taos and buy a band of sheep and settle down, for I thought I had enough money, if properly handled, to make me a good living.

At this Jim laughed heartily and said: "Yes, you'll settle down with a band of sheep when you are too old to straddle a horse and your eyes too dim to take in an Indian. I have often thought of the same thing," he continued. "I have a place picked out now about fifteen miles east of Fort Bridger on Black's Fork, near the lone tree. There is where I am going to settle down after I make this trip. I can then sit in my door and with a good glass I can see Fort Bridger that was named for me and which I feel proud of to-day."

Jim Bridger made this trip north with Boseman's train into the valley where the town of Boseman now stands, without the loss of a man or beast on the entire trip, and returning to South Platte, married an Indian woman of the Arappahoe tribe, went to Black's Fork and took up a ranch within five miles of the lone pine tree. Here he lived with his Indian wife for about five years, when she died, leaving two children, a girl and a boy, which I have been told he sent to school, gave them a good education, and they now live, I think, in the state of Missouri.

CHAPTER XXVI
THROUGH TO BANNOCK.—A DANCE OF PEACE.—FRIGHT OF THE NEGROES.—A FREIGHT TRAIN SNOWED IN AND A TRIP ON SNOW-SHOES.—SOME VERY TOUGH ROAD AGENTS

While I was at Fort Kearney another long train of emigrants came along, en-route for Bannock, Montana. They did not know just where Bannock was, and through the influence of Jim Bridger and Gen. Kearney, I was offered employment in guiding them at seventy-five dollars per month, with provisions.

I told them I did not know where Bannock was, but that I could take them to any portion of Montana they asked to go, I was not long making the bargain and making preparations to get started. We went back over the same road as far as Fort Bridger that I had come only a short time before. There was not a person in the entire train that had ever seen a hostile Indian, and very few of them had ever traveled outside of their own state. The most of them were from Indiana, and most of the men had families, and I presume they were fleeing from the draft; that being the time of the late war.

I experienced a great deal of trouble in getting those people organized and trained in a manner to enable us to protect ourselves against the hostile Indians.

In this train there were two negros, whose names were Joe and Bab. Joe was driving a team for his grub and Bab was cooking for two families for his grub. The people of the train fell into the habit of calling me Captain, and every time I would ride along where this Joe or Bab were, they would invariably salute me by lifting their hats or by taking them off entirely and then they would say: "Marse Capting, de ye see any Injuns?"

One day my scouts came in from the south and reported seeing a band of Indians, about ten or fifteen in number, two miles away and coming direct for the train. I struck out alone at full speed in that direction to ascertain what kind of Indians they were, there being another man whose business it was to take charge of the train at any time I was away, and in case of an attack or danger of such, it was his business to corral the train and prepare for battle.

I had only gone a half mile when I met the Indians, and they proved to be Arapahoes. I was personally acquainted with all of them and asked them to go to the train with me, telling them it was just over the ridge. This they agreed to do, saying: "We will go to the train and then all will go out and kill some buffalo this evening."

We rode leisurely along until in sight of the train, and the moment the people saw me riding with the Indians on each side of me, they felt sure that I had been taken prisoner, and all the hustling and bustling around to get those wagons corralled, beat anything I had ever seen, and they were all so badly excited that it was no use to try to hello at them.

They were afraid to shoot at the Indians for fear they might shoot me, or if they did not shoot me, they were afraid that if they should shoot the Indians they would retaliate by shooting me down.

The wagons being corralled, we rode around the entire train. I left the Indians and rode inside of the corral and told the people that these were peaceable Indians and were all friends of mine, and that I wanted every man, woman and child to come out and shake hands with them. Quite a number hesitated, believing that I had been taken prisoner by the Indians and had been compelled to do this in order to save my own life, and believing that those Indians wanted to murder the entire train.

But after reasoning with them for a while I succeeded in convincing them that the Indians were peaceable. Then they all went out and shook hands except the two darkies, who were not to be found any where about the train at that time. I then told the man whose duty it was to look after the train in my absence, to drive about three miles and camp, describing the place, and that I would go with the Indians and kill some buffalo, so that we might have fresh meat, telling him to have each family cook a little bread extra for the Indians, and that they would furnish meat enough to do to-night and to-morrow, and was off for the buffalo hunt.

The Indians told me there was a band of buffalo about two or three miles ahead of us near the road.

We pushed on, on the main road, and sure enough right in the little valley where I had told the captain to camp, we saw a band of buffalo feeding. We all made a dash for them, and succeeded in killing five fat buffalo, and on the ground, enough for the entire train.

As soon as the train was corralled and the stock turned loose, we appointed four men, who claimed to know something of butchering, to cut up and distribute the meat among the people of the train. Up to this time the darkey cook had not been seen since I came over the hill in company with those Indians. A certain lady in the train said she thought that when he saw the Indians coming he had run off and hid in the sage brush, but after the fires were started he crawled out of one of the wagons where he had been hid, and claimed that he had been asleep all this time and did not know anything about any "Injuns," but it was a difficult matter to make the people in the train believe this yarn. I had the Indians build their fire outside of the corral, and while they were preparing their meat I went around and collected bread enough of different ones in the train for them, also a bowl of molasses. After all had their supper over I proposed to the Indians that we have a dance.

This dance is what they call a dance of peace, and is carried on in a manner like this: They—or all that wish to participate in the dance—form in a circle around the camp-fire, singing, or rather humming, a certain tune. I went to the people of the train and told them that the Indians and myself were going to have a peace dance, and all that wished to see it could come to the camp- fire and look on. I think every man, woman and child came out to see the dance, which lasted about two hours. After the dance was over one of the young Indians in the crowd came to me and said if I would interpret for him he would be pleased to make a speech for my friends, providing they were willing for him to do so. When he told the other Indians he was going to make a speech they all sat down in a circle around the camp-fire, seventeen in number, and were perfectly silent. I told them that this young Indian wanted to know if they would care to hear him make a speech. All were anxious to hear him, which would be something new to them. I told them that he would make the speech in his own language and I would interpret it word for word as near as I knew how.

When I told him they would be pleased to hear from him he walked up to me, laid his hand on my shoulder, and said:

"I have known this friend of mine a great many years. A long time ago when he use to come to our village, we always killed a dog, and after we would have a feast on dog meat, we always smoked the pipe of peace, and all of the Arapahoes are his friends."

He continued this manner of speaking about fifteen minutes, to the amusement of the entire train, and when he took his seat he wanted some one else to speak, but no one would attempt to respond to him, thus winding up the amusements for the evening.

In a conversation that evening with the Indians, they told me their business out there, which was to keep the Sioux Indians off of their hunting ground.

The Sioux and they were on friendly terms, but sometimes the Sioux would steal over on their hunting ground. They proposed to accompany us through the dangerous part of the country.

The morning following I told the men in the train of the generous proposition which the Indians had made me, and told them if they would furnish the Indians with bread they would keep them in meat. I also told them that we were now in the most dangerous part of the Sioux country, and that as long as those Indians were with us we were in no danger whatever from the fact that when the Sioux saw those Indians with us we were supposed to be their friends, and they dare not trouble us in the least.

This, however, was more than agreeable to the entire train, relieving the scouts of their duty, also the night guards. I made arrangements with the Indians to travel three days, and we then pulled out. Just when we were almost ready to start, one young lady in the crowd said to me; "Captain, I want to ask you one question, and will you tell me the truth?" I said: "Most assuredly I will." She said: "I want to know whether it was true that when you visited those Indians they always killed a dog and ate the meat?"

I told her it was true as gospel, and said we always considered dog meat the finest in the land, and only the chief and his most intimate friends were able to afford dog meat. She said she was astonished to hear me talk in such a manner. She said: "The most laughable part of the proceedings the evening before was the action of the darkey cook, Bab, who stood away back in the outer edge of the crowd when you and those Indians were dancing. You could have knocked his eyes off with a frying-pan and not have touched his face."

All went well. The Indians traveled with us three days as they had agreed to, which brought us to the head of Bitter creek. We killed a few buffalo all along the way, and when the Indians were ready to leave us they had killed all the meat that the train could take care of.

This being as far as they had agreed to accompany us, they were to start back the following morning and that night we had another peace dance. The Indians invited all in the train to participate in the dance, but none would take a part; so they and myself had the dancing to ourselves again The next morning when they were ready to leave us I told the people in the train to all come outside of the corral, both old and young, and form in line so those Indians could shake hands with all of them, telling them that they had done us a great favor in escorting us through the dangerous part of the country, and that this shaking hands they considered a great token of friendship.

This request was complied with, and the Indians all passed down the line of people, shaking hands with each one. After they were done shaking hands with all the train they all came and shook hands with me, mounted their ponies, and rode away as fast as their horses could run.

We pulled on for Fort Bridger, all going smoothly, for we were in the Bitter creek country and had no fear of Indians in that section. The day we arrived at Fort Bridger we sent four men on ahead to ascertain, if possible, where Bannock was. Here they met, by chance, some men from what was then called East Bannock and from them we learned just where Bannock was located, it being on a west tributary of the Missouri river. We also learned from these parties that there was a great excitement at this time over mines that had been struck some eighty miles east of Bannock, on what was known as Alder Gulch, or Stinking Water, but they were not able to advise us as to whether or not we could get there with wagons.

Now I knew just where we wanted to go, and we took what was known as the Landers cut-off, and pulled for Fort Hall, reaching the fort without encountering any trouble with the Indians or otherwise. The second day after passing Fort Hall, while we were crossing Snake river, we met a crowd of miners just from Alder Gulch, on their way to Denver, Colorado, for their families. From them we learned where Alder Gulch was, and those miners spoke in such high terms of the richness of that place that a great many in the train wanted to go there instead of going to Bannock, while others wanted to go to Bannock, that being where they had started.

That night they took a vote to decide as to which place they should go, which resulted in favor of Alder Gulch, so we pulled for Alder Gulch instead of Bannock.

We were now in the Bannock country. I did not hear of any depredations being committed by the Indians, but I used all precautions possible in order to prevent a surprise by the redskins.

Every few days we would meet a little squad of miners, all telling exciting stories about the richness of Alder Gulch. They were going home to their families with the expectation of moving them out there the following spring; most of their families being in Denver, Colorado. This all helped to create an anxiety among the people to push on and get through as quick as possible.

They moved somewhat faster now than before, reaching Virginia City, Montana, about the last of September, this being the trading point for Alder Gulch. Here we stopped and the train paid me off.

I stayed around there about three weeks. One day while I was at Virginia City two men, Boon and Bivian, who owned the only store of any note in Virginia City at that time, came to me and said that they had a train of twenty-two wagons some where on the road, but just where they did not know, and they wished to employ me to go and pilot it in, as their men with the train were all inexperienced in that line of business, and not acquainted with the road, not having been over any part of it before, and they were afraid that through carelessness they might fall into the hands of Indians.

The train was loaded, principally, with flour, bacon, sugar, coffee and tobacco. Flour was then worth twenty-five dollars per hundred, bacon forty cents a pound, and other things in proportion. On the twentieth of September I took two horses and started off to meet the freight train.

Three days from the time I left Virginia City I crossed the summit of the Rocky Mountains and it was snowing hard. I thought it doubtful whether or not they would be able to cross the mountains this winter, but I went on, and met them between Fort Hall and Soda Springs. I gave the wagon-boss a letter which Boon and Bivian had sent him, and after reading the letter he asked me if I thought they could cross the range this fall. I told him that it was about one hundred and eighty miles from there to the summit, and if he could make that distance in ten days he would be able to get through, but if not, he could not cross the mountains this fall. He said it would be impossible to make it in that length of time, as the cattle were all getting very poor and weak and the teams very heavily loaded. The next morning I struck out, taking another man with me, to try and find if possible, another ford on Snake river some thirty or forty miles above the old crossing, knowing if I could do that it Would save us two or three days' travel, and might be the means of our getting across the mountains that fall. I told the wagon-boss that I would meet him at Fort Hall, so in company with one other man, I struck straight across the country for Snake river. The second day about noon we reached the river, and that afternoon we succeeded in finding a good ford, which we called the Island ford, there being a little island just above.

We camped on Snake river bottom that night, and the next morning about daybreak we were on our journey for Fort Hall, reaching the fort one day ahead of the train. Here we waited until the train arrived. From Fort Hall we struck out for Snake river. This was all an open country, with the exception of sagebrush. The first night after leaving the fort snow fell four inches deep on the valley, and I felt satisfied then that we would not be able to cross the mountains that winter. The next day the snow all melted in the valley, but hung low at the foot of the mountains.

The third day after leaving Fort Hall we reached Snake river, and were successful in getting across without any mishap whatever. This new ford is near where Pocatello, Idaho, now stands. The first night after crossing the river we camped on a little stream, which I gave the name of Rock creek, and I am told that it is still known by that name. That night the snow fell one foot deep. I told the wagon-boss the next morning that he was at his journey's end for the present fill. We unloaded one wagon and he took one wagon to haul his camping outfit and provisions for the winter, and returned to the river bottom for the purpose of wintering his stock there. Another man and myself went to work to make two pairs of snow shoes, for which we had to use the side- boards of a wagon, there being no timber suitable in reach for that purpose. We were three days preparing for this trip, by which time the snow had settled.

All being in readiness the morning of the fourth day in this camp I, accompanied by two other men started on horseback, one man going along to bring the horses back, and the other to accompany me across the mountains. We rode to within ten miles of the summit of the mountains. Here the snow was nearly two and a half inches deep. Our horses were unable to get anything to eat except the branches of quaking asp trees that we cut and carried to them. The next morning we saddled our horses, one of my companions started back again, and we mounted our snow shoes and started to climb the mountain, this being my second attempt to travel on snow shoes. I was somewhat awkward at this new undertaking, and you can rest assured that I was tired when I reached the summit of the mountains, which took the greater part of the day. Each had a pair of blankets and enough provisions strapped on his back for the trip.

After reaching the summit of the mountain and starting down on the other side we found it much easier traveling. We worked hard all day and made what we thought to be twelve miles, camping that night in the fir timber. It was a cold, disagreeable night, with our one pair of blankets each, we consoled ourselves that it was much pleasanter than to have been here afoot and alone, and no blankets at all. The second day's travel after crossing the summit of this mountain we met a freight train on its return to Salt Lake City. This train was owned by a man named Goddard. It had been across the mountains with a load of freight and was returning, like our train on the opposite side and was unable to proceed farther, having to return to the low lands for the purpose of wintering the stock. We abandoned our snow shoes and procured conveyance to Virginia City. Messrs. Boon and Bivian were glad to know that their train was safe from the hands of the hostiles, but they said they would lose ten thousand dollars by not getting it across the mountains that fall. These men having a room at the rear of their store where they slept and did their cooking, kindly proposed that I should stop and winter with them, which hospitable offer I accepted.

At this time a stage ran from here to Bannock and from Bannock to Boise and from Boise to Salt Lake City, and the news was coming in every day of both stage and train robberies along this line, and it actually got so bad that it was not at all safe for a man to step outside of his own door after dark, if it was known that he had any money. These robbers were known in those days as "road agents."

CHAPTER XXVII
ORGANIZATION OF A VIGILANCE COMMITTEE.—END OF THE NOTORIOUS SLADE—ONE HUNDRED DOLLARS FOR A "CROW-BAIT" HORSE.— FLOUR A DOLLAR A POUND

About this time what was known as a vigilance committee was organized at Virginia City, and other points along the stage line, for protection against desperadoes. During the winter I was not out much, and all the news I could get was from persons who came to the store to trade.

One morning in the latter part of January I went out after a bucket of water at daylight, and happening to cast my eyes up a hillside I could see sentinels walking to and fro I could not understand it. On returning to the house I mentioned the matter to Messrs. Boon and Bivian. They smiled and said: "We understand all that," and they explained the whole thing to me. One of them said: "There will be some fun to-day," and the other replied: "Yes, a little hemp-pulling."

"Yes," responded the other, "that is what I meant." And then—in our western vernacular—I "tumbled to the racket."

By the time we had breakfast over people were beginning to come in to trade, and happening to look down the street I saw forty or fifty men all well armed come marching up the street in the direction of the store They marched up to a large gambling house, called the Shades. There they halted while some of them went in and returned, bringing with them a man by the name of Jack Gallagher.

There was a log cabin immediately across the street with a fireplace in it, and to this house they marched Gallagher and put him inside.

Leaving a strong guard around the cabin, the balance of them started out as if hunting some one else. In a short time they came marching another man to the cabin by the name of Boone Helm, who had one hand tied up. It seemed to comfort Gallagher to know that he was going to have company on the long trip by the short route, and "misery likes company."

The third man was brought in a few minutes later whose name was Hank Parrish, the fourth and last that day being Clubfoot George.

They were all placed in the log cabin under a strong guard.

About the middle of the afternoon the crowd reassembled at the cabin jail, took the prisoners out, and marched them up the street. Mr. Boone and I walked down the street by the side of the crowd, and after they had gone one block, for some reason they came to a halt, when Boone Helm sang out in the most profane language he could have uttered, saying: "Hang me if you intend to, or I will have to go and warm my sore hand."

They marched on up the street to where there was a new log house that had been recently built and not yet covered. That had been prepared for this neck-tie party by placing four dry goods boxes in a row in the house. The four men were led in and placed on the boxes and a rope placed around each of their necks thrown over a joist above and made fast to a sleeper below.

While they were tying the rope around Jack Gallagher's neck—his hands already having been tied behind him—a perfect stream of oaths was pouring from his lips, and about the last words he uttered were: "I hope to meet you all in the bottomest pits of hell." These words were uttered not more than a minute before the box was kicked from under him.

After this little hanging-bee everything was quiet until near spring, when there came to town a man by the name of Slade, who was full of noisy whiskey, and started in to paint the town red. This man was the same Slade that used to be stage agent on the Overland road. He was also the same man that in the year 1852 cut an old man's ears off while he was tied to a snubbing post in a horse corrall, where he had been taken by the cowardly curs that were at that time in the employ of Slade simply because he, Jule, would not vacate the ranch where Julesburg was afterward established. After severing both ears from his head they shot him down like a dog while he was tied and helpless.

While in Virginia City this time Slade made threats against several people, and during his spree did something, I never knew just what, and a warrant was sworn out and placed in the hands of a marshal for his arrest. The marshal found him in a gambling house, and in some way managed to get him into the court-room before he suspected anything, not reading the warrant to him until they were in the court-room.

When informed that he was under arrest, Slade did not wait to hear the warrant read, but jerked it from the hands of the officer, tore it in two, wadded it up in his hands and threw it on the floor and stamped on it with his foot. Then he turned and walked out, and was in no wise backward in telling the officer, as well as the judge of the court, what his opinion was of such proceedings.

About the middle of that afternoon the Vigilantes, some twenty in number, came to where Slade was standing, took him in charge, and marched him off up the street. I happened to be standing near when they took him in tow and followed close in the rear while they were marching him off to the place of execution. I don't think that he drew three breaths during that time but what he was pleading for his life.

He told them after he was on the dry goods box that if they would release him he would leave the United States just as soon as he could get away. I have seen men die in various ways, but I never saw a man die as cowardly as this man Slade. When he found they were determined he begged and plead for them to let him live until he could see his wife; he said it was for a business affair. They did not wait for anything, but as soon as they were ready they kicked the box from under him, thus ending the life of another of the worst men that ever lived.

The awful life of this man is another story that would be too long to give here.

It seemed as though as soon as the arrest was made some of Slade's friends had started to inform his wife, from the fact that just as they were carrying the body from the gallows to the hotel she was seen coming across the hill as fast as her horse could carry her. I was told afterward that had she only got there before the hanging took place he never would have hanged, for parties that knew her said that before she would have seen him hanged she would have shot him herself. I was standing in the hotel where the body lay when she came in. She stood silently looking at the corpse for a few minutes, and then turning to the crowd that was standing around, said: "Will some one tell me who did this?" No one answering her, she repeated the question, and finally the third time she repeated the question at the top of her voice. At this I turned and walked out, and that was the last time I ever saw her. This was the last hanging we had that winter and spring.

In the latter days of April Messrs. Boone and Bivian employed me to cross the mountains and take letters to the wagon-master, and also to assist him in crossing the Rockies, so taking one pair of blankets, ten days provisions and a pair of snow shoes on my back I started afoot and alone across the mountains. The fourth day after leaving Virginia City I came to the foot of the main divide, and up to this time I did not have to use my snow shoes. Where I camped that night the snow was two feet deep, and the next morning there was a crust on it strong enough to bear me up until I went six or seven miles farther on, when I commenced to break through.

Then I put on my snow-shoes, and in a short time I was at the summit of the mountain. After reaching the top, the country being open and all down hill, I had fine traveling while the snow lasted, making a distance of about forty miles that day. Then I abandoned my snowshoes, and in two days more I was in camp on the river bottom where the stock had been wintered.

The wagon-master informed me that he had lost about one-third of the oxen, which had stampeded and ran off in a storm; also my two saddle horses, and his one and only saddle horse had gone with the cattle. He said they had been gone about six weeks, so I struck out to Fort Hall to try and buy a horse to ride to hunt up the lost stock.

I succeeded in buying a very poor excuse of a horse for a hundred dollars, that under any other circumstances I would not have accepted as a gracious gift. But it was "Hopkins' choice," that or none. Mounting my crow-bait, I struck out in a westerly direction to look for the stock.

Three days' ride from the fort I struck plenty of cattle sign. They were apparently heading for Wood river, and after following their trail about two miles, I discovered two horse tracks, which convinced me it was the stock I was looking for. The next morning I found them and the cattle were all there with the exception of three. One of my horses was there, but the other one was missing, the wagon-master's horse was also there. I succeeded in catching my horse and turned loose the one I had bought and left him there for wolf-bait, provided they would eat him, mounted my saddle horse, and turned the stock in the direction of camp. It took me five days to drive them to our camp on the river, making ten days in all since I had started out. We stayed there three weeks longer, and the grass being good, by that time the stock was looking well.

All this time we were expecting a Mormon train on the other side would cross over and break the road as they were not loaded, but not seeing any sign of them, the wagon-boss got tired of waiting, and hitching up, pulled about twenty miles to the edge of the snow.

We were two days making this twenty miles. Here we stopped, but the wagon-master and I started next morning on foot for the summit. While we were on the mountain we could hear the other train coming so we walked on to meet it and see if we could assist them in any way. They were taking a very wise plan for it; two men riding ahead on horseback, others were driving about forty head of loose stock behind them, all followed by the wagons.

They got to our camp that night about dark. This tram broke the road in good shape for us, and the following morning the boss put all of the oxen to half the wagons and pulled across. It took us nearly all day to get out of the snow on the other side, thereby taking us three days to cross the mountains.

I traveled with the train three days after crossing the mountains, and then I left and rode on to Virginia City, knowing that Boone and Bivian would be anxious for information.

This was the first train of the season, and when it arrived flour was worth one dollar per pound, bacon fifty cents, and everything else in proportion.

CHAPTER XXVIII
TWENTY-TWO THOUSAND DOLLARS IN GOLD DUST.—A STAGE ROBBERY.— ANOTHER TRIP TO CALIFORNIA.—MEETING WITH GEN. CROOK.—CHIEF OF SCOUTS AGAIN

After the goods were unloaded and the stock rested up for a few days, the train was started back to Salt Lake City to load with flour and bacon. After it had been gone five days Mr. Boone and I started to follow it, expecting to get to the Mormon city ahead of the train and have the cargo purchased by the time it would arrive.

Mr. Boone took with him on this trip twenty-two thousand dollars in gold dust, on pack-horses. But in order to get away from Virginia City with it and not be suspected, we packed up three horses one night, behind the store, and I started that night with a pick and shovel tied to each pack, as if I were going prospecting. I went to where I thought would make a good day's ride for Boone, and camped. He overtook me the next night, and he said he would not have had it known how much dust he had with him for three times that amount.

We made the trip to Salt Lake all right, however, but in a few days after we learned that the stage-coach that left Virginia City at the same time we did was robbed and every passenger killed. These passengers were seven successful miners that had made all the money they wanted, or rather what they considered a handsome little stake, there being eighty thousand dollars in the crowd, and they were on their way home somewhere in the East.

The driver was the only one that escaped, he claiming to have jumped off from the stage. I saw the stage when it came into Salt Lake City, and it was riddled with bullets and blood spattered all over the inside of the coach.

There was a man by the name of Brown driving the stage at that time, and many people believed, in fact it was the general impression at the time, that the driver was in with the robbers. This robbery and massacre occurred in what is known as Beaver canyon.

During my stay at Salt Lake there came in from Virginia City a young man by the name of Richard Hyde, to buy cattle. Mr. Boone recommended him to me as being a fine young man and very shrewd for his age. After having some little acquaintance with him and he had told me his business, also what profit there was in it, he and I formed a co-partnership for the purpose of buying cattle and driving them to Virginia City. We bought one hundred and ninety- two head of all sizes, and by the help of two other men, we drove them through, losing only five head, which was considered excellent luck.

We stopped about ten miles below town, and after setting a price on our cattle, I remained with them while Mr. Hyde went to look for buyers. He was gone nearly a week, and when he returned he had sold nearly all the cattle. We were well pleased with the result of our venture, and I am told Mr. Hyde kept the business up for several years until he made an independent fortune, and I am told, at this writing—1899—that he is somewhere in Iowa doing a large banking business.

As soon as the cattle were all delivered and we had settled up, Mr. Hyde and I struck back for Salt Lake City, he to buy more cattle, and I on my way to California.

Near Ogden I fell in with an emigrant train of twenty-two wagons bound for California. As soon as they learned who I was, having heard of me back at Fort Kearney, they insisted on my traveling in company with them, and there being some fine looking young ladies in the train, I accepted the invitation and joined them.

These families were from Illinois and Ohio, and I can truthfully say that I never traveled with or saw a finer crowd of people than these were, and I never was in a company that I regretted leaving as I did those people, for they all seemed more like brothers and sisters to me than strangers.

The majority of them bought small farms in Solano county, California, and settled down. I remained with them until after the holidays, then left and struck out for San Francisco. This was the beginning of the year 1865.

After remaining in the city a few days I concluded one day to take a ride out to the fort and see if any of my acquaintances were there. I only found one person that I had been acquainted with before, and that was Capt. Miller. He showed me a number of letters from his brother officers out in Arizona, all saying they were having a great deal of trouble with the Indians in that country. I returned to the city, bought two more horses and commenced making preparations to go to Fort Yuma by way of Los Angeles.

The day before I was to start I was walking down Sampson street near the American Exchange Hotel, where I was stopping while in the city, when I heard a voice across the street that sounded familiar, say, "Hello chief." I looked around and who should I see but George Jones, who was then coming on a run to me; and you can rest assured that I was glad to see him, as it had been nine years since I had met him. He told me of his trip back to Fort Klamath the time that he accompanied me to San Francisco and returned with the mail; of the hardships that he underwent on his way back, and also his various speculations after leaving the service and said that it seemed that everything he turned his hand to went against him.

I told him my intention was to go to Arizona and secure a position as scout, and he at once made up his mind to go with me, and it is useless to say that I was well pleased with his decision from the fact that when he was with me I always knew just what to depend on.

It was in the fore part of February when we started on this long and tedious trip, and we made up our minds to take our time to it. From here we went to Los Angeles, and there we stayed four days to let our horses rest, and while there we lived principally on fruit.

From Los Angeles to Fort Yuma it is called five hundred and fifty miles and the greater part of the way it is over a desert country. From Los Angeles we struck across the Mojave desert, crossing the extreme south end of Death Valley to avoid the sand desert, and made our way to the Colorado river without any mishap, but sometimes having to ride as much as forty miles without water for our horses.

When we struck the river we traveled down on the north side until just below the mouth of the Gila we crossed the Colorado, where Jim Beckwith and I had crossed a number of years before. We had not gone far after crossing the Colorado when we came to the Yuma Indians, spoken of before as not wearing any clothing. Here George Jones declared that he had gone far enough, saying he had found a place that he had been looking for for a long time where people did not have to wear clothing nor till the soil for a living. And he added: "This is good enough for me."

The next day at noon after crossing the river we reached Fort Yuma. We rode up to the guard and asked if Lieut. Jackson was stationed at this fort. The guard replied that he was, and directed me to his quarters. I walked up to his door and rapped. He came to the door, but did not recognize me as my hair had grown out long and my beard was all over my face, but in his usual kindly way he asked what he could do for us. I asked him if my friend and I could get our dinner.

By this time his wife had recognized my voice and came to the door, and as she was approaching him he asked if she could let those two gentlemen have their dinner.

"Why, Lieutenant, don't you know who that is you are talking to?" she said. "I do not," he replied. "Why," said she, "that is the boy scout."

It is useless to say that we were taken in to dinner and our horses taken care of, and while at the dinner table I told the Lieutenant our business there. I told him that I had come there with the intention of getting a position as chief of scouts, and that I would not accept a position unless my friend Mr. Jones could get a place with me. He told me that he had no doubt but that we would both be able to get a position, as they had lost five scouts inside of the last month.

After dinner Lieut. Jackson excused himself, and telling us to remain at his quarters until he returned, he took a walk to the General's quarters. He returned in about an hour, saying Gen. Crook wished to see us both at once at his quarters, and we, in company with the Lieutenant, walked over to the General's tent, and to my astonishment, I was introduced as Capt. Drannan.

The General's orderly and the officer of the day were both in his room and he told them he wished to speak to us on private business, and they at once withdrew. Then the General commenced to question me in regard to fighting Indians, and I did nothing for the next two hours but answer questions.

Like all other successful officers, he did not want any dead-heads around him, and I presume that is why Gen. Crook was such a successful Indian fighter.

He requested us to call at his quarters at nine o'clock the next morning, after which he called his orderly and told him to show us quarters for the night and also to care for our horses. That evening while George was away looking after our horses I was taking a stroll around the fort, when by chance I met Gen. Crook taking his evening walk, and he asked me what I knew about this friend of mine. I told how I had seen him tried on various occasions and that I had never seen any signs of his weakening yet. I also told him that if I accepted a position as scout, I wanted George Jones with me, for I knew that I could depend on him under any and all circumstances. The General told me that he had been having very hard luck this summer, having lost all his best scouts by their falling in the hands of the Apaches. He also told me that he had one scout that fell into their hands and was burned at the stake. The next morning at nine o'clock Jones and I were on hand at the General's quarters. The first question he asked me was on what conditions I wished to go to work and what I expected per month. I told him that heretofore what scouting I had done I had gone as an independent scout, and that I would go to work under no other conditions.

He asked me what I meant by an independent scout. I said I meant so much per month, rations for myself and horse, and all horses I captured from the Indians to be my own. If I don't suit you, you can tell me so and I will quit, and when you don't suit me I will call for my money and quit at once.

He said that was fair enough, but I told him that I would not go to work under any consideration unless my friend Mr. Jones could have employment too.

I hired to Gen. Crook for one hundred and twenty-five dollars per month, to go to work the following morning. After the bargain was made the General said to me: "You must bear in mind that you're in a different country now to what you have been accustomed to working in, and altogether a different climate as well." He proposed sending a man with me that he said was thoroughly posted in the country, knowing every watering place, as well as the different runways of the Indians in the whole, country, and he added that he would not expect any benefit from us for at least ten days, as it would take this man that length of time to show us over the country.

At this I withdrew from the General's quarters, and he and George soon made a bargain. George was to receive seventy-five dollars per month. The balance of the day was spent in making preparations for our prospecting tour, as we termed it.

CHAPTER XXIX
FIND SOME MURDERED EMIGRANTS.—WE BURY THE DEAD AND FOLLOW AND SCALP THE INDIANS.—GEN. CROOK IS PLEASED WITH THE OUTCOME.—A MOJAVE BLANKET

The following morning I ordered ten days' rations for three of us. When we were ready to start Gen. Crook called me aside and told me the nature of the man who was to accompany us, saying that there was not a watering place nor an Indian trail in the whole territory that he did not know, and said he: "If you don't see any Indians or fresh sign of Indians he will show you all over the country. But he is the scariest man of Indians you ever saw in your life."

This man's name was Freeman. When we were ready to start Freeman asked me what course I wished to take. I told him that I would like to go in the direction that we would be the most likely to find Apaches. I pointed in the direction of a range of mountains, telling him that by ascending them he would be able to show me where the different watering places were in the valley by land marks, and we struck out southeast from the fort in the direction of the middle fork of the Gila river. The first night we camped on what was then called the Butterfield route, some thirty-five or forty miles from the fort. This season there were a great many emigrants passing over this route from Texas and Arkansas to California, and Gen. Crook said the Apaches were giving them much trouble on this part of the road, and if they continued to be so bad he would have to send one or two companies of soldiers out there for the protection of the emigrants. The second morning out we passed a ranch owned by a man named Davis, who had lived there two years. He told me that the Apaches had never given him any trouble from the fact that he had gotten the good will of the chief when he first went there by giving him numerous little presents of different kinds.

He told me that although isolated from the world, he was doing well, from the fact that most all of the people passing there patronized him. This family was from Indiana. After I had told him who I was and what would be my business, he insisted on my staying over night with him when convenient, saying that it would not cost me a cent. Thanking him for his hospitable offer, we rode on, keeping the Butterfield route. Late that afternoon we met a train of sixteen wagons on the way to California. The people told us that the day before they had seen where five wagons had just been burned. I asked how far it was, and they thought it was twenty-five miles from where we met them. When we heard of this we pushed on, thinking there might be some dead bodies there and that we could bury them. On arriving at the scene, sure enough we found three dead bodies two hundred and fifty yards from the burned wagons; one of them being that of an old man, and the others, two boys twelve and fourteen years of age. The Indians had not stripped the bodies nor mutilated them, only they were all filled with arrows. The dead bodies were all dressed in home-made jeans. We found a few pieces of wagon boxes that had not been burned and dug as good a grave as we could in the sand, giving them as good a burial as we could under the circumstances. This being done, we took the trail of the Indians, which led off in a south-westerly direction. I felt confident that it had been at least three days since this depredation had been committed. My object in following them up was to see if we could get any evidence of white prisoners in their camp. For the first ten or fifteen miles they kept on the roughest, rockiest ground they could find, all of which led me to believe they had expected to be followed. The next morning we came to where they had made their first camp. All the evidence we could see of white prisoners in their charge was a few pieces of calico torn up and scattered around their camp-ground. We followed the trail until we came to where they had made their second camp, and here we found the waists of two women's dresses, one being somewhat larger than the other. The two dress waists we took along with us. Here the Indians had changed their course somewhat, and our guide said in the direction of their main village, but I did not consider myself well enough posted to go too near their main village. I told the guard to lead us off south of west from Fort Yuma, which he did, and late that afternoon we saw six Indians traveling east, and I told the boys that they were scouts for the main band and that they were going out to look for emigrants. When we first got sight of them they were traveling up an open valley. I told the boys that we would keep a close watch of them, and if they should camp alone we would have their scalps before morning; but just one look from Freeman and I was convinced that he did not approve of this scheme. George said to him: "You can take care of the horses can't you, and if everything is favorable, Cap and I can take care of the Indians." Late in the afternoon I told them what course to travel, and taking advantage of the ground, I pushed on to see the Indians go into camp. When I started the guide told me there was water about a mile above where the Indians were, and that they were pulling for it. He said there was a fine spring of water in a little bunch of timber, and that the Indians always camped there when they were going to and from their hunting ground. Sure enough, when they came to this little grove they all dismounted and turned their horses loose entirely, then commenced to roast their antelope meat for supper. I hurried back to meet my companions, and we succeeded in getting within a quarter of a mile of the Indians. By this time it was getting dark.

We picketed our horses and sat down to eat our cold lunch, after which we started down to the camp, but were very cautious how we traveled. When in sight of the camp-fire we could see them all plainly sitting around it. We lay silent and watched them and their movements. In a few minutes two of them got up and went out to where their horses were and drove them all up together to less than one hundred yards of where we lay. It was so dark we could not see them, but could hear them talking very distinctly. After having rounded their horses up together they returned to the fire. Thinking they would lie down in a short time, for they did not seem to suspect any trouble that night, we started to crawl down to their camp, all abreast. After our guide, Freeman, found that I was determined to attack them he seemed to muster up courage and come right to the front like a man. My object in crawling near their camp so soon was to see in just what position they lay before the fire went out, and when the last one laid down we were within fifty yards of them. I told the boys we had a soft thing of it, for each of us had two revolvers and a good knife, and the Indians were all lying close together with their feet towards the fire. I told them we would wait two hours as near as we could guess the time and then they would be asleep; that then we would crawl up and send them to their happy hunting-ground. After waiting until we thought they were asleep we crawled down to their camp, again all three abreast, George on my right and Freeman on my left; and so we drew near, their fire had not gone entirely out, and a little breeze now and then would cause it to blaze up just enough so that we were able to get their exact positions. I told the boys to watch me and when I raised to my feet for both to raise and draw both revolvers as we would then be right at their heads, and for each man to stick the muzzle of each of his pistols to an Indian's head and fire; George to take the two on my right and Freeman the two on toy left, and I to take the two in the middle, and after firing each man was to jump back two jumps, so in case one of us should miss one of his men that we would be out of their reach, thereby enabling us to get all of them without taking any chances ourselves.

George said that at the first click of his pistol one of his men raised up in a sitting position, and he only got one the first shot. Freeman and I each got our two Indians the first shot; but George having both his eyes on one, the other rose to his feet. George and I took two shots each at this other Indian before we could get him down. It was mostly guess work, for it was so dark that we could scarcely see him.

As soon as we were satisfied that we had all of them we started out to look for their horses, but it was so dark that we could not find them, so we found our way back to where our own horses were. Freeman and I laid down to rest, while George got on a horse and kept circling the camp so as not to let any of the horses get away during the night. He kept this up until the morning star arose, and seeing that all the horses were there, laid down to rest. As soon as it was beginning to get light Freeman and I arose, started a fire, and sat around until after sun-up, when we got breakfast, made some coffee and then called George, and all enjoyed a good square meal once more.

After breakfast we scalped our Indians and found that we had eight good half-breed horses and a number of good horse-hair robes. I asked our guide how far we were from Fort Yuma and he said straight through it was one hundred and twenty miles, but the way that we would have to go it would be at least one hundred and fifty miles. I concluded we had better pull out for the fort so Freeman and myself rode ahead and George followed up the rear, driving the loose horses. We did not see any more Indian sign that day. Late in the evening I was riding along when I ran on to a young antelope. I shot him and we had fresh meat for supper for the first time since we left the fort. The next day we crossed a big Indian trail going east. The trail looked to be about two days old, but as our rations were beginning to run short we did not attempt to follow them, but pushed on to the fort, making as good time as possible, returning on the eleventh day from the time we started out.

I reported our success to the General. He was well pleased with the result of the trip, and when I reported the burying of the dead bodies, he thought we had better return to the spot, taking with us some good coffins, and give them a more decent burial, but on consulting the doctor, concluded in that extraordinarily hot climate it would be utterly impossible to bury them after so long a time, and the idea was abandoned.

I showed the two dress waists that I had found at the Apache camp to the General, also to Mrs. Jackson, but we never got any information of any white prisoners being taken there at that time.

The General was pleased to see the Indian scalps, as he said they were the first scalps that had been brought in for two months.

Gen. Crook now made up his mind at once to send Lieut. Jackson out on the road with two companies of cavalry, and George Jones and myself were to accompany them as scouts.

When we were ready to start Lieut. Jackson asked me if I didn't want more scouts, but I told him that I thought we could get along this trip with what we had.

We took the Butterfield route and followed that road until we were in the St. Louis mountains. This seemed to be at that time, a favorite part of the country for the Apaches to commit their depredations upon emigrants. We traveled very slowly as we had to pack our entire outfit on burros, and our saddle horses having to live altogether on grass, consequently we could not hurry. Early in the morning of the sixth day of that trip George and I started out in advance of the command, one to the right and the other to the left of the road, and if neither of us should see any signs of Indians we were to meet at the crossing of a certain stream only a few miles ahead of the command; and in the event of either of us arriving at the stream and waiting half an hour and the other did not make his appearance, he was to return at once with his force of scouts to the command. On arriving at the appointed spot and finding that George and his assistants were not there, we waited until we were convinced he was not coming and at once returned to the command.

On our return we learned that shortly after starting out that morning George had run on to a big Indian trail. Supposing it to be the same band of Indians whose trail we had crossed when returning from our other trip, he had reported to the command at once, and the trail being fresh, he, taking four other men, had started in pursuit, leaving word with Lieut. Jackson for me not to be uneasy about him nor attempt to follow him, but to remain with the command until I heard from him again.

While Lieut. Jackson was yet talking relative to the matter, I received a message from George saying that he had the Indians located some five miles from the road and wanted me to come and look the ground over before the command should start.

I at once mounted, and piloted by the man who had brought the message to me, rode to where George was. On arriving there I found the Indians so situated that it was impossible to ascertain the number from the fact that in this extraordinarily warm climate the Indians do not use any wick-i-ups or lodges, so that the only method by which we could make an estimate of their number was by counting the number of fires they had end calculate each fire to represent a certain number of Indians, this being our method of estimating them when in wick-i-ups, we reckoned their number to be one hundred and fifty.

Where these Indians were camped it would be utterly impossible to make an attack without being discovered long before reaching them, they being in a large valley.

After a thorough examination of the camp and surroundings by looking through a glass, we concluded that the best plan would be to return to the command and have it move up to within two miles of the Indians and remain there until after dark, then leave it to the Lieutenant whether he should make the attack on foot or horseback.

I remained to watch the movements of the Indians and see whether they were reinforced during the day and to report at dark, George returning to the command. The soldiers moved up that evening to within two miles of the Indian camp I remained at my post until it was so dark that I could not see through my glasses any longer, when I mounted my horse and rode to the command, having made no new discoveries. After explaining the situation as nearly as I could, the Lieutenant concluded to make the attack on foot some time between midnight and daylight the next morning, and to attack them from two sides at the same time.

The Lieutenant taking half the men and making the long march, which would be about one and a half miles farther than the others would have to march, leaving his orderly sergeant in charge of the other half of the command. I piloted the Lieutenant and George piloted the orderly. Here Lieut. Jackson invented some new style of signal to what I had seen before, by taking a tea cup and pouring powder in it and when he was ready to make the charge he was to set the powder on fire, which would make a flash, and in case the orderly was ready, he was to signal the Lieutenant in the same manner.

We made the circuit and marched up to within one hundred yards of the Indians, but could not make the attack until near daylight, the Lieutenant thinking it was so dark that the soldiers were in danger of killing each other, which was all perfectly true.

When the time arrived for the attack, which was just at daybreak, the Lieutenant gave his signal, which was answered at once by the orderly, and the Lieutenant led the way by going in advance of the force, and I think it was the quickest fight I ever saw. I did not count the Indians that were killed myself, but was told that there were between 190 and 200 found dead on the battlefield. They seemed to raise up as fast as the soldiers would cut them down, and I think there were two cut down with the sabres where one was shot. As soon as the battle was over, or when we could not find any more Indians to kill, George and I got our horses as quick as we could and went out after our horses, but they had taken fright at the firing and were scattered all over the country. That evening the Lieutenant moved back to the road at the head of a nice little valley where there were plenty of fine grass and good water, saying that he would make this his headquarters as long as he was out on this road.

The Lieutenant having five men wounded in this engagement, he wanted some one to carry a dispatch to headquarters requesting the General to forward an ambulance, and George Jones being a light man who could stand the ride better than any one in the crowd, the Lieutenant chose him to make the ride. It took us five days to come from Fort Yuma, and George took three horses and made the round trip in seven and one-half days. We remained here in this camp something like three months, but did not have another fight of any consequence with the Indians during our stay in this place. The Apaches quit their work in this portion of the country, thus enabling the emigrants to pass unmolested. In about one week after George Jones had returned from his trip to headquarters, Lieut. Jackson, George and myself went out around the foot of the mountain on a scouting tour. We were riding in sight of each other, when the Lieutenant signaled us to come to where he was. On arriving there he told us to keep our eyes on a certain ridge and we would see a little band of Indians rise over the top of the hill in a few minutes, saying he had just got sight of them while crossing the ridge beyond but could not tell just how many there were.

We secreted ourselves in a little thicket of timber where we would be concealed from their view, and in a few minutes they hove in sight. We counted them and found that there were eleven of them. Lieut. Jackson said to me: "Cap, shall we try them a whirl or not?" I said: "Lieutenant, I will leave that with you. If you feel like it we will give them a round." The Lieutenant said: "All right. I want to try my mare anyway and see if she is any good or not."

He was riding a mare of fine breeding, as black as a coal and as fleet an animal as there was in the whole command. By this time the Indians had crossed over the ridge and were then traveling up a little ravine, and by keeping ourselves secreted they would cross the ridge near us. Just as they turned over the ridge referred to, we were to make the charge. I was riding a roan horse that I had bought in San Francisco that could run like a deer, for when in this business I would not ride a horse that was not swift, but I never had him in an engagement of this kind. Being very hard-mouthed, I thought he was liable to run away with me, and I did not know whether he would run in the opposite direction or after the Indians. The Lieutenant and Geo. Jones said that if he would only run after the Indians they would follow me up closely.

As soon as the last Indian had passed over the ridge out of sight we made a charge, and that black mare went like she was shot out of a cannon. The

Indians were all armed with bow and arrows, but they did not attempt to use them. They did not suspect anything wrong until they heard the clatter of our horses' feet within a few yards of them and when they turned to look back we all had our revolvers ready and turned loose to firing and yelling, and for the next half mile we had a lively race. I had thought up to that time that there wasn't a man on the plains or in the Rocky Mountains that could beat me shooting with a pistol while on the run, but I must confess that Lieut. Jackson on his black mare could shoot more Indians in the same length of time than any person I was ever out with, and it seemed that as fast as the Lieutenant would shoot one Indian down his mare would turn and take after the next nearest. The Lieutenant fired six shots and killed five Indians and wounded the sixth one, while riding at full speed, and in this country in places the sage brush is waist high to a man. In this engagement I got four Indians, having to shoot one Indian three times before I got him down, and George Jones killed three. Not one of them escaped. Lieut. Jackson said he could not see why it was that they did not offer to defend themselves, when they had four to one to start with, for the Apaches have always been considered the bravest tribe of Indians in the entire West, and they had been known at different times to fight soldiers man to man. The last Indian I killed was beyond doubt the best horseman I had ever seen among the Indians, for he was first on one side of his horse and then on the other. It seemed as though he could almost turn under the horses belly while on the dead run, and he would swing himself around under his breast, rendering it almost impossible to deal him a fatal shot, for he frisked around so fast that a person could not get a bead on him.

We arrived at camp that evening just at dark. During our absence a train of emigrants consisting of twenty-one wagons had camped near our quarters. They wanted an escort of twenty or twenty-five men to accompany them to Fort Yuma, which they were willing to board free of charge while on the trip.

Those emigrants were from Dallas, Texas, and apparently well-to-do people. On learning that the Lieutenant was out on a scouting tour, they prepared a nice supper for the three of us. The following morning the Lieutenant detailed twenty men in charge of a sergeant, to escort the emigrants to Fort Yuma. George Jones went along as a scout and I remained with the command. They were ten days making the trip, as the emigrants having ox teams, traveled slowly. On the return of the escort the Lieutenant concluded to move some fifty miles south on this road, where we made our headquarters while we remained in this section of country, being on a tributary of the Grand river, which runs down through the western part of New Mexico.

One day while I was out on a scouting tour I ran on to a little band of Navajo Indians on their way to the St. Louis Mountains for a hunt. They had some blankets with them of their own manufacture, and being confident that the Lieutenant had never seen a blanket of that kind, I induced them to go with me to our quarters to show their blankets to the Lieutenant and others as well. I told the Lieutenant that he could carry water in one of those all day and it would not leak through. We took one of them, he taking two corners and I two, and the third man poured a bucket of water in the center of it, and we carried it twenty rods and the water did not leak through it. The Lieutenant asked how long it took to make one of them, and the Indian said it took about six months. He bought a blanket for five dollars, being about all the silver dollars in the command. The blanket had a horse worked in each corner, of various colors, also a man in the center with a spear in his hand. How this could be done was a mystery to all of us, as it contained many colors and showed identically the same on both sides.

By this time our three months' supply was running short, and Lieut. Jackson commenced making preparations to return to headquarters with his entire command. We pulled out for the fort, and did not see an Indian or even a fresh track on our way.

When we arrived at the fort and Lieut. Jackson made his report Gen. Crook was more than pleased with the success we had met, and I succeeded in getting George's wages raised from seventy-five to one hundred dollars per month, unbeknown to him.

It was now in the fall of the year, and the General decided to send us back again with two companies of cavalry and one company of infantry, calculated more for camp and guard duty than for actual service.

After we had rested up a month or such a matter the General had six or eight mule teams rigged up, also fifty burros for pack animals, and started Lieut. Jackson back again with three hundred soldiers.

CHAPTER XXX
A WICKED LITTLE BATTLE.—CAPTURE OF ONE HUNDRED AND EIGHTY-TWO HORSES.—DISCOVERY OF BLACK CANYON.—FORT YUMA AND THE PAY MASTER

We traveled very slowly and cautiously, and at the foot of the mountains, one hundred and fifty miles from Fort Yuma, we met a freight train from Santa Fe loaded with flour and bacon, principally, bound for Tombstone, Arizona. This train was owned by a man named Pritchett; but he was generally known as "Nick in the Woods." His party had had a fight with the Indians in the mountains the third day before we met him, and he had lost several mules killed and two of his teamsters were wounded. He informed us that the mountains were swarming with Indians, so the Lieutenant sent one company ahead of the command, George Jones and I going as scouts.

The advance company was under command of an orderly sergeant, who was instructed that if we met no Indians before reaching our old quarters we were to stay there until the command came up. On the third evening, just as our company was going into camp, and Jones and I were taking a survey from the hill near by, we saw a band of Indians coming leisurely along and evidently bound for the same camp ground that the soldiers were. Jones hurried down to inform the sergeant of the situation, I tarrying long enough to become positively convinced that the reds might get their camp fixings mixed with ours. So I put spurs to my horse and rode down to camp as quickly as I could. During this time the sergeant was flying around like a chicken with his head cut off to have his company ready to meet the Indians, and he barely had time to get his men all mounted when the reds came in sight, not forty rods away. George and I had ridden our horses very hard all day, consequently took no hand in this engagement, but rode to the top of a little hill close by where we could see the whole affair.

In this fight the Apaches showed their blood by standing their ground better than any Indians I have ever seen in a battle. They did not offer to retreat until the soldiers were right up among them, there being some sixty Indians and one hundred soldiers.

This was beyond doubt the wickedest little battle I had ever witnessed, but it did not last long. In the engagement three soldiers were killed and five wounded, and nine horses killed and nine wounded. There were twenty-seven good Indians left on the battle-field, and none of the Indian horses were captured. Those that the Indians did not drive away took fight and ran after them.

The soldiers followed until after dark, but did not find any more dead Indians. We remained in this camp until the Lieutenant came up with his command. He regretted that he did not come on himself ahead of the command, thinking that had he been there the result would have been quite different.

On his arrival he made a detail of eight men to assist in scouting, informing them that they were relieved of all guard duties while serving in that capacity, which is a great relief to a soldier, especially when in an Indian country. I was appointed captain or chief of scouts and George my first assistant The Lieutenant selected what he thought to be the best men he had in his command and they afterwards proved themselves to be just what he had expected. On starting out I did not make any reserve of scouts, but sent four with George and took the other four with me.

The fourth day after starting, about noon, I saw a band of Indians in camp ten miles from the Lieutenant's quarters. I knew this to be a new camp, as I had been over the same ground only two days previous. The Indians were camped in a valley nearly a mile wide that had not a stick of timber on it, except the few small willows that grew along the little rill that ran through the valley, consequently I could not get close enough to ascertain the number of the Indians until after dark. In the meantime I telegraphed the Lieutenant to hold his men in readiness or to move on at once as he thought best.

As soon as he received my message he mounted two companies of cavalry and pushed on to the place where I had told the messenger to meet me on his return.

While the messenger went to headquarters, in company with one of my scouts I went down near the Indian camp to try to ascertain if possible their number, leaving the other two scouts in charge of the horses. The only way we could get at the number was to count the fires and make an estimate in that way. The Indians seemed to be nervous and much disturbed that night from some cause; continually little squads of them would walk from one fire to another. After we had crawled around something like two hours and made our estimate, we returned to our horses and comrades, and I never was more surprised in my life than when I got back and met Lieut. Jackson there with his command, for I did not think sufficient time had passed for him to come that distance. I sat down and explained the lay of the ground as best I could, nothing being in the way except the little creek that carried the water across the valley, and I told him that about one hundred and fifty yards below the Indian camp the horses would be able to jump it. I also told them that I estimated their number at two hundred.

The Lieutenant said: "I think I will attack them at once," and asked me if I had their horses located. I told him I had. He then gave orders for all of the men to muffle their spurs, and he asked me to take my four men and as soon as the charge was made to make a dash for the horses, cut them off and stampede them. So we made the start, my scouts and I on the extreme right of their entire command. The Lieutenant had explained to the command that he would give the word in an undertone, each corporal to take it up, and they also had orders to hold their sabres up in a way that they could not make any noise. Being good starlight that night, one could see fairly well. We rode within less than one hundred yards of the Indian camp before the word was given to charge. When we were in sight of the horses we raised the yell and they all started, and we did not let them stop until at headquarters the next morning at daybreak. At this haul we got one hundred and eighty-two horses.

The Lieutenant returned with his command at ten o'clock the same morning, and he told me that he didn't think a dozen Indians escaped.

In this engagement he did not lose a man, and only a few were wounded, but five horses were hurt, and those he had killed after returning to headquarters, claiming that in this warm climate, where the flies were so bad, it took too much attention to cure them.

The two days following were days of rest with us, very little being done in the way of scouting. On the morning of the third day after the battle, George and his force went out to make a tour around the camp, and Lieut. Jackson, myself and four scouts went out to try to kill some deer, as we were getting very hungry for fresh meat, having been so long on bacon that we were all sick and tired of it. That day we killed four deer, and that night we camped six miles from our quarters. The next morning the Lieutenant sent to headquarters for ten pack animals, and we remained to hunt. In two days we killed all the game we could pack to camp on the ten animals. On our return the Lieutenant said to me: "This part we will have to keep to ourselves, for if we tell the General that we were out hunting and spent three days on the trip he would swear until everything around would turn blue."

After this we made two and three day scouting trips. While out on one of these, I found where the Apache stronghold was; down in a deep canyon, which since then has been known as Black canyon. From all appearance the greater part of the tribe was there. This canyon was tributary to the Colorado, and the hardest place to get into I have ever seen in the Rocky Mountains.

After making as good an investigation as the surroundings would permit, I returned with my scouts to the command to report. In making my report I said: "Lieutenant, I cannot half describe that canyon to you, for it is beyond any doubt the blackest looking place I have ever seen in all my travels." I told the Lieutenant that I would like to have him go with me and view the place before he moved his command. The canyon was fifty miles from our quarters. That same night George Jones returned with his four scouts, and the morning following we started out with the entire scout force, taking four days' rations with us. On the morning of the second day we came in sight of the canyon. The Lieutenant took a good look at it through his glasses, after which he said: "Captain, I think you named it well when you called it a Black canyon, for it looks as if it would be impossible to enter it on horseback." That day and the next was spent in trying to find where the Indians entered the canyon, and we at last discovered that they entered it from the east and west with horses, by descending a very abrupt mountain, and they were strung up and down the canyon for five miles. After the Lieutenant had made examinations of the location we started back to headquarters.

The Lieutenant and I fell back to the rear in order to have a private conversation relative to the situation. He said: "To be honest with you, I don't think it safe to go in there with less than two thousand soldiers, especially at this time of the year. If the Indians are as strong as they look to be, and have the advantage of the ground that they seem to have, it would only be sport for them to lie behind those rocks and shoot the soldiers down as fast as they could enter the canyon. This is the first time I ever went out hunting Indians, found them, and had to go away and let them alone. To tell the truth, I don't know what to do, for if I report to the General he will come at once with all his forces and accomplish nothing when here."

The Black canyon is in the northwest corner of Arizona, where it joins on to California and Nevada. Since that time there have been more soldiers killed in that place than in all the balance of Arizona territory.

After he had thought the matter over for a day or so he decided to move the command up near Black canyon, catch small parties out from there, and try in that manner to weaken them, or he might succeed in drawing them out, and in that way be able to get a fight out of them on something like fair ground. But in this the Lieutenant was very much disappointed, for they were too smart to come out.

George Jones and myself, each with our company of scouts, started out to locate some place suitable for headquarters, with instructions that anywhere within twenty miles would be satisfactory. I was out six days but did not find what I considered a suitable location. Jones was more successful. Within about ten miles of the canyon he found what he thought to be a suitable location, but said it would be impossible to get to the place with wagons. So the wagons were corralled and left at our present location in charge of a sergeant, with thirty infantrymen.

Loading the entire pack train, we started for Howard's Point, that being the name George had given the new camp.

Upon arrival at our new camp the Lieutenant put out pickets all around camp one mile away, keeping them there day and night while we remained. The scouts for the next six weeks were almost worked to death, without accomplishing much of anything, from the fact that we were too close to the main body of Indians to catch them in small squads, for in going out to hunt they would not go into camp until twenty or thirty miles from their headquarters, and our plan was to catch them in camp and attack them either in the night or just at daybreak in the morning.

One morning after being here ten days, the whole scout force started in two squads, with the understanding that we keep in about one mile of each other, so that if one squad should encounter a band of Indians the other could come to the relief.

After traveling about ten miles we heard shots in the direction where I knew George was with his four assistants, and turning in that direction, we put our horses down to their best speed, and were soon at the scene of action, but owing to the roughness of the ground we could not make as good time as we desired. When in sight of the contestants I saw that George was on foot, a comrade on each side of him, and they were firing as fast as they could load and shoot. He had run into those Indians, about twenty in number, hid in the rocks, and they had opened fire on the scouts, killing two of his men the first shot, and shooting George's horse from under him, leaving him afoot. When we arrived I ordered my men to dismount and take to the rocks, leaving the horses to take care of themselves, as the Indians were on foot and we could make better time in that immediate vicinity than we could on our horses. We had a hot little fight, but succeeded in driving the savages back. After the battle was over we tied our dead comrades on one horse and packed them to camp, changing off with George and the scout whose horse the dead bodies were tied on, letting them ride our horses part of the time. That night we dug graves and gave the two comrades as decent a burial as circumstances would permit. George felt very sorry over losing the two scouts because they were in his charge, but he was not to blame in the least.

In this little battle we got six Indians, and they killed two of our men and three horses. Lieut. Jackson thought it would now be advisable to increase the number of scouts and have a sufficient force together to be able to protect ourselves, for we were to remain here a month longer, and if in that time we were not able in some way to get at the Indians we would return to the fort and wait until spring.

Two weeks later I was out on a scouting tour when I saw a small band of Indians coming out of Black canyon and making their way westward. When they were within ten miles of our headquarters I got to count them, finding there were forty in the band, all on foot. I decided that they had started on a hunt and I would keep my eye on them to see where they would camp for the night. By this time I had all the water in this region located, and when I would see a band of Indians late in the evening I could tell about where they would camp.

As soon as I had decided where those would camp I telegraphed to Lieut. Jackson the situation. Where these Indians camped was within six miles of our quarters, but a miserable place to enter with horses, but I thought we could ride within a mile of the place on horseback.

The Lieutenant, however, was well acquainted with the ground, and as soon as he read my message he mounted his cavalrymen and started, and met me within a mile of the Indian camp. Dismounting, he and his men started on foot to the camp, and he told the soldiers to walk lightly, and when in sight of the camp to get down and crawl, but to be very careful not to break a limb or twig. I was very much disappointed in not getting to see this fight, for after I had sent my message to headquarters my horse fell with me and dislocated my right knee.

Lieut. Jackson said that he had never seen Indians fight harder in the dark than they did. He had three to their one, and said if it had been daylight he thought they would have held the soldiers in check for some little time. He did not think that he got all of them. In this action he lost— two men killed and seven wounded, two of whom died afterwards from their wounds.

I was laid up for a month with my knee, having to go on crutches most of the time, and it has given me more or less trouble since, even up to the present time. After we had arrived at our headquarters the Lieutenant concluded that as it was getting late, we had better move in the direction of the fort, and we started, making ten miles a day, and keeping out a strong force of scouts, thinking they might be able while in the mountains to capture small bands of hunting Apaches, but no more Indians were seen.

When we were out of the mountains we doubled our distance, making about twenty miles a day. Having no other way to travel than on horseback, my knee swelled badly, and when we got to Mr. Davis' ranch, which was forty miles from Fort Yuma, I had to stop and rest a few days. This was, however, a very desirable place for an unmarried man to stop, for Mr. Davis had some young daughters who were very attractive. I remained there a week, until I got the swelling reduced in my leg, and Mr. Davis hauled me to the fort in a wagon, taking at the same time a load of watermelons and tomatoes, which grew abundantly in that country. When I arrived at Fort Yuma Gen. Crook told me to take good care of myself, also saying he was highly pleased with the success of the past season, and he said: "If I live until spring I am going to see that Black canyon of yours that Lieut. Jackson has told me so much about."

During this winter we got a weekly mail established from Fort Yuma to Los Angeles, I had been here over eight months and had not seen a newspaper since I came, and when this mail line was established nearly every man subscribed for a paper of some kind, and the fort for the first time was blessed with plenty of reading matter, and we were able to gain a little knowledge as to what was going on in the civilized parts of the United States.

In the fore part of the month of December the officers put the men to work cleaning and straightening things up in general about the fort. We were all confident there was something up, but just what was not known. After everything was in proper shape it was whispered around that the paymaster would be in in a few days. On hearing this I asked Lieut. Jackson if it was true, and he said it was, and he also informed me that from this on we would have a regular pay day; and this was not all either, but that we were to have two more companies of cavalry and one of infantry, and said he: "The General is talking of sending you and me to California to buy horses, but that will not be decided upon until the paymaster comes."

It was the twentieth of December when the paymaster came, and also the three companies of recruits spoken of by the Lieutenant. This was the first pay day the soldiers had had for over a year, and the boys all had plenty of money, but a-poor show to spend it, as there were no saloons or gambling houses there, so they amused themselves by gambling among themselves, and one could go all around the fort and see all kinds of games running, and there was money flying in the air.

CHAPTER XXXI
TO CALIFORNIA FOR HORSES.—MY BEAUTIFUL MARE, BLACK BESS.—WE GET SIXTY-SIX SCALPS AND SEVENTY-EIGHT HORSES.—A CLEAN SWEEP

It was about the first of January when Gen. Crook ordered Lieut. Jackson and I to go to California to buy fifty head of cavalry horses. With an escort of twelve men we headed for Los Angeles, expecting to be able to procure the horses there, which we did, and were back at Yuma in a little more than a month preparing to give Apaches more of our warm social attention. In this campaign Lieut. Jackson was to take the lead with two companies of cavalry and one of infantry, and take the same route as the season before. Gen. Crook was to follow in a month, taking no wagons, but a pack- train of one hundred animals. Only Mexicans were employed this time as packers, and the captain of our train was named Angel, but he didn't look it.

It was arranged between Gen. Crook and I that I was to have twelve scouts and select them myself. The General sent a sergeant with me to take the names of the men I wished to secure, and then he gave me permission to go into the corrall and select two horses for each of my men, taking anything that did not belong to a commissioned officer. In the afternoon of the same day Lieut. Jackson came to me and said: "Captain, I have a present for you if you will accept it. I want to give you Black Bess."

This was the beautiful mare that he rode the year before and of which I spoke previously.

It was a very acceptable present indeed, and I was surprised to learn that he would part with her, but he walked down to the stable and turned her over to me. He had never ridden her when going into a fight except the time of which I made mention when out on the scouting tour. He said to me: "She is too fine an animal for me, and if you will train her a little she will be a perfect companion to you."

This black mare proved to be the most intelligent animal that I had ever owned in my life, and there was nothing she seemed to dislike so much as the sight or even the scent of an Indian. Often when out scouting I have got off of her and let her feed at the end of a picket rope while I would lie down and sleep, and the moment she would see or scent anything strange she would come to where I was lying and paw until I would raise up and look in the direction of whatever object she had seen or heard, and in less than three months she was the pet of the entire command. She would follow me like a dog anywhere I would go.

We pulled out for the mountains, and went something like one hundred and fifty miles from Fort Yuma before making a halt for a permanent camp-this being the fore part of February, 1866-and as soon as we were fairly settled we began active work.

We had only been there a few days when George Jones came in and reported having seen the trail of a band of Indians coming from the direction of Black canyon. George, myself and four other scouts started out immediately to take the trail, which was ten miles south of our quarters. We camped on their trail that night on account of the country being too rough to travel after night, but the next morning we were off early and followed the trail all day. Just before sundown we halted on a high ridge, when I took a look through my glasses over the country. About twelve miles away I saw an Apache camp. The course they had traveled that day brought them about as near our quarters as where we had struck their trail, and from this I came to the conclusion that they were either looking for the command or were expecting an attack.

Now the country between us and the Indians was very rough, but I told the boys that we must get there that night, and as quickly as possible.

I could see the country between the Indians and headquarters, and they were not more than fifteen miles from there, although we were about twelve miles away, and about the same distance from the Indians.

Knowing that Lieut. Jackson would be anxious to hear from me, I sent one man back to camp to report to him, with instructions as to the course to move, also for him to throw up a rocket every mile or so, that I might know where to send my next messenger to meet him. Myself and the other four scouts started for the Indian camp, and it took two hours and a half the best we could do to reach it.

When we were within a quarter of a mile of them, that being as near as we thought it safe to ride, we dismounted, and leaving two men in charge of our horses, the other three of us started to crawl down to their camp, at least near enough to find out about their number.

They had not lain down for the night nor had they any guards out with their horses, but were sitting around the camp-fire smoking and apparently enjoying themselves.

No doubt if we could have understood their language they were then laying plans to capture the first emigrant train that might come that way. The moon was shining brightly, and we had a splendid chance to have stampeded their stock, but I did not think it best from the fact that it would put them on their guard, which would be to the detriment of the cavalry when they should arrive. We decided not to disturb them until the cavalry came up, knowing that the command would lose no time in getting there, and that it would be before daylight if it was possible.

We counted the horses of the Indians as best we could by moonlight, and made out eighty head of them. We could not make out just the number of Indians, but estimated them at seventy-five, After ascertaining as near as we could the lay of the ground and the general situation, we returned to our horses, and all started in the direction that we expected the command to come from. After we had ridden about a half mile I stopped, and George Jones started on with the other scouts to meet the command. After riding five miles they met Lieut. Jackson coming with two companies of cavalry and the entire scout force; and long before I expected them Black Bess told me by her actions that they were coming.

The Lieutenant formed his men in a triangle on the ridge, his object being to pocket the Indians; in other words, to bunch them up or prevent them from scattering. While he was forming his men and giving instructions, I told my men where the horses were and that we must get to them about the time the cavalry made the attack on the Indians. I told them that no doubt the horses would have ropes on them and the first one that I come to I would take him and lead the way. "And when you hear the first shot, all raise the yell, for by doing that we will be able to make the stampede, and if nothing goes wrong we will keep the stock going until we reach headquarters." When I got to the horses about the first one I stumbled onto was a white one, with a long hair rope on; I caught him and led the way, and he made a good leader for the others to follow.

We got to the horses a few moments before the soldiers got to the Indian camp, and at the first shot we all raised the yell, and as I led the white pony away all followed, and we did not halt until we were five or six miles off. Here we came to a small stream that meandered through a little valley. There we stopped awhile to let our horses drink and rest, and while there we counted our horses and found that we had seventy-eight.

We reached camp about six o'clock the next morning, but the soldiers did not get in until noon. When the fight was over the Lieutenant put out a strong picket guard and remained there until morning in order to catch the Apaches that might be secreted in the sage-brush.

When daylight came he succeed in jumping up eleven, which he considered ample pay for staying there a few hours. In this fight sixty-six Indians were killed, besides we got all their horses, blankets, ropes and such other articles as they had.

We did but little in the way of scouting for the next few days. Lieut. Jackson said that we had made a good beginning and we did not want to do much before Gen. Crook came. "For," said he, "we will have all the fighting we want when the General gets here."

The morning of the third day after the fight we started out with the entire scout force in squads of four, there being three squads, with the understanding that we were to keep in from one to three miles of each other, and all to camp together at night.

We took along with us four days' rations, but a scout is expected to live on four days' rations for eight days if it becomes necessary, for when he starts he never knows just where he is going or when he will return.

It was in the afternoon of the third day that I ran on to an Indian trail that appeared from the number of horse-tracks to be about twenty in the band. We could tell that they had passed there that day, so we followed the trail; and it was not long until the other two pulled in towards me, and we were soon near enough that I could signal to them, or they to me, and shortly we all met on the trail.

We had not followed long before we came in sight of the Indians riding leisurely along, and we then set it down that they were a band of Apaches on their way to the Oscuro Mountains for a hunt. They went into camp early that night on account of water, and after supper they amused themselves by running foot-races. I was tempted several times before dark to make a charge on them, but knowing that we could accomplish our end better by waiting until after dark, we held back until they had all turned in for the night. They did not lie down until about nine o'clock, and by this time the boys were all getting anxious for a fight. We waited about an hour after they had all lain down and then we started to crawl down to their camp. We agreed to use our knives and sabres, George Jones and I each having a big knife, all the rest having sabres.

Our idea for this was to prevent any of our own party from being shot accidently; but each man had his pistol in his left had with instructions not to use it except in case of emergency. We crawled into the camp undiscovered as the Indians had no dogs along to give the alarm.

Previous to this I had told the boys that I could crawl all over an Indian and not wake him up, and I came near demonstrating it that night. They were apparently asleep and badly scattered, two in a place.

I had told the boys not to strike until they saw that I was just in the act of striking; that when they saw me raise up for each man to spring to his feet and get his Indian the first lick if possible, and not to let up as long as they could see one kick.

It being bright moonlight we could see each other very plainly, and we crawled right in among them, there being no order whatever in their camp. When I came to where there were two lying with their backs together, I made up my mind that that was too good a chance for me to let pass; so I looked around to see if the boys had their men selected, and seeing that they had, and that they were all watching me and the Indians also, I raised to my feet, and placing my right foot between the two Indians, I aimed to sever the first one's head from his body, which I came near doing, for he only just quivered after I struck him. At that they all began the work of blood and death.

The second one I attacked I had to deal the second blow, as I also did the third one. Up to this time I had not heard a word from any one of my companions, but there had been a continual ringing of sabres all around me. Just as I had done up my last Indian George sprang to my side and said: "Cap, we have got every one of them." We counted them and found that we had killed twenty-two, and after examining their blankets and other "traps," we knew that we had got them all.

They had killed a fine buck deer during the day and had only cooked enough of it for their supper, so we had plenty of fresh meat, for a while, at least; so while George and some of the other scouts went for our horses, which were about a quarter of a mile from camp, the remainder of us built a fire and began roasting venison. This was the first fresh meat we had on the trip.

The morning following we gathered up the horses and found we had twenty-two, and we started two of the men to headquarters with them, and also sent a message to Lieut. Jackson to the effect that we were going in east of Black canyon to see what kind of a country it was. We were out seven days longer, making ten days in all, but we did not make any new discovery.

When we returned to headquarters I learned that Lieut. Jackson had received a dispatch from Gen. Crook, to the effect that he would soon be on with more supplies and men.

The Lieutenant advised me to work close to quarters, as the General was likely to be on any day, and said it was hard to tell what he would want to do when there.

CHAPTER XXXII
SOME MEN WHO WERE ANXIOUS FOR A FIGHT AND GOT IT.—GEN. CROOK AT BLACK CANYON.—BAD MISTAKE OF A GOOD MAN.—THE VICTIMS

After the events of the last chapter I remained in camp most of the time, and sent my assistants out in different directions, with orders to return the same day.

In ten days Gen. Crook made his appearance, with two companies of cavalry and one of infantry.

The next day after his arrival after having talked the matter over relative to Black canyon and the country surrounding it, he asked me how far it was to the noted place. I told him it was what we called fifty miles. The General said: "There is where I want to go. Those men I brought out with me are anxious for a fight. I brought them out here to fight, and I will see that they get it." He told me that the day following he wished me to accompany him to that country, saying: "You can take as many of your scouts along as you like, and I will make a detail of twenty men to do camp duty."

We started out the following morning for Black canyon, taking along my entire scout force. In the afternoon of the second day I piloted Gen. Crook to a high ridge, where, with his glasses, he could overlook the whole country. He could see Black canyon and the perpendicular wall of rock on the opposite side for miles and miles, in fact, as far as he could see with his glasses. After he had looked the country all over he asked me where we could get into the canyon. In answer to this question I said: "General it is easy enough to get into it, but the question is where to get out."

He said: "We surely can get out where we go in if we only have sense enough to keep our eyes open." So I told him that I would show him the next morning. We returned to camp and I started out on foot to find some fresh meat, and had gone but a short distance when I ran on to a band of wild turkeys, and killed two fat gobblers. Turkeys seemed to keep fat in that country the year around, as those that I killed were very fat. During the time

I was out hunting George Jones had taken two other scouts and had made an entire circle of our camp, and not seeing any Indians or fresh sign we felt safe from any attack that night.

The next morning we did not move camp, but leaving the twenty men detailed for camp duty in charge of the camp and stock, I took my entire scout force to escort Gen. Crook to Black canyon. When we came to where the trail started down the bluff, he asked me how far I had been down. I told him about a mile, but did not let him know that Lieut. Jackson was with me at the time, knowing that the General wanted the glory of being the first officer to investigate and take in the situation of Black canyon. He asked me if it was safe for us to go down that far. I told him it was not at this time of day as we could not go that far and back without being seen by hundreds of Indians.

He decided not to look any further, but we returned to our camp and made preparations to start back to headquarters the next morning. He did not say anything to me as to what he thought of Black canyon that evening, but next day on our way back to headquarters he asked me if I thought there would be grass enough where we camped the night before for three or four hundred head of stock for three or four days. This led me to believe that he intended moving a part of his command to that place.

As soon as we were back at headquarters he told me that if any of the horses belonging to the scouts had shoes that needed resetting to have it attended to at once, and also told me to have the scouts pick out the very best horses for the trip.

During the time that these preparations were in progress, Lieut. Jackson in a private conversation told me that Gen. Crook was going to move up with a portion of the command near Black canyon and try to get into it. I told him that he could get in there easy enough, but had my doubts whether or not he would be able to get out with half the men he took in.

After having completed our preparations we pulled out for the Camp on the Mountain, this being the name given the camp by some of our men when we were out before, and I am told that the springs where we camped still go by that name. We started with two companies of cavalry and one of infantry, taking a pack-train to carry the supplies.

The first night at Camp on the Mountain Gen. Crook threw out a strong picket guard, and the next morning he told me to place my men both above and below the trail that they were to travel in descending the mountain into the canyon. I had examined this part of the country and was thoroughly posted in all the ways and by- ways of the Black canyon, which I knew the

General was not, and I told him that there was no danger from above, from the fact that it was at least six miles to the next place where the Indians could climb the bluff, but this didn't seem to satisfy him, so I placed my scouts according to his directions. This, he said, was to protect his rear.

I took my stand farthest down the hill from any of the scouts, being about half way down, and had my men scattered along on the mountain side, both above and below. This I did so that in case any of my men should see danger from above they would report to me at once and I would report to Gen. Crook.

After I had my men all placed and was at my stand I saw two companies of cavalry coming down the bluff supported by one company of infantry. When they got to where I was stationed, it being what we termed a bench on the mountain, they halted, and Crook and Jackson held a council in which Lieut. Jackson advised Gen. Crook to send the infantry ahead as "feelers," but the General thought just the reverse, saying: "I will feel my way with the cavalry." So they started down the mountain single file.

After they had been gone about two hours, or it seemed that long to me at least, I heard the firing commence; but I could tell from the direction that they were not yet down to the foot of the mountain. The firing continued about an hour, but I could not get to see any of the battle, for I dared not leave my post for fear that some of the scouts might come to report to me, and in case I was away he would not know what to do.

At last I saw the cavalry coming back up the mountain, some on foot, some leading their horses, and a very few riding. The Indians were being held in check by the infantry in order to give the cavalry a chance to get out of the canyon with their horses.

As well as I can remember, in this fight Gen. Crook lost forty-two men killed, twenty-one wounded, and sixty horses killed.

That night I heard one sergeant ask another in the presence of Gen. Crook when the dead would be buried, but the question was not answered. The next morning the General told me to take as many men as I wanted and see if I could recover the dead bodies. I said. "General, if you will wait until night I will take my men and if there are any dead bodies left on the battlefield I will try and get them, but I do not propose to take my men and stick them up for a target to be shot at by the Indians when they have no show whatever, for I will not ask my men to go where I will not go myself."

He said: "Suit yourself about it," and turned and walked away.

That night I took my entire scout force, besides twenty soldiers that volunteered to go along, and descended the mountain. We worked hard all night, and all that we could find was twenty-one bodies, and that day they were buried, after which we commenced making preparations to return to headquarters.

Up to that time I had not had a chance to talk to Lieut. Jackson concerning the battle in Black canyon, as we had both been busy ever since. When on a march it was my custom to ride ahead of the army, so the morning that we were ready to start back I had given my orders to the scouts, had mounted, and was just ready to start, when Lieut. Jackson said: "Wait a minute, Captain, and I will ride with you."

The reader will understand that by this time the Lieutenant and I were as intimate friends as though we were brothers, and when he told me anything I could rely upon it, and I had always made it a rule to be punctual with him. If he would ask me a question I would always answer it the best I could, and if I asked him for any information, if he knew he would tell me. And here I would like to say that while Gen. Crook bore the name of being a great Indian fighter, I know for a fact that Lieut. Jackson planned more victories two to one than Gen. Crook did himself, and had it been in the Lieutenant's power to have kept those soldiers out of Black canyon, they never would have entered it.

That morning after we had ridden a short distance he mentioned the fight and said: "Cap, that was a horrible affair." I said: "Lieutenant it was not half as bad as I thought it would be, for when I saw you go down there I did not expect to see half of the boys come back." He said: "Had it not been for the infantry coming to our rescue just when it did not a horse would have come out of the canyon, and but very few soldiers."

I asked him where the next move would be and he said that Gen. Crook was going to return to the fort and we would go farther out on the road to protect the emigrants, who would soon begin to move toward California. For the next two or three days everything was undergoing a change around camp; rigging up packs and fitting up in general.

The soldiers who had their horses killed were mounted on the choice horses that we had captured from the Indians, which made very fair cavalry horses.

As soon as we had completed our arrangements Gen. Crook started back for Fort Yuma, much wiser than he came, while we pushed farther out on the Butterfield route, with two companies of cavalry and fifty infantry-men.

We traveled four days from our old camp before making a general halt. The evening of the fourth day just a short time before we were ready to go into camp the scouts came in and reported having seen a small band of Indians only a short distance west of us, and they said they had watched them go into camp.

I reported to the Lieutenant and he started with one company of cavalry after them, leaving orders for the command to go into camp at the next water, which was about a mile ahead of us. This proved to be a small hunting party, and they in some way discovered us before we got to their camp. When we came in sight of them we were about a quarter of a mile away from their camp and they had their horses all packed and were beginning to mount. We gave chase, but they had the start of us so that we only got two out of the band, but we crowded them so close that they had to leave their pack- horses, and we got all of them, there being twenty.

I captured a fine American horse that showed good breeding. He was a sorrel, with white hind feet and a white stripe on his face and branded C on the left shoulder. I made the Lieutenant a present of this horse, and he afterwards proved to be a very fast animal, as the Lieutenant told me several years after, that during the winter months he kept the soldiers nearly all broke with that horse. He told me that he proved to be the fastest half mile horse he ever saw.

CHAPTER XXXIII
THE MASSACRE AT CHOKE CHERRY CANYON.—MIKE MALONEY GETS INTO A MUSS.—RESCUE OF WHITE GIRLS.— MIKE GETS EVEN WITH THE APACHES

The emigrants now begun to come along and we were kept busy night and day looking after the small bands of Indians that were continually making murderous forays in spite of all we could do to prevent.

With only three hundred soldiers and twelve scouts, and a country over one hundred miles in extent to guard, the service was exacting, and our lot was not altogether a happy one.

One day in July, in company with George Jones and John Riley, I started out in the direction of Black canyon to see if I could locate any small band of Apaches that might be prowling around. We traveled all day, and not seeing any Indians or sign of them, concluded to return to camp and get some much needed rest, and did so. It now seemed that there were no Apaches near us so I went to Lieut. Jackson's tent to report to him, intending to then lie down and rest for the day at least. He had just rolled out of bed, but he looked worn and haggard as if he had had a bad night of it. He asked me what news I had and I said good news, as we had seen no Indians or any fresh sign, but that I was worn out, having been almost constantly in the saddle for twenty-four hours. I asked him if he had any news and he said he had, and bad news too. The Indians had attacked a train in Choke Cherry canyon, burned all the wagons, but how many persons they had murdered or how many had escaped he could not tell me, as there were no scouts in camp at the time.

He wished so know if I could spare some men to go and bury the dead and locate the Indians. I replied that George Jones and John Riley were there, but that like myself, they were very much fatigued. He said he wanted them for another purpose. Then I offered two men, good and fresh, Jim Davis and Mike Maloney. But I had some uneasiness as to Mike. Not that there was any doubt about his bravery but he was so utterly incautious. However, I decided to go with them myself, as tired as I was. So as soon as I could get a bite to eat and a fresh horse saddled, we were off and on the way to Choke Cherry canyon.

Lieut. Jackson asked me when he could expect to hear from me. I told him that if I succeeded in locating the Indians in a body I would report to him at once, but if not he might not hear from me until my return. So we shook hands and he retired to his tent.

I directed Mike to go straight to the canyon and to keep on the east side until he came to the trail leading to Agua Caliente, and then take that trail direct for Sand Point; and when near the point to signal me by barking like a cayote, and that I would answer him by gobbling like a turkey; that he must meet me at Sand Point at three o'clock sharp, and if he was not there at that time I would know that something was wrong. I also told him to be careful and not run into an ambuscade, but above all not to be taken prisoner. Then I asked him if he could bark like a cayote. His answer was: "Sure, Captain, it's mesilf that can make a bloody cayote ashamed of himself bairking, and I belave ye's is afraid for me, but O'ill tell ye now there's no bloody Apache in all Arizony that's goin' to take this Irishman prisoner. I'm sure they don't want me schalp anyway, for me hair is too short."

I told Jim Davis to go to Wild Plum Ridge and then follow the trail to Sand Point, for him to signal me the same manner as Mike and I would answer him in the same manner.

Everything being understood between us we separated, each taking his appointed route, and I striking direct for the late emigrant camp. Before I got there, however, I ran onto the trail of apparently three Indians and concluded to follow them up. I had not gone a great distance away until I espied them in a little ravine a short distance away and they were having a scalp dance. I tied my horse secure from observation and then commenced to crawl upon them. They were circling two scalps that they had hung upon sticks stuck in the ground, every now and then drawing their bows as if going to shoot at them. I crept along cautiously, expecting that the Indians would be so absorbed in their scalp dance that I would get in close pistol shot before they discovered me; but in this I was mistaken, for when yet a long rifle shot away they espied me, and the moment I saw I was discovered I opened fire with both pistols, which caused them to flee in hot haste, leaving the two scalps hanging on the sticks. I went up to where they were and found that one scalp was that of a woman and the other that of a man.

I was now certain that there had been some emigrants murdered, and I soon made up my mind that about the first thing to do was to locate the bodies and bury them; but on consulting my watch I saw that I must hurry if I made Sand Point by three o'clock. Just as I had turned and started back to my horse, who should come up but Jim Davis. He had been trailing the Indians, which brought him over in my direction, and when he heard the shots he had come with all haste thinking that I was in trouble. We both turned and rode on to Sand Point, arriving there about half past three, but no Maloney was in sight, so after giving the signal agreed upon and receiving no answer, we made up our minds that he was in trouble, and we struck out to find his trail.

While we were on our way to hunt Maloney's trail Davis said: "Captain, I believe those Indians had two prisoners with them, and I think they are both women, judging from their tracks and other indications; see here what I found while I was trailing them." And he showed me two pieces of calico of different color. He thought that they had been dropped by the prisoners in the hope that some white person might find them and follow. He also said that there were small twigs broken off along the trail, which would indicate that they expected a search for them.

When Maloney left us he made direct for Sand Point, but before he reached there as he was riding along he discovered a small shoe track, he dismounted and tried to follow it, but it seemed that the tracks extended no farther. This confused him greatly, and he said to himself: "Be the loife of me it was only just there that I saw the thrack, and it's sure I am that she could not have flew away. Oh! here it is again, and begorra I belave it's the thrack of a white woman, for sure I am that no dhurty spalpeen of an Injun could iver make such a dainty thrack as that. Sure and I'll look in that bunch of brush, perhaps it's there she is, the poor crayther."

He made his way up to the brush cautiously with a pistol in each hand, and just as he peered in two Indians sprang upon him and grabbed his arms, which caused his pistols both to be discharged up in the air. They quickly bore poor Maloney to the ground and soon had him bound hand and foot. They then drove a stake into the ground and tied Mike to it, and began to gather brush for the fire. This did not suit him a bit, but all he could do was to hurl an avalanche of words at them, which, of course, they did not understand and to which they paid no heed.

"Ah, ye dhurty divils," said Mike. "Ye's have took me pistols both away from me. Ye's know I can't hurt ye's without me guns, so what's the use in ye's tyin' me like a hog, ye dhurty blackguards. Let me loose and Oi'll be afther lavin' ye's. Oi'll do it be the boots that hung on Chatham's Hill. I do belave they are goin' to burn me alive. O, ye bloody haythens; let me loose and Oi'll fight the pair of ye's if ye's have got me pistols."

The Indians by this time had the fire started, but Mike still retained his nerve, cussing the red fiends by all the powers in the Irish vocabulary.

Davis and I were pushing on with all possible speed in the direction of the place we expected to find Maloney's trail, when we heard two pistol shots in quick succession further up the canyon, so we put our horses down to their utmost in the direction from whence the sound of the shots came.

After running about two miles we came in sight of a small fire a short distance away that seemed to be but just kindled. We dashed up at full speed and found Mike tied to a stake and two Apaches piling brush on the fire. We fired at the Indians through the gathering darkness, but only killed one, and the other one made off about as fast as you ever saw an Indian go. Jim kicked the fire away from Mike and cut his bonds before he was burned to speak of. I asked him how he came to be taken prisoner by just two Apaches, and his story ran like this:

"Oi'll tell ye, Captain, it was on that sage-brush hill there while I was ridin' along I saw a thrack in the sand and sure I was that it was not the thrack of an Injun for it was a dainty little thing and the hollow of the foot didn't make a hole in the ground like an Apache's and Apaches niver wear shoes, aither. Well, I got off me horse and stharted to follow the thrack, and whin I got to that bunch of brush the dhurty rid divils sprang out on me like a pair of hounds, tied me hands and fate, and was tryin' to burn me aloive whin ye's came up."

"Well, Mike," said I, holding up the scalp of the Indian we had killed, "here is one Indian that will not bother you again, but be more careful next time."

We were all of the opinion that there was a woman alone somewhere in those hills that had escaped from the Indians when they burned the emigrant train, and we decided to keep up the search until morning; so we agreed on the following search: To separate about a quarter of a mile apart, and to commence circling a large hill or knob close by covered by a dense growth of sagebrush that in some places was as high as a man's head when he was on a horse, and every few rods to hallow, that in case she was secreted around there in hearing of us she would answer, and in case any one found her he was to fire two shots in quick succession, when the other two would go to him immediately.

We made almost the entire circuit of the hill, hallowing every little while, when I finally thought I heard a faint answer. I called again and then listened intently, and I was sure I heard an answer, after which I turned and rode in the direction from which the answer came. After riding a few rods I called again, when I heard the faint answer quite near, and I soon found a young girl of about eighteen years. She was overjoyed at seeing me, but was too weak to rise. I asked how she came there, and she said that the train in which her family was traveling had been attacked by the Indians. The people, or a part of them, had been murdered and the wagons burned, she and her younger sister had been taken prisoners, and when night came they were tied hand and foot and staked to the ground, and all laid down for the night.

"After we thought that the Indians were all asleep," she said, "I made a desperate effort and freed one of my hands, although it cost me a great deal of pain. After I was free I soon released my sister and we then ran for our lives. We had got but a short distance when the Indians discovered our absence, and raising the yell, started after us. My sister outran me and I soon hid in a little thicket and they missed me, but I fear they have overtaken her."

I asked her what her name was and she said it was Mary Gordon, and her father's name was Henry Gordon. He was sheriff of their county in Illinois for two years before starting west. I now fired the two shots to call Jim and Mike, and they were not long in getting there.

As soon as Mike came up he said: "Sure, Captain, and wasn't I after tellin's ye's that it was no bloody spalpeen of an Apache's thrack that I be follerin' lasht avenin'?"

Miss Gordon now seemed just to have realized that she was alone in a wild country, for she wrung her hands and said: "Oh! what shall I do in this desolate country without a relative or a friend; it would have been better if I had been killed when my poor father and mother were. O, kind sir, what will I do?" and she sobbed as if her heart would break.

I told her not to grieve, that we would protect her and see that she got safely to civilization, and that we would also try to find her sister. I asked her if she was not very hungry and she said she was, as she had eaten nothing for almost thirty-six hours. At that Mike said: "Sure, Captain, it's meself that has a pairt of me rations lift, and Oi'll go and get it for the poor crayther, and Oi'll bring the horses at the same toime," and he started off muttering to himself, "Ah, them Apaches, the dhirty divils; I'd like to kill ivery wan o' thim."

He soon returned with the horses, and handing me his rations, he said: "Sure, Captain, it's mesilf that thinks I'd better be afther takin' a look around here-abouts, as thim durty haythens might be afther playin' us the same game as they did me last evenin'." I told him it was a good scheme, that we might go up to the top of the hill and take a look as it was then most day, and if there were any Indians around they would be astir and that he had better let Jim Davis go with him, but he said no, for Jim to stay with me and the young lady and see that no "bloody blackguard of an Apache got her again," so I cautioned him to keep his ears and eyes open, and he struck out.

When Mike had gone Miss Gordon turned to me and asked my name. I told her my name was William F. Drannan, but I was better known on the plains as the Boy Scout.

"Oh, kind sir," she said, "are you the Boy Scout? I have often heard my father speak of you, and he said you were liable to put in an appearance when one least expected it. I thought of you a thousand times yesterday and to-night, but I had no idea that you were in a thousand miles of here."

I told her that I was at present scouting for Gen. Crook, who was at Fort Yuma, but that Lieut. Jackson, with three companies of soldiers, was stationed but a few miles west of us.

We had been waiting for Mike Maloney's return about two hours and were beginning to get uneasy about his delay and speculating as to what caused his absence so long, when we heard two pistol shots. This was always our signal to call a companion; so telling Jim to look after the young lady, I swung myself into the saddle and was off like the wind in the direction from whence the call, as I supposed it to be, came. It was now getting daylight, and when I got to the top of the hill I looked down to the south and I could see a fire. I did not hesitate, but went down that slope through the heavy sagebrush like smoke through the woods. As soon as I was near enough to distinguish objects around the fire I saw Mike bending over some object, and when I rode up to him, to my great surprise and delight, I saw it was a young girl. Mike was beside himself with excitement.

It appeared from his story that upon reaching the top of the hill after he had left us he came in sight of the fire and concluded to investigate; so riding down as near as he thought safe he tied his horse and commenced crawling. He soon saw that there were but two Indians and to his horror he saw that they had a white girl tied to a stake and were preparing to burn her. He crept up to within about twenty yards of them and fired, killing one of the Apaches, and as the other one turned to see what was up he fired again, killing the other one; then brandishing his pistol over his head he dashed up to the fire, exclaiming: "O, ye murtherin bastes, I'm avin wid ye's now; Oi'll learn ye's how to stake a poor divil down to the ground and thin try to burn him." Then he went up to the girl, cut her loose from the stake, and she raised up in a sitting posture, "Would ye's moind lettin' me help ye to yer fate, Miss?" said Mike. "O, I'm so tired and weak I can't stand," said the girl. "They have almost killed me dragging me over the cactus."

Just as I came in sight Mike fired two shots as a signal for us to come to him, but I was there almost before the echoes died away in the mountains.

When I rode up Mike was most beside himself with glee; his tongue ran like a phonograph, and within five minutes he had given me the history of the whole transaction and had invoked a curse on the whole Apache tribe from all the saints in the calendar.

I told Mike that we had best get the girl on one of our horses at once and be off to where Jim and the other girl were, and from there on to headquarters, for there was no telling how many more of the red devils there might be lurking around. "Faith, Captain, and it's right ye are this toime, too," said Mike, "and it's me own horse she can ride, the poor damsel." So saying he led his horse up and we assisted the young lady to mount.

As soon as we were fairly started I asked the girl her name and she said it was Maggie Gordon. She also spoke of her sister having been taken prisoner along with her, and when I told her that Mary was safe, her joy knew no bounds. This news so revived her spirits that she talked quite freely with us on the way over to where Jim Davis and the other girl were. When we got to near where they were Mary looked up and saw us and exclaimed, "Oh! there's Maggie!" and when they met there was the most pathetic scene of greeting I ever witnessed.

As soon as they had a good cry in each others arms we gave Maggie something to eat, after which we put the girls, one on Jim Davis' horse and one on mine, and headed for camp, arriving there in the afternoon.

We did not go to the late emigrant camp, as we could do nothing toward burying the dead, burdened as we were by the two young women, so Lieut. Jackson sent a platoon of soldiers out to do that last act of charity.

There were four families besides the Gordon family murdered, and those two young ladies were the only ones that escaped, so far as we knew. When the next emigrant train came along we sent the Misses Gordon on to Fort Yuma, and from there they drifted on into California, and I never heard of them again.

CHAPTER XXXIV
MASSACRE OF THE DAVIS FAMILY.—A HARD RIDE AND SWIFT RETRIBUTION. —A PITIFUL STORY.—BURIAL OF THE DEAD.—I AM SICK OF THE BUSINESS

We remained here for some weeks yet, piloting and escorting emigrants through the mountains, but having very few scraps with the Indians. When the emigrants quit coming and our provisions had run very low, we made preparations to return to Fort Yuma. But to make sure that no more of the crawling trains would be winding along that way this season, myself and another scout, with two days' rations, started on a little scurry eastward. But a tour of four days developed no further sign of emigrants or Indians, so the scout and I returned to find the command all ready to start. We were just about taking up the line of march for Yuma when a teamster on his way to Phoenix with a load of freight, drifted into camp and informed us to our horror, that the Indians had attacked the Davis ranch, killed the old man and his two sons, treated the old mother and the two daughters shamefully, and then pillaged the place and drove off all the stock.

I had no sooner ridden into camp that night than an orderly came and took my horse and said: "Lieut. Jackson wishes to see you at his tent immediately." I knew that there was something very unusual the matter or he would not have called me to his quarters until I had had my supper. On approaching his tent I saw that he was much excited. He told me what was up, and said it was strange the Indians would come down there that season of the year and commit such depredations as that. After he had laid the whole matter before me just as he had it from the teamster, he said: "Send the very best men you have on their trail." I told him I would go myself and take George and two other men with me.

I was convinced before finishing my talk with him that it was not the Indians that had committed the depredation, but that I kept to myself.

Just as I walked out of the Lieutenant's tent I met George and told him that we had a long night's ride before us, to pick out two of the best men we had, also to take the best horses—we had, and to change my saddle to Black Bess from the horse that I had been riding that day. I also gave orders to have everything in readiness by the time I was through supper, which did not take long, although I was very hungry. The boys were all on hand by the time I was through eating, and we mounted and rode away for the Davis ranch. The way we had to go to reach the ranch was about twenty miles down grade and inclined to be sandy all the way. We were all well mounted and we scarcely broke a gallop until we reached the Davis place.

A pitiful sight was there. The old lady and her three daughters had carried the old gentleman and two boys into the house and laid them out on benches in the best manner possible, and to say that it was a heart-rending scene does not begin to express it.

When I stepped into the house Mrs. Davis pointed to the dead bodies and said: "Captain, if you will avenge their death I will be a friend to you as long as I live." I told her that I would do all I could, that I was in a great hurry to get on the trail of the perpetrators, and I would like her to give me all the information she could relative to the matter.

She then led the way into a private room and related the whole circumstance, telling me how the Indians had come there, decoyed her husband and two sons to the barn and there shot them down, then rushed to the house, and before the inmate had time to shut and bar the door, came into the house, caught and tied her to the bed post, and then disgraced her three daughters in her presence. Then they gathered up all the horses and cattle about the ranch and drove them across the desert.

In the direction she said they had started it was eighty-four miles to water, but I did not believe for a moment that they would attempt to cross the desert in that direction.

After I had gained all the information I could, I said: "Mrs. Davis, those were not Indians, but Greasers or Mexicans, and I will capture them before twenty-four hours if I live."

I started one man back to camp to tell Lieut. Jackson to take the trail direct for Aw-wa-col-i-enthy, which in English means hot water, (Agua Caliente).

Lieut. Jackson had become over anxious as soon as we left and had started after us with one company of cavalry. My messenger met him five miles from the Davis ranch, and there he turned in the direction of Agua Caliente.

In starting out from the ranch I took the trail of the stock, and after we had gone quite a distance I called George to my side and told him it was not Indians we were following, but a crowd of cut- throat Greasers, and we didn't want to have a fight with them until the soldiers arrived if we could help it, but that we would fight them before we would allow them to escape.

I had never told George until now what all they had done, and when I related to him the whole affair he said: "We will not allow one of them to escape." We could see that they were turning in the direction of Agua Caliente and had made this circuit merely to throw any one off that might attempt to follow.

This was what I thought when I dispatched the Lieutenant to come to Hot Springs.

It was twenty-seven miles straight through on the road from the Davis ranch to Agua Caliente, but the way we went that night we supposed it was about forty miles, making sixty miles that we had to ride that night, while the soldiers if they started direct from camp would only have to travel thirty-five miles.

Finally the trail made a direct turn for Agua Caliente and I again "telegraphed" the Lieutenant to hurry up with all possible speed and try to reach the place before daylight, my object being to catch them in camp, as our horses would be too tired to run them down after they were mounted on fresh horses.

My second messenger did not see the Lieutenant at all on the road, for unbeknown to me he had started from headquarters soon after we did, and after having met my first courier, had pushed on with all possible haste.

When George and I were within a mile and a half of Agua Caliente we met some of the stock feeding leisurely along the direction of their old range. We examined them closely and found that they were the Davis stock.

We had not gone much farther until Black Bess raised her head, stuck her ears forward and commenced sniffing the air. I told George to watch her, and he said: "We must be near them." So we dismounted, took off our spurs, picketed our horses, and started cautiously towards their camp.

When we were within three hundred yards we could see the glimmer of their fires that had not entirely gone out, evidence that they had not gone to bed till late. We crawled so near that we could see the outlines of the fiends lying around the few coals that were yet smoldering. Now and then a chunk would blaze up as if to show the exact positions of the murderers.

After satisfying ourselves that this was the party we were in pursuit of, we returned to our horses.

I told Jones to mount his horse and not spare him until he met the soldiers; and to hurry them up so we could catch the Greasers in bed; and

I said to him as he was mounting: "If you do not return with the soldiers before daylight I will take chances of holding them here with Black Bess until you do return." But he had not gone more than two miles and a half when he met the soldiers coming in a stiff gallop.

George reported that we had the outlaws located, and the Lieutenant gave orders for the soldiers to muffle their spurs and sabres and to be quick about it.

I did not have to wait long until Black Bess told me they were coming, for when they got near me I could not keep her still.

Upon the arrival of the soldiers I told Lieut. Jackson the particulars of the murder as given to me by Mrs. Davis, and also where the murderers were. He divided his men, sending fifty around on the opposite side of the camp, giving them half and hour to make the circuit, George piloting them, and I the other fifty. When the time was up we rode down, both squads arriving almost at the same time. Just one word from the Lieutenant and the Greasers were surrounded, and us with our pistols drawn.

The outlaws seemed to be sound asleep, but when we commenced to close in on them they woke, and the first one that jumped to his feet had his pistol in his hand, but when he looked around and saw the situation he dropped his pistol before the Lieutenant had time to tell him to drop it.

It was not yet daylight, but their being a very bright moon, one could see first rate. All the Mexicans were soon on their feet and begging for their lives. Lieut. Jackson being able to speak Mexican asked if any one in their crowd could speak English, but they said they could not speak a word in that language. He then asked them in Spanish who their Captain was, and a big, rough, greasy looking fellow said he was the Captain.

The Lieutenant then told him to form his men in line out on the road, saying: "I will give you five minutes to prepare to die." He then turned to his orderly and told him to relieve them of their arms, and they gave them up without a word of protest. He then told them all to stand in a line and when the five minutes were up they must die. During all this time their Captain was pleading for their lives and making all kinds of promises, but the Lieutenant turned a deaf ear to them, not even answering them.

When the five minutes were up the order was given, "Platoon No. 1, front face. Make ready. Take aim. Fire." And all of the scoundrels fell at the first round, although some of them had to be shot the second time to get them out of their misery.

This being done they were taken about a hundred yards away and buried in the sand.

By that time it was daylight and Lieut. Jackson made a detail of twenty-four men to assist George and I in driving the stock back to the Davis ranch. The rest of the company returned to, headquarters, but went by way of the Davis ranch to assist in burying the bodies of the old gentleman and the two sons. Lieut. Jackson told me that when he arrived at the ranch and saw the dead bodies and heard the sad story of the wife and mother and of her daughters, he said it was more than he could stand. He made a detail of six men to dig the graves and he returned to headquarters and moved the entire command down there and they all attended the funeral.

After the funeral was over Mrs. Davis called me to one side and said: "There is one more favor I wish to ask of you before you leave." I asked her what it was. She said as she was keeping a boarding-house she would have to keep travelers, and that she would like to have us leave a man to look after the stock until such time as she could get some one to work for her. I told her that if the Lieutenant did not object I would leave a man with her that would take as much interest in the stock as if they were his own, and that she would find him a perfect gentleman at all times.

I called Lieut. Jackson aside and mentioned the matter to him. He told me to leave a man and that he would also detail a man to stay, which he did then and there. I asked George Jones to stay, which he was willing to do.

Mrs. Davis asked us to send her a good, trusty man and she would pay him good wages, and she said she would write to her brother, who, when he came out, would close up her business there as quickly as possible, and they would return to the East.

Arriving at the fort and finding no idle men, Lieut. Jackson wrote to San Francisco for a man, and in about three weeks he came, and he proved to be a good one, as Mrs. Davis told me several years afterwards.

It was nearly a month after we arrived at the fort before George Jones came. The next day after he arrived he told me that he had just received a letter from his father, who was then living somewhere in the state of Illinois, and had written him to come home as he wanted to emigrate to Oregon the following spring, and wanted George to pilot the train across the plains and over the mountains to the country where big red apples and pretty girls were said to grow in such abundance.

George had made up his mind to accede to the wishes of his father, and as we had been there twenty-two months and both were tired of the business, and having made up my mind to quit the scouting field, I talked the matter over with George for two days and concluded to accompany him to San Francisco; so we went to Gen. Crook and told him we were going to quit and go away.

He asked what was the matter, if anything had gone wrong. We told him there was nothing wrong at all, but we were tired of the business and had made up our minds to quit. He said he was very sorry to have us leave, but if we had made up our minds to that effect there was no use saying any more. He asked me how many head of horses George and I had. I told him that there had been over one hundred head of horses captured, and that many of them had been used by the soldiers all summer, but if he would let George and I select thirty-five head from the band of captured horses he could have the rest of them. This he agreed to, so there was no falling out over that.

Having settled up with Gen. Crook and everything arranged, in a few days we were ready to start.

The day before our departure for San Francisco we went around and visited with all the boys in blue, telling them we were going to leave, and that for good. They expressed their regrets, but bade us bon-voyage and good luck for the future.

CHAPTER XXXV
BLACK BESS BECOMES POPULAR IN SAN FRANCISCO.—A FAILURE AS RANCHER.— BUYING HORSES IN OREGON. THE KLAMATH MARSH.—CAPTAIN JACK THE MODOC

George Jones and I pulled out for San Francisco, via Los Angeles, this being the regular mail line at this time, and we made the trip to the City of the Golden Gate inside of a month.

As soon as we arrived at San Francisco we commenced selling our horses at private sale. We put up at what was known as the Fashion Stable, which was kept by a man by the name of Kinnear, whom we found to be a perfect gentleman, and who rendered us almost invaluable assistance in disposing of our horses. This was the first stable that was built on Market street. As soon as our horses were sold Jones boarded the steamer for New York. When we separated here, having been so intimately acquainted for so long, the separation was almost like that of two brothers, and we had not the least idea that we would ever meet again in this world.

I remained in the city three months, not knowing what to do or where to go. During this time I spent much of it in training Black Bess, as I found her to be a very intelligent animal, and she would follow me like a dog wherever I would go when she had the saddle on, and during that winter I taught her to perform many tricks, such as to lie down, kneel down, count ten, and tell her age. I could throw my gloves or handkerchief down and leave her for hours without tying her and she would stand there until I would return, and no one could come near them or take them away, nor would she allow a stranger to put his hand on her. One day I came to the barn and Mr. Kinnear asked what I would take to saddle Black Bess up and let her follow me to Wells, Fargo & Co.'s express office and back to the stable again without touching her on the way.

I said: "Mr. Kinnear, if it will be any accommodation to you I will have her follow me up there and back and it will not cost you anything."

"All right," he said, "about one o'clock come to the stable, for I have made a bet of fifty dollars with a man from the country, that you could make her follow you from the stable to Wells, Fargo & Co.'s express office and back to the stable and not touch her."

Wells, Fargo & Co.'s express office was a distance of eight blocks from the stable, and on my return I found quite a crowd there waiting to see the performance. I threw the saddle on the mare, put the bridle on her just as though I was going to ride, took my whip in my hand, and started down the sidewalk and the mare walked down the street. Montgomery street was always full of teams at this time of the day, and also the sidewalk crowded with people, but I walked near the outer edge. She would pick her way along the street among those teams as well, apparently as though I was on her back and at the same time would keep her eyes on me all the time. On arriving at the place mentioned, I took my handkerchief from my pocket and threw it down at the edge of the sidewalk, walked into the office and remained five minutes or more, and when I came out she was still standing with her head over the handkerchief as though she was tied. I picked the handkerchief up, started back down the sidewalk, and she took the street, keeping her eyes on me all the time until we reached the stable. The farmer was somewhat wiser, but about fifty dollars short in actual cash, but vowed he would not bet again on a man's own game.

On my return several different men asked me what I would take for her, but I informed them money would not buy her from me. Before putting her in the stable I had her perform several tricks, and then bow to the crowd, which by this time had grown to more than a hundred people.

I had now lain around so long that I had become restless, as it never did suit me to loaf about a town, so I concluded that I would try ranching. I had enough money to buy a good ranch and stock it, not thinking that it required any great amount of skill. So I started up the Sacramento river to look for one. After I was out most a month, this now being the last of February, 1867, I found stock looking well and found a man that wanted to sell out his stock and ranch. He had three hundred and twenty acres of land and one hundred and fifty head of cattle, some chickens, a few hogs, and a very few farming implements. After I had ridden around over the ranch several days and looked at his stock, and finding the range good, I asked his price. He wanted nine thousand dollars. I believed that this would be a nice quiet life, and although I did not know anything about raising stock, yet I thought I would soon catch on as the saying goes, so I made him an offer of eight thousand dollars, which offer he accepted. He was to leave everything on the ranch but his bed and clothing and a few little keep-sakes that he had about the house.

Now I started in to be an honest rancher, believing that all I would have to do was to ride around over the range occasionally and look after my stock, take things easy, and let my stock grow into money, as I had heard it said that stock would while one was asleep.

I stayed on this place until the spring of 1872, ranching with very poor success, by which time I had learned to a certainty that this was not my line.

When a man came along and wanted a cow I always sold him one. I would take his note for the price and, as a rule, that was all I ever got.

In the spring of 1875 a man named Glen came into that country from Jefferson county, Missouri, and to him I sold my entire possessions. I got out of that scrape by losing my time and one thousand dollars in money, but I had five years of almost invaluable experience in ranching and stock-raising.

In those days this was what we called a Mexican stand-off. I lost my time and money, but had my life left. Nothing occurred during this five years of my life more than the routine of business that naturally belongs with this kind of life, so I will pass over it. I had such poor success ranching that I don't like to think of it myself, much less having it told in history.

Leaving here I went to Virginia City, Nevada. This was in the palmy days of the Comstock, and everything was high. After looking around for a few days and seeing that horses were valuable, I started for Jacksonville, Oregon, to buy horses for the Virginia City market. On my arrival at Jacksonville I met a man by the name of John T. Miller, who was a thorough horseman, and was said to be a great salesman, which I knew I was not myself. I could buy, but I could not sell to advantage like some other men.

I formed a partnership with Miller, and we were not long in gathering up eighty-five head of horses in Jackson county and starting to market with them.

I was back to Virginia City in a few days over two months from the time I had left there, and Mr. Miller proving to be a thorough salesman, we soon disposed of our entire band at a good figure, and in less than one month from the time we arrived at Virginia City we were on our way back to Oregon.

After we returned to Jacksonville we settled up and had cleared eleven hundred dollars each on the trip. That beat ranching all hollow. Now Mr. Miller proposed to me that we go into horse raising. He said he knew where there was a large tract of swamp- land near Klamath Lake. Swamp and overflown land belonged to the state, and this swamp-land could be bought for a dollar an acre by paying twenty cents an acre down and twenty per cent yearly thereafter until it was paid.

Miller being a thorough horseman, I thought I might succeed better in the horse business than in cattle. So in company with him, I started over to look at the land, and being well pleased with the tract, I made application for it at once. This land was located just on the outer edge of the Modoc Indian reservation. Miller being acquainted with all the Modocs, he and I, after I had concluded to settle, rode down to Captain Jack's wick-i-up, which was a distance of two miles from where I proposed settling. Captain Jack was the chief of the Modoc tribe, and I found him to be a very intelligent Indian, and he made a very good stagger towards talking the English language.

When Mr. Miller introduced me to Chief Jack—or Captain Jack as he was called—and told him that I was going to be a neighbor to him, he said, "All right, that's good, and we be friends, too." I told him yes, and if the white men did not treat him well to let me know and I would attend to it. Jack then asked Mr. Miller where Mr. Applegate was, he being agent for the Modoc tribe, and lived in the neighborhood of Jacksonville, Oregon. Miller told him that he did not know. Jack said: "My people heap hungry and Applegate no give us anything to eat, no let us leave reservation to hunt; I don't know what I do."

Mr. Miller told Jack that he would see Applegate and tell him of their condition. The next morning Miller started back to Jacksonville and I remained on the land selected to be my future home.

Every few days Jack would come to my place to ask my advice as to what he should do, saying: "We no got anything to eat for three moons (three months). He tell me he come bring beef. He no come, no send beef." Finally Jack came to my camp one day and said: "I don't know what I do, no meat, no flour, wocus nearly all gone."

I told Jack that I would go home with him and see for myself, not knowing but that his complaints might be without foundation. I mounted my horse, and riding over with Captain Jack, my investigation proved to a certainty that he had been telling me the truth all this time, for they were almost destitute of anything to eat, there being nothing in the entire village in the line of provisions but a little wocus, or wild rice.

Jack said: "Agent no come next week and bring something to eat, I take all Injuns, go Tule Lake and catch fish. What you think?"

I said: "Jack, I do not know what to say, but you come home with me and I will give you one sack of flour and I have a deer there, I will give you half of that, and by the time you eat that up perhaps the agent may come with provisions." A few days later Jack came to my house and said: "Agent no come to-morrow, I go Tule Lake, take all Injuns. Plenty fish Tule Lake, easy catch them." To this I did not reply. I dare not advise him to leave the reservation, and at the same time I knew they were almost in a starving condition and were compelled to do something or sit there and starve; and here I would say that in this case Captain Jack was not to blame for leaving the reservation. I just state these few facts merely to show that while the Indians are as a general rule treacherous and barbarous, at the same time, in many cases no doubt similar to this one, they have been blamed more than was due them.

As the old adage goes, I believe in giving the devil his just dues, and I do not believe that Jack would have left the reservation at that time had he been supplied with provisions sufficient to live on.

I do not pretend to say whose fault this was, but merely state the facts as I know them.

CHAPTER XXXVI
THE MODOC WAR—GEN. WHEATON IS HELD OFF BY THE INDIANS—GEN. CANBY TAKES COMMAND AND GETS IT WORSE— MASSACRE OF THE PEACE COMMISSION

Two weeks later I went out to Linkville to buy some groceries. This place was fifteen miles from where I had settled, and the nearest trading post or settlement to me, telling my two hired men that I would be at home the next day or the day after at the outside.

The store was kept by a man named Nurse. He told me he had a band of mares that he would sell cheap, and insisted on my staying over night with him, saying that he would have them brought in the day following, which I agreed to do, and the next morning he started his men out to look for the mares. They did not get them gathered up until the afternoon, and Mr. Nurse and I were in the corral looking at them, when a man rode up at full speed, his horse foaming all over, and said in a very excited tone that the Modoc Indians had gone on the war-path and had murdered most all the settlers on Lost River and Tule Lake, the latter being only twenty miles south from Linkville. The courier that brought the news to Linkville said that the soldiers had come down to Tule Lake and fired on Captain Jack without any warning whatever, which we learned later to be all too true.

The Indians had scattered all over the country, and had killed every white person they ran across for two days and then fled to the lava beds. This put an end to the horse trading. Mr. Nurse said that some one would have to go to Jacksonville and report at once, for they were not strong enough there to protect themselves against the Modocs, but no one seemed willing to tackle the trip, and I told them that if no one else would go, I would go myself. It was now near sundown, and it was called one hundred miles to Jacksonville from there. I started at once, going part of the way over the wagon road and the remainder of the way on the trail.

I arrived at Jacksonville the next morning before sun-up. The first man I met was the sheriff of the county, who was just coming out to feed his horses. I related my story to him in as few words as I could, and told him to raise all the men he could. I had my horse taken care of and went to bed, for I was very tired; with directions to wake me up in time to eat a bite before starting. At four o'clock that afternoon they woke me, they having sixty men then ready to start and one hundred ready to follow the next morning.

Among the balance who were ready to start was Mr. Miller. When I led my horse out he asked if that was the horse I had ridden over from Linkville. I told him I had nothing else to ride. He went to the stable and got another horse and insisted on my changing my saddle, but I told him I would ride my horse to the foot of the mountains and then change, which I did.

We reached Linkville the next morning at nine o'clock, and Mr. Nurse gave us breakfast. That afternoon we went down to Tule Lake and buried three dead bodies, being of the Brotherton family, the father and two sons, and the next day we buried four more, after which I left this squad and returned to my ranch to get my two hired men away, which took me three days. By the time I had got back to Linkville the news had spread all over the country of the outbreak of Captain Jack and the Modoc tribe, and Gen. Wheaton had moved his entire force down to the lava beds, where Captain Jack had his forces concentrated.

Gen. Ross and Col. Miller had moved in, but I do not know just the exact number of men they had in their command. After this scare I could not get any men to work on the ranch, so I abandoned it for the time being and stayed around Linkville about a week, when I received a message from Gen. Wheaton to come to his quarters immediately. This message was carried by one of his orderlies. I complied, the orderly returning with me. I was not acquainted with Gen. Wheaton, nor had I ever seen him before. When I was introduced to him he asked me if I knew Captain Jack, chief of the Modoc tribe. I told him that I was well acquainted with him and all of his men. "Now," said he, "I'll tell you what I wish to see you about. Col. Miller recommends you very highly as a scout, and how would it suit you to take charge of the entire scouting force, and organize them to suit yourself and start in at once?"

I said: "General, I have tried hard to quit that business. In the first start I went at it for the glory in it, but having failed to find that part of it, I have become tired. I will not answer you now, but to-morrow morning at nine o'clock I will come to your quarters, at which time I will have my mind thoroughly made up." I left his quarters and went over to Col. Miller's. I told the Colonel that the General had sent for me. He urged me in the strongest terms to take hold of it, saying that there was not a practical scout in the entire command. Finally I promised him that I would again enter the scouting field.

The next morning I was up early and had breakfast with Col. Miller. After obtaining the pass-word I saddled Black Bess, and at nine o'clock was at Gen. Wheaton's quarters.

I left Black Bess standing about twenty paces from the General's tent, took one of my gloves and stuck it on a bush, and went in to see Gen. Wheaton. I told him that I had decided to start in scouting for him, and I suppose I was in his tent about half an hour talking matters over about the scouting business. All being understood, I started out to get my mare, and saw quite a crowd had gathered around her, and one man in particular was trying to make up with her. Just as I stepped out of the door I heard him say, "This must surely be Black Bess. I wonder who owns her now." And until he called the mare's name I had not recognized him, and it struck me that it must be George Jones, but not being sure, I said: "Is that you, George?" He said: "Yes, and that's my old friend Capt. Drannan." This was a surprise to us both. It was the first time that we had met since we separated at San Francisco in the fall of 1866, at which time we had both decided to quit fighting Indians, but here we both were again in the field. After a good square shake and giving a hasty synopsis of our experiences during the time we had been separated, George asked if I was going into the scouting field again. I told him that I had just accepted a position as chief of scouts with Gen. Wheaton. I then asked him what he was doing for a livelihood. He said that he had joined the Oregon Volunteers, and asked me if I did not think I could get him relieved. "For," said he, "I would rather work with you than any one else. We have been together so much we understand each other."

He told me his Captain's name and that he belonged to Col. Miller's regiment. I did not lose any time in seeing Col. Miller and telling him that I would like very much to have him relieve George Jones from his command, as I must have him for my first assistant.

This was the first time that Col. Miller had heard of George Jones being a scout, and he wrote out the release at once and went out and had Gen. Ross sign it and gave it to me.

George and I went to work at once to organize our scouting company, drawing our men mostly from the volunteers. About the time that we were thoroughly organized it was reported that the Pah-Utes and the Klamaths were all coming to join Captain Jack. This lava bed where Captain Jack was fortified, was sixty miles from the Klamath reservation, but the Pah-Utes were one hundred and fifty miles away, and it both surprised and amused me when those old officers would tell me that they expected the Pah-Utes any time. Being afraid of an attack from the rear, we had to scout a strip of country about forty miles long every day, and all the arguments that I could produce were of no avail. After going through this routine for about a month Gen. Wheaton concluded to take Captain Jack by storm. Captain Jack was there, and had been all the time, in what was called his stronghold in the lava bed, being nothing more or less than a cave in the rocks, sixty yards long, and from ten to thirty feet wide, there being one place in the east side where a man could ride a horse into it, and numerous places where a man could enter with ease. Down on the east and south sides are numerous holes in the rock just large enough to shoot through. Captain Jack had his entire force in there, had killed all of his horses and taken them in there for meat, and through the Klamath Indians had got a good supply of ammunition.

After Gen. Wheaton had made up his mind to take the stronghold by storm, he asked if I could give a description of the place. Up to this time there had not been a shot fired at the soldiers by the Indians, and I had a number of times passed in gunshot of the main entrance, and I know that the Indians had recognized me, but because I had befriended them they would not shoot at me.

I drew a diagram of the cave in the best style that I could, showing the main entrance and the natural port holes, and when I submitted it to the General, I said: "General, you can never take Captain Jack as long as his ammunition lasts, for he has the same kind of guns that you have, and the majority of his men have pistols also, and all that he will have to do is to stand there and shoot your men down as fast as they can come."

But the General thought different. The day was set for the attack, and on Wednesday morning the storm was to commence. The army had its camp one mile from Jack's stronghold, so the soldiers did not have far to march. About sunrise the whole command marched down and turned loose on Jack, and were soon bombarding him in great shape. This was kept up for three days and nights, when Gen. Wheaton withdrew, having lost sixty men and something over twenty wounded, as I was told by Col. Miller afterwards, but Jack did not come out.

A short time after this Gen. Canby came over and took the entire command. He brought with him a minister by the name of Col. Thomas.

The second day after Gen. Canby arrived he asked Gen. Wheaton, in the presence of quite a number of officers, how many men Captain Jack had with him.

Gen. Wheaton said; "My chief scout could tell just the number that he has, but I think some sixty-three or sixty-four warriors."

"And you had fifteen hundred men in that three days' fight?"

Gen. Wheaton said he had.

"And you got whipped? There was bad management somewhere," said Canby; and he concluded he would take Captain Jack by storm, but postponed it for a month, this bringing it into the foggy weather in that country, and in that time of the year it is the foggiest country I ever saw. I have seen it for a week at a time in the lava bed that I could not tell an Indian from a rock when twenty paces away. And this was the kind of weather Gen. Canby was waiting for. He marched down to the lava bed and placed his howitzer on the hill about a quarter of a mile from Jack's stronghold and commenced playing the shell. This was done in order to give the infantry a chance to march down to the main entrance of the cave and there shoot the Indians down as fast as they came out.

Three days and nights this was kept up, but not an Indian came out, and Gen. Canby drew off, losing over one hundred men killed, but I never knew the exact number wounded.

When Gen. Canby found he could not take the Modocs by storm, he sent to Yreka, Cal., for a man named Berry, who was a particular friend of Jack's, or rather Jack was a particular friend to him. On Mr. Berry's arrival at headquarters Gen. Canby asked him if he thought he dare go to Captain Jack's stronghold. Mr. Berry replied that he would provided that he went alone. I never knew just what Mr. Berry's instructions were, but, however, I accompanied him to within two hundred paces of the main entrance to the cave, in order to direct him to the proper place, and he chose his time to go after dark.

I remained there until after he returned, which was before midnight. A few days later I learned that there was to be a council meeting between Gen. Canby, Rev. Col. Thomas and Captain Jack, and in a conversation with Col. Miller he asked me my opinion in regard to the matter. I told him that I did not understand all the particulars, as I had heard but little about it.

He then told me that Gen. Canby and Col. Thomas, with George Meeks as interpreter for them, and Meek's squaw as interpreter for Captain Jack, were to meet Jack next Sunday morning for the purpose of effecting a treaty with the Modoc tribe, they to meet Jack at a certain place, without escort or side arms. After the Colonel had told me of the council and manner in which they were to meet Captain Jack, I said: "Colonel, do you really believe they will go?"

"Go," he replied. "Gen. Canby will go if he lives till the time appointed for the meeting."

I could not think that Canby would do such a thing, and I told Col. Miller that there was one thing he could depend upon, if they went in that manner they would never return alive. I also told him I did not consider Mr. Berry showed good judgement in letting Captain Jack choose his own ground for the council and agreeing to meet him without escort or side arms.

That afternoon Gen. Wheaton sent for me, and I responded to the call at once. When I arrived at the General's camp he opened the conversation by saying: "Captain, have you heard of the meeting that is to take place between Gen. Canby and Captain Jack?"

I said: "No, General, I had heard nothing of it." This being a little white lie, for it had been told me in confidence by Col. Miller. I asked what the object of the meeting was, and when and where it was to be.

He said it was for the purpose of effecting a treaty with Captain Jack, and was to be held in a little glade or opening on the other side of Dry Lake canyon, this being about one mile south of headquarters, and within a quarter of a mile of Captain Jack's stronghold. Said he: "Gen. Canby and Rev. Col. Thomas, accompanied by George Meeks and his squaw as interpreters, are to meet Captain Jack there without escort or even side arms. Now, Captain, tell me seriously, what you think of this affair."

I said: "General, they may go, but they will never return."

The General then asked me if I would have a talk with Gen. Canby. I told him that if Gen. Canby asked for my opinion in the matter I would give it just as frankly as I would to you, otherwise I had nothing to say, for Gen. Canby was a man that seemed to feel too much elevated to speak to a scout, except just to give orders. Gen. Wheaton told me that he would see Gen. Canby himself and have a talk with him. This was on Friday previous to the Sunday on which they were to meet in council.

In the afternoon of the same day it was reported that there had been Indians seen along Tule Lake. I mounted my horse and started with a platoon of soldiers and a sergeant, and when we had advanced about twelve miles I was riding about two hundred yards in advance I saw something dodge into a bunch of sarvis brush. Beckoning to the sergeant, he dashed up to my side and said: "What's up, Captain?"

"I got a glimpse of something just as it ran into that patch of brush, and I think it was an Indian."

He had his men surround the brush and I went to scare the Indian out. I searched that patch of brush thoroughly, but could find no Indian or anything else, and the boys all enjoyed a hearty laugh at my expense.

The sergeant proposed that we all have a smoke, so we turned our horses loose to graze. The sergeant lit his pipe, threw off his overcoat and laid down to rest. As he cast his eyes heavenward in the direction of the top of the only pine tree that stood in that patch of brush, he exclaimed: "Captain, I have found your Indian." Of course we all commenced looking for the Indian, and I asked where he was, whereupon he told me to look up in the pine tree, and on looking I beheld an Indian with whom I was well acquainted, as he had been to my ranch several times in company with Captain Jack.

I asked him to come down, telling him that I would protect him if he would, but he would not utter a word, nor would he come down. I tried for at least a half hour to induce him to come down until I had exhausted all the persuasive powers I possessed, but to no avail.

I told the sergeant that I had treed his Indian, and now he could do as he pleased with him, and the sergeant ordered him shot down, after which we returned to headquarters, this being the only Indian seen on the trip.

The next morning Gen. Wheaton sent for me to come to his quarters, which I did, and in a conversation with him he asked me if I was still of the same opinion concerning the council meeting as when I talked with him before. I told him that I was, that I had not seen or heard anything to change my mind in the least. He then said: "I had a conversation with Gen. Canby and Rev. Col. Thomas, and Col. Thomas scoffs at the idea you advance, claiming that they were going in a good cause, and that the Lord would protect them." I told the General that George Jones and I were going to see that meeting. He said that would not do, for it was strictly forbidden. I assured the General that I would not break any rules, but that I would see the meeting. I had given my scouts their orders until ten o'clock the next day, and when dark came Jones and I were going to the bluff on this side of the canyon and there secrete ourselves, where, with a glass, we could see the whole proceeding and not be discovered by the Indians.

The reader will understand that a scout is, in a certain measure, a privileged character.

As soon as it was dark Saturday evening George and I went to the place mentioned and remained there until the time arrived for the meeting. About nine o'clock that morning the fog raised and the sun shone brightly, making it one of the most pleasant mornings we had experienced for some time, thereby giving us a good view of the grounds of the proposed meeting, and we could see Captain Jack and another Indian there waiting. I could recognize Jack's features through the glass, but the other Indian I could not. In a short time we saw Gen. Canby, Col. Thomas, George Meeks and his squaw coming. When they reached the lower end of the little opening one hundred and fifty yards from where Captain Jack was standing, they dismounted, tied their horses and walked slowly in the direction where Captain Jack was standing, and every few steps Gen. Canby would look back, apparently to see if any one was following them. On arriving at the spot they shook hands with Captain Jack and the other Indian, and probably fifteen minutes elapsed when Captain Jack dropped his blanket from his shoulders to the ground and suddenly turned and picked it up. This, I believe, was a signal for an attack, for the next moment I saw smoke from a number of guns from the rocks and could hear the reports also. Col. Thomas, Meeks and his squaw started on the run, but Gen. Canby fell in his tracks, a victim at the hands of Captain Jack and his followers. Col. Thomas only ran about ten steps, when he fell. Meeks ran nearly one hundred yards, when he fell, and the squaw escaped unhurt, but badly scared, I presume.

As soon as Gen. Canby had fallen George Jones asked if he had better go to headquarters and give the alarm. I told him to go with all possible speed. George reached camp twenty minutes ahead of me. The other officers could not believe that he was telling the truth, but when I arrived and told them that the entire crowd had been killed, with the exception of the squaw, they were thunderstruck, and by the time I was through telling them the squaw was there.

I do not know just how many soldiers were sent to recover the dead bodies, but that day there was a general attack made on Captain Jack, which was kept up from day to day almost as long as the war lasted.

When it was foggy, as it was nearly all the time, the Indians almost invariably got the best of the soldiers, from the fact that they would come out without any clothing on their bodies with a bunch of sage-brush tied on their heads, and their skins being so similar in color to that of the lava rocks, that when the fog was thick, at a distance of thirty or forty yards, it was impossible to distinguish an Indian from a rock. There were more or less soldiers killed and wounded every day until the end of the war.

One day only a short time after the assassination of Gen. Canby and Col. Thomas, the soldiers were attacked in Dry Lake canyon by the Modocs and were getting badly butchered up.

As I rode along Gen. Wheaton dashed up by my side and said: "Where can those Indians be and what kind of guns have they? I have been losing men all day and there has not been an Indian seen." I told the General I would try and locate them and let him know just where they were. Taking George Jones and another man by the name of Owens with me, I rode around on the opposite ridge, dismounted, and leaving my horse with the other boys, I crawled down among the rocks. I had on a buckskin suit and could not be seen much easier than a Modoc when in the lava beds. They kept up a continual firing, and now and then I could hear a bullet whiz near me. After I had crawled about sixty yards as cautiously as I could I raised on one knee and foot and my gun was resting across my leg while I was peering through the fog to see if I could get sight of any Indians, and listening to see if I could hear an Indian's voice. I had remained in this position about five minutes when a ball struck me on the shin-bone, just below the boot top. It appeared to me that I could have heard it crack at a hundred yards. Never before in my life had I experienced such a miserable feeling as at that time. I thought that my leg was broken into atoms. I started to crawl back up the hill, taking the same route that I had come down, and when I had ascended the hill near enough to the boys so they could see me, George Jones saw that I was hurt.

He dropped his gun and ran to me at once and said: "Captain, are you badly hurt?" But before I had time to answer him he had picked me up bodily and was running up the hill with me.

When he got to where our horses were he said: "Where are you shot?" I said: "George, my left leg is shot off." "What shall we do?" said George. I told him to put me on Johnny, that being the name of my horse, and I would go to headquarters. He said: "Let me pull your boot off," at the same time taking hold of my boot. I caught my leg with both hands to hold the bones together while the boot was being removed from the leg, thinking that the bone was shattered into small pieces. As soon as George had succeeded in removing my boot from my foot, he turned the top of the boot downward to let the blood run out of it. "Why," said he, "your leg is not bleeding at all." I then commenced feeling my leg, but could not feel or hear any bones work, so by the assistance of George I got my breeches-leg up and there the ball stuck just between the skin and the bone of my leg, and the boys had a good laugh at my expense.

When I had learned that my leg was not broken, George and I crawled down together into the canyon, and located the Indians. We got so near that we could see the flash from their guns through the fog. We then ascended the hill, mounted our horses, rode back and reported to Gen. Wheaton. But the Indians had the advantage over the soldiers from the fact that the soldiers' could be easily distinguished from the rocks.

About one week later, George Jones, a young man named Savage, and myself, went on just such another trip. It was our custom when going into the canyon to leave one man in charge of our horses until we returned, and in this case we left Savage with three saddle horses and instructions to remain there until we returned. On our return we found poor Savage mortally wounded, and he only lived a few minutes. He had two balls through his body. It seemed that he had tied the horses and come to the top of the hill to look for us or to warn us of danger, and while there had been shot down by the Indians.

This was the first scout I had lost since I had entered the scouting field at this place. By the assistance of Jones I got the body on my horse in front of me and carried it to headquarters and reported to Gen. Ross, who was acquainted with Savage's family, and he sent the body to Jacksonville for interment. A few days later, George, myself and four assistants started out to meet a pack-train that was coming in from Yreka, Cal., with supplies. We met the train twelve miles from headquarters and told the man in charge that he would either have to cross the lava beds or go around forty miles. He decided to take chances in crossing the lava beds in preference to going so far around. We told him that he would be running a great risk, for we were satisfied that Jack was running short of provisions and that he had men out all the time foraging, and we knew that if the Indians happened to discover this train they would make a desperate effort to capture it, or at least a part of it. There were fifty animals in the train and only three men. When we started across the lava beds I took the lead, and George and our other men in the rear. In case of an attack on either, he was to fire two shots in quick succession as a signal for assistance, for the fog was almost thick enough that day to cut in slices with a knife. The man in charge of the train started a young man ahead with me to lead the bell-horse, placing another young man about the center of the train.

It was a miserably rough country across these lava beds, and we had to travel very slowly.

The man in charge dropped back in the rear of the train, thinking that if we were attacked it would be at the rear.

The reader will understand that in crossing this hell-hearth it was necessary for the pack-animals to string out single file.

CHAPTER XXXVII
THE CRY OF A BABE.—CAPTURE OF A BEVY OF SQUAWS. TREACHERY OF GEN. ROSS' MEN IN KILLING PRISONERS.— CAPTURE OF THE MODOC CHIEF

When we were across the lava beds, or "Devil's Garden," as the place was commonly called, I told the man who was leading the bell-horse to stop and wait until the other animals had come up in order to see whether we had lost any. This was within a mile of headquarters. The man in charge, also Jones and the other scouts, came up, but the young man who had been riding in the middle, also four mules and their packs, as the saying is, "came up missing."

The train went on to headquarters, but Jones and I returned along the trail to see if we could find the missing man. One of us, however, had to leave the trail and scout along on foot.

After following the back-track two miles I found where the four mules had left it. It was now late in the evening, and we were within less than a mile and a half of Captain Jack's stronghold. We tied our horses there and started out, caring but little about the mules and their packs; it was the man that we were looking after. We had not gone more than fifty yards from the trail when we found the body.

The poor fellow had been stoned to death, his head being beaten out of shape. This the Indians had done to prevent an alarm. They had evidently been hidden in the lava rocks and had managed to turn those four mules from the trail, and the fog being so thick that a person could not see any distance, the man did not notice that he was off of the trail until too late; and when once off the trail a few paces it was impossible for him to get back again. The mules and packs were never seen again. The Indians, no doubt, took them to the cave, used the provisions, killed and ate the mules and saddle-horse which the man was riding. We took the body to headquarters, and the next day it was started to Yreka, Cal. I do not remember the name of this young man, but he lived near Yreka.

Gen. Wheaton was now fighting, the Indians every day, and at night kept a strong picket guard around the cave. About this time it was reported that Gen. Wheaton had received orders to take Captain Jack if he had to exterminate the entire tribe.

The feeling was getting to be very strong against Captain Jack in regard to the assassination of Gen. Canby, Col. Thomas and George Meeks, the interpreter. One evening in a conversation with Gen. Wheaton he asked me how long I thought it would take to starve them out. I said: "General, if they took all their horses in the cave, which I believe they did, and we know for a fact that they got some cattle from the Klamath river, I think it will be May or June before you will be able to starve them out."

He said that every Indian that came out of the cave single-handed or otherwise would not live to get through the picket line, saying that he had a double picket line now around the entire cave, both day and night.

The next morning after this conversation with the General, one of my scouts came in from Rattlesnake Point and reported having seen the tracks of twenty Indians, where they had crossed the road on the east side of the lake, and they were all small tracks.

I reported this to the General, telling him that Jack was a pretty smart Indian, for he was sending his women and children away so as to make his provisions last as long as possible.

George Jones and I started out, accompanied by two platoons of soldiers, to capture the Indians. We had no trouble in finding their trail, and in running them down.

It so happened that our escort that day were all Gen. Ross' men and were all friends to young Savage, who had recently been killed by the Modocs. After following the trail about ten miles we came in sight of the Indians on Lost river. We did not see them until we were near them and had no trouble in capturing the whole outfit. There were twenty-two, all squaws and little girls. I was personally acquainted with all of those Indians, and knowing so well the cause of all this trouble, and just what brought it about, I could not help sympathizing with the women and children. In fact, I had felt from the very start that this trouble was all uncalled for. Among the crowd was one young squaw who spoke pretty fair English for an Indian in those days. I was well acquainted with her, and told her that we would have to take them all, but that they would be treated as prisoners. She did not seem to understand the meaning of "prisoners."

I explained to her, and she in her own tongue explained it to the rest of the crowd. I told her that we would have to take them back to headquarters.

She said: "We heap hungry, long time no eat much. Maby white man no give us anything to eat. 'Spose no eat purty soon all die." I assured her that they would have plenty to eat as long as they behaved themselves and gave the soldiers no trouble.

They all seemed to be perfectly willing to surrender and go back to headquarters, so we started back via Tule Lake. When we reached the mouth of Lost river I turned the prisoners over to the two sergeants who had charge of the two platoons of soldiers. George and I wanted to make a circuit around in the direction of Clear Lake, thinking, of course, that the prisoners would be perfectly safe in charge of the soldiers, especially those little girls. George and I did not get to headquarters that night until ten o'clock, and the first thing I heard when I got into camp was that the Indians had tried to run off into the tules while coming down Tule Lake, and they had all been shot down by the soldiers, I went at once to see Gen. Ross relative to the matter, for I could not believe it. The General confirmed the report by saying every one of them had been shot. I said: "General, that is the most cowardly piece of work I ever heard white men accused of in my life. Will you please tell the men who did that cowardly piece of work, that they had better never be caught out with me when I have the best of it, for I would much prefer shooting such men down, to shooting helpless women and children."

This conversation caused a great deal of talk of a court-martial, but it all blew over, I suppose, on account of Captain Jack murdering Gen. Canby. The next conversation I had with Gen. Wheaton, I asked why the picket guard let those Indians pass through the picket line, and speaking as though I thought they had passed boldly out through the line; he said:

"I cannot see into it myself."

I said: "General, that is the way the Indians will all get out of there, and at the final surrender you will not have six warriors in the cave. From this on you will find that they will gradually desert Jack, for the squaws told me that they were getting very hungry."

It was reported around that Captain Jack and three other Indians would be hung if caught alive, this being the orders from headquarters. The other three were Schonchin, Scarfaced Charlie and Shacknasty Jim, these being Jack's council or under chiefs.

When this report came, Gen. Wheaton told me that if it was necessary he would make another detail of scouts, for he would not under any consideration have the Indians escape. I told the General to give himself no uneasiness in regard to that part of it, for we would run down all the Indians that crossed the picket line, but I must know what I should promise a prisoner when I captured him. I asked if I should promise them protection or not, for if there was no protection, I would not bring them in. He assured me that all prisoners caught after this would be protected as prisoners of war until tried and proven guilty.

What the General meant by that was those who might be proven guilty of being directly interested in the murder of Gen. Canby and Col. Thomas.

I now put George Jones on the night shift. He had the entire charge of night scouting, and he and his assistants rode all night long. In the morning I started out with my assistants and rode all day; so it was impossible for the Indians to get out and away without our getting track of them, and if they left a track we were sure to capture them.

We kept this up for about three weeks, when I made a change; George and I doing the night scouting alone, and leaving the day scouting for the other scouts.

One night we were out near Dry Lake, about five miles from headquarters, and there came up a cold fog. We built a little fire to warm by, and shortly after we had started it we heard what an inexperienced man would have called two cayotes, but we knew they were Indians and were in different directions and this was their signal for meeting.

We mounted our horses and rode in the opposite direction, but before we left we gave a yelp in a laughing sort of manner to make the Indians believe that we thought it was cayotes. We rode quietly away about three hundred yards from the fire, dismounted, tied our horses and crawled back near the fire. All this time the Indians had kept up their cayote barking and were drawing near the fire. It was some little time before they dared approach, but after they had looked carefully around, I suppose they thought it had been campers who had stopped, built a fire and then pulled out, for it was not the custom of scouts to build a fire, which the Indians well knew, they finally ventured up to the fire and were warming themselves. Seeing that they were both armed with rifles, and the chances were they both had pistols, we made up our minds not to take any chances, so I proposed to George that we should shoot them down, just as they would have done us if we had not understood their signal.

Of course if it had been daylight it would have been quite different, but three jumps away from the fire and they would have been safe from us. We were sitting side by side not more than forty yards from them. I told George to take the one on the right and I would take the one on the left, and when he gave the word I would fire with him. We raised our guns, and when he gave the word we both fired, and the two Indians fell to the ground. We waited about five minutes to see whether they would rise or not, and believing we had killed them both, we approached them. One of them was dead and the other was just about dead, so we took their guns and pistols and reported to Gen. Wheaton.

The next morning he said it was a mystery how the Indians would get out and the men on picket would not see them. He said: "I cannot see through it."

About a week or ten days later George and I were coming in just before daylight, when we heard a baby cry on the hillside only a short distance from us. We stopped and listed until we had located it. George dismounted, and I held his horse while he crawled up to see where it was, and found that there was quite a number of squaws and children there. I told him that it would be a matter of impossibility for them to get away from us and the grass so high, for we could track them easily, so I left him there to keep watch and see which way they moved so that we would know how to start after them, and I would ride to headquarters, about two miles away, for assistance to help capture them when it was daylight. I rode slow until so far away that I knew they could not hear the clatter of my horse's feet, and then I put spurs to my horse and rode with all speed to headquarters. When I passed the camp guard he challenged me and I gave my name. I could hear it carried down the line from one to another, "There comes the Captain of the Scouts, there is something up." Rather than wake up a commissioned officer, I woke up my entire scout force, and was back to where George Jones was just at daylight. He said that the squaws had moved in the direction of Clear Lake. There was a heavy dew and we had no trouble in finding their trail and following it; in fact, at times we could ride almost at full speed and follow without difficulty. We had only gone about four miles when we came in sight of them, six squaws, a little boy, a little girl and a baby. When they saw me coming they all stopped. I rode up and asked them where they were going. They could all speak a little English.

There was one in the crowd named Mary, with whom I was well acquainted, who said: "We heap hungry, too much hungry, we go Clear Lake catch fish." I told her that we would have to take them prisoners and take them all back to headquarters and keep them there until we got all the Modoc Indians and then they would have to go on to the reservation. "No, too much hungry, you all time fight Captain Jack, Injun no catch fish. All time eatem hoss. No more hoss now; Injun eatem all up, eatem some cow too. No more hoss, no more cow. Injun all heap hungry."

It was some time before I could make them believe that they would be fed when at headquarters, but they being acquainted with me and knowing that I had been a friend to them in time of peace. I finally succeeded in getting them to turn and go to headquarters. These were the first prisoners that had been taken to the General's quarters during the Modoc war.

Gen. Wheaton was away from his quarters, so I left the prisoners in charge of George Jones and the other scouts, with instructions to let no one interfere with them while I went to hunt the General.

I soon found him and with him returned to where the Indians were. The General asked me to question the one of them that talked the best English and had done the most talking, concerning the number of men that Captain Jack had in his stronghold. When I asked her she said: "Some days twenty men, some days thirty men, no more, some go away. No more come back, some shoot, by and by he die. Two days now me not eat. Injun man, he no eat much."

From this we inferred that they only had a little provisions left, and the men that did the fighting did the eating also. They were given something to eat at once, and I don't think I ever saw more hungry mortals. I told the General that it would not be long until they would all come out, but that I did not think they would come in a body, but would slip out two or three at a time. The General thought it so strange that they were stealing out through the picket lines and the guards not seeing any of them.

Some three weeks later than this, it being about the first of June, 1873, George and I had been out all night and were coming into quarters, being a little later this morning than common, and when we were within about one and a half miles from quarters we crossed the trail of three Indians. I got down and examined the tracks closely; there was one track quite large and long, another not quite so large and the third was quite small. I told George I was not afraid to bet twenty dollars that they were the tracks of Captain Jack, his wife and little girl. We pushed on to headquarters with all possible speed and reported to Gen. Wheaton. He asked my reason for thinking that it was Captain Jack. I told him from the fact that it suited for his family. I was well acquainted with both him and his squaw, and I told the General that Jack himself had an unusually long foot. He asked how much of an escort I wanted and if I would go at once. I told him I would, and I wanted two platoons. He directed his orderlies to report as soon as possible with two platoons of cavalry, and I gave my horse to George, telling him to change our saddles to fresh horses at once. As soon as it was noised around that we had got track of Captain Jack, the scouts all wanted to accompany me, but I told them that their services could not be dispensed with at camp for one hour, for it was getting now where the thing must be watched very closely. George rode up on a fresh horse and was leading Black Bess with my saddle on her. I mounted and we were off again in pursuit of Captain Jack, but as we rode away Gen. Wheaton expressed himself as being doubtful as to its being Captain Jack.

When we struck the trail of the three Indians, I had one platoon to ride on each side of the trail, keeping about fifty yards away from it, and in case we should miss it or get off, we would have a chance to go back and pick it up again before it would become obliterated.

This was one of the prettiest mornings that we could have had for the occasion. The fog disappeared with the rising of the sun, and in many places we could look ahead and see the trail in the grass for fifty yards. In those places we put our horses down to their utmost. George and I were both very hungry, having had nothing to eat since the evening before, and we had been in the saddle all night, but an old scout forgets all this when he gets on a fresh Indian trail and becomes somewhat excited. After we had gone about six miles we came to a gravel country for a mile and a half, and it was slow and tedious tracking across this, for many times we had nothing to go by only as they might turn a little pebble over with their feet or step on a little spear of grass and mash it down, and this was very thin and scattering on the ridge. However, as soon as we were across the gravelly ridge, we again struck grass and we let our horses out almost at full speed, knowing very well that as soon as the dew dried off it would be slow and tedious tracking. After we had ridden about twelve miles, and just as we raised the top of the hill, on looking across on the next ridge we saw the three Indians, and sure enough, it was Captain Jack, his squaw and little girl. About this time he turned and saw us coming. He stood and looked at us for a moment or so and the three all turned and started back to meet us. We both pulled our pistols and dashed up to him at full speed.

When we were close enough, I could see that he had a smile on his face, and I knew that he had recognized me. When we rode up to him he said: "Good mornin. Long time no see you," and at the same time presented the gun with the breech foremost.

As I took the gun, I said to him: "Jack, where are you going?"

He replied: "O, heap hungry, guess go Clear Lake catch fish."

I said: "No, Jack; you are my prisoner. I will have to take you back to Gen. Wheaton."

He replied: "No, me no want to go back, no more fight, too much all time hungry, little girl nearly starve, no catch fish soon he die." But when he saw that he had to go, he said:

"All right, me go."

So I took the little girl up behind me, and George took the squaw up behind him and Jack walked.

It was in the afternoon when we returned to headquarters with the prisoners, and there was no little rejoicing among the soldiers when they learned for a certainty that I had taken Captain Jack prisoner.

That afternoon a runner was started to Yreka with a dispatch to headquarters to the effect that Gen. Wheaton had taken the notorious Captain Jack prisoner. As a matter of fact, an old scout is never known in such cases. They, as a general rule, do the work, but the officers always get the praise. Although Gen. Wheaton had the praise of capturing Captain Jack, he had but little more to do with it than the President of the United States.

CHAPTER XXXVIII
STORY OF THE CAPTURED BRAVES.—WHY CAPTAIN JACK DESERTED.— LOATHSOME CONDITION OF THE STRONGHOLD.—END OF THE WAR.—SOME COMMENTS

That evening I had a long conversation with Captain Jack, and from him I learned the exact number of Indians in the cave. He said there were twenty women, and maybe thirty children and twenty-two warriors. He said they would not stay there long for they had nothing to eat, and their ammunition was nearly gone.

I must admit that when I learned Jack's story of the way that he had been both driven and pulled into this war, which I knew to be a fact myself, I was sorry for him. He said that after the Indian agent would not send them anything to eat he was forced to go away from the reservation to catch fish to keep his people from starving, for which purpose he was at the mouth of Lost river when the soldiers came there. One morning before the soldiers fired on him without even telling him to return to the reservation or giving him any warning whatever. He said that he did not give orders for his men to kill any white men that morning, but they all got very angry at the soldiers for shooting at them. "That day," said he, "I go to lava bed, my men scout all over country, kill all white men they see."

After I was through talking with Jack, Gen. Wheaton sent for me to come to his quarters, as he was anxious to learn what information I had obtained. When I told him the number of Indians yet in the cave and that they had nothing to eat, he asked me what would be my plan for capturing the remainder. I told him that if I was doing it, I would capture the entire outfit without losing a single man, but that it would take a little time; that I would not fire on them at all, but would double the picket line, and it would not be many days until they would surrender, and in case some of them did slip by the guards, we would pick them up before they got twenty miles away.

The following morning a council was held in camp, and all the commissioned officers were present. Now Captain Jack had been captured, and according to reports, the other Indians were nearly starved out, so that morning they did not open out on them at all.

The third day from this it was reported by a citizen who had passed over the country that day, that he saw Indians up on Tule Lake. It being late in the afternoon, nearly dark in fact, when I heard the report and it not being from a scout, I questioned closely the man who was said to have seen them, but did not get much satisfaction from him, so naturally discredited the report. But for fear there might be some truth in it, the next morning by daybreak George Jones and I were scouring the country in the vicinity of Tule Lake. After having ridden some little distance we ran upon the trail of six Indians, who as we supposed had passed the evening before, and were evidently plodding along in the direction of Lost river. This was without doubt the trail of four bucks and two squaws. After we had followed this trail a few miles we found where they had stopped, built a fire, caught, cooked and ate some fish. We knew they were not many miles ahead of us, in fact, the fire had not entirely gone out. From here on we had plain sailing, and the nearer an old scout gets when on the trail of an Indian the more anxious he gets, so we sped along up the lake four miles further, and were on them before they knew it; they were all on the banks of the river fishing.

In this outfit there were Scarfaced Charley and Black Jim, their squaws, and two other Indians. The moment we saw them we both drew our pistols, but concealed them from their view by hiding them under our coats. When we approached them they all said, "Good morning."

I did not see any guns near them nor did either of them have pistols. Scarfaced Charley said: "We like go reservation; too much hungry, my squaw nearly dead, ketchem some fish her, purty soon go."

After I had informed him that I would have to take them all back to Gen. Wheaton's quarters, Charley said: "What for?" I said: "Charley, I will take you all back to headquarters, give you all plenty to eat, and when we get all the Modoc Indians they will be taken to the reservation." "All right, me go now," said Charley, as he started, eager to be off on the journey for headquarters.

I asked them where their guns and pistols were, and they said: "O, me hide them in lava bed, too much heavy, no like carry." So George Jones took the lead, the Indians followed him, and I brought up the rear. I could see that they were very weak from hunger, but they plodded along, encouraged by the thought of getting something to eat at Gen. Wheaton's quarters.

We arrived there at noon, and when I turned them over to the General and told him their names, he said: "It is with the greatest of pleasure that I receive them. Now if I only had just one more I would be satisfied. That one is Schonchin. I would then have all the ring leaders."

Up to this time I had not learned what would be the fate of those Indians directly interested in the assassination of Gen. Canby and Col. Thomas, and I must admit that I was terribly surprised when Gen. Wheaton informed me that they would all be hanged. From those Indians I learned that Captain Jack and his council were not on good terms, having had a falling out while in the cave, and they would not speak to each other while at Gen. Wheaton's headquarters. The cause of the trouble grew out of a proposition by Captain Jack to surrender, and he had been talking surrender for two weeks past, but the rest of them were in favor of fighting to the last. Mary, the squaw, told me that they at one time came near putting Jack to death for cowardice, and that was the reason he had deserted them, knowing that his life was in danger in the cave.

From this on we captured one or two Modocs every day. The fourth day after the last band referred to was captured, one of my scouts reported having seen Indian tracks at the head of Tule Lake, but could not make out the exact number, I had just lain down to take a nap, it being early in the morning, and I had been riding all night, but George and I saddled our horses and were off for the head of Tule Lake, Gen. Wheaton promising to send a company of soldiers after us at once.

We struck the Indian trail about twelve miles from headquarters, this being the first band that had escaped from the west side of the cave.

As soon as we discovered their trail we put spurs to our horses and sped along up the river, for the trail was plain and we experienced no trouble in following it, and just above the Natural Bridge on Lost river, we came on to them. Some were fishing, some were cooking the fish they had caught, and others were eating fish. It seemed that each one of them caught, cooked and ate their own fish. Seeing no arms we rode up to them. There were twelve of them, and among them was Sconchin, the other councilman who the General was so anxious to get hold of. Sconchin said: "Go Fort Klamath, all Injun heap hungry, now ketchem fish, eat plenty, by and by go to fort."

I had George Jones turn and ride back to hurry the soldiers up, for I did not deem it a safe plan for two of us to try to take the whole crowd prisoners, for even though they had no arms they might scatter all over the country and then we could not get them only by killing them, and that I did not want to do. While I am in no wise a friend to a hostile; I believe in giving even an Indian that which is justly due him, and I must admit that all through this Modoc war I could not help, in a measure, feeling sorry for the Modocs, particularly Captain Jack, for I knew that through the negligence of one agent and the outrageous attack upon Jack by the squad of soldiers on Lost river, while there catching fish to keep his people from starving, he had been driven and dragged into this war, and I do not believe to-day, nor never did believe, that Captain Jack ought to have been hanged.

I have often been asked, since, what I thought of the arrangements Mr. Berry made for the meeting of Gen. Canby, Col. Thomas and Captain Jack, but I have always refrained from answering that question any farther than that it seemed to me that a school boy ten years of age should have known better than to have made such a bargain as he did, knowing the nature of Indians as well as he claimed to.

But to my story—I stayed there and engaged the Indians in conversation while George was making tracks back over the same road that we had just come to hurry the cavalry up. I learned from them that there were no more able-bodied men left in the cave, and there were some twenty or thirty squaws and children, besides several warriors that were wounded. In about an hour from the time George started back, the soldiers made their appearance.

I told the Indians that we would have to take them prisoners and take them back to headquarters. This, however, was not pleasant news to them. They objected to return with us until I had informed them that they would be fed and protected until such time as we could get them all, and they having been acquainted with me before, we were successful in persuading them to return peacefully to the General's quarters.

It was late in the afternoon when we returned, and I at once reported to the General the number of Indians, also that Schonchin was in the gang, and that I had learned that there were no more able-bodied men in the cave. I told him that from what I could learn, I thought it perfectly safe for three or four men to enter the cave and secure the few remaining Indians. The General said: "I will think the matter over until morning."

That evening the officers held a council and it was decided that in case the following morning was fair, Col. Miller and the Colonel from California whose name I do not remember, myself, and two soldiers would make the attempt to enter the cave, I going as a guide more than anything else.

Next morning about ten o'clock when the fog had raised and the sun came out most beautifully, we made the start for the cave. Although I had never been inside of the cave, I had no serious trouble in finding the main entrance to it, but we found it so dark inside that we had to use lanterns. We had not proceeded far until we could see the fire. I proposed to the others that as I was acquainted with the Indians to let me advance alone, and I can truthfully say that just such another sight I never saw before nor since.

There was a number of wounded Indians lying around; here were the bones of their horses that they had killed and eaten, and a smell so offensive that it was really a hard task for me to stay there long enough to tell them what we wanted of them. As soon as I commenced talking to them the squaws and children began making their appearance from every direction.

I told them my business, and if they would go with me they would be fed. They were not only willing, but anxious to go.

By this time the other men were there, and when they were all gathered up, Col. Miller sent two men back to camp for stretchers to carry the wounded Indians to headquarters. They were all taken out that day. I do not remember the number of wounded bucks that were in the cave, but there were thirty-two squaws and forty children.

Now the bloody little Modoc war that had lasted so long at the cost of many lives, was brought to an end. This was glorious news to the surviving ones among the volunteers, and the next day they were making preparations to return to their respective homes, or rather Jacksonville, where they would be discharged, and they again could say their lives were their own. This being the last days of June and my services not needed any more, I asked the General when the hanging would take place. He said that it would be about the twentieth of July.

CHAPTER XXXIX
AN INTERESTED BOY.—THE EXECUTION
OF THE MODOC LEADERS.—NEWSPAPER
MESSENGERS.—A VERY SUDDEN DEPUTY
SHERIFF.—A BAD MAN WOUND UP

I went from there to Yreka to rest up a while. During my stay there, one morning while I was waiting for my breakfast, I was glancing over the morning paper, when a bright-eyed little boy about nine years old, entered the restaurant, walked up in front of me and said: "Is this Capt. Drannan, the scout?" I said: "Yes, my little man. What can I do for you?" He said: "I am going to school and I have to write a composition to read in school, and my mother told me to see you and you might be able to assist me in getting up a piece on the Modoc war." I asked the bright little fellow his name. He said his name was Johnny Whitney. "Where is your father and what does he follow for a living?" "My father is dead, and my mother takes in washing to support herself and children."

That afternoon I spent in assisting the little fellow to prepare his composition. I remained there at Yreka about ten days, during which time I received a letter from George Jones, who was then at Jacksonville, requesting me to meet him at Fort Klamath about four or five days before the hanging was to take place, and also requesting me to bring all my saddle horses. I succeeded in getting up quite a party of business men and citizens of Yreka and we started out across the Siskiyou Mountains. After the first day's travel we found game plentiful and we had a pleasant trip. We had all the game and fish we wanted, which afforded plenty of amusement for the pleasure-seekers of the crowd, which was the main object of this trip with a majority of them. We arrived at Fort Klamath five days before the hanging was to take place. The next day after we arrived a crowd came in from Jacksonville, and among them were Gen. Ross, George Jones, J. N. T. Miller and three newspaper reporters, one of whom represented the San Francisco Chronicle, one the San Francisco Examiner, and one the Chicago INTER-OCEAN. Col. Miller came to me and asked if I would like a job of carrying dispatches from there, either to Jacksonville or to Ashland, saying: "The

Chronicle man has not found a man yet that he could trust the dispatches with."

The reporter had told Mr. Miller that he would pay one hundred dollars for carrying the dispatch, and in case he was first to the office, he would also pay one hundred dollars more in addition to that. From there to Jacksonville it was one hundred miles and a wagon road all the way, while to Ashland it was but eighty miles, of which sixty miles was only a trail. This I had passed once in company with J. N. T. Miller. I was introduced to the reporter by Col. Miller, with whom I soon made arrangements to carry his dispatches. He asked me how long it would take me to ride to Ashland. I told him I thought it would take about eight hours with my three horses. He said if I went to Ashland I would have no competition on the trail as the other riders were both going to Jacksonville.

The day before the hanging was to take place I hired a young man to take two of my horses and go out on the trail, instructing him to leave one of them picketed out at Cold Springs, and the other one to take to Bald Mountain, which was thirty miles from Ashland. At this place I wanted Black Bess, and he was to stay there with her until I came and to return, get my other horse, and meet me at Jacksonville.

When the time arrived for the hanging and the prisoners were led to the scaffold, each dispatch carrier was mounted and standing on the outer edge of the crowd, ready at the moment he received the dispatch to be off at once. When the four Indians were led upon the scaffold to meet their doom, each of them were asked, through an interpreter, whether or not he wished to say anything before being hung, but they all shook their heads with the exception of Captain Jack, who informed them that he had something to say.

He said: "I would like for my brother to take my place and let me live so I can take care of my wife and little girl."

The carrier for the Inter-Ocean was the first to get his dispatch, the Examiner the second, I receiving mine just as the last Indian was hung, and now for the race to see who gets there first. It was eleven o'clock when we started. We all traveled together for the first twenty miles, where I left the wagon road and took the trail for Ashland. Now I had sixty miles to ride over a trail and they had eighty miles over a wagon road. At this junction where the trail left the wagon road I bade the other couriers good-day, telling them that in case they beat me they must treat to the oysters when we met at Jacksonville, and I sped away and lost no time in getting from there to Cold Springs, where I found my other horse picketed out as I had ordered. I dismounted, threw my saddle on the other horse, which was apparently feeling fine, mounted him and was off again, leaving the other horse picketed at the same place, so my man could get him on his return. My horse took a long sweeping gallop and kept it up for about twelve miles, by which time he was beginning to sweat quite freely, and I commenced to urge him and put him down to all I thought he would stand. When I came in sight of Black Bess she raised her head and whinnied to me. The young man was lying asleep and holding her rope, while she was grazing near him. Again I changed my saddle from my other horse to Black Bess, and gave the young man instructions to start at once and lead my horse slowly so as to prevent him from cooling off too fast. I mounted Black Bess and now I was on the homestretch. I did not urge her any for the first few miles until she commenced sweating freely, after which I commenced to increase her speed, and fifteen minutes after six I rode up to the telegraph office and handed my dispatch to the operator, who started it on the wire at once. I led my mare up and down the streets to prevent her from cooling off too quick, and when it was known where I was from, everybody in town had about forty questions to ask relative to the hanging of the four Modoc braves.

On leaving the telegraph office I asked the operator to let me know when the first dispatch started from Jacksonville, and while at supper he came in and told me that the Examiner had just started their dispatch over the wire, which was just one and three-quarter hours behind me in getting to the office. The next day I rode to Jacksonville, and the day following the balance of the crowd came in from the fort. Among them were the three reporters, all well pleased with the time their bearers had made in carrying their dispatches, and that night we all had what in those days we used to term "a-way-up time."

The balance of the Indians who were taken prisoners in this Modoc war were afterwards taken to Florida and placed on a small reservation, which, I presume, was done on account of the bitter feeling that existed among the people of that section of the country toward this tribe on account of the assassination of Gen. Canby, Col. Thomas and George Meeks, the interpreter, as well as the many other people that were murdered on Lost river and Tule Lake.

While at Jacksonville a man came to me named Martin, who was a merchant and resided in Oakland, Cal., who wanted to hire me to go out in the mountains some twenty miles from Jacksonville and look after a man named McMahon, saying: "There must be something wrong with McMahon, for he is the most punctual man I ever dealt with; he promised to be here three weeks ago to pay a certain party fifty dollars, but has not been seen nor heard from since."

McMahon owned a band of sheep and was ranging them out in the mountains. Mr. Martin gave me directions, and the next morning I started out for the sheep ranch. I had no trouble in finding the place, but the cabin and surroundings showed that no one lived there. I spent the balance of this day and the next in riding over the sheep range, but could see no one, and only about twenty head of sheep.

On my return to Jacksonville I went by way of Bybee's ferry, on Rogue river, and learned that about three weeks previous to that time a band of two thousand head of sheep had crossed over the ferry, driven by two men. Now it was almost a foregone conclusion that some one had murdered McMahon and driven his band of sheep away, and when I returned to Jacksonville there was no little excitement about the city in regard to McMahon. Some of the business men and citizens with whom I was well acquainted, prevailed upon me to accept an appointment as deputy sheriff, and start out and track the band of sheep up if possible and capture the thieves and murderers, the sheriff himself being very busy just at that time, it being near time for court to sit in that county. After receiving my appointment and taking the oath of office, I struck directly for Bybee's ferry, and for the first twenty miles beyond the ferry I experienced no trouble whatever in keeping track of the sheep, finding a number of people who had seen them, and all gave the same description of the two men who were driving them.

Leaving the settlement, I went into the mountains, spent five days tracking sheep here and there in every direction between Rogue river and Umpqua. Finally they struck off on to the breaks of the Umpqua and were soon in the settlement again, and I was able to get the description of the two men, which coincided with the description given by others.

I found the sheep within about twelve miles of Canyonville, and a young man was herding them who I soon learned to be what might be called a half idiot. He told me that his name was Buckley. I had quite a pleasant chat with him and spent about two hours with him, lounging around, talking about his sheep. I asked if he had raised his sheep, and where his winter range was.

He said he had not owned the sheep but a short time. I asked him if he had bought them here in this country. He said he had not, but got them on the other side of the mountain in the Rogue river country. I asked him if he owned them alone, whereupon he informed me that he had a partner in the sheep business. I asked him what his partner's name was, and he told me it was John Barton. I asked where his partner lived, and he said that he lived down on the Umpqua river and was running a ferry.

Now I was satisfied that I had found the sheep and one of the men and as good as got the other one where I could put my hand on him at any time. I rode down to Canyonville and telegraphed Mr. Manning, the sheriff, that I had found the sheep and one of the men and had the other one located. He answered me by saying that I would have help the following day from Roseburg, that being the county seat of Douglas county, which is sixteen miles from Canyonville, where I then was and which was in the same county. I waited patiently the next day for assistance, but it did not come. Late that evening I went to the constable of that precinct and asked him to go with me and assist in making the arrest, but he refused, saying: "That man Barton is a hard case. I don't want to have anything to do with him." I did not tell him the particulars of the case, and I must admit that I did not know enough of civil law to know that it was necessary for me to be armed with a warrant to go and make the arrest. On the refusal of the constable to accompany me, I at once walked down to the stable and ordered my horse saddled, and inquired the way to John Barton's place. The proprietor of the stable told me how to go.

So concluding to tackle him alone, I mounted my horse just after dark and started for Barton's Ferry. I found the place without difficulty, and although I rode very slowly, I got to the river some time before daylight. I tied my horse in the brush and walked the road until daylight. As soon as it was daylight I saw the house on the other side of the river, and kept my eye on it until just before sunrise, when I saw the smoke commence to curl up from the chimney, and in about fifteen minutes I saw a man come out in his shirt sleeves and bare-headed. I at once mounted my horse and rode down to the river and halloed for him to bring the boat over as I wished to cross the river. He answered by saying: "I'll be there in a minute as soon as I get my hat and coat." He stepped into the house, got his hat and coat and came across. When he landed I walked on to the boat and asked if he was Mr. Barton. He said that was his name, and in a second he was looking down the muzzle of my pistol, and I informed him that he was my prisoner. He asked me what for. I said for the murdering of McMahon.

"Have they found the body?" were the first words that fell from his lips, which he doubtless would not have uttered had I not caught him off his guard. I told him they had, which was false.

"You want to take me away with you and not let me see my wife and bid her good-bye?"

I informed him that I would, telling him that she could come to see him if she liked. He offered all manner of excuses to get back to his house. After I had listened awhile I gave him two minutes to get off the boat and take the road, which he did at once. I did not try to put the handcuffs on him alone, not wishing to give him any drop on me whatever.

I made him take the road ahead of me, and we started on our way for Jacksonville. After we had gone some two miles in the direction of Canyonville an old gentleman and his son overhauled us with a wagon, and I had the old man put the handcuffs on him, after which I allowed him to get into the wagon with the other two men and ride to Canyonville. When I put him in the little lock-up which they had there for such occasions and went and hunted up the constable and asked him to look after Barton until I would return. I could get no satisfaction from him, so I went to a merchant in town and related the whole circumstance to him and asked him to keep a watch or tell me of some one whom I could hire to look after him that I could rely upon. He assured me that he would look after a man, put him there to watch and then we would be sure that he would be safe. I then mounted my horse and was off for Buckley, who I found without difficulty, arrested him, and started on my way back to Canyonville.

He came so near admitting the crime that I was sure I had the two guilty men. I got back with my prisoner just in time to take the stage for Jacksonville. Leaving my horse at the livery stable, I instructed the liveryman to send him at once to Jacksonville and I would pay all charges. I handcuffed both prisoners and had them shackled together, put them in the stage and started to Jacksonville with them. I wired the sheriff that I had both of the guilty parties and would be at Jacksonville on the stage, which was due about six o'clock the next morning.

The sheriff and his deputies met us that morning at the edge of town. It had been noised around that I would be in and they were somewhat afraid of a mob, but we succeeded in getting to the jail all safe, and not until then had I the faintest idea that I had stepped beyond my official duty in arresting those men without a warrant and bringing them into another county.

These were the first white prisoners that I had ever had any experience with. I had taken so many Indian prisoners that never required any red tape, I naturally supposed that the same rule would be applicable in this case, but I got away with it just the same. That afternoon we took the young man off to himself, and when he was questioned by the district attorney and a certain doctor, whose name has slipped my memory, he admitted the whole affair, and told us just where to go to find McMahon's body. When he told us this the doctor drew a diagram of the ground. Buckley said we would find a tree a certain distance from the cabin that had been blown out by the roots, and in that hole we would find the body covered up with brush and chips thrown on top of the brush. After giving this valuable information we at once started out to hunt for the body.

It was now late in August and a little snow had fallen on the mountains in the fore part of the night. By the aid of the diagram we went to the ground after night, built up a fire and waited till morning. As soon as it was light enough to see, the doctor took the diagram out of his pocket, looked at it and said: "It should be near here." He then turned, and seeing a tree that had been blown over, said: "There is a tree that answers to the description." We walked to the tree and at once saw the toe of one of the dead man's boots protruding through the brush. The doctor when gathering wood the night before to build a fire, had walked almost over the body and had picked up two or three chips of wood from the brush which covered the body. We waited some time before the crowd came with the wagon. After they arrived the body was uncovered, loaded into the wagon and hauled to Jacksonville, arriving in time for the coroner to hold the inquest that afternoon, and the following day the body was buried.

The time having been set for the preliminary examination, Barton's wife and her father arrived in Jacksonville the day before the time set for the trial, and his father-in-law employed an attorney to conduct the case in court in his behalf. When Barton was brought into court he waived examination, but it was quite different with Buckley. When he was brought in for trial the judge asked him if he had counsel. He said he did not, nor did he want any, but the judge appointed a lawyer to take his case.

The lawyer took the prisoner off into a room in company with the deputy sheriff and they were gone about twenty minutes. When they returned the lawyer stated that the prisoner wished to plead guilty and receive his sentence so he could start in at once to work it out. Barton never had a trial, for he starved himself to death and died in jail. The jailor told me that for seventeen days he did not eat or drink but one spoonful of soup.

CHAPTER XL
IN SOCIETY SOME MORE.—A VERY TIGHT PLACE.—TEN PAIRS OF YANKEE EARS.— BLACK BESS SHAKES HERSELF AT THE RIGHT TIME.—A SOLEMN COMPACT

I remained in Jacksonville until about the first of December, 1874, when I received a letter from Lieut. Jackson, who was yet at Fort Yuma, Ariz., stating that there was an opening for me there, and asking me if I knew where George Jones was at that time, and telling me if possible to have him accompany me, as he would insure us both employment in the scouting field upon our arrival.

George was now living twelve miles from Jacksonville. Being sick and tired of idling away my time around town, I rode out to pay George and his parents a friendly visit before taking my leave for Arizona. I found them in rather good circumstances on a small farm on Bear creek, near Phoenix, and a pleasant visit I had with them at their beautiful little home, during which time I showed the letter to George that I had received from Lieut. Jackson. He expressed a desire to accompany me on the trip, but as his parents were now getting old and childish, he did not like to leave without their consent, he being their only son.

Two days later George informed me that he had the consent of his father and mother to go to Arizona, to be gone one year, after which time he was going to quit the business for all time. But we have quit the business before, and then I related the conversation I had with Jim Bridger some years previous at the time I first made up my mind to quit the scouting field.

The time being set for the start, I returned to Jacksonville for my other two horses, clothing, bedding and other traps such as belong to an old scout. All being in readiness, we bade Mr. and Mrs. Jones good-bye and started on our way for Arizona and aimed to reach San Francisco by Christmas. We had five horses in our outfit, I having three and George two. We arrived in San Francisco on the twenty-first of December.

The next morning we were walking up Kearney street near the Lick House when we met the reporter for the Chronicle who I had ridden for at the time of the hanging of Captain Jack and associates at Fort Klamath. The reporter expressed himself as being very glad to meet us, and insisted on our taking a stroll over to the Chronicle office and meet the proprietors of the paper, whose names were DeYoung, their being three brothers of them.

As we had not changed our clothing, having our traveling suits on I insisted on deferring the matter until the next day, but this he would not hear to. As that would not work I tried another plan by telling him that we had not yet had our breakfast, but he told us that he had not yet been to breakfast, and proposed that the three of us take breakfast together, or rather invited George and I to take breakfast with him, which we did, seeing that there was no chance to evade him.

After breakfast we accompanied him to the CHRONICLE office, which at that time was located on the corner of Kearney and Pine streets, and here we met all three of the DeYoung brothers. After being introduced to them and spending some two hours with them, Charles DeYoung, the eldest of the three brothers, gave us a cordial invitation to take dinner with him at his own residence, saying that dinner would be ready at six o'clock. This, I think, was the first time in my life that I had ever heard a six o'clock meal called dinner. Thanking him for the kind offer I excused myself as I was in my traveling suit, and the very thought of entering the private residence of one of the popular men of the city almost paralyzed me. But my excuses were all fruitless. He would not even consider "No" as answer, and some of them were with us until time for dinner, as he termed it, but what I would have called supper.

With as bold a front as possible we accompanied Mr. DeYoung to his residence, which we found to be a fine mansion on California street. On arriving at his residence we met there some ten or twelve other guests, both ladies and gentlemen. Now the reader can have a faint idea of the embarrassing position in which we were both placed at that moment, and I can truthfully say that at the moment I entered that mansion I would have given three months' wages to have been away from there. George Jones had on buckskin breeches and I had on a buckskin suit, while the guests were dressed in style. I tried to offer some apology, but at every attempt it seemed that I only made a bad matter worse.

We were treated with the greatest respect while at this place, and were asked many questions by the other guests relative to the Modoc war, the capturing of Captain Jack, etc., and the following morning quite an article came out in the Chronicle concerning George Jones and myself relative to the position we held in the Modoc war.

We remained there until the last day of December, on which day we started again on our journey for Arizona, via Salinas, Santa Barbara and Los Angeles. Here we lay over and let our horses rest four days, after which we proceeded on our journey via San Diego, which at that time was a very small place. From there we struck for the Colorado river and followed down the river to Fort Yuma.

This route we took in order to avoid crossing any of those sand deserts. We were about five weeks making the trip, and reached Fort Yuma without any accident or mishap whatever, and learned that the Indians were worse in Arizona than when we left them several years before, as they were most all armed with rifles, instead of bows and arrows, and many of them had pistols.

Lieut. Jackson told me he had lost more men the last year out than in any other two seasons since he had been in Arizona. He had received orders to take four hundred cavalrymen and one hundred infantrymen and go into the mountains and follow the Indians from place to place the coming season. The Lieutenant told me that there had been a settlement started the last year about ninety miles from the line of Arizona and Sonora, Mexico, and they were not only troubled with the Indians, but the Mexicans also came in there and stole their stock and run it across the line.

Gen. Crook was still in charge of the command, and wanted me to accompany Lieut. Jackson, saying: "I do not expect you to do any hard service yourself, but want you to take charge of the scout force and handle it to suit yourself."

If my memory serves me right, it was in the latter part of March, 1875, when we made the start for the mountains. For the first hundred miles our supplies were hauled on wagons, but the balance of the way they had to be packed on animals.

On our way out we passed near Salt River Valley, that being settled up now with Americans. I started to ride out to the settlement to ascertain something of the nature of the depredations committed there lately. I dressed in teamster's clothing and tied a pair of blankets behind my saddle before starting to the settlement. It was late in the evening, just about sunset, and I was riding leisurely along, being within six or seven miles of the settlement, when suddenly I came upon three Mexicans, just cooking supper. They saw me as quick as I saw them, and I thought I was in for it. I was too near them to attempt to get away, so all that I could do was to make the best I could of it, take my chances and trust to luck. When I rode up I spoke to them in my own language and one big burley looking Mexican said: "No indetenda English," meaning I don't understand English. They then asked me in their tongue if I spoke Spanish, which I understood as well as they did, but I shook my head as if I could not understand a word they said.

I dismounted, untied the blankets from behind my saddle, threw them down near the fire on which they were cooking supper, but did not unsaddle my mare. I was riding Black Bess, and one of them got up and walked around her and examined her closely, and when he returned to the fire he said: "Esta ismo muya wano cavia," meaning that is a good horse. Another one in the crowd said he had in his pocket just ten pairs of ears that he had taken from the heads of Yankees, and this would make the eleventh pair. Now I thought my time had come, but I had been in tight places before and had always managed in some way to get out.

While it looked very blue, still I made up my mind that when it came to the worst I would get at least one or two of them while they were doing me up. I did not pretend to pay any attention to their conversation, yet at the same time I could understand all that was uttered by them. I learned that there were ten in the gang, and the other seven had gone that night to the settlement for the purpose of stealing horses, and were liable to return at any time. While I was lying there on my blankets I heard them lay their plans to kill me in case I went to sleep, or if I got up and started to my horse they were to shoot me before I got away. Now the reader can rest assured that this was getting to be a serious affair with me, for I knew that these Mexicans could handle a pistol with good success, while they are as a rule experts with a knife, the latter being a Mexican stand-by. This was a little the closest place that I had ever been in. If I attempted to leave they would kill me as sure as I made the start; if I stayed there until the other seven returned, then I would not have a ghost of a show for my life.

I laid there by the fire as though I was worn out entirely, listening to their talk, and more than once heard the big rough- looking Mexican boast of a pair of Yankee ears that he would take from my head.

Their supper being ready, they sat down to eat, but did not invite me to sup with them. They all three ate out of the same frying pan and poured their coffee out in tin cups. Two of them had their backs turned toward me, while the other one sat on the opposite side of the frying pan that they were eating out of and facing me, but they were paying but little attention to me. Black Bess was feeding close by and on the opposite side of them from where I lay. Now I made up my mind that I would make a desperate effort to extricate myself from this trap, for to stay there I knew meant death and I would rather take my chances with those three than with the entire gang.

They were all sitting flat on the ground, each had a pistol on him and their guns all lay within a few feet of them. My only show for escape was to kill two of them at the first shot and then I would have an equal show with the other one, but now was the particular part of the work. Just one false move and the jig was up with me, but it was getting time that I should be at work for the other seven were likely to be there at any moment. I carefully reached around under my coat tail and got hold of both of my pistols, and just as I did so, as good luck would have it, Black Bess shook herself very hard and caused them to turn their eyes toward her, and it could not have happened in a better time. I was on my knees in an instant, and leveling a pistol at each of the two with their backs towards me, I fired, and being almost near enough to have touched either of them with the point of the pistol, it was a sure thing that I would not miss them. After firing the first two shots I was on my feet in an instant, by which time the third man had taken a tumble to himself and was on his knees and had his pistol about half out when I fired both pistols at him and he fell back dead. By this time one of the others had staggered to his feet and had his pistol out, but, fortunately, he seemed to be blind, for he fired his pistol in the opposite direction from where I stood. I turned and dealt him his fatal dose.

I tried to catch their pack horses but missed one of them, and as time was precious, for I did not know what moment the seven would come, I took their rifles, broke the stocks off of them, took their pistols along with me, mounted Black Bess, rounded up their horses and started for the train, and I lost no time in getting there, and as I sped across the country on Black Bess after the nine captured animals I felt that I could congratulate myself on getting out of the tightest place I had ever been in, without even a scratch.

When I arrived at camp and reported to the Lieutenant he at once started two companies of cavalry out to try and cut the other seven off, instructing them to watch every trail and every watering place within fifty miles, closely.

I changed horses and started with George Jones and six other scouts, and the last words that Lieut. Jackson said to me as I was ready to ride away was: "Don't spare horse flesh, but run them down Cap, if it is possible, and let us break up this thieving band. I would rather kill one Mexican any time than two Apaches."

Across the country we rode at a rapid rate, but were not able to reach the spot until after daylight. The Mexicans had been there ahead of us and removed everything but their dead comrades, those they did not attempt to remove or even bury, leaving them for the wolves that roved the country in search of food.

We were soon on their trail, which was easily followed, as they were driving a large band of stock. About the middle of the afternoon we came in sight of them. When they first saw us we were so near them that they deserted their band of stock and ran for their lives. We gave chase, but could not get any nearer. We followed them until dark, our horses being badly jaded, and I had now been in the saddle for two days and one night in succession, so we made camp for the night. The next morning a detail of six men was made to drive the stolen stock back to the settlement where it belonged, there being some forty head of horses and mules. The balance of us returned to the trail, lay over and rested one day. This put a stop to the Mexicans troubling the settlement for some time.

Pulling on for the mountains, the second day we saw the ruins of two wagons that had been burned, but could get no trace of the teamsters. The supposition prevailed that they were taken prisoners by the Apaches. The Lieutenant established his headquarters fifty miles from where he had his quarters when we were out before, and now active work commenced, for there was plenty of it to be done.

We had only been there a few days when two of my scouts came in one evening and reported having seen about twenty Indians ten miles from camp and traveling west. The scouts all being in, George Jones and I and four other scouts and one company of cavalry started in pursuit. We had no trouble in striking their trail, and there being a good starlight that night and the country somewhat sandy, we were able to track them easily. We had not followed the trail more than two miles when we passed over a ridge, and I looked down the valley ahead of us and could see the glimmer of their fire. Here the soldiers stopped, and I and my scouts went on in the direction of the fires, which we supposed to be about half a mile away but which proved to be nearer two miles. When we were near the camp we dismounted and crawled up. We located the horses, which were mostly standing still at the time and two or three hundred yards from camp. I "telegraphed" the soldiers to come at once.

Taking the balance of the scouts we rode slowly and carefully around, getting immediately between the Indian camp and their horses, I telling George Jones that as soon as the soldiers started to make their charge to follow me with the horses. But this time the Indians were awake before the soldiers were on them and opened fire on them, killing three horses and wounding two the first round, but only one soldier was wounded, and the sergeant in charge told me afterwards that he got eighteen Apaches out of the crowd, and we got twenty-seven horses. We got back to headquarters about noon the next day and learned that Lieut. Jackson had gone in a different direction after another band of Apaches, which he overhauled and got twelve scalps from their number.

Now we started for a trip on the east side of Black canyon, six scouts and one company of cavalry, with twenty-two pack animals, calculating to be gone about ten days. On the fifth day of our trip George Jones, myself and two other scouts were riding leisurely along about one mile in advance of the command when just as we raised to the top of a little rocky ridge we came face to face with a band of Indians, making a surprise to both parties. I could not tell which party fired first, but we gave them one round and seeing that there were too many of them for us, we wheeled and started back down the hill. As we did so George sang out: "My horse is shot," and just at that time the horse fell. George threw himself clear of the horse and when he struck the ground he lit running, and at his best licks, too. The rest of us dropped behind George to protect him until we were off the rocky ground. The Indians held their distance all the way down the hill, not stopping to reload their When we were at the foot of the hill the three of us that were mounted, in order to give George Jones a chance to ascend the hill, turned and gave them another volley. Here I fired three shots and got two Indians and then spurred up by the side of George and gave him a chance to jump on behind me, which he did. Just as we raised to the top of the hill we met the command, who had heard our firing and came to our relief, and they met the Indians face to face. At this the Indians changed their minds very suddenly, and it is useless to say that they were on the back track much quicker than I could tell it. The soldiers went in hot pursuit of them and got nine of their number. From there we struck off in a south-westerly direction, thinking that when we struck the main road we might run on to some emigrants en- route for California.

We struck the main road fifty miles south of the Lieutenant's quarters. Here we laid over two days, thinking that there might be an emigrant train come along that we could escort through to headquarters, this part of the road being in the heart of the Apache country, and the most dangerous for emigrants from the fact that it is all a timber country and over mountains which, in places, are very rocky, thereby giving the Indians all advantage over the emigrants.

The evening of the second day, just as we were sitting down to supper, I received a message from Lieut. Jackson for George Jones and myself to come to headquarters at once, but he did not state why he required our presence there. As soon as supper was over we started. The dispatch bearer thought it was at least sixty miles, but we had supposed it was not more than fifty, each of us having two saddle horses.

At one place on the road the cayotes turned loose, and it sounded as if there must have been a hundred, all barking at once, and George Jones remarked: "Above all things that I have dreaded while in this business is being shot down and left on the plains for my bones to be picked up by those sneaking wolves, and now Cap, I will make this agreement with you; in case that either of us happen to be killed, which is liable to happen any day, the surviving one is to see that the other is buried if in the bounds of possibility."

I said: "George, we will shake hands on that," which we did, and I added: "You can also rest assured that if ever you are shot down while in company with me, no Indian will ever scalp you as long as I have the strength to stand over your body, nor shall the cayotes ever pick your bones if I live long enough to see that you are buried," and the reader will see later on that I kept my promise.

CHAPTER XLI
WE LOCATE A SMALL BAND OF RED BUTCHERS AND SEND THEM TO THE HAPPY HUNTING GROUNDS.—EMIGRANTS MISTAKE US FOR INDIANS.—GEORGE JONES WOUNDED

Just at sunrise we made our appearance at the Lieutenant's quarters, and he informed us that the Indians had made an attack on the settlement on the east side of the San Antonio desert; had killed two families, taken two little girls prisoner and captured a lot of stock from the settlers.

This report had first reached Gen. Crook at Fort Yuma, and he had dispatched the news to Lieut. Jackson. This being a strange country to the Lieutenant, having never been over it and knowing that I had been through it twice, once with Uncle Kit Carson and another time in company with Jim Beckwith, he insisted on my going out in that section to investigate the matter and see whether or not the report was true.

The day following George and I started with four assistants for the settlement. Each of us took two saddle horses and one pack animal for each two men, with ten days' rations. From there to the settlement was about seventy-five miles.

Knowing just where the majority of the Apache force was concentrated, we took rather a circuitous route in-stead of going direct to the settlement in order to ascertain whether the depredations were committed by Apaches or Pimas.

The fifth day out we struck the settlement, but did not cross the Indian trail, which led me to think that the work was done by Pimas and not Apaches.

When we arrived there no one could tell us how many Indians there were nor what they looked like, but when I came to find out the truth of the matter there had been no families massacred, nor had the two girls been taken prisoners, but there had been two boys killed that were herding stock.

We remained there one day in order to learn what we could in regard to the trouble and then struck the trail of the Indians and followed it two days, but it was so old that we gave it up, as it was then twelve days since the depredations were committed and we knew that the Indians were a long ways off by that time. We took a different route on our return, and the second day we saw a small band of Indians traveling toward the settlement, which we had left four days previous. We started in pursuit of them and struck their trail before it was dark. I was confident that they would camp at the first water they came to, which was about seven or eight miles from there, so we staked our horses out on good grass, sat down and ate our lunch while we waited for the clear moon to make its appearance and light us across the country where we might find the noble red men of the plains and entertain them for a while at least. We thought that it would take us about all night to track them up by the light of the moon, find their camp and play them just one little tune of "How came you so?"

About ten o'clock the moon arose, but we waited until it was two hours high, giving our horses a chance to fill up, after which we mounted and took the trail of the Pimas, which we had not great trouble in finding.

After we had followed the trail about seven miles we came to their horses, but could see no signs of any camp, and we at once made up our minds that the Indians were not far away, but that they had either built no fire or the fire had gone entirely out, for we could see no signs of any.

Dismounting, George took one man with him and I took one with me, leaving the other two with the horses, and started out in different directions to look for their camp. After wandering around about an hour I found where they were camped, and they were sound asleep and lying in a row but each one separate. We then returned to our horses and in a short time George came in. It was now getting high time that we were at work, for it was beginning to get daybreak, so after I had explained how they laid, five of us started for them, leaving one man with the horses. They were lying about two hundred and fifty yards from where we had stopped with our horses. We crawled up abreast until within ten feet of the Indians, and each scout drew both his revolvers, sprang to his feet, and I need not say that we made quick work of those redskins. Only one got to his feet, and he did not stand a second until there were three or four bullets in his body, but not one of us got a scratch in this fight.

Now the fun was over and we were not afraid to speak out, so we called out for the man that we left in charge of our horses to bring them over, and we gathered some wood and built a fire.

It had been several days since we had had fresh meat, but the Pimas had been kind enough to kill an antelope that day, and as they had only eaten of it once, we had a feast that morning, which we enjoyed very much.

We gathered up the guns and ammunition that belonged to the Indians, which, by the way, was the best armed lot of Indians I had ever seen. Each one of them had a good rifle and a Colt revolver, and one of them had the handsomest knife I ever saw. Had we not run on to them no doubt they would have done some devilment in the white settlement the following day. We reached headquarters in three days.

It was now time for the emigrants to begin to travel over the Butterfield route, and Lieut. Jackson started one company of cavalry across to the opposite side of the mountain some sixty miles away to protect the emigrants, and George Jones and I both accompanied them. We established our quarters about a half mile from the road at the foot of the mountains on the south side.

The next day after we struck this place George and I started out to scout over the country to see whether or not there were any Indians in the country and also ride out on the road and look for emigrants.

The second day out we climbed to the top of a high ridge, and by looking through the glass we could see a large emigrant train coming, which we thought to be about twenty miles distant. We knew very well where it would camp, and by riding briskly we would be able to meet it by dark; so we rode on and reached the emigrants about sunset. They were just corralling their wagons for the night, and when they saw us coming they took us for Indians and every man went for his gun. As soon as we saw them start for their guns we both took off our hats and waved them over our heads, when they saw that they were needlessly alarmed. This train was from Texas, and the name of the captain was Sours, and it was beyond doubt the best organized train I ever saw on the plains; everything seemed to move like clock work.

When I told Capt. Sours who we were and what our business was and that as soon as they got to our quarters they would have an escort, he said: "I am indeed very glad to know that there is some protection out here for emigrants, but as for ourselves we do not need it much, for every man in my train has seven shots, and some of them three times that number."

We stayed with them that night and the next morning pulled out for our quarters. We remained there for a month, but did not see any Indians during that time.

At the end of the month there came along a large train from Arkansas and Texas. We escorted it across the mountains expecting that this would wind up the emigrant travel across there for the season. When we arrived at Lieut. Jackson's quarters he started George and I and two other scouts out towards the Salt river valley settlement, telling me that he would move down near Mrs. Davis' ranch and there he would wait until he should hear from me. The third day out we made camp early on account of water, and after deciding on the spot where we should pitch our camp for the night George rode off to a high ridge near by to take a look over the country. He was not gone long before he made his appearance riding at full speed, and announced that there was a large band of Indians coming direct for our camp, and would be on to us before we could saddle up and get away.

"Get your horses boys," were his first words, and every man made a rush for his horse, but before we could get saddled the Indians hove in sight, and not over half a mile away.

"There they are," said George as he jumped on to his horse again, "and there must be at least sixty of them."

I was not long in making up my mind what to do. We all got our horses saddled and were mounted just in the nick of time to get away for we were not twenty yards from camp when they were close on to us.

Down the ravine we went with the Apaches in hot pursuit of us. I yelled out to the boys to turn to the left across the ridge and when we were over the turn we stopped and gave them a volley, and picked off the leaders as they came in sight. I saw a number of them fall, but it did not appear to check them in the least. They were coming too thick and we wheeled and were off again with some of them within at least thirty yards of us, but we gained on them gradually. Finally George Jones sang out: "I am shot through the arm." I reined my horse up by his side and asked if his arm was broken. He said it was, and I could see it was hanging down and the blood almost streaming off his fingers. I asked if he felt sick, and he said he did not.

Of course all the time this conversation was going on we were putting our horses down to their utmost. George said; "I am all right if I don't get another shot," so I told him to take the lead and not to spare his horse. I also told the other boys to fall back to the rear so we could protect him, as he was badly wounded and the Indians were holding their own pretty well.

On looking ahead I saw another little ridge and I told the boys that when we were over that to all turn and give them two shots each, and for each to be sure to get his Indian. This order was carried into effect and they were so near us that I think each shot did its work. This brought them to a halt and they did not crowd us any more; it was soon dark and we escaped without any further mishap.

After we could hear no more of them we rode to the top of a ridge where we would have a chance to protect ourselves in case of another attack, and dismounted to ascertain the extent of George's wound, and as the excitement died down he commenced feeling sick at his stomach. I gave him a drink of whiskey from a bottle that I had carried in my canteen at all seasons, and this was the second time the cork had been drawn from the flask. When we got his coat off and examined his wound we found that the arm was broken just below the elbow. Using our handkerchiefs for bandages, we dressed the hurt as best we could, corded his arm to stop the flow of blood and then pulled out for headquarters, arriving there just at daybreak.

I took George to the surgeon, who set the bone and dressed the arm up "ship shape," after which he gave him something to make him sleep.

After seeing George in bed I at once repaired to the Lieutenant's quarters and found him just arising. He asked me if I was too tired to make another chase, and I told him I would be ready as soon as I could eat my breakfast. He said in one hour's time he would have two companies of cavalry ready to start.

After breakfast I changed horses, and taking four other scouts, started out to pilot the cavalry to where we could take the trail of the Indians. On this trip each scout took four days' rations, and about one o'clock that afternoon we struck a plain trail that we followed at a lively gait until nearly dark; the scout force riding from one to two miles ahead so in case we should get in sight of the reds we could telegraph back to the command, or should the Indians attempt to give us another chase we might be able to run them up against the soldiers, where they would find amusement for a while.

We followed them for two days but never got sight of them. They had turned and made their way back in the direction of Black canyon and we gave up the chase, but we were sure that in the running fight we had with them that evening we had killed at least thirteen, as we found that many newly made graves when we went back to take their trail.

We returned to headquarters and I found George doing splendidly, and the next day we all pulled out for Fort Yuma. The first day's travel took us to Mrs. Davis' This was the first time I had seen her or any of her family since the next day after the funeral of her husband and two sons in the fall of 1866.

Mrs. Davis insisted on George staying there with them until his arm was well, which kind and hospitable offer he accepted, remaining two months. We put in our time that winter as usual when wintering at the fort, doing nothing.

CHAPTER XLII
"WE ARE ALL SURROUNDED."—A BOLD DASH AND A BAD WOUND—MRS. DAVIS SHOWS HER GRATITUDE.—THE MOST OF MY WORK NOW DONE ON CRUTCHES

It was the last of February or first of March, 1876, that we started for St. Louis Valley. I had visited this valley twice, but had come in both times from the opposite direction to which we would have to enter the valley in going from camp, consequently I was at a loss to know just which direction to go from camp to strike the valley where we wanted to enter it, but we struck out southeast, taking twenty days' provisions with us. The ninth day out we came in sight of the valley from the west side. It being about noon, water being handy and no end to the grass, we stopped there for dinner and to let our horses graze After I had taken a squint through my glasses, I called the Lieutenant to me and handed them to him.

He sat and looked for a long time, and when he took the glasses from his eyes he said: "That is beyond any doubt the prettiest sight I ever saw in my life." There were small bands of bison scattered here and there all over the valley, elk by the hundreds and deer too numerous to mention, but not an Indian nor even a sign of one could be seen in this lovely valley.

"I have made this trip unnecessarily," said he, "for I had expected to find many little bands of Indians in this valley hunting, but in that I am disappointed." We then turned back for headquarters as quick as possible, making the entire trip without seeing an Indian or even a sign of one.

Some time in June the Lieutenant started out in command of two companies of cavalry to cross the mountains to protect the emigrants, George Jones and I ahead with four assistants.

The Lieutenant having told us where he would camp that night, it was the duty of the scouts to make a circuit of the camp before dark. On arriving at the appointed place, George and I started to make a tour of the camp, leaving the other scouts at the camping place. It was about sunset when we saw a band of Indians as we supposed about four miles from where we were to camp that night, and about one mile and a half from where we then were. We put spurs to our horses and headed for the Indian camp, as we were desirous of ascertaining about their number and getting the location of the ground before it was too dark. When we were within about a quarter of a mile, it being nearly dark, we were just in the act of tying our horses, intending to crawl up near their camp, we heard a rumbling noise back in the direction from which we had just come. I crawled quickly around the hill and saw another band of Indians coming directly toward us, who were making their way as we supposed to where the other Indians were camped. I got back to my horse in less time than it took me to crawl away from him, then we mounted and got away as we supposed, undiscovered, and rode up a ravine and in a direction that we would not be seen by the Indians. Not thinking ourselves in any immediate danger, we did not hurry. After riding up the ravine only a short distance, just as we rounded a curve, we were brought face to face with another band of Indians. This was, I think, a small band that had left the main band to hunt for game and were just getting into camp, but we did not make any inquiries as to what success they had in hunting, nor did we ask whether they had been hunting at all.

The moment we saw them we drew our pistols and commenced firing, and they returned the fire. We were almost entirely surrounded by Indians, and I saw that it was no place for me, so I sang out to George: "Let's breakthrough their ranks." "All right," said he, and we drove the spurs into our horses with all vengeance, riding about fifteen feet apart and succeeding in getting through unhurt, and away we rode for quarters, closely followed by the redskins Now we thought we were safe, and each in his own mind was congratulating himself, when a ball struck me in the left hip which paralyzed my whole side and wrecked my whole nervous system. I sang out to George to drop behind and whip my horse, for now I had no use whatever of my left leg, and it took all the strength in my right leg to hang on to the horse. No quicker said than he was behind my horse and doing all in his power to urge him, and telling me for God's sake to hang on a little longer.

The soldiers had just rode into camp and were dismounting when they heard our firing, and remounted and started in that direction, but as it was getting dark and the country strange to them they could not make very good time. They met us about half way between the camp and the Indians, the reds still in hot pursuit of us. The Lieutenant ordered a charge, and he had his men so trained that when he said charge they did not stop shooting as long as there was an Indian to shoot at.

By this time I was so sick that George had to help me off my horse, and leaving two men with me, he went on after, and overhauled the command before they got to the Indian camp, where they found the Indians ready for battle, and here I think the Lieutenant got the worst of the fight, for when he made the attack the Indians attacked him in the rear. The men had to carry me in their arms to camp, as they had no stretchers in the outfit, and there I lay four weeks before an ambulance came. I was then removed to Fort Yuma. George Jones took charge of the scout force after I was wounded.

I told George then that if I should be fortunate enough to get over my wound I would quit the business for all time. After remaining in the hospital at the fort about two months I was able to get around on crutches. Mrs. Davis having heard of my misfortune, came over in company with her brother to see how I was getting along, and insisted on my going home with them and remaining until such time as I could ride on horseback, which kind offer I accepted, with the consent of the doctor, he giving me a supply of medicine sufficient to last me several weeks.

I remained there until after Christmas, when George came after me, and by this time I was able to walk with a cane. I then returned to Fort Yuma, having made up my mind to draw my pay and quit the business.

George also being tired of this kind of life, had concluded to return to his home in Oregon. When I made our intentions known to Gen. Crook he asked me how I would ever be able to get to civilization, for the mail was yet carried on horseback and I was not able to ride in that way. He insisted on my remaining with him the coming season, and if I should not be able to ride I could stay in camp and give orders to the other scouts. I asked George what he thought of the matter, and he said: "I will leave the matter with you, if you stay another season I will, or if you say leave I will quit also." However, we decided after talking matters over to stay there one more season, and that would end our scouting career, both vowing that we would quit after that, and in our contract this time with the General we agreed to stay until the coming January, and George and I were to have two-thirds of all the property captured during this campaign.

CHAPTER XLIII
POOR JONES MAKES HIS LAST FIGHT.—HE DIED AMONG A LOT OF THE DEVILS HE HAD SLAIN.—END OF THIRTY-ONE YEARS OF HUNTING, TRAPPING AND SCOUTING

About the first day in March, 1877, we started out on our summer's campaign. I was now able to mount a horse by being assisted, but had to be very careful and only ride a short distance, and very slow at that. The third day on our trip from the fort George reported having seen the trail of quite a large band of Indians traveling westward almost parallel with the road, but said they had passed about two days before. I asked the Lieutenant to give me his camping places that night and the next one, which he did. I then told George to select four men from the scout force, take two days' rations and see if he could run down the Indians and to telegraph me when they changed their course or when he had them located.

George was on their trail before noon and before sunset he had them located, only a short distance from the place where I had been wounded the year before. I got a dispatch from him just as I was ready to turn in for the night, and by one o'clock I received another dispatch stating that there were about eighty in the band, and well armed, and among them about twenty squaws and their children. This was something we had never seen among the Apaches before. Lieut. Jackson asked my opinion of their having their families with them. I told him I thought they must be on their way to Sonora to trade, as at that time the Apaches had never traded but very little with the whites.

They might be out for a hunt, but it was not customary when on such a trip to have their families with them. Upon the receipt of the second dispatch from George, Lieut. Jackson started out with three companies of cavalry, and arrived at the spot near daybreak. I was told afterwards that George had been crawling around all night getting the location of the Indians, the general lay of the ground and to ascertain the best plan of attack, knowing it would be so late by the time the Lieutenant would arrive that he himself would have no time to spare, and he had a diagram drawn on a piece of envelope of the camp and surroundings, also had their horses located. When the Lieutenant was ready to make the attack George took four of the scouts and started to cut the horses off and prevent the Indians from getting to them, but it seemed as though when the cavalry started to make the charge the Indians' dogs had given the alarm and a part of the Indians had made for their horses. At any rate when daylight came George was found some two hundred yards from the Indian encampment, with both legs broken and a bullet through his neck, which had broken it and four Indians lying near him dead, which he no doubt had killed, and his horse lay dead about a rod from where he lay. No one had seen him fall nor had heard a word from him after he gave the order to charge for the horses. About the middle of that afternoon they returned to camp with George's body and seven others that were killed, and nineteen wounded soldiers. They had killed thirty-seven Indians and had taken all the squaws and children prisoners. After I had looked at the body of that once noble and brave form, but now a lifeless corpse, I told the Lieutenant that I was ready to leave the field, for there was not a man in the entire army that could fill his place, and without at least one reliable man in the field it would be impossible to accomplish anything.

The dead were buried about two hundred yards north of the spring where we had camped, and I saw that George Jones was put away in the best and most respectable manner possible considering the circumstances by which we were governed at that time. We buried him entirely alone, near a yellow pine tree, and at his head we placed a rude pine board, dressed in as good a shape as could be done with such tools as were accessible to our use. On this board his name was engraved, also his age and the manner in which he came to his death, and the same is also to be seen on the yellow pine tree that stands near the grave of this once noble friend and hero of the plains.

My brave and noble comrade,
You have served your country true,
Your trials and troubles are ended
And you have bade this world adieu.

You have been a noble companion,
Once so trusty, true and brave;
But now your cold and lifeless form
Lies silent in the grave.

While your form remains here with us
In this wicked dismal land,
Your soul has crossed the river
And joined the angel band.

The prisoners that were taken here Lieut. Jackson sent to Fort Yuma and placed under guard, as Gen. Crook had made up his mind to capture all the Apaches he could and try in that way to civilize them, but he made a total failure in regard to this particular tribe of Indians.

I informed George's father and mother of his death as soon as I could get a letter to them, telling them as soon as I returned to the fort I would draw his pay and send it to them, which I did. When I talked to Lieut. Jackson of quitting he said he could not spare me until the summer's campaign was over, so I remained with him.

We moved on and established our quarters at the same place as the year before, and a more lonesome summer I never put in anywhere than there. I was not able to do anything more than stay in camp and give orders until late in the season. Lieut. Jackson had two more engagements that season, but I was not able to be in either of them.

The first one the soldiers killed nine Indians, and the other time the Indians made an attack on him while he, with twenty of his men, were escorting an emigrant train across the mountains. In this engagement the Lieutenant did not lose a man, and only three horses, and killed twenty-three Indians and gave them a chase of about ten miles.

It was now getting late in the fall and Lieut. Jackson pulled out for the fort, and by that time I was just able to climb on my horse without assistance. We arrived at Fort Yuma about the first of November, and there I remained till the first of June, 1878.

Before I left I made Mrs. Davis and her family a farewell visit. Two of her daughters were then married and lived near their mother, and all seemed to be in a prosperous condition. After a pleasant visit with the Davis folks I returned to the fort and commenced making preparations to leave, but was delayed in starting at least a month on account of some soldiers who had served their time out and were going to return with me. I told my old friend Lieut. Jackson the day before starting that I did not think that there was another white man in the United States that had seen less of civilization or more of Indian warfare than I had, it now being just thirty-one years since I started out with Uncle Kit Carson onto the plains and into the mountains.

When I left the fort this time it was with the determination that I would not go into the scouting field again, and I have kept my word so far, and think I shall thus continue. I started out from the fort with twenty-three head of horses, and I packed the baggage of the four discharged soldiers in order to get them to help me with my loose horses.

CHAPTER XLIV
A GRIZZLEY HUNTS THE HUNTER.—SHOOTING SEALS IN ALASKAN WATERS.—I BECOME A SEATTLE HOTEL KEEPER AND THE BIG FIRE CLOSES ME OUT.— SOME REST

On my arrival at San Francisco the first thing was to get rid of my surplus horses. During the time I was selling them I made the acquaintance of a man named Walter Fiske, who was engaged in raising Angora goats, about one hundred and twenty miles north from San Francisco, and who was something of a hunter also. Mr. Fiske invited me to go home with him and have a bear hunt.

Being tired of the city, I accompanied Mr. Fiske to his ranch. He said he knew where there was a patch of wild clover on which the grizzlies fed, so we were off for a bear hunt. We soon found where they fed and watered. They had a plain trail from their feeding place to the water. Mr. Fiske being hard of hearing proposed that I stop on the feeding ground and he would take his stand down on the trail, and in case I should get into trouble I could run down the trail, and if he were to get into a tight place he would run up the trail to where I was. I took my stand and had not been there long until I saw, just behind, in about twenty feet of me, a huge grizzly bear coming for me on his hind feet. I did not see a tree that I could get behind or climb, so I took out along the trail as fast as I could, the grizzly after me. For the first fifty yards I had to run up grade and then I turned down hill. When I reached the top of the hill I commenced to hallo at the top of my voice, "Look out Walter, we are coming!" Walter was sitting only a few steps from the trail and the moment I passed him I heard the report of his gun. I jumped to one side and gave the bear a shot. I got in two shots and Fiske four. After receiving this amount of lead the bear ran but a short distance and dropped dead. All of the shots were near the bear's heart. We dressed him and started home and we had bear meat enough to last for some time to come. In the mean time Mr. Fiske had told me about a man four miles from, his place who had a ranch for sale, consisting of three hundred and twenty acres of deeded land, one hundred acres in cultivation, eighty bearing fruit trees and two acres of a vineyard. He said the place could be bought cheap, and he also told me that there was a vacant quarter section adjoining this land that I could take up, and I would have the finest goat ranch in the country. Mr. Fiske and I took a trip down and found the owner very anxious to sell. After looking the ranch over and getting his figures, I made him an offer of four thousand dollars for everything, which offer he accepted, he reserving nothing but one span of horses, his bed and clothing. We then went to Santa Rosa, the county seat, to get an abstract of title and a deed to the property, and now I am once more an honest rancher. While in Santa Rosa I hired a man and his wife by the name of Benson, by the year. Mr. Benson proved to be a good man and his wife a splendid housekeeper. All went well for about five months, and having filed on the quarter of vacant land adjoining me, of course I had to move over there. I had noticed a change in Benson's appearance, but had not thought much about it till one Saturday I sent him to haul some pickets over to my preemption claim. That night, having company, I did not go to the cabin on the claim, but stayed on the other place. Benson was not at supper that evening, but I paid no attention to it nor thought it strange, supposing he was just a little late getting home. The next morning I noticed that he was not at the breakfast table, and I asked Mrs. Benson why Mr. Bensen didn't come to his breakfast. She asked if I had not told him to stay on the preemption claim that night. I told her that I had not and that I had the key and he could not get into the house, and besides there was no feed there for the mules. She commenced to feel uneasy then. So as soon as breakfast was over I took one of my hired men and started out to hunt for him. We struck the wagon trail and tracked him around for some time. He had traveled in a terribly round about way. We finally came to him where he had run his team against a tree, and when we came upon him he was down in front of the mules whipping them around the fore legs trying to make them get down and pray. He did not notice us until I spoke to him and told him to quit whipping the mules. When he looked at me I could see that he was perfectly wild. It took us both three hours to get him back to the house. I sent for the constable, who took him to Santa Rosa and from there he was taken to the insane asylum. His wife went East to her folks, and I was told afterwards that he got all right.

I next tried a Chinese housekeeper, but John Chinaman had too many relations in the country. There would be two or three Chinamen there almost every week to see my cook and would stay one or two nights. It was not what they ate that I cared for, but what they carried off.

I tried ranching there for three years and during that time I had three different men with their wives, but there was always something wrong, too far from church or too far from neighbors, so I came to the conclusion that a man had no use with a ranch unless he had a wife. In the mean time I had proved up on my preemption, and had all my land fenced in with a picket fence made of red wood pickets. I had also got sick and tired of ranching, not but what I had done fairly well, but it was too much bother for a man that had been raised as I had. I went to San Francisco and placed my land in the hands of a real estate agent for sale, and it was but a short time when he sent two men out to look at it. This was the fall of the year when my fruit was just beautiful and the grapes ripe in the vineyard, and we were not long in making a trade.

In less than one month I was without a house or home, so I placed my money in the bank and arranged to get my interest semi- annually, and made up my mind to take things easy the balance of my days.

About one year from that time I succeeded in getting up a hunting party, and we went up into the mountains in Mendocino county, where we found game in abundance, deer, elk and bear. I stayed out in the mountains nearly three months, during which time I killed the largest grizzly bear I have ever seen, weighing net, eight hundred and sixty pounds. This bear I killed at one shot, and it is the only grizzly that I ever killed at one shot in all my hunting. We also killed ten large elk. One man in the party killed an elk that the horns measured from tip to tip, five feet and four inches, and those horns can be seen at the Lick House in San Francisco. He sold them for fifty dollars.

I remained in San Francisco until in the spring of 1886, when there was a party fitting up a schooner to go sealing on the coast of Alaska, and I was offered a job as shooter. I agreed to go with them and they were to pay me two dollars for each seal that I killed. The first of April we started, and were twenty-two days getting to where there was seal.

Now this was a new business to me, and my first seal hunting was near the mouth of the Yukon river. The captain anchored about twenty miles from land. There were six sealing boats with the schooner, the shooter had charge of his boat, and there were two or three other men to accompany him. One of my boatmen was a Frenchman and the other a German; they were both stout and willing to work. While I received two dollars a piece for all the seals killed, they only got one dollar each, making in all four dollars each that the seals cost the company.

In the morning the captain gives each man his course and instructions to return at once when the signal cannon is fired. The first morning that we started out we went about four miles before we saw any seal, when we ran on to a school sleeping on the water. The two boatmen pulled up among them and I turned loose to shooting them and got six out of the outfit before they got away from us. Shooting seal out of a boat reminded me very much of shooting Indians when on a bucking cayuse, as the boat is always in motion, and it is all that a person can do to stand up in it when the sea is any ways rough. That day I killed nine seal and we were called in at two o'clock, as there was fog coming up, and we just got in ahead of it. We had fair success sealing until the last of August, when my crew ventured a little too far and the wind changed so that we did not hear the cannon and the fog caught us. Each crew when starting out in the morning always took supplies along sufficient to last twenty-four hours. This time when we got caught in the fog the wind had changed on us, so we tried to remain as near the same place as possible, but this time we had to guess at it as we could not always tell just which way the tide was going. This was beyond any doubt the worst trip that I ever experienced, the fog was very cold and our clothing wet. We were out three days and nights and then were picked up by another schooner. The captain of the schooner that picked us up heard the firing of our cannon that morning and we were picked up about noon. He at once set sail for our schooner, firing the signal cannon every half hour, reaching our schooner just as it was growing dark, and the captain and crew had given us up for lost. We stayed out until the last of September, when we sailed for San Francisco, and this wound up my seal hunting.

There was only one other man in the crew that killed more seal than I did during the season, but I made the largest day's killing of any one in the crew, that being twenty seven. But one season was enough for me in that line of business. I concluded that I would much rather take my chances on dry land.

In the spring of 1887 I took a trip to the Puget Sound country and found Seattle a very lively place; in fact, as much so as any place I had ever seen in my life. After remaining in Seattle about two months I concluded that I would try my hand at the hotel business, as that was something I had not tried, so I bought out a man named Smith, who owned a big hotel on the corner of South second and Washington streets, just opposite John Court's Theatre Building, paying Mr. Smith sixteen thousand dollars for the property, and besides this I spent one thousand two hundred dollars in repairing and fitting it up in shape. I gave it the name of "Riverside House." Here I built up a good business in the hotel line. In fact, inside of six months from the time I opened up I had all that I could accommodate all the time, and this was the first time in my life that I had been perfectly satisfied.

I had all the business I could attend to, and was making money, and as fast as I could accumulate a little money I invested it in different parts of the city in good property.

In the month of May, 1889, two brothers named Clark, from Chicago, came to my hotel for the purpose of buying me out, but I told them my property was not for sale, as I was satisfied and liked the business and did not think I could find a place that would suit me better; but about the first of June they returned and made me an offer of twenty thousand dollars. I told them that I would not sell at any price, as I was satisfied and intended to remain there as long as I lived. On the morning of the sixth of June, 1889, my clerk came to my room and woke me up, saying that there was a fire in the northern part of town and that the wind was blowing strong from that direction. I dressed at once, and when I got out on the street I could see the fire about a half mile from my property, but had not the faintest idea that it would ever reach me, although the excitement was running high on the street. I returned to the hotel, washed, and was just eating my breakfast when one of the waiters came and told me that he could see the fire from the door. I told him he must be mistaken, but he went and looked again and came back and told me that the fire was getting very close. I ran to the door and saw that it was then within one block of my hotel. Now I saw that my property was sure to be burnt, so I sent my clerk up stairs to see whether or not there were any lodgers in the rooms, and I made a rush for the safe and only just had time to get it unlocked and the contents out when the fire was on us.

That fire wiped me out slick and clean as I did not have a dollar's worth of insurance on the property. Any business man would have known enough at least to have a few thousand dollars of insurance on that amount of property, but I had never seen a fire before in a city and thought it folly to insure, and did not find out my mistake until it was too late. During the next six months I had a number of offers of money to build a brick hotel on my lots, but I could not think for a moment of borrowing the money for that purpose.

I remained in Seattle for nine months, during which time there was a great decrease in the value of property, and I sold my lots where my hotel had stood at a very reduced price. I tried various speculations on a small scale during this time, but with very poor success.

By this time I had spent and lost in speculation about all the money that I had realized for my property, and the outside property that I owned I could not sell at any price. Since that time I have wandered around from pillar to post, catching a little job here and there, and at this writing I am temporarily located at Moscow, Idaho, which is situated in the heart of the famous Palouse country, one of the greatest countries on the globe for the growing of wheat, oats, barley, rye, flax and vegetables of all kinds.

And now kind reader, begging your pardon, I would say that I have been two years making up my mind to allow my life to go down in history to be read by the public, as notoriety is something I never cared for. One reason, perhaps, is that I was brought up by noble and generous-hearted Kit Carson, who very much disliked notoriety, and I do not believe that there ever was a son who thought more of his father than I did of that high-minded and excellent man.

I have had many opportunities to have the history of my life written up, but would never consent to anything of the kind. Finally, however, I decided to write it myself, and while it is written in very rude and unpolished language, by an old frontiersman who never went to school a day in his life, all he knows he picked up himself, yet it is the true history of the most striking events, trials, troubles, tribulations, hardships, pleasures and satisfactions of a long life of strange adventure among wild scenes and wilder people, and in telling the story I hope I have interested the reader.

It is not strange that in the wilderness, where all nature sings, from the fairy tinkle of the falling snow to the boom of a storm- swept canyon; and from the warbling of the birds to the roaring growl of mad grizzlies; and from the whispers of lost breezes to thunder of thousands of stampeding hoofs—it is not strange that among all that, even a worn and illiterate old hunter should try to sing, if nothing more than the same sort of a song that the dying sachem sings. So I beg you bear with

THE OLD SCOUT'S LAMENT

Come all of you, my brother scouts,
And join me in my song;
Come, let us sing together,
Though the shadows fall so long.

Of all the old frontiersmen,
That used to scour the plain,
There are but very few of them
That with us yet remain.

Day after day, they're dropping off;
They are going, one by one;
Our clan is fast decreasing;
Our race is almost run.

There were many of our number
That never wore the blue,
But, faithfully, they did their part,
As brave men, tried and true.

They never joined the army,
But had other work to do
In piloting the coming folks,
To help them safely through.

But brothers, we are failing;
Our race is almost run;
The days of elk and buffalo,
And beaver traps, are gone.

Oh, the days of elk and buffalo,
It fills my heart with pain
To know those days are passed and gone,
To never come again.

We fought the red-skin rascals
Over valley, hill and plain,
We fought him in the mountain top,
And fought him down again.

Those fighting days are over;
The Indian yell resounds
No more along the border,
Peace sends far sweeter sounds

But we found great joy, old comrades,
To hear and make it die,
We won bright homes for gentle ones,
And now, our West, good-bye